The story of Josephine Cox is as extraordinary as anything in her novels. Born in a cotton-mill house in Blackburn, she was one of ten children. Her parents, she says, brought out the worst in each other, and life was full of tragedy and hardship – but not without love and laughter. At the age of sixteen, Josephine met and married 'a caring and wonderful man', and had two sons. When the boys started school, she decided to go to college and eventually gained a place at Cambridge University, though was unable to take this up as it would have meant living away from home. However, she did go into teaching, while at the same time helping to renovate the derelict council house that was their home, coping with the problems caused by her mother's unhappy home life – and writing her first full-length novel. Not surprisingly, she then won the 'Superwoman of Great Britain' Award, for which her family had secretly entered her, and this coincided with the acceptance of her novel for publication.

Josephine gave up teaching in order to write full time. She says, 'I love writing, both recreating scenes and characters from my past, together with new storylines which mingle naturally with the old. I could never imagine a single day without writing, and it's been that way since as far back as I can remember.' Her previous novels of North Country life are all available from Headline and are immensely popular.

'Josephine Cox brings so much freshness to the plot, and the characters . . . Her fans will love this coming-of-age novel. So will many of the devotees of Catherine Cookson, desperate for a replacement' *Birmingham Post*

'Guaranteed to tug at the heartstrings of all hopeless romantics' *Sunday Post*

'Hailed quite rightly as a gifted writer in the tradition of Catherine Cookson . . .' *Manchester Evening News*

By Josephine Cox

THE EMMA GRADY TRILOGY
Outcast
Alley Urchin
Vagabonds

QUEENIE'S STORY
Her Father's Sins
Let Loose the Tigers

Angels Cry Sometimes
Take This Woman
Whistledown Woman
Don't Cry Alone
Jessica's Girl
Nobody's Darling
Born To Serve
More Than Riches
A Little Badness
Living A Lie
The Devil You Know
A Time For Us
Cradle of Thorns
Miss You Forever
Love Me Or Leave Me
Tomorrow The World
The Gilded Cage
Somewhere, Someday
Rainbow Days
Looking Back
Let It Shine
The Woman Who Left
Jinnie
Bad Boy Jack

JOSEPHINE

COX

Tomorrow the World

First published in hardback in 1998 by
HEADLINE BOOK PUBLISHING PLC

First published in paperback in 1999 by
HEADLINE BOOK PUBLISHING PLC

This edition published in paperback in 2017 by
HEADLINE PUBLISHING GROUP

1

Cataloguing in Publication Data is available from the British Library

ISBN 978 1 4722 4570 0

Typeset in Times by Avon DataSet Ltd, Bidford-on-Avon, Warwickshire

Printed and bound in the UK by Clays Ltd, St Ives plc

Headline's policy is to use papers that are natural, renewable and recyclable products and made from wood grown in well-managed forests and other controlled sources. The logging and manufacturing processes are expected to conform to the environmental regulations of the country of origin.

HEADLINE PUBLISHING GROUP
An Hachette UK Company
Carmelite House
50 Victoria Embankment
London EC4Y 0DZ

www.headline.co.uk
www.hachette.co.uk

Someone once said life was a wonderful adventure.

As a child I knew poverty and violence, and my only saving was the stories I wove around me, a cocoon in which to hide.

It was never easy, but I would not want to change my life in any way. I owe a great debt of gratitude to the people I knew then, and now, whether they be good or bad; and others, family and friends, who lift my spirits when I'm low, and comfort me when I'm sad.

So many people have touched my life: family and friends; neighbours; readers; professionals who shape and build my career; and so many more. People I hold dear to my heart. Some I will never meet, such as those who write to me from across the world, whose every word I cherish.

My big brother Sonny has been there for as long as I can remember. He was called 'Sonny' because as a child he was always smiling. He likes a pint, and he likes to sing, and we love him very much.

God bless you, sweetheart. Get well soon, and we'll have you dancing in the aisles before you know it.

Contents

Part One

1850–51

SECRET LOVE

Chapter One

'Are you afraid of me?'

'Never!'

'Then trust me.' A charming, confident fellow, Peter Doyle had the mistaken idea that every woman in the world fancied him. 'The snow's coming down heavily,' he told Bridget, 'you'll never get through on foot.' He'd had his eye on Bridget ever since she came to work at Weatherfield Grange. 'I insist on taking you home.'

'No thank you, sir.' Wise beyond her years, Bridget always felt nervous in his presence.

'You *are* afraid of me!' His smile was wonderful, but he had a certain naughty gleam in his eye, and judging from the way he moved his hand inside his trousers, he also had a rising bulge that would not be contained. It was a long time since his wife had shown him any favours. A man had to get his pleasures wherever he could.

As a rule he had no difficulty in persuading even the shyest of creatures into his bed. But Bridget Mulligan was not like the others; at only twenty years of age, she was delightfully fresh and different. It was no wonder he wanted her but, as yet, he had not managed to worm his way into her affections – or her bed, more was the pity! Still, there was time enough yet. He was a patient man.

'It's very kind of you, sir,' Bridget said, 'but I don't need to put you to any trouble because a friend of the family is collecting me any minute now.'

'Really, my dear?' Suspicious, Peter scrutinised her pretty features.

'It's a standing arrangement.' When needs must, Bridget lied beautifully. 'If it snows, like today, I'm to wait for him at the gate – and I must not accept a ride home from anyone else.'

'Quite right, my dear,' he grudgingly conceded. Secretly, he thought it was downright wicked, especially when he could have been giving her the best 'ride' of her life. Damn her eyes, and damn her friend with her!

For what seemed an age he stared at her; the smile frozen to his face, and the member in his trousers straining to burst forth. When she nervously returned his smile, he gave a shrug, a little laugh, then turned abruptly and left the room.

'Good shuts!' she hissed, relieved that he'd given up. 'Randy old bugger, I know what you're after, but you can whistle in the wind till kingdom come, for all you'll get from me.'

As she made her way down the back path to the servants' gate, Bridget was shocked to see how the weather had deteriorated since midday. Now, at half past six in the evening, the wind was sharp and bitter-cold, driving the snow into her face.

'Jesus, Mary and Joseph!' Cook rushed by, her coat above her head, and her long skirt flapping round her ankles. 'I wouldn't let a dog out on a night like this!' A fat lady, too layered with lard to catch a cold, she was never without a nip of gin in her pocket, and as she paused at the gate, she sneaked a swig from the flask. 'That'll keep the goosy pimples away,' she chuckled. Returning the flask to her pocket, she set herself against the wind and cut a crooked path home. She was soon out of sight, but the sound of her voice raised in song told its own merry tale.

Bridget laughed. 'Drunk as a lord tonight, and crotchety as

hell tomorrow. We'll all suffer in the morning, you can be sure of that.' Still, she had a fondness for the dear soul, and anyway, what was life all about if a lady of Cook's responsibilities couldn't have a nip or two of gin when the fancy took her?

Bridget looked up at the dark and laden sky. 'I don't like the look of it and that's for sure.' Wild and spiteful, the night air cut through her hooded coat. 'By! It's bloody freezing!' Drawing her coat tighter about her, she glanced back to the house; it looked warm and cosy, with the lights blazing a path through the night. 'Happen I should have let him take me home after all.' Thinking of his disappointed face made her smile again. In truth, she would rather run naked in a storm than let a man like Peter Doyle have his way.

Coming to the gate in a hurry, she lost her footing and slid to the ground. 'Damn and bugger it!' Now she was wet to the bone, her boots letting the snow in. And to make matters worse, as she tried to struggle up, she realised with a sinking heart that she had turned her ankle.

She had two options. She could either bear the discomfort of her ankle and press ahead, or she could try and get back to the house.

A pleasant thought struck her.

If she was to go back to the house, Harry might be there. But no, Harry wasn't back from Manchester yet. She knew that, because she'd been watching for him all day. It was strange how she missed him whenever he was away.

Feeling ashamed, she chastised herself. 'Bridget Mulligan, shame on you! Here you are, thinking pleasant things of Harry, and you a married woman these past four months.' She had no right even to *look* at another man, let alone miss him. Not when she had a loving husband like Tom.

'Maybe Tom will come for me,' she thought aloud. But there wasn't much chance of that, she reminded herself. Tom was at the quarry, taking delivery of new rolling stock. Before he left this morning, he had warned her he might not be home until later than usual.

'Aw, well.' Brushing herself off, Bridget sighed. 'I'm not going back to the house, not with the squire after me at every turn, and I don't mean to sit here and freeze to death.'

As she struggled on, Bridget was afraid she might fall into some deep ditch and be lost for ever. The landmarks were rapidly disappearing beneath a blanket of snow and it was becoming increasingly difficult to see where the lane was. 'The squire was right after all,' she groaned, her teeth chattering uncontrollably, 'though I would never give him the satisfaction of telling him so.'

With the wind howling and the snow lashing down, Bridget didn't hear the cart coming up behind her.

'Whoa, boy!' Catching sight of the small, forlorn figure in front, Harry Little drew back on the reins. 'Easy there . . . whoa!' A strong young man in his early twenties, Harry had no trouble bringing the horse to a halt. Dropping the reins, he leaped from the cart and hurried forward.

'Bridget! What the devil are you doing out in this weather?' He was angry, but that was nothing new. Bridget had a way of making him angry; mostly because she was married to someone else and not to him.

Relieved, and utterly exhausted, Bridget fell into his arms. 'Harry! Oh, Harry, you don't know how glad I am to see you.'

He gently shook her. 'Have you gone mad? What possessed you to set out on such a wild night?'

'I didn't know it was this bad.'

'You should have waited. You know I would always see you home.'

'I know.' She had no intention of telling him how the squire had offered and she had refused.

'Well, this is no time to argue the point. Come on.' Effortlessly lifting her into his arms, he carried her over the rough ground. 'Good God, woman! You're soaked to the skin!'

Bridget made no reply. The feel of his strong arms about her made her feel safe and warm.

Harry Little was a contradiction to his name; he was a tall, powerful man, lean and lithe, but as gentle as a lamb. He had a thick mop of brown hair and hazel eyes, an easy smile, a quick temper, and a heart as kind as any you could hope to find.

'There!' Placing her on the seat at the front of the wagon, Harry took a blanket from a box under the seat. 'That should help keep you warm.'

Watching Harry tuck the blanket round her legs, Bridget couldn't help but smile. He was like a mother hen. 'I'm sorry,' she said. 'I know it was stupid of me to try and make my way home in this weather.'

He climbed on to the seat beside her. 'So why did you do it?'

Bridget shrugged. 'It's Friday and I wanted to get home, that's all. And now I've turned my ankle.'

'Hmm!' Clicking the horse on, he skilfully manoeuvred the cart to the highest ground; pitting his strength against the elements was no easy matter. 'Hold on tight,' he warned. 'There's no way round this lot, Bridget. We'll have to plough right through it.' The weather was worsening by the minute, and Blackburn town was a good six miles away.

Sneaking a glance at Bridget, Harry couldn't help thinking how pretty she was. With that long, thick brown hair and big brown eyes, she had the bright, wondrous look of a child. Even now, with just her cold, pink nose poking above the blanket, her goodness shone out, and not for the first time he realised how much he loved her.

'I'm surprised the master let you out at all,' he said. 'If he had any sense he'd have made you wait until I got back, or at least offered to take you home himself.'

'He did.' Bridget suspected that Harry already knew.

'I thought as much.' The wind was howling so loudly that he had to yell to make himself heard. 'Fancied his chances, did he? The lecherous bugger!'

Just then the cart struck a boulder and the impact threw them sideways. 'Jesus! That's all we need.' Harry climbed from the seat and took stock of the situation. 'Part of the wall seems to have broken away,' he called back. 'It must have given out under the weight of snow.' Squaring his shoulders, he began digging into the rubble with his bare hands. 'Got to clear a way here,' he shouted. 'Stay where you are, and keep well wrapped up.' The wind was like a cold, hard blade slicing through him.

Glancing up, he was angered to see Bridget climbing down from the cart. 'No! Stay there!' Waving his arms, he gestured to her not to come any further.

Pretending not to hear, Bridget ignored him. In no time at all, she was beside him, pulling her weight with his to roll back the large boulders that blocked their way.

'You're a stubborn little devil,' Harry told her, but he admired her determination all the same, especially when he knew she was in pain from her ankle.

With the way partially cleared, Harry helped Bridget back to the cart and lifted her on to the seat. That done, he checked on the horse. 'God willing, we'll soon have you out of this,' he told the tired creature, and for his reward he got a wet, grateful nose nuzzled in his face.

'Is he all right?' Bridget, too, was concerned about the horse.

'He's a big strong feller, used to all manner of weather.' Harry clambered on to the seat and took up the reins once more, adding pointedly, 'And he knows how to be patient, whereas you, you young bugger, couldn't sit still if your life depended on it.'

'It doesn't though – does it?' The danger they were in was all too apparent.

'It well might, unless we can keep going.' He knew they would have to negotiate some deep rutted tracks, invisible under the drifting snow, before coming to level ground.

Images of Tom coming home and not finding her there turned Bridget's stomach. Her husband was a good man, but he was a stickler for routine; discipline, pattern and good order, that was Tom. So much so that if one day was too different from the one before, he could be impossible to live with.

Reaching out, Harry squeezed her hand. 'Don't you worry, sweetheart,' he told her. 'I'll get you home.'

'I know you will.' Harry had a habit of calling her sweetheart. Tom never did, and that was a shame because when Harry did it, it made her feel warm all over. But then Harry and Tom were like chalk and cheese. Harry was twenty-two and Tom only four years older, but there was a world of difference between them. Harry was full of spirit, always smiling and cheerful, while Tom took life too seriously, rarely smiling, and always looking for the next problem. But the thought of Tom was strangely reassuring. She did love him, she told herself. In fact, she told herself this time and again, as though wanting to believe it.

'Tom's bound to worry if I'm not home when he gets back from the quarry.' What she meant was, that Tom would throw a tantrum. That was his usual way of dealing with things that upset his precious routine.

Harry urged the horse on, gently tapping its rump with the whip. 'Come on, feller, get the young lady home and it's worth an extra bag of hay to you.'

The weary horse made a valiant effort, but deep down Harry

was worried. If the wind kept up at this rate, they might not get through this side of morning.

'How about if we turned back?' Bridget was no fool. She knew the road well. She also knew the dangers.

'Too late for that.' Harry had given it a passing thought, but with the walls collapsing into their path and the road possibly blocked behind them, it was not an option. 'Wrap that blanket tight about you,' he advised. 'With luck, the heavens will ease up and smile on us. All the same, from now on, if I ask you to stay on the cart, I'd be obliged if you'd do as you're told. Two of us out there breaking our backs is downright reckless. If one of us gets hurt, there's always a chance the other can fetch help.'

'Sorry.'

'So you should be.'

There was a lull between them, before he suddenly reached out and took her hand in his. 'It's me that should be sorry,' he apologised. 'I ought never to have started the journey. I should have taken you back to the house there and then. Trying to get you home on a night like this is sheer bloody lunacy!'

Opening the blanket to encompass him, Bridget huddled close. 'You'd die before you would admit it,' she said, 'but I know you're frozen through. Please, Harry, share the blanket. We can keep each other warm.' Her face was so close to his, she could feel the stubble on his chin. 'And no arguments.'

Harry wasn't about to argue. In fact, with Bridget's small soft body next to his, he was the happiest man in the world.

When they got as far as Samlesbury, Harry called the horse to a halt. 'Just as I thought,' he told Bridget. 'With few hedges along these lanes and only low-lying shrub beyond, there's nothing to stop the snow from whipping across the fields. We ought to be standing right in the middle of the lane but it's impossible to be sure. Looks like the whole area is buried under four feet of snow.'

'What can we do?'

'I'm just wondering where we are exactly, and whether there are any farms hereabout.'

'There *is* a farmhouse somewhere along this lane, I've seen it on my way home.' She always thought how pretty it was, with its thatched roof and bull's-eye windows.

Rubbing his hands together, Harry encouraged the blood to circulate faster. 'We'll be hard pressed to find it in this lot.'

'What then?'

'One thing's for sure. We can't go on, and we can't go back.' Turning the blanket away, he climbed down. 'You stay where you are,' he told her. 'And I mean, stay . . . where . . . you . . . are!'

'Don't worry.' Her quiet smile reassured him. 'Anyway, somebody has to look after the horse.'

He looked at her and, for one precious moment, his love shone in his eyes. Then, just as quickly, his features were grim. 'Get down under the seat. It's important to keep warm. Wrap the blanket tight about you.' He made certain she was tucked securely underneath the seat, with the blanket covering her from top to bottom, until only her eyes peeped out. 'I'm going to scout ahead. If there is a farmhouse like you said, I'll find it.'

Sorry eyes stared up at him. 'I'd rather come with you, even if it is reckless.'

He shook his head. 'You drive a man crazy, Bridget Mulligan!' Strong, lean fingers caught hold of her. 'Will you do as I ask? Or must I tie you to the cartwheel?'

'All right. But what if you get hurt? How am I supposed to know?'

He answered with a grin. 'Oh, you'll know all right because I'll shout and yell until you find me.'

'What about me? I might be frightened here in the dark all on my own.'

He shook his head. 'Not you,' he declared with a smile. 'Anybody else, maybe, but not Bridget Mulligan!'

Taking the spare lamp from the box under the seat, he lit it from the one he had hung on the shaft. 'I'll be as quick as I can,' he promised. 'Meanwhile, do as I say. If I come back and find you've gone off looking for me, I'll track you down and give you the smacking you deserve.'

Bridget laughed out loud. 'You wouldn't dare!'

Without answering, he put up the collar of his overcoat, and tightened the straps of his boots, and set off.

As Bridget watched him go, she couldn't help but wonder how Tom might cope in these circumstances. Like Harry, Tom was a strongly built man and probably just as capable of dealing with an emergency as Harry was. But, as far as she was aware, the circumstances had never arisen for him to be put to the test, whereas Harry had proved himself more than once, in particular last year when there had been a bad fire at the Grange. Cook had gone into fits and the master was worse than useless. But Harry had quickly ushered everyone outside. He sent the pot boy running for the brigade, and by the time they arrived, Harry had organised the staff with a line of water buckets to prevent the fire from spreading. Afterwards, the brigade officer commented on his calm nerve and organising ability. 'You did well,' he told Harry, and offered him a job, should he ever leave Weatherfield Grange.

Curled up beneath the seat, Bridget thought about the two men. What if she had married Harry instead of Tom? But Harry had not asked her, whereas Tom had pursued her right from the day she dropped her purse in the puddle outside the market. Tom had retrieved it and given it back, and after that he had set his cap at her. Not a day passed when she didn't receive a note, or a box of chocolates, or a posy of flowers, until in the end she fancied herself in love with him.

But it was a peculiar love. Quiet and predictable. Going home to Tom was like going home to a stern father, accompanied by a feeling of guilt without quite knowing why. It wasn't at all how she felt whenever she saw Harry; with him, she had the most wonderful glowing feeling inside.

Bridget had no way of knowing what time it was, or how long Harry had been gone. 'It seems like he's been gone for ever,' she murmured. 'I hope he's all right.'

Straining up from her cramped position, she peered ahead. The snow was blinding. She cupped her hands round her mouth and called his name.

Her only answer was the howling wind and the hush of snow as it fell about her. She tried again, this time louder.

Still no answer. Now she was really concerned. If he was in trouble or hurt, it was obvious she would not hear his calls for help, and he had been gone for such a long time. 'I have to find him!'

Impatient, she climbed down from the cart – and immediately sank up to her knees in snow. 'Damn it, Harry, where are you?' She called again but there was still no answer.

Her teeth were chattering and her limbs were beginning to set. With great difficulty, she managed to make her way to the front of the cart to the horse. 'Oh, you poor thing,' she groaned; the creature was wet and bedraggled, head hanging low, his big brown eyes looking at her appealingly. His beautiful lashes were speckled with snow and the water trickling down his face made him look as though he was crying. 'I know,' she said, putting an arm round his thick neck, 'it's a bad situation. All we can do is put our trust in Harry.'

Harry had strapped a horse blanket over the animal, and by now it was heavy with snow. Bridget shook it off as best she could, then slid it higher over his withers. 'It won't keep you dry,' she told him, 'but it might keep the worst of the wind off you.' The wind was worsening, swirling the snow and sending it into a frenzy. 'Harry won't let us come to any harm,' she assured the frightened creature, 'and I won't leave you, I promise.'

He seemed to understand. Snorting, he pushed his nose into her shoulder.

'Be patient,' she coaxed. 'He'll be back soon.' Wrapping both arms round the animal's wide shoulders, she snuggled up. 'We'll keep each other warm,' she promised, and, for what seemed an age, that was what they did.

Then at last Bridget saw the hazy glow of a lantern as Harry made his way back. 'Thank God,' she murmured.

She pushed her way through the snow to meet him. 'Oh, Harry! You've been gone so long.' The force of the wind sent her into his arms. She made no move to free herself, nor did he want her to. She felt herself blushing. The insane idea that Tom might see them made her break away.

'I thought I told you to stay put,' Harry said gruffly, though he was greatly relieved to see her. He had been frantic in case she wandered off. 'We'd best get started,' he urged. 'We've a way to go yet.'

'You found the farmhouse then?'

Harry shook his head. 'No, I didn't. It's like all hell cut loose out there.'

With his arm tight about her waist, he helped Bridget back to the cart; he might have carried her over the snow-laden ground, but his legs were weakened by the long, heavy trudge, and his back felt as though it was cracked right down the middle. More importantly, he had to preserve what strength he had left. Who knew what lay ahead?

'Where are we going?' It was increasingly difficult for Bridget to make herself heard against the noise of the wind.

'There's a barn about a mile away. It's not the best place in the world, but it's got four walls and a roof. If we make it there, we should be all right till morning.'

'If there's a barn, surely the farmhouse can't be far away?'

'Probably not, but I couldn't find it and I've searched as far as I can tonight,' Harry answered. 'It's impossible trying to find anything in this blizzard.'

Bridget nodded in agreement.

Harry urged the horse forward. 'Hang on,' he warned Bridget, 'we're in for a rough ride,' and sure enough, the cartwheels ran straight into the ruts. Thankfully, though, the mighty heart of that brave, weary horse soon carried them on to smoother ground.

As they fought their way through, Bridget clung to the sides of the seat, wishing she was home with Tom, and then wishing she could stay with Harry for ever. Right now it seemed as if they were the only two people left in the entire world, and nothing else mattered. Then she chided herself, and once again her mind turned to Tom, and her thoughts became bleak and confused.

The journey to the barn seemed to take for ever. There were times when she feared they would never make it. But, after a struggle, Harry got them there safely.

'Hold the lamp up,' he said, and Bridget did as she was told without question.

It took an age for Harry to open the great doors; the snow had piled up against the timbers, holding them fast. Summoning all his strength, Harry put his back to the doors, straining his muscles until they felt as though they were being wrenched from his frame. With agonising slowness, the doors began to creak apart.

As soon as the opening was wide enough to drive the cart through, he returned to where Bridget waited. 'Sit tight,' he told her. 'A few more minutes and we'll be in the dry.' He took up the reins and gently urged the weary horse to make one last effort.

Once the cart was inside the barn and the doors were closed behind them, Harry quickly unshackled the horse, while Bridget scouted round.

'Harry, look!' She pointed to a pile of grey blankets on a rail. 'At least we'll be warm.' Plucking the top blanket from the pile, she shook it hard, dropping it with a scream when a fat brown rat fell out and scurried away. 'He's probably more startled than I am,' she said boldly, but her voice was shaking with fright.

After a further look round, she'd found two hurricane lamps, a sizeable length of thick, strong rope, a billycan filled with cold, rank tea, horses' tack and throw-overs, and any amount of dead rabbits, tied by their feet and strung from the rafters. There was also a loft above, filled with last summer's hay.

'The horse won't go hungry,' she said with a satisfied smile as she came to lend a hand with the unshackling. 'Not with all that hay up there.'

Once the horse was dried off and led into a railed-off section in the corner of the barn, he seemed contented enough, especially when Harry gave him a generous bite of hay. 'I'm sure the farmer won't mind,' he said, patting the animal fondly.

Bridget, too, expressed her gratitude to the horse. 'You're a brave old feller,' she said, both arms round his neck. 'Thank you for getting us here safely.'

Harry watched her as she stretched up to embrace the horse, and he thought how delightful she was, small and perfect, with an honest, warm heart and a kindness that belied her tender years. Whenever he looked at her, like now, he felt the anguish of a love that could never amount to anything. Bridget was happily married, while he was hopelessly tied by an aged mother and a selfish sister. They both relied on him, and always would. There was no time or opportunity in his life for anyone like Bridget, and even if she had been a free woman, he could never have asked her to share his burden. He pulled off his cap and ran his hand through his hair. Maybe it was just as well she *was* happily married, he thought philosophically. Funny how Fate had a way of sorting things out for the best – or the worst.

Suddenly aware that she was being watched, Bridget spun round. When she saw Harry looking at her, she smiled shyly. He was so handsome, standing there, one arm stretched to the upper rail and his foot placed on the lower one. His skin was tanned from his work in the open air, and his hair lay rough and unkempt. He looked like a Gypsy from the roads, she thought fondly.

For a long, poignant moment they gazed at each other, a river of words between them, and not one uttered.

With Tom surfacing in her mind, Bridget was the first to look away. 'What now?' she asked softly, not daring to look at Harry. Even after their shared ordeal, Bridget suddenly felt oddly embarrassed.

Sensing her discomfort, he was once again the Harry who had driven them here – organised, efficient, and slightly aloof. 'For a start, you'd better get out of those wet clothes,' he suggested. 'There's a measure of privacy back here. When you've done that, wrap yourself in one of these blankets. They're a bit rough, I'm afraid, but better than nothing, eh?' Taking the thick, prickly blanket from the rail, he placed it behind him over the trestle and strode away. 'I'll leave you to it then.'

'What about you?' Bridget knew he, too, was soaked and chilled to the bone.

'Don't worry your pretty head about me,' he answered. 'I've work to do. Besides, it won't be the first time my clothes have had to dry on me.'

'If yours dry on you, then mine can dry on me.' Bridget was adamant.

He laughed out loud. 'Just like I said before,' he grinned, 'you're a stubborn little devil, and that's a fact. While you're drying off, I'll find somewhere comfortable for us to sleep.'

'And after that?' She eyed him with defiance.

'All right.' His smile was charmingly boyish. 'After that, I'll think about getting *both* our clothes dry. Satisfied now?'

Bridget relaxed and nodded.

'Good.'

After a while, wrapped in a blanket, Bridget joined Harry among the bales of hay in the loft.

'I'll be away for help as soon as daylight breaks,' he promised her. 'The farmhouse can't be above a mile or two away, if that.' Taking off his boots, he wiggled his toes and sighed. 'That's better. Damned things are wet to the insides.' Taking a blanket, he wrapped it about his bulky form. 'Snuggle up,' he told Bridget, settling down beside her. 'We'll keep each other warm.'

Snuggling up to Harry gave her a strange, wonderful feeling. 'Harry?'

'Hmm?'

'If, as you say, the farm can't be above a mile or two away, why couldn't you find it?'

'In this weather, a mile or two might as well be a hundred miles. I yelled until my throat was sore, but the wind was so fierce, I couldn't even hear my own voice. As for the farmer, he's probably got his hands full rounding up his animals. A few hours out in this little lot and they'd all be frozen stiff.'

'But wouldn't the lights from the farmhouse be visible?'

'Maybe the poor devil has run out of paraffin, or used all his candles, or he could be saving supplies, in case this weather sets in for a long period.'

'Do you think it will?' Once more, Tom crept into her thoughts. He had never set a hand against her, but she was wary of him.

Harry tried to reassure her. 'Don't worry, Bridget. I promise you, one way or another I'll have you home sooner than they can send out the search parties.'

'I know you will.' A part of her wished this adventure would never end. Another, more responsible, part of her was afraid of the consequences. 'And I'm not worried.'

'Good.' Gazing down on her upturned face, he said, 'I'll do everything I can to get you home safely. All I ask is that you trust me.'

Bridget smiled up at him. 'I do.'

'Are you warm enough?'

'Mmm.' Just a small, quiet sound, but she couldn't trust herself to say any more. He was too near and her heart was thumping too loudly.

Not daring to light a candle with all the hay and straw about, Harry had opened the barn window just wide enough to let a trickle of moonlight creep in. The soft, silvery glow bathed her face, and he was taken aback by her quiet beauty. He had to look away. 'Go to sleep now,' he said. 'It'll be daylight before we know it.'

'Goodnight, Harry.'

He didn't answer, and he did not look at her. With her warm body so near, he could not trust himself.

For a long time he lay awake while Bridget slept, his mind on how he was going to keep his promise to her.

'I *will* get you home, sweetheart,' he murmured, his gaze on her sleeping face, 'though I'd give my soul to keep you with me.'

Bridget stirred but didn't wake, although somewhere deep in her subconscious she heard him.

The night seemed long and tortuous to Harry. He couldn't sleep, but dared not move for fear of waking Bridget. His arm ached where she lay, and his heart ached even more.

He looked at her for an age, then he turned away for a moment, and when he glanced back, she was awake, her eyes gazing up at him. 'Harry,' she said. One word softly spoken, that was all, but it told him all he wanted to know.

Crying out like a man in pain, he caught her close to him. When she folded her arms about his neck, he groaned with the sheer pleasure of it. 'Oh, Bridget! I do want you so.' Suddenly the truth was out, and there was no hiding his love. 'I've always wanted you.'

Fired by the passion of the moment, Bridget clung to him, her whispered words shocking, even to her own ears. 'Take me,' she said. 'Please, Harry, love me. We may never get the chance again.'

The loving was beautiful.

Like two shy children they removed each other's clothes. They fondled one another's nakedness, teasing and caressing. 'You're everything I imagined,' Harry said, his gaze roving over her young figure; lying there in the half light, her body glowed with a silk-like sheen, the round, taut breasts standing proud and erect, the nipples dark and rich against the milk-white fullness of her skin. Down below, between the pale thighs, dark, tightly curled hair shaped into a perfect pyramid. And here she was, his for the taking.

Unable to suppress his need for a moment longer, he raised himself above her and prepared to enter her.

Bridget watched his every move. Silhouetted against the moonlight, he made a wonderful sight, lean and strong, his skin warmed by the sun and his muscles honed by his work. When he lowered himself, he trembled with excitement, his large, shadowy member hardened by a desire that had lain too long asleep.

For a moment they gazed into each other's eyes, and then she felt him penetrate, and her heart leapt. Gasping with delight, she gave herself to him.

She thought how Tom had made love to her many times, but never like this.

Tenderly, he pushed open her legs, wider now, so that he could feel every part of her. Wonderfully aroused, she began to move beneath him, her mouth on his, skin melting into skin. Sensations she had never known before flowed through her body.

Wave after wave of pleasure coursed through her. Faster now, until her heart raced like a wild thing.

Suddenly, all too soon, it was over.

Exhilarated, she lay beneath him, her eyes coveting his face, while he held her in his arms, murmuring gentle longings in her ear, keeping her safe all night long.

Dawn was just beginning to colour the skies when Harry donned his clothes and boots. 'I'm shutting you in,' he told her. 'Get a few more hours' sleep. Don't set foot outside this barn and you'll be safe enough.' Safer than she had been with him, he thought bitterly. Bridget had placed her trust in him, and he felt ashamed. They had let their feelings run away with them, and now, in the daylight, he could see how wrong it had been.

'Don't be too long, will you?' Bridget wondered why he was acting like a stranger. Why didn't he say anything about last night? Maybe he was embarrassed, like her.

'I'll be back as soon as I can.'

When he had gone, Bridget got out from under the blanket and quickly dressed. 'Brr!' The cold air invaded her every pore. 'Set to work, my girl!' she told herself. 'That'll keep you warm, and there's more than enough to do before he returns.'

The first task was to check the horse and make certain he was all right. 'Looks like you were born to it,' she laughed; lying on his side, he stared up at her with big lazy eyes. 'You can't stay there,' she warned. 'Harry's gone to get help and, God willing, we'll be on our way home soon.'

A sense of sadness overwhelmed her. Sinking to her knees, she looked into those big, placid eyes. 'Harry is a very special person, but I think he's ashamed of what we did last night. I feel ashamed too. It was wrong, because I have a husband, and he has an elderly mother and sister to care for. Even if we loved each other madly, it could never come to anything, could it? The truth is, we should have been more responsible.' Rubbing her face against the horse's, she sighed. 'I don't suppose he will ever speak of it, and neither will I.' Maybe that would be just as well, she thought wisely. If word of this ever got out, their lives would be turned upside down. And however fond of him she was, it wouldn't be right. Too many other people could be hurt, and she didn't want that.

She and Harry would always know that they were more than good friends. For all their sakes, that would have to be enough.

Chapter Two

Tom Mulligan was a good man but, like most men, he liked to have the upper hand. 'What do you mean, you're not coming? I've already told them we'll be there. It's Freddy Derngate's leaving party, all the quarrymen are taking their wives, and besides,' he gave her an appreciative look, 'I want to show you off.'

Bridget had told him she didn't feel well enough to make the long trek to the other end of town to the George Inn, a rambling old place that reeked of booze and beeswax polish.

Bridget put a fresh mug of tea before him. 'Why don't you go on your own?' she suggested. 'Explain that I'm not well enough to come along. From what you tell me, they're a decent lot. I'm sure they'll understand.'

Tom was appalled. 'Go on my own? I'll do no such thing!'

Bridget knew when to remain silent and she remained silent now, her gaze roving round the tiny kitchen. She noticed how the stairhole door needed a coat of paint, and even the gas hob was looking the worse for wear. Feeling his gaze on her, she sipped her tea avoiding his eyes. What could she do? Where could she turn? One weak moment, that was all, and it had cost her dear.

'Look at me, Bridget!' Now he was angry as well as disappointed.

Startled, Bridget looked at him, praying he could not read her thoughts, or the guilt on her face.

'Did you hear what I said?'

'No, Tom, I'm sorry.' She gave him a feeble smile. 'I wasn't listening. Like I say, I don't feel well, but if you really want me to come, I will.' She knew from experience that if she was to get her way and stay behind, the idea must come from him. Experience also told her she had to be wily. 'If I get worse, we can always leave early.'

Regarding her over his mug, he observed worriedly, 'I must admit, angel, you do look washed out.'

An endearment! Bridget was heartened. 'Don't worry, Tom,' she answered cagily. 'I'll be all right, as long as we can leave early.'

'We can't do that, Bridget,' he protested. 'Leaving early would be worse than if we didn't go at all.'

'Then we'll stay until the end. Whatever you say, Tom.' For effect, she gave a deep, withering sigh that brought him swiftly to her side.

With his arm about her shoulders, he looked at her with concern. 'What a pig I am! Here's you, feeling unwell, then there's me wanting to drag you out on a cold March day to get your death.'

'I'll be fine,' Bridget insisted. 'Give me ten minutes and I'll be ready for off.' She made to rise from the chair but he held her there.

'The only place you're going, my girl, is your bed.' He put the palm of his hand on her forehead. 'If you were to ask me, Bridget, I reckon you've got a temperature.' His mind was made up, albeit reluctantly. 'That's it! You're not leaving this house tonight, and neither am I.'

'But what about Freddy Derngate's party?' Bridget asked. 'You just said all the quarrymen were going. Won't it look bad if you don't turn up?'

'Bugger Freddy Derngate, and bugger the party! You come first.'

'No.' Bridget looked suitably concerned. 'I won't have them saying you couldn't go and see a mate off. I'll come with you, and no more argument.' With that, she got up and went towards the stairs.

In two strides he was there. 'All right. This is what we'll do. You go to your bed, and I'll show my face at the party. On one condition though.'

'Oh?' Just then, with it all going her way, Bridget dared not say too much.

'Before I leave, I mean to fetch Nelly Potts from next door. She's worth her weight in gold, is Nelly. There's nothing she doesn't know about women's upsets, if you know what I mean.' Lowering his gaze, he looked embarrassed. 'I'll only feel right if I know she's here keeping an eye on you.'

This was an unexpected development and not one which Bridget welcomed. But she had to play along. 'All right,' she conceded, 'if it puts your mind at rest.'

Half an hour later, Bridget was tucked up in bed, and Tom was presenting himself for her to admire. 'What do you think?' He had on his brown cord trousers and a dark jacket that had seen better days but with his thick build and upright stance he made a presentable sight. 'You don't reckon I look too dandy in these smart clothes, do you? The truth now.'

'Course you don't look dandy. What a thing to say.' Bridget thought he was a good-looking man. No doubt the other men's wives would think so too, she mused.

For a wicked moment she wondered how Tom would react if confronted by an attractive lady who took a naughty fancy to him. She smiled to herself. There was no doubt in her mind. He would blush and stammer, look the other way, and come running home to her at the first opportunity. A quarryman he might be, and gruff with it, but when it came to women other than her, he was a mouse.

'What about the rest of me then?'

'You look grand to me, Tom Mulligan.' His hair was larded down, and except for the long, thick sideburns that almost covered his ears, he was cleanly shaven.

'So you reckon I'll do?' His pale blue eyes smiled down on her.

'You'll do just fine,' she said. 'Now be off, and don't worry. After a good, long sleep, you mark my words, I'll be skipping about like a two-year-old.' In fact, the minute he went out that door, she'd be out of bed and right behind him down the street – once she'd squared things with Nelly Potts.

'Right.' Reassured, he thumped one fist into the other. 'I'll fetch Nelly.' He rushed off, closing the door behind him with a resounding thud.

Bridget winced. 'Hark at that! And me needing my rest,' she chuckled.

When the reason for all this charade came back to torment her, the smile slid from her face. 'There's nothing to smile about, Bridget Mulligan!' she chided herself. 'And well you know it!'

It seemed only a moment before Tom returned, with Nelly by his side. 'Here we are then,' he announced. 'Nelly says she'll be happy to stay with you until I get back.'

'An' don't forget the shilling for me trouble,' Nelly promptly reminded him.

While he fished in his pocket, Nelly stood before him, not moving until he flipped the coin into her grubby fingers. 'One silver shilling, and not a farthing more.'

'That'll do. Yer can be on yer way now.'

Nelly was a stout, scruffy person of fifty years and more, though some who knew her from the old days said she must be nearer seventy, an idea she hotly denounced as being 'a spiteful bloody lie, made up by them as are jealous of me young looks!'

Nelly Potts was anything but young. She walked with a peculiar bent, and possessed a smile that was frightening to man and beast alike. Her features were manly and coarse; she had a wide, cavernous mouth, empty of teeth, and a red, rough tongue that licked at her lips until they were sore and cracked. Her voice was shrill and curiously musical.

'Well, go on then!' she urged Tom. 'I'm here now, and I'll not be messed about!' Ambling across the room, she came to the bed. 'And what's up with you? Filled yer belly with a young'un, has he? Making yer feel rotten to the core, is it?'

Bridget might have stopped her, but when Nelly got started, no one else could get a word in.

'Oh, aye. I know all about that, seeing as I've 'ad more than me fair share o' young'uns meself. Mind you, they're all of 'em long gone now, an' thank the good Lord for small mercies, that's what I say.' She gave a cheeky grin. 'Trouble is, all the men 'ave gone an' all. The buggers couldn't handle me, that was the truth. I were too much woman for 'em, do yer see?' And while she spoke, her eyes twinkled with memories of long ago.

Bridget gave her a small, crafty wink. 'I'm just a bit under the weather, that's all, Nelly.' It was the sort of informative wink that one woman could give another, and the understanding was clear.

Nelly rose to the occasion. Turning to Tom, she screeched, 'Are you still here? You'd best be off, young man. This is women's business.'

Uncomfortable in her presence, Tom shuffled his feet. 'Right then.' Sidling past Nelly, he placed a kiss on Bridget's cheek and quickly departed with the words, 'Look after her, Nelly. I'm not sure what time I'll be able to get away.'

'Stay away as long as you like,' Nelly called back. 'We've no need of you here.'

A moment later they heard the front door close.

'Now then, Bridget Mulligan.' Grinning like a Cheshire cat, Nelly settled herself on the edge of the bed. 'What little game are you playing, eh?'

Scrambling out of bed, Bridget confessed, 'I need a few hours to myself, and it was the only way I could get him out of the house.'

Nelly's face opened with surprise. 'Aah! Got yerself a boyfriend on the side, 'ave yer?' The old face crinkled like a dried prune. 'Lucky divil!'

'No!' Bridget was shocked that Nelly had twice hit so near the truth. 'You've got it wrong, Nelly. I love Tom. He's a good man, and I would never do anything to hurt him.' Not any more, she wouldn't anyway. Once was more than enough, and now, because of it, she was in terrible trouble.

'Well, if it isn't a boyfriend, what is it? Are you planning some sort of surprise? His birthday, is that it? And you want him out of the way so you can get it all ready?' Standing up, Nelly rolled back her sleeves. 'Where's the food? I'm a dab hand at laying out a party table, so I am.'

'Wrong again, Nelly.' Bridget was already halfway dressed. 'It's Fanny.'

Nelly frowned. 'Fanny who?' Her memory wasn't what it used to be.

'You met her that day she called here, and the two of us went out shopping. You asked me about her at the time, and I told you, she lives on Montague Street. Oh, you *must* remember her, Nelly. She's taller than me, a bit on the thin side, wiry brown hair—'

'Yer mean Fanny Higgins! Aye, yer right. I *do* remember. What's more, I've heard a lot about her since then. Common as muck, it seems. According to some, she's had two kids by different men, then gave the poor little sods to the Gypsies.'

Bridget gave her a withering glance. 'Shame on you, Nelly. That's all hearsay, and you know it! As far as we know, Fanny's only crime is to keep herself to herself.'

'Aye,' Nelly was shamefaced, ''appen yer right. Mind you, it's her own fault! When a woman on her own turns up out of nowhere, never talking about where she's come from or what she's been up to, well, it's only natural for folk to gossip. What they don't know they'll make up. It's human nature, is that.'

Bridget knew it only too well. 'Tom's the same. He's never liked her, not from the moment I brought her home after she fainted in the street. She told us then that she had ideas of starting up her own dressmaking business. He couldn't wait to get her out of the house.'

'Ah well, that's because she mentioned setting up on her own. Men don't like to think a woman can look after herself. It makes 'em feel useless.'

'Tom really took against her. When I got back from seeing her safely home, he said I was never to see her again, but I have. And I mean to go on seeing her. She's been a good friend to me, and whatever Tom says, I won't turn my back on her now.'

Nelly rubbed her hands with delight. 'Now I can see why you wanted to get him out of the way. You're off to Montague Street, aren't you? You could wait until Monday morning when Tom's at work, but that won't do because she needs you right now . . . on a Saturday. Whatever it is, it can't wait, can it? So it must be summat important.'

'It is.' More important than you'll ever know, Bridget thought.

Nelly rolled her eyes as if thinking hard. 'Let me guess now. The silly cow's got herself into some kind of trouble, and she needs your help. I'm right, aren't I?'

Bridget felt so ashamed she could hardly look the older woman in the eyes. It wasn't Fanny who was the silly cow who'd got herself into trouble, it was her! And it was her who needed help.

'Fanny and I have to talk, yes, you're right, but she isn't in any trouble that I know of.'

Nelly was not convinced. 'I expect there'll be a *man* at the bottom of it,' she declared knowingly. 'There allus is. Some man will have had his wicked way with her and left her with a swollen belly, you wait and see if I'm not right. Men! Bah! As far as they're concerned, a woman is good for only two things, bedding and cooking.' Lowering her gaze to Bridget's belly, she giggled, 'I might have known it weren't *you* in the family way!'

Bridget paused in pulling on her stockings. 'Why do you say that?'

Bold as brass and too thick-skinned for her own good, Nelly explained, 'If yer don't mind an old lady saying—' she could always fall back on her age when it suited her – 'yer old man might be big and strong, but in my experience it's the skinny ones who reach the spot – if yer know what I mean. Anyway, you've been wed long enough to be made with child afore now, don't yer think?'

Bridget was deeply shocked. 'What I think is, it might be better if you didn't say any more.'

'Oh? A sensitive issue, is it? Mind you, I'm not surprised.'

'Nelly!'

'His brother were the same, as I recall. Wed eight years and never managed to fill her belly, not once! In the end she buggered off with some man who gave her eight brats one after the other.' Tutting with disgust, Nelly muttered, 'All I can say is, she must have been wrong in the bloody 'ead.'

'Goodnight, Nelly.' Disturbed by Nelly's words, Bridget escorted her down the stairs. 'Thanks for your help.'

A cunning old bird, Nelly had other ideas. 'Why don't I hang on here till yer come back?' she offered slyly. 'I can maybe do a bit o' cleaning or summat. There's nobody waiting for me at home, worse luck. And besides, happen you'll want somebody to confide in when yer get back, eh?' Her meaning was all too clear, and Bridget couldn't help but smile at her nerve. She knew the old dear meant no harm. All the same, there was no time to waste. If Tom returned before she did, there'd be hell to pay.

'Thanks all the same, Nelly, but no.' There was one other thing. 'I would appreciate it if yer didn't mention any of this to Tom, knowing how he feels about me being friendly with Fanny.'

Bending forward intimately, Nelly replied in a whisper, 'My lips are sealed, you can depend on it. I mind me own business, and I ask others to do the same.' There was nothing Nelly enjoyed more than a good gossip, Bridget knew. 'O'course,' Nelly added, 'I was hoping to earn a few bob doing you a favour or two. Cleaning and scrubbing, like, yer know what I mean?'

Bridget searched out two silver coins from her purse and dropped them gently into the old woman's gnarled hand. 'Not a word, Nelly. Or I might be tempted to tell Tom what you said – about him not "reaching the spot", if you know what I mean?' A little smile lifted the corners of her mouth. 'If I was to let on what you've been saying about him, I reckon he might just string you up from the nearest lamppost.' He might, too, thought Bridget. Not having made a child with her was one of Tom's deepest regrets, and one that had been the source of much anguish to them both.

Nelly's eyes grew wide and frightened. 'Whoooh,' she breathed. 'We wouldn't want that now, would we, eh? Not when we know how to keep us mouths shut, eh?'

'I'm glad we understand each other, Nelly.' Bridget was satisfied she wouldn't tell. 'Come on now, we'd best make tracks. I must get back before Tom, or he'll have all manner of questions to ask.'

'That's right, m'dear.' Now that she'd got three shiny coins tucked away in her skirt pocket, Nelly was pleased as punch. 'Don't forget though, I'm a good listener – that is, if you've got a mind to talk about it when yer get back.'

'I'm sure Fanny won't want me discussing her business with anyone,' Bridget told her, 'but it's good of you to be so concerned, Nelly.'

The houses down King Street were all the same: two or three bedrooms, a back yard with an outside lavvie, and a fire range that did everything from boiling a kettle to warming the bedpan. Like Bridget, most folk took a pride in their homes, making them cosy and welcoming.

Not Nelly though. Her curtains hung in holes, and her rugs were threadbare, but she paid no mind. As long as she had enough to keep her gin bottle topped up and a fire to warm her bony knees, she was content.

'It's a good job you don't know why I'm really going to Fanny's,' Bridget muttered as she went away down the street, 'or it would be all over Blackburn by morning.' Nelly was a good soul, but a terrible gossip.

Behind her, Nelly's voice sailed through the air. 'Don't forget what I said. If there's trouble brewing, two heads are allus better than one. I know what I'm talking about, lass. I've had a lot of experience in these things.'

Smiling to herself, Bridget pretended not to hear. Least said, soonest mended, she thought.

Going at a brisk pace, over the bridge and left into Montague Street, Bridget frequently glanced about, worried that Tom might be making his way back to see if she was all right. He was like that. Sometimes he could be the sweetest soul, while other times he could be a hard-headed and self-opinionated pig.

Fanny lived right at the top of Montague Street, on the right-hand side, just before the Preston New Road. It was pleasant, long and steep, with wide pavements and houses with big bay windows; on the corner was a warehouse where the rag-and-bone man kept his goods, and after that a row of curious little shops. There was a grand old inn situated to the right; this was Fanny's favourite haunt. Bridget wondered fleetingly if she might be there now. Women who frequented such places were viewed as coarse and easy, which was one reason why Tom insisted that she should put as much space between herself and Fanny as possible.

At first glance, Fanny's house looked as though no one was home. The downstairs curtains were closed and there was no sign of any lamplight from inside.

Twice Bridget knocked, and twice she thought she heard sounds from inside. Encouraged, she clenched her fist and banged on the door, louder this time. 'Fanny, it's Bridget!'

The scuffling seemed to go on for an age before the door edged open and Fanny's narrow face peeped out. 'What the devil are you doing here at this time of a Saturday?' She looked up and down the street. 'Does Tom know you're here?'

Bridget shook her head. 'I need to talk,' she said softly. 'I'm worried sick.'

The door opened wide enough to admit her. 'You'd best come in then.'

In the hallway a stout, red-faced man was hurriedly pulling on his coat. 'Come on, shift yer bleedin' arse,' Fanny cried, giving him a hefty shove. 'I told yer never to show yer face again, and here yer are, same old trouble.'

'I want you to marry me,' the man wailed, paying no attention to Bridget. 'I've told you time and again, and still you give me no answer.'

'That's because yer still wed to *her*, yer useless article!'

'I'll get rid of her, I've told you!'

'She'll not be got rid of, and well you know it, Bill Norman!

She's got a comfortable home and money enough to buy what she wants. Why the hell should she give it up so *I* can have it, eh? Tell me that, yer silly old sod!'

'I'll tell her, once and for all. I'm not frightened.' Though he appeared to be quaking at the very thought of her.

'Don't talk bloody daft! If she were to come through that door now, you'd mess yer bleedin' self!'

'If I do get rid of her, will you wed me, Fanny? Will you say yes?'

'I'm still not decided.'

'How can you not be decided? You've had two years to make up your mind, and still you keep me hanging on. We're none of us getting any younger, Fanny. I'm warning you, I'll not wait for ever.'

'Did I turn yer away just now?'

'Well, no, you didn't, and I'm glad of it.'

'And did I let yer have yer way with me?'

He laughed. 'I'll say you did.' The smile fell away. 'But I do so want to wed you, Fanny. Say yes and be done with it.'

'And if I said yes, what would yer do, tell me that?'

'I'd go straight back and tell her.'

'Liar! You're scared to death of the old battleaxe. Admit it, yer bleedin' coward!'

Bill dropped his gaze, his voice trembling as he confessed lamely, 'You don't know what she's like, Fanny darling. She's got a fearful bloody temper.'

'Oh, has she now? Well, in case yer didn't notice, so have I.' Opening the door, she propelled him on to the pavement. 'Now piss off afore I *really* lose me temper.' Fanny slammed the door and turned to Bridget. 'Daft bugger, he never learns. Come into the parlour.'

The parlour was well furnished and cosy, and whenever Bridget visited, she always felt at home. 'You were a bit rough on him, weren't you?' she chuckled. 'Poor soul. He doesn't know whether he's coming or going.'

Fanny burst out laughing. 'Oh, he knows *that* all right,' she giggled. 'I've had the randy devil upstairs in bed for the past hour, and I can tell yer from experience, Bill Norman may not know much, but he knows when he's getting his oats.'

Bridget smiled. 'I didn't mean that, you devil.'

Rising from her chair, Fanny made her way into the kitchen, from where she continued the conversation. 'I had to throw him out, he left me no choice. I'll be old and grey afore he plucks up the courage to tell that old boot where to go. She robs him blind to line her own pocket and he daren't refuse her anything. Honest, gal, I'll bet she's got more money tucked away than I'll ever have in the whole of me miserable bloody life. And what does he do? I'll tell yer!'

Returning with two mugs of hot tea laced with a drop of brandy, she handed one to Bridget and the other she balanced precariously on the edge of the fender. 'I'll tell yer what he does, he works day and night on that farm of his. He digs the ground, plants the vegetables, coaxes 'em to grow and then digs 'em up when they're fat and ripe for market. Then he stands behind that blessed stall all day every day, six and sometimes seven days a week, come rain or shine. Then he carries the takings home for the walrus to grab and never sees it again. I ask yer! What kind of goings on is that for a grown man?'

'Poor Bill.'

'Poor Bill nothing!' Fanny scoffed. 'He deserves everything he gets.' She chuckled wickedly. 'Well, maybe not *everything*, but if I didn't let him have his oats now and then, *I'd* have to go without an' all, and what have *I* done to deserve that, eh? Besides, it helps to keep him dangling. A carrot for a donkey, if yer know what I mean.'

Her own troubles pushed to the back of her mind, Bridget took a gulp of the tea and was pleasantly surprised at the warm flush that spread through her. 'Would you really want to be a farmer's wife though her?' she asked, absent-mindedly cradling the cup in her hands. 'Think about it, Fanny. Outside in all weathers, mud and rain; plucking chickens for market.'

Fanny smiled knowingly. 'Don't be daft,' she said. 'We'd not be wed two weeks afore that place was on the market. I intend to be a lady, not a bleedin' skivvy. What's money for if it's not to be spent?'

Content in each other's company, they sat quietly, sipping their drinks, Fanny reflecting on life and Bridget wondering if it might be kinder not to trouble Fanny with her own problem, yet desperate to confide in her.

In the event, it was Fanny who broached the subject.

'I'm sorry, Bridget, luv,' she said. 'There's me going on about that fat old bugger and there's you come all this way to talk about, well, whatever it is that's worrying yer. So, come on. Out with it.'

Feeling pink all over, Bridget took another sip of her tea, then carefully placed the cup far enough away from her so that she would not be tempted to drink too much of it and lose her wits. Never one to mince words, she came straight out with it. 'I'm carrying,' she said. 'And it's not Tom's.'

Fanny gawped at her. 'Carrying somebody else's baby? Yer never are!' Her eyes were nearly popping out of her head. 'By! I'd have bet me life that you weren't the sort to cheat on yer old man.'

'It was the first, and last, time.' Images of Harry came into her mind, but she pushed them aside. 'It was a terrible mistake.'

'Aye. We all say that, don't we, eh?' Leaning forward in her chair, eyes pink from the brandy, Fanny was unnervingly direct. 'If it don't belong to Tom, who the bloody hell *does* it belong to?'

'I don't want to say.' She would keep Harry out of the picture if she could.

'Well I never!' Smiling from ear to ear, Fanny sat back in her chair. 'O' course, it's that randy old bugger yer work for, ain't it?' Clenching her fists she suddenly realised the seriousness of the situation. 'Tom's found out, ain't he? That's why yer here. The bugger's thrown yer on the streets, ain't he? By! I've a bloody good mind to take meself up to the big house and give that master o' yourn the sharp edge o' my tongue.'

'It weren't Mr Doyle.'

'Eh?' Fanny was puzzled. 'If it ain't Tom, and it ain't the master, who else is there?' Suddenly the light dawned. 'My God! It's Harry Little, ain't it? I knew he fancied yer. I saw it in his face that morning in the grocer's when he walked in and took you by surprise. I reckoned then you had a soft spot for him too, an' now I know.'

There was no use denying it. Bridget knew Fanny would keep ferreting away until the truth was out. 'I'm really worried, Fanny. I can't eat or sleep, and I can hardly look Tom in the face any more. He's sharp. He'll know there's something going on.'

'What? Yer mean he doesn't know?'

'That's why I'm here. What should I do, Fanny? If I confess about what happened between me and Harry, there'll be murder, I know it. Tom's a quiet sort of man, but if he thought I'd been bedded by another . . .' She visibly shivered. 'Oh, I daren't imagine what he'd do.'

'It's easy. Don't tell him.' As far as Fanny was concerned, most things were black or white.

'How can I not tell him?'

'Tell him you're with child, but let him think it's his.'

'I can't.'

'What d'yer mean, yer can't? Unless you and Harry mean to run off together, I don't see what choice you've got.' Eyeing Bridget closely, she asked, 'Have yer told anybody else?'

'Not a soul. I wasn't even certain myself until a few days ago when I started feeling sick and unwell. I was hoping it might all be my imagination, but I know it isn't. I had to come and see you today, Fanny. I've got no one else to confide in.'

'Hmm. So you've not told Harry then?'

'No.' She had hardly spoken to him since the night of the storm, and she would not allow herself even to think of her feelings for him, so great was her shame.

'D'yer mean to tell him?'

Bridget lowered her gaze. 'No.'

'Yer must be fond of him though, or yer wouldn't have let him get yer in such a pickle.'

'If it hadn't been for the storm, it would never have happened.'

Fanny smiled, but not unkindly. 'I've heard some excuses in my time, gal, but never that.'

Bridget had to smile too. 'I know, but it's true. When we got snowed in, it just sort of . . . happened.' It all came back to her, the closeness of Harry, the scent of him, the way she felt when he put his arm round her. So good. So different from when Tom was that close.

Closing her mind to it, she went on, 'We slept in the barn for some hours before Harry could go for help. We didn't get home until the next morning.' So many lies, she thought, so much deceit. 'I never did tell Tom I'd been in the barn with Harry. He thinks I waited at the big house until someone brought me home. It worked out all right really, because Tom got snowed in too, and as luck would have it, I got home only minutes before he did.'

'Let me get this straight. You've been made with child by Harry Little. Nobody knows but you and me. You haven't told Tom, and yer don't want to. Moreover, you've no intention of telling Harry either.' Suddenly a knowing look came over Fanny's face. 'Ah!' There was relief in her voice. 'I see what yer after. You've come to yer friend, Fanny, because you think I might know somebody who could help rid yer of the little brat. And, as it happens, I do know a certain woman. She don't come cheap, mind, but I can help you there, because I'm not short of a bob or two. Anyway, gal, if yer can't help yer friends, who the bleedin' hell can yer help, eh?'

Bridget's face had lost colour with every word. 'No! I don't want to be rid of it! I want to keep the baby. It's my flesh and blood. I want to hold it in my arms, and see it grow up to be a fine young person. Oh, no. I could never harm it.'

Exasperated, Fanny groaned out loud. 'Well, I'm buggered! You've got me foxed now, an' no mistake. If yer don't tell Harry, an' yer don't tell Tom, an' suddenly there yer are with a belly the size of God's hill, there'll be no hiding it.' She sighed. 'Oh, gal, whatever will yer do? Tom's no fool. He'll know when his wife's about to drop a young'un on his bleedin' doorstep.'

Bridget felt more confused than ever. 'I can't tell Harry,' she said quietly. 'We did wrong and that's an end to it. It's best if he doesn't know the consequences. He's got enough with his old mammy to look after. I won't saddle him with more responsibility.'

'He saddled you!' When Bridget blushed to the roots of her hair, Fanny apologised. 'Sorry, luv. I've a wicked tongue. So what will yer do then?'

'I don't know.' But just talking it through with Fanny made her feel much better. 'What would you do?'

'I'd tell my old man it was his.'

'I *can't* do that.'

'Why can't yer?'

'Because Tom and I have been wanting a baby ever since we were wed, and it's not happened. Tom's like his brother, d'you see? He can't make babies. It's just the way it is. Tom knows that, and it drives him crazy.'

'He might be wrong.'

Bridget shook her head. 'No. We've tried so hard to make a baby. But it never happened, and Tom says it never will.'

'If yer tell him, he'll think he's struck lucky at long last.'

'I could never lie to him like that, not without him knowing. He'd be suspicious, I just know he would, and anyway, I couldn't live with it. I couldn't let him think he was the father when he wasn't. It would drive me insane, every day, every minute, seeing them together, knowing how I'd deceived him.' Bowing her head, she murmured, 'Tom can be difficult at times, but so can anyone. But he's always been good to me, and he's such a proud man. He doesn't deserve to be treated like that.'

'You've too much of a bloody conscience, that's the trouble.'

'Maybe.'

'Me, I'd let him think what the devil he liked, as long as it saved *my* skin. But I do see what yer mean, gal. And when all's said an' done, happen yer right after all.'

Bridget looked up with sorry eyes. 'I hope so, but whichever way I go, it means trouble.'

'Well now, it seems to me you've two choices left.'

'Go on.' Advice was what she had come for, and here it was.

'You either pack yer bags and leave him. Or yer tell him the truth.' She took Bridget's hand in hers and said kindly, 'Whichever way, even if he kicks yer arse out the door, yer allus welcome to move in with me, gal, yer know that, don't yer?'

'I know. You're a good friend.'

'So. What's it to be?'

Bridget's mind was made up. 'I have to tell Tom the truth. It's the only way I can sleep at night.' Her heart fluttered with fear.

'So. When am I to make yer bed up?' Fanny asked in her blunt way. The look on Bridget's face made her bite her tongue. 'You're sure about this, gal?' she asked more gently.

'There's no other way, I know that now.' She felt relieved and afraid all at the same time. 'I think I've known it all along.' She looked at the mantelpiece clock. 'I'll have to get back now.' She rose from her chair and Fanny walked her out to the hallway.

'I'm here if yer need me, allus remember that. Yer a brave little bugger, I'll give yer that. Braver than I am, that's for sure.'

'I'm not brave,' Bridget confessed. 'I'm frightened sick.'

'Go on. Off with yer, me beauty, and if he gives yer trouble, get yer arse over 'ere.'

Bridget hugged her tight. 'I don't know what I'd do without you.'

'Oh, you'd manage. You've got what it takes. And yer not the only one with a little secret.' Pointing to her own stomach, Fanny confided, 'I'll bet mine will be here weeks afore yours.'

When Bridget's face opened with astonishment, Fanny laughed. 'That's right, me beauty. We're a pair o' softies together, because I couldn't get rid of *mine* either.'

There was laughter, and a few tears, and after a while Bridget went on her way, a wiser, braver woman.

The truth had to be told, and the consequences faced up to, and if Tom chose to throw her out on the streets, she wouldn't blame him for it.

The party had gone with a swing. They were merry to a man, and now, with the evening drawing to a close, Tom prepared to leave. 'I'd best be off,' he told the hard-drinking quarrymen. 'The missus hasn't been too well, as you know, and even with Nelly watching over her, it's not right to leave her for too long.' He'd had a good night, and now it was time to go.

'Aye, and I'd best be away an' all,' Dave Grundy declared. 'Me own wife's due to birth any minute. She'd skin me alive if it happened tonight while I were here having a bloody good time.'

Laughter greeted his remark, but Ted Louis, a burly fellow with a nasty scar across his lip, had something snide to say. 'We all know about that,' he guffawed, his sly gaze going to Tom, whom he disliked. 'There's not one of us here who ain't fathered a heap o' young'uns – all except for Tom Mulligan.' His lips curled in a sneer. 'I reckon 'e don't know how to do it right. Happen one of us should show him, eh?'

A terrible silence fell on the party, all eyes on Tom who had turned to face his tormentor.

'Leave him be, Ted,' one man warned. 'It ain't his fault. It could happen to any one of us.'

'Naw!' Ted was obviously looking for a fight. 'Not if you're a man, it couldn't.' By now Tom was making his way across the room, his hard, glittering eyes fixed on the burly man.

'Shut your mouth!' Dave Grundy gave Ted a push. 'It ain't his fault, I tell you! It runs through the family. Him and his brother both.'

Tom grabbed Ted by the throat. 'You bastard! I'll have your bloody head off your shoulders!' But before a fight could start, the two of them were quickly separated.

'Go home, Tom,' one of the men said quietly. 'He's a loud-mouth. Don't let him goad you.'

Ted was manhandled out of the back door, and Tom out of the front.

'You're a better man than he'll be any day of the week,' Dave Grundy told Tom. 'Remember that, and get off home to your wife.'

Struck to the heart, Tom went on his way, bitter and disillusioned. It wasn't the first time his manhood had been questioned. And if men like Ted Louis had their way, it would not be the last.

Chapter Three

A week passed, and still Bridget had not dared talk to Tom about the child. Since coming home from the party, he had been in the worst and darkest mood she had ever seen. She didn't know what was bothering him, and was afraid to ask. She was even more afraid to make her dreadful confession, and so, growing ever more anxious, she kept it to herself. But with her belly rising like new-baked bread, she knew she couldn't hide the truth for much longer.

On Saturday morning she went to market as usual, and there, while queuing for a hank of pork, she saw Mrs Louis, a kindly soul who had more children than she could count and whose loud-mouthed husband was disliked from one end of Blackburn to the other.

'Oh, I'm so sorry, Mrs Mulligan,' she greeted Bridget without preamble. 'Ted bragged about how he taunted your husband at the leaving party. Ooh! He's a wicked man at times, and I told him so!'

Bridget was about to ask what she meant when Mrs Louis swung round to display a large, colourful bruise on her cheek. 'I got this for my trouble,' she said loudly. 'Fists and mouth, that's Ted Louis, and God only knows what I ever saw in the brute!'

'Mrs Louis, I—'

'Even the kids are frightened of him. I've a bloody good mind to sod off and leave him to rot. It would serve the bugger right, that it would!' With that, and before Bridget could get a word in, she gathered her numerous children and marched them off. 'Mouth and fist, that's all he knows!' she muttered as she went. 'Getting wed to that one was the worst thing I've ever done in my life.'

Bridget found herself being stared at by other women in the queue. Embarrassed and confused, she gave them a feeble smile and slipped away, with the intention of coming back when the queue had dispersed.

In the teashop she hid herself in a corner with an iced bun and a jar of sarsaparilla. 'Poor Mrs Louis,' she mused aloud. 'Wonder what she was getting at?' When a family at the next table gave her a curious look, she pretended to stare out of the window.

Ten minutes later she left the tearooms and returned to the market. She didn't go back for the pork; instead she bought two fat and juicy fish. An hour after that, what with being caught up in the hustle and bustle and feeling uncomfortable with the growing weight of the shopping bags, Bridget decided to make her way home. As she disembarked from the bus, the heavens opened and she was soaked to the skin.

Tom was already home. 'I finished early,' he said, a world of sadness in his eyes. 'I can't settle somehow.' The truth was, he couldn't stomach working alongside Ted Louis; he was even considering looking for another job.

Bridget thought about what Mrs Louis had told her, that she rued the day she had married Ted Louis, and how he used his fists on her. Tom had never once done anything so bad. In fact, he was a better husband than most, which was why she loathed herself for what she had to tell him. But not yet. Not the way he was.

'Are you ill, Tom?' She had noticed lately that he wasn't eating or sleeping well, and now although he was talking to her his thoughts seemed far away. 'Do you think you should see a doctor?'

Suddenly he was looking at her, *really* taking notice. She was so small and pale, he thought, with her rain-soaked hair peeping from beneath her beret, and her knuckles white from the weight of the bags. 'I reckon it's *you* who has need of a doctor,' he said, crossing the room and taking the shopping bags from her. 'You look tired out, lass.' He headed for the kitchen with the bags. 'I think we could both do with a hot brew, so sit yourself down.' He turned and looked at her. 'There's summat I need to tell you.'

A few moments later he returned and they sat by the fire with a mug of hot tea each. 'I've been thinking of moving away from here. What do you think to it?'

Bridget was shocked. 'You've lived here all your life,' she reminded him. 'How can you move away? You've got a steady job here, and good work isn't all that easy to find, you've said so yourself many times.' This had all come at the wrong time. So much was rolling up on her, she couldn't think straight. 'Besides, where would we live?'

'Trust me,' he said. 'I know what I'm doing. So, is it yes or no?'

After a moment she asked, 'Is this anything to do with Ted Louis?'

'What the bloody hell's Ted Louis got to do with it?' He leaped up, his mood abruptly ugly. 'Who's been talking?' he demanded. 'What's been said? Come on, out with it.'

Bridget relayed what had happened at the market. 'I never did get to find out what she meant, but it was something to do with you and Ted Louis. That's all I know.'

He visibly relaxed. 'Aye, and that's all you *need* to know.' Thrusting his hands into his pockets, he turned away. 'We had a bit of a row. Something and nothing, and that's the top and bottom of it. A simple row that men have, if you know what I mean. There are times when men like Ted Louis need to be put in their place, that's all. Nothing for you to worry about, so let that be the last I hear of it.' With that, he put on his coat and cap and left the house.

Wishing she had never come across Mrs Louis, and content enough to accept Tom's word that it was 'something and nothing', Bridget unpacked the shopping bags. When that was done, and the kitchen tidy, she went upstairs to lie down. 'Just a few minutes,' she promised herself. 'Then I'll make him a nice fish tea.'

She felt restless. Something was obviously playing on Tom's mind, and if it wasn't to do with that awful Ted Louis, she wondered if the cause was closer to home.

A frightening thought came to her. 'No,' she decided, 'there's no way he could have found out about me and Harry.' Tom had few dealings with country folk, and because of the long, hard hours Harry worked up at the big house, he was not a familiar face in the local inns.

Bridget relaxed and let herself drift off to sleep.

It was late when she woke. 'Oh, my God!' The clock on the mantelpiece stared back at her. 'Quarter to six!' Rolling out of bed, she rubbed her eyes and straightened her clothes. 'I must have sunk into a deep sleep. Don't let him be home yet. I need to keep him sweet-tempered. There are things I have to tell him tonight; *bad* things. And may God forgive me. By the end of the day, Tom will know what a shameful thing I've done.' Her heart lurched. 'Tell the truth and shame the devil, that's what my mother always said.'

A deeper despair came over her. 'Oh, Mam, I wish you and Dad were here with me,' she whispered. 'If I ever needed anyone, it's now.' But they were gone; taken in a bitter winter that had swept through Lancashire, leaving many dead in its wake. It had been a long time ago, but the pain of their loss never really went away. An old grandmother had brought her up, but then, the day before Bridget's sixteenth birthday, the old woman was gone too.

After that she was on her own, and soon learned to fend for herself. Life had not been easy, and one way or another Tom had been her saviour.

'And this is how I repay him,' she whispered sadly. But she would not deceive him any more, whatever price she had to pay. She would never again do that to him.

When she came downstairs, half expecting to see him sitting there, Bridget was astonished to find he hadn't been home. 'Where can he be till this time?' she wondered. A smile flitted across her features. 'Hopefully making his peace with Ted Louis.'

Putting all else out of her mind, she set about creating a meal fit for a king. She cooked the potatoes until they were soft right through, dropped a knob of butter and a good measure of milk into the pan and let them steep, turning them occasionally to make certain every potato was rolled in the simmering mixture.

She prodded and coaxed the cabbage in the salted water until the rich green leaves were cooked to the point where they would crunch on the teeth while melting on the tongue. The fish was deboned and rolled, then placed in a skillet of milk, covered with herbs, and gently steamed over the hot fire.

Returning to the potatoes, she took up a round-headed instrument and began mashing until the potatoes were light and fluffy, and tasted delicious. Bridget had been taught to cook by her grandmother, and had never forgotten the old ways.

The kettle was boiling, and the table made a pretty sight, covered with her best white cloth and set for two, with a jar of ale for him and a measure of cider for her. 'It might be the last meal we have together if he takes my news badly,' she said sadly. 'We'll just have to wait and see.'

By seven thirty everything was ready. The aroma of food wafted on the air and carried to every room in the house. The fire blazed cheerily in the hearth; the house was warm and cosy, and in her best blue dress Bridget was a sight to behold. Her brown hair was combed loosely about her face, and her eyes shone with the glow of a woman carrying a new life inside her.

'Dear God,' she sighed, gazing into the flames. 'Please let it be all right.' Yet, in her deepest heart, she could not imagine how Tom would ever forgive her.

For one wonderfully precious moment, she let herself think of the child; *Harry's* child. Would it look like him? Would it take after her? Or would it carry the marks of them both? More importantly, did it really matter? Surely all that mattered was that it should not suffer because of her.

Thirsty after her rush of work, Bridget poured herself a glass of cider and sat by the fire, her gaze going occasionally to the door. She wondered how long Tom might be, hoped he would be back before the meal started to spoil.

The minutes ticked away.

The cider made her feel relaxed, and the heat from the fire was mesmerising. She glanced up at the mantelpiece clock. 'Ten minutes to eight. Where is he?' Her eyelids grew heavy. She began to feel sleepy.

Closing her eyes, she thought of Harry. How could a woman love two men at the same time? she asked herself. But she did, and it was a strange thing.

When the clock chimed the hour, she sat up with a jolt. 'Tom!' But he wasn't home yet.

The aroma filling her nostrils had been warm and teasing. Now it was drier, tinged with the smell of burning. Quickly she got up and inspected the contents of the range where she had earlier arranged the meal on two plates, each plate then covered by another, turned upside down.

Taking the plates out, Bridget uncovered them to find the meal shrivelled and inedible. 'Ruined!' Disappointment brought a rush of anger. 'Damn and bugger it, Tom! Why didn't you tell me you'd be gone all this while?'

Carrying the plates to the midden, she scraped them clean. 'Spoiled! All spoiled!' Somehow the sum of her life was lying on those plates, she thought sadly. And anger turned to despair.

With the entire evening and all her efforts wasted, she busied herself by washing the pots and pans, and then stacking them away. 'Where can he be?' Now she was concerned. This wasn't like Tom at all. 'Ten o'clock. He's been gone for hours!' Normally, he would always tell her where he was going and how long he was likely to be. Never before had he just taken off and stayed out for this length of time.

Hurrying down the passage, she opened the front door and looked up and down the street. There was no sign of him. In fact, for a Saturday night it was very quiet, except for Molly McBride who was rolling down the street singing an old Irish ditty. On seeing Bridget she called out, 'Goodnight, me beauty,' and promptly fell in the gutter.

Rushing out, Bridget hauled her to her feet.

'Sure, I'm drunk as a lord,' Molly laughed. 'What's more, I don't care if I am!' And she went on her way, singing words so randy they would have made grown men blush.

It made Bridget laugh out loud, and for one brief moment her own troubles were forgotten.

Tom had never been to the Swan Inn before. He chose it because the quarrymen did not frequent it. The inn was further out of town than the usual drinking haunts, and normally he would not have travelled so far for a drink either, but on this occasion a tuppenny bus ride was not much to pay for a few hours away from prying eyes.

The truth was, Ted Louis's sneering comments had cut him deep. At first he had thought he was man enough to put it out of his mind and get on with his life, but now he knew differently. He had to make a new life, get away from here, find a place where he and Bridget were not known. He felt as if every man-jack around here was watching and waiting to see if he could father a child. The more he thought about leaving the area, the more the idea appealed to him. They could start again and, who knew, maybe things would change and he might turn out to be a 'real' man after all.

'Ain't it time yer went home to your wife and kids?' The kindly innkeeper was impatient to shut up shop. 'Everybody else has gone, and I'll be closing the doors soon.' He thought Tom looked like a man in trouble. 'You ain't run off, 'ave yer?' he asked carefully. 'Yer ain't done nowt wrong, I hope. I mean, the authorities ain't after yer, are they? I don't want no trouble here. I run a clean premises, I do.' He shook his head and his jowls wobbled from side to side. With his bright red face he looked like a half-set jelly.

Tom shook his head. 'I've done nothing wrong.' That was the pity of it all. Whatever misfortune had been handed down to him was none of his doing.

'Won't she be worried about yer?'

'Who?'

'The missus! Won't she wonder where you are?'

'Probably.'

'An' don't yer care?'

'Maybe.' He loved Bridget, but deep down he was bitter. No doubt she was fertile as a cow in season, while he didn't have it in him to make her with child. It was a wicked thing for a man like himself, big and strong, and able to do everything else demanded of him. He often wondered whether she was laughing at him behind his back, but no, Bridget wasn't like that, and he should be ashamed of even thinking it. 'I dare say she is wondering where I am,' he said thoughtfully. 'As a rule, I tell her how long I'm likely to be, but not this time.'

The innkeeper smiled knowingly. 'I see. Been naughty,

'ave yer?' He gave a sly little wink. 'Got a bit o' fluff on the side, 'ave yer?'

Tom laughed out loud, but it was a sad sound. 'Who'd want me? Naw. I want no other women. Not when I've already got one of the best.' He bowed his head. 'Trouble is, I don't deserve her.'

'Seems to me you're luckier than most. Go on, get off home to her, you bloody fool, afore some other gent tries to steal her away.'

'She wouldn't even *look* at another gent.' His mood darkened. 'Besides, if she did, I'd probably slay her alive – him too.' The thought of Bridget with another man turned his soul inside out. He was no lover of violence, but just thinking about it brought murder to his mind.

'Get off home, I say.' Impatient to be rid of him, the innkeeper made his way round the counter. 'I'm shutting shop now.'

'She can wait!'

'Oh, aye, an' what about yer kids? The poor little buggers will be wondering where their daddy's got to.' He reached into a jar of liquorice sticks and pulled out a handful. ''Ere, they'll enjoy these. Take 'em with my compliments.' When Tom grabbed his wrist, he drew back, startled. 'I meant no offence, matey. Pay for 'em if it worries you that much.'

'Bugger you, and bugger your charity. I don't need it! What's more, there are no bloody kids waiting back home, d'you understand?' He laughed insanely. 'No kids, and not likely to be!'

The landlord was relieved. For a moment he'd thought he was in for a beating. 'No kids? That ain't nothing to worry about,' he quipped. 'Me? I've got more than enough. If you were to steal a couple of 'em right from under me nose, I don't suppose I'd even notice.'

Tom looked at him with scorn. 'Then you're a bigger bloody fool than you look.' He drained his whisky, slammed the glass down on the counter, and moved towards the door.

Now it was the turn of the landlord to do the grabbing, and he did, with some considerable force. 'That'll be two bob. Cough up quick and then clear off, before I call the bobbies.'

Dipping into his waistcoat, Tom threw the coins across the counter, then departed without another word.

'And good riddance to yer!' Bolting the door behind him, the landlord went up the stairs two at a time, into the bedroom, where his fat, idle wife was waiting, arms open, to welcome him.

Not so, Bridget.

She waited up until she could hardly keep her eyes open, then she tidied the kitchen and left a cheese sandwich between two plates in the centre of the table. 'It isn't much of an offering,' she sighed, 'not compared to that wonderful meal.' But the meal was thrown away, and she had no intention of cooking anything else tonight. So, with a sorry heart, she went to her bed.

As she settled down between the sheets, she thought of tomorrow and what she must tell him. 'Oh, Tom! I did so want to tell you tonight. But it can wait,' she muttered resignedly. 'I don't suppose one day will make much difference.'

But she couldn't sleep. Her mind was too restless. Her heart too guilty.

When in the early hours Tom came into the room, she was still wide awake, though pretending to be asleep.

Leaning over her, he twice called her name, and each time she lay perfectly still, eyes closed and breathing heavily, as though in a deep slumber. Eventually, he climbed in beside her, rolled over and was soon fast asleep. 'Thank God,' she whispered.

She slept in fits and starts, dreading the morning and the confrontation that must follow.

Dawn was breaking when she got out of bed to go to the lav. When she came back, he was waiting for her. 'Let me hold you,' he said, turning back the sheets and inviting her in.

Reluctantly, she went to him.

'I want you so much,' he murmured, taking her into his arms. 'I wanted you when I came home, but you looked so peaceful, I couldn't bear to disturb you.'

As they coupled, he feverishly and she afraid to respond, Bridget suffered all manner of emotions; she felt warmed and needed, her guilt compounded, knowing how soon she must destroy his trust in her.

Tom quickly went back to sleep. Raising her eyes to the heavens, Bridget asked for divine help to do what must be done today. But oh, how she wished none of it had happened.

Lying there, afraid and insecure, she thought of Harry. Since that night she had kept her distance from him, scurrying out of his way whenever she saw him approach. He made no attempt to seek her out, and she was glad of that. On the one occasion he unexpectedly met her in the kitchen, both their tongues were tied, and though he gave a nervous smile, neither of them spoke. What was there to say? For different reasons, each had suffered because of that night and, as far as Bridget was concerned, nothing he could say or do would ever rid her of the shame she felt.

Eventually she crept out of bed, quickly washed and dressed, and hurried downstairs. She needed to be on her own for a time, before Tom followed and the truth was out. Everything must be straight in her mind. There must be no going back now.

In the kitchen she made herself a cup of tea, but could eat nothing. She felt nauseous. Mornings were always bad, and today was no exception.

Every little sound made her turn her gaze towards the stairway, expecting to see Tom there, tousle-headed and sleepy. He worked so hard in the week, Sundays were always an excuse to lie in.

Going to the back door, she flung it open. Outside the sun was shining, and in the distance she could hear church bells chiming.

Sundays were always a delight. But not today. Today was a nightmare, with no escape.

She went to fetch her tea and then stood by the door for what seemed an age, gazing at the scene before her. The back door opened into a long, meandering alley, open to the elements at both ends; if she looked to the left, she could see the canal wall, with the main body of the canal and a stretch of wasteland beyond. If she looked to the right, her gaze fell on the bridge and the canal as it turned away and out of town.

This was the view she favoured, her heart delighting in the scene. In this area of King Street, where houses lined the street and rows of chimneys pumped dark, foul smoke into the air, there was little room for beauty. But the bridge was surprisingly pretty, gently curving over the canal, with fluted bricks and narrow pavements. Grime from the mill chimneys had darkened the stone, but it didn't matter. The bridge stood proud, and nothing, not smoke, or the ravages of time, or even the drunks who occasionally emptied the contents of their stomachs over it, could destroy its appeal for Bridget.

Presently, when a cloud covered the sun, making her shiver, she closed the door and went back into the kitchen. Placing her empty cup on the pot sink, she went softly to the foot of the stairway and listened. 'Slumber of the innocent,' she murmured. 'Sleep as long as you like, Tom. I haven't the heart to wake you.'

She noticed that Tom hadn't touched the cheese sandwich she had left for him. She threw it into the midden. She washed the plate and her cup, and then took up all the rugs and hung them outside on the wash line. Leaving them to blow and dance in the breeze, she swept and polished the downstairs like a thing possessed; it sped away the hours and helped take her mind off things.

As a rule, Bridget never did her laundering on Sundays. Today was different. Searching for every soiled article and even some that didn't really need washing, she swept them up and threw them in the dolly tub. Taking up the three-legged stick that Tom had made for her, she plunged it into the water again and again, twisting and turning as if her life depended on it.

When the dirt was thrashed out of the clothes, when they were rinsed umpteen times and wrung between her strong fingers, Bridget ran them through the mangle. When every drop of water was squashed out of them, she left them folded in the bucket and turned her hand to other things.

In the parlour, she black-leaded the fireplace and swept the floor. She scooped the dirt into a sheet of newspaper, which she then set in the hearth to make a paper flower. Finally she dusted every inch of the furniture, inside and out.

She did the same in the sitting room, and when that was done she lit a fire in the range, boiled the kettle on the gas ring, filled the bucket with hot water and got down on her knees to scrub the floor. She punished herself, scrubbing every inch of the flagstones until the sweat ran down her face and back; scrubbing and scraping over and over again as though purging the sin from her soul.

Afterwards, she took the beater to the rugs and thrashed them until they hung subdued on the line. Then she took them back inside and laid them on the floor in their usual places. Hands on hips, she inspected her work. She felt no satisfaction or sense of achievement, only an awful emptiness inside.

Exhausted and grubby, she went to the sideboard and took out a clean skirt and blouse. In the kitchen she washed herself at the pot sink, brushed her hair, and put on her clean clothes. 'All right, Tom,' she whispered, 'I'm ready for you now.' She looked at the clock. It was nearly midday.

Quietly, she prepared the Sunday meal – skin the chicken and put it in the oven, peel the potatoes and quarter the cabbage; make the pastry for the apple pie, and get the sauce ready. All done. Now to put out the tablecloth and lay the table.

She was engrossed in checking the simmering vegetables when Tom crept up to her and grabbed her round the waist. She almost died with shock. 'Tom! I didn't hear you come down.'

Laughing, he swung her round, shivering with delight when her hair brushed his face. 'You're so lovely.' With her brown eyes and small, round face, she was like a frightened child. In fact he thought he had never seen her look so young and innocent. But then, he had never really taken the time to look at her as a man should look at a woman. He had wanted a wife to keep house for him and to produce a child. Now, with a new life planned, he felt good, almost as though he was being given a second chance.

Gripping her shoulders hard, he grew serious. 'Bridget, there's something I need to tell you,' he said. 'But first, I must eat.' His features softened. 'I'm starving, brought from my bed by the smell of food.' He glanced hungrily at the range top where the pan lids were rising with the steam. 'Besides, what I have to say will sit better on a full stomach.'

The first thing that came to Bridget's mind was that maybe he had heard something about her and Harry. But no. How could he? If not, what then? She had to know. 'You'd better tell me now, Tom,' she urged. 'It sounds serious.'

'It is serious,' he confirmed, 'but wonderful in a way.'

'Tom! Please, I want to know.' She thought it ironic that they were both harbouring secrets.

'It's just that I've been doing a lot of thinking and, as it concerns you, it's only right that I should tell you what I've decided. And I will, when I've eaten,' he said firmly. His face broke into a smile. 'I hope you've baked an apple pie.' In the whole of Lancashire, there was no one who could bake an apple pie like his Bridget, he thought proudly.

The meal was a nightmare for Bridget. She picked at her food, but Tom thoroughly enjoyed it. He ate half a chicken, a mound of fluffy potatoes, and a heap of cabbage. When she served up a generous portion of apple pie, he swallowed it down and asked for another. 'You spoil me,' he grinned, and poured himself a glass of cider.

When, a full hour and a half later, he had finished eating and drinking, she pushed the crockery to one side. 'Now then, Tom, what have you got to tell me?'

'Ah!' Leaning back in his chair, he sighed with satisfaction. 'That was a meal for any man.' He patted his round stomach. 'D'you know, Bridget, last night when I rolled you beneath me, it seemed to me you were more of an armful than I remember.' Laughingly, he teased, 'You've been eating too much apple pie behind my back, is that it?'

Bridget could only look at him in horror. She had been wondering when he would notice her swelling stomach, and now that he had and she was presented with the chance to explain herself, she was utterly speechless.

Blissfully oblivious, he chattered on, 'Not that I mind. You needed a bit more meat on you. I've told you before, a man likes a woman with curves to fill his arms.'

'Tom.'

'Yes, my beauty?'

'You had something to tell me.'

'Ah! Now then!' Getting out of his chair, he began pacing the room. 'I think we've been here long enough. We've had very little good fortune in this house.' Swinging round he looked her in the eye. 'So I've decided it's time to leave it all behind us.'

'What are you saying?' He had mentioned this before, but she hadn't believed he was serious. They had always been happy enough here.

'It's decided.' His words were clipped with anger. 'I have no intention of explaining my reasons to you or anyone else. While I'm head of this household, you'll do as I wish.'

'But *why*?' It didn't make any sense to her. 'We've always been comfortable here.'

'We're leaving, and that's an end to it. I want us to make a new start somewhere else.' His tone softened. 'Look, Bridget, I realise it will be a terrible upheaval, but nothing worthwhile is ever easy. And besides, it's what I need, something new and challenging to occupy my mind. And don't talk about the quarry, or my work, because I'll find other work easy enough, and so will you. Leaving here will be good for us, Bridget. We could even take a little holiday before we settle down.'

Shocked into silence, Bridget stared at him, at his shining blue eyes and the boyish way he was grinning at her. She had never seen him so excited. She was intrigued, and then she felt angry. How dare he make decisions like this without talking it over with her first?

Suddenly, like a slap across the face, she remembered her own shameful secret, and the anger turned to fear. This was the time to tell him about her and Harry, and the child that had been made out of wedlock. The moment was right and she must seize it with both hands.

Taking a deep breath, she said, 'Sit down, Tom. I have something to say.'

'Oh aye! I'm sure you have.' He didn't see the worried glint in her eyes or hear the tremor in her voice. 'But I'm warning you, Bridget, my mind's made up and you won't change it, whatever argument you come up with. I've been through them all, and there is nothing to keep me here.' Except a child, he thought. Only that. Nothing else.

'Please, Tom. Sit down.'

For a moment he looked at her, and then he sat down facing her, his arms folded in front of him.

Bridget swallowed hard. 'When I've told you what's on my mind, you might want to throw me out on the streets. I pray you won't do that. Instead, I hope you will find it in your heart to forgive me. And, though I don't deserve it, maybe I can hold on to the love and trust you have always given me.'

Tom sat forward in his seat, a look of confusion on his face.

She went on, 'I know the biggest disappointment in your life has been that we never made a child together, and that's why it's especially difficult for me to say what's on my mind.' She wondered how she could go on with Tom's puzzled blue eyes staring at her, his fists clenched on the table in front of him as though ready to fight off some awful thing that was about to attack.

'Go on.' His face was set like stone. 'Let's hear the rest of it.'

Afraid but determined, she said, 'You remember the night of the storm, when you were snowed in at work and didn't get home until the next morning?' He nodded slowly. 'You never knew, but I got home only minutes before you. It was snowing when I set off for home but I didn't think it would be much, and anyway I was anxious to be home in case you worried about me.' As he always did, she thought regretfully. 'Before I knew it, the snow was falling from the skies like it was the end of the world. The wind was fierce, blowing the snow every which way, half blinding me, until I could hardly see where I was going.'

As Bridget conveyed the mood of the night, it all came alive in her mind, and she was carried back there, to Harry's arms. She felt her face grow hot and pink, and bent her head so Tom would not see. Dear God, forgive me, she prayed silently. Her tongue was so dry with fear it stuck to the roof of her mouth, but she must not stop.

'I was found in great difficulties,' she said. 'I had lost all track of which way I was heading, and by this time I couldn't even find my way back.' How could she tell him that the master of the house had made advances to her and that was why she couldn't go back? Tom might think she had encouraged him, especially when he knew what she and Harry had done.

'Who was it found you?' Tom's voice was harsh.

Reluctant to betray Harry, Bridget didn't answer.

'Dammit, woman! I asked who was it found you?' The question was put so loudly and with such force, it struck the fear of God into her.

'It was Harry. If he hadn't found me, I might have frozen to death.' She was visibly trembling, her guilt alive in her eyes. She had not wanted to reveal Harry's name, but what choice had she? Tom would discover his name one way or the other whether she told him willingly or not.

'Go on.' Tom's voice was so low she could barely hear him.

'We had to take shelter in a barn . . . I . . . we . . .' The sweat was running down her back. She wanted to run from here, like the coward she was, but she remained, as she knew she must. 'We huddled together to keep warm, then, some time in the night . . . we made love . . .' Her voice faltered. Tears rolled down her face and fell over her hands. 'Oh, Tom! I'm carrying his child. I would give anything for it not to have happened. It's *your* child I want, not his. Never his!'

There! It was said.

The silence in that little room was so thick she could hardly breathe. She dared not look up. She stared at the pattern in the rug and thought how she had not beaten it hard enough on the line because there was a small ball of fluff in one corner.

When it came, it was with such force that she was knocked to the floor, her nose spurting blood where his fist had split the skin. 'You filthy little whore!' Standing over her, he reached down and put his two hands on her shoulders. Lifting her as if she was no more than a rag doll, he made her look at him, his face so close to hers she could see the small pink blood vessels in his eyes.

'Please, Tom,' she pleaded, 'let me make amends. I can. Please believe me …'

Her voice trailed away as he took hold of her by the throat, his words rasping in her ear. 'You let another man touch you . . . like *that*!' As he spoke he shivered. 'Trash! Nothing but trash!' With a wide sweep of his arm, he sent her flying against the sideboard. 'I can't even bear to look at you. Get out of my sight!' Grabbing her up, he swung her towards the door. 'You'll take nothing but what's on your back.' Crazed with jealousy and disgust, he gave her a sharp, cruel jab in her back. 'I ought to choke the life out of you. Then I should string you up on a lamppost and let the dogs tear you to shreds!'

In all his life he had never felt such fury, and such shame. Oh, the shame! His wife had been with another man. A man who had given her a child, when he never could. Something had snapped inside him and he wanted to kill.

Torn and bleeding, Bridget tried to keep some semblance of dignity. 'I don't blame you for hurting me . . . I deserve it. I'll do as you say, Tom. I'll go now, and I won't ever come back.'

He looked at her face and was deeply touched. Her big brown eyes gazed at him, tears trembling on her lashes and her nose bloodied and bruised where he had hit her, and with a great rush of sorrow he felt less of a man than he had ever felt. Some inner voice told him that she need not have been honest; she could have lied, and he might never have known. But honesty was her way. That was part of the reason he had fallen in love with her; that and her warm, childish smile.

When she turned to go, he wondered how he would ever manage without her. This house which had been their home and where they had known much happiness would be empty and cold. He would be all alone. Oh, he could go away as he had planned but somehow, without her, it seemed a futile thing to do. Besides, where would Bridget go? How would she manage? Loathing mingled with love, and he was lost in a sea of emotion.

'Will you go to *him*? The truth now!'

Bridget shook her head. 'No.'

'Why not?'

'I don't love him, not the way I love you.'

'So, you *do* love him?' Jealousy raged like an inferno inside him.

'In a way, yes. But it isn't the same.'

'I don't understand you any more.' Moving away from her, he walked up and down the room, his fists clenching and unclenching as he fought to control the tide of loathing he felt towards these two people, for they had turned his world upside down. The loathing showed in his voice. 'Does *he* know you're with child?'

Bridget's answer was given swiftly, and with the smallest glimmer of hope. 'He has no idea.'

Tom laughed aloud, startling her. 'What kind of justice is it when one man makes a child without even knowing it while the other craves to know the joy of being a father and never will be?'

Bridget thought it wise to say nothing, but her heart went out to him.

'Do you intend telling him?'

'No.'

He turned to stare at her. 'You realise I can never forgive you.'

'I know.' In pain and weakened by his attack on her, Bridget felt herself falling. Pushing herself upright, she pressed her weight against the door.

Ignoring her obvious distress, he resumed his pacing, up and down, like a caged animal, his mind working and weaving, and his fists doing the same. And then suddenly he was beside her, drawing her into his arms and thrusting her into the armchair. 'I don't want you walking the streets looking like this.' Gesturing to her bruises and cuts, he felt only a fleeting remorse. 'I don't want folk knowing what's been going on in this house. If this gets out you'll be looked down on by every God-fearing woman in

Lancashire – though you will have brought it on yourself! As for me, no doubt I shall be laughed at for the failure I am.'

He squeezed a cloth under cold water and threw it into her lap. 'Tidy yourself up. Keep your mouth shut about what's happened here tonight and, God willing, we might be able to salvage something from this bloody awful mess.'

For a moment Bridget wondered if he had found it in his heart to forgive her.

The coldness in his voice told her he hadn't. 'For the sake of your soul and my sanity, we need to keep everything as it was. Stay here. Have the child by all means, and raise it as ours.'

'Oh, Tom. I'm so glad!' Her eyes shone with joy, and for the moment nothing else mattered but that he had agreed to raise the child as his own. 'You won't regret it,' she promised. 'I'll be a good wife to you. As long as I live, I swear I'll never give you cause to feel ashamed.'

'It's too late for all that,' he snapped. 'What I've agreed to do carries a condition with it.'

'What condition?' She didn't like the look on his face, a kind of insane satisfaction.

'You must never speak to anyone of its real father.' Grabbing her roughly by the shoulders, he shook her hard. 'Not one word! Not even to the child itself.'

'All right, Tom. I'll abide by that condition.' What else could she do?

'And so you should!' He was smiling unpleasantly. 'As far as the world outside these four walls is concerned, your bastard will have been fathered by me, Tom Mulligan!' With a stiff finger he jabbed himself in the chest. 'Let them think that Tom Mulligan is as good as any man among them!' A flicker of fear swept over his features. 'Do you understand what I'm saying? Do you?'

'Yes, Tom. I understand.' It was what Bridget had hoped for, but not this way, with cruelty and hatred and self-serving pride.

'And do you agree?'

She took a moment to think it through.

Where was the harm? Harry was not in a position to take on a child, and if she left here, without money and without a place to go, what would become of her? What would become of the child? How would they live? The prospect was frightening. On the other hand, Tom was offering her a way out, offering to take on another man's child and to give them both a home. Clearly, the need to make himself seem a man among men outweighed his outrage at being cuckolded.

A thought suddenly came to her. Of course! That was what Mrs Louis had been talking about when she said her husband had taunted Tom at the party. Ted Louis must have sneered at Tom about him not having fathered a child up to now. And that must be the reason Tom had decided he wanted to move away. Yes! It was all becoming clear. This was a way of showing them all, and he could not do it without her help. In a way it gave her a measure of satisfaction.

'You haven't answered me!' His voice penetrated her thoughts. 'Do you agree?'

'Yes,' she answered quietly. 'I agree.'

'Good!' Straightening himself to his full height, he flexed his shoulders, as though he'd just been relieved of a heavy burden. 'Now then, woman, when I get back, I want to see you washed and cleaned up. We've still got a deal of talking to do, but first, I have other business to attend to.' He narrowed his eyes. 'You'll never know what you've done to me this day, Bridget Mulligan.'

'Where are you going?' Anxiety betrayed itself in her eyes.

'You've already done your worst,' he answered angrily. 'Now it's my turn.'

Realisation dawned. 'No! Don't go to him. Please, Tom, leave it be.'

'Oh no!' He smiled wickedly. 'There are scores to settle.'

'Violence won't solve anything.'

'Maybe not.'

'Then please, don't go.'

'Oh, you'd like that, wouldn't you? You'd like me to cower from him, pretend nothing happened.' The sneer slid from his face. As he raised his arm, Bridget instinctively backed away. She was too late. A hard blow to the side of her head knocked her sideways. He looked down on her as she fell. 'The time when you could tell me what to do is over,' he growled. 'Remember that. And remember this, too. I've always been too proud a man to link with whores, so I'll thank you to stay out of my bed. While I'm away from this house, I want you to move all signs of yourself from the bedroom. It finishes here, Bridget. For as long as we live, there can be nothing between us, except the man you deceived me with and the bastard you forced on me.'

Bridget watched him leave. 'Oh, dear God. What have I done to that good man?' For that was what he had been, a good man, a good husband and a good Christian. Now, like a wounded animal, he was out for revenge and it was a terrible sight to see.

As he went down the street, Tom recalled the look on her face when he told her it was all finished. 'Tears are no good now, my beauty,' he whispered unforgivingly.

He had treated Bridget's tears with contempt.

Now, as the tears fell down his own sorry face, he realised how she must have felt.

Without warning, the heavens opened and the rain lashed down, soaking him to the skin. He seemed not to notice. Holding his head high, and with his heart set like stone against her, he angrily wiped away the scalding tears. 'Scores to settle,' he muttered, quickening his steps. 'Without pride, a man is nothing!'

* * *

The rain lashed down and brought a darkness that turned day into night, but Harry barely noticed. He stood outside his father's house, his thoughts going back to a night some three and a half months ago; the most wonderful night of his life, and the worst.

'Better get inside,' he muttered. 'Mother will be wanting her medicine.' Yet still he stood there, his gaze on the house, his heart soothed by its familiar presence. Here in this place he had known a measure of sanctuary. Not now, though. Now, the house and all inside it were like an albatross round his neck.

Straddling the corner of Ainsworth Street, the building was many years old. Its ancient roof dipped at one end, and at the other the brickwork was so higgledy-piggledy, one layer was no longer distinguishable from another. It had been in Harry's family for three generations. His grandfather had built it, and his own father, Silas, had been master of it for nigh on forty years. Silas had fathered three children here; Alice, now nearly twenty-five, was the first-born, followed two years later by Harry, and then three years later came their younger sister Fay.

All three children were born in the very room where Harry's mother now spent most of her waking days. All her births had been bad, each taking its own particular toll on her health. The last one had weakened her heart, until now she barely had the strength to lift herself up. Maud had never been a strong woman, but she was brave. It was not in her nature to bemoan her lot in life. She dearly loved both her daughters – Fay, with her bright smile and homely ways, and Alice, with her lofty ideas and delusions of grandeur. But Harry would always be her favourite. He was reliable and loving, with a deep, quiet nature and a well of goodness in his soul.

Maud knew Harry's every mood. As a rule, there was nothing he could hide from her. Lately, though, she sensed there was something preying on his mind and, try as she might, she could not persuade him to confide in her.

Her eyes strayed to the window. 'Where are you, lad?' she muttered. Maud had always called him 'lad', and as the years rolled on, taking with them the best part of her senses, she found pleasure in hanging on to the old habits. It helped her feel that life was not altogether passing her by.

Outside, Harry stood, a lone, sad figure, his right hand in his pocket, holding the bottle of medicine he had been sent to collect. He looked up at the old house and wondered if he would ever be free of his responsibilities. 'Oh, Bridget,' he sighed. 'If only it could have been different.' But it wasn't, and unless he was to lose everything he knew and clung to, it never would be. His mother was old and feeble, and with his father working so hard it was up to Harry to look after her. Being the peevish, bone-lazy person she was, Alice increasingly shifted more and more of the work and responsibility on to his shoulders.

As for his younger sister Fay, she had made a new life as a teacher at the Blackburn orphanage; bright and generous, she would have gladly given up her work to take care of her mother, but Harry would have none of it. 'You're too young and talented to waste your life,' he insisted. In the end, secure in the knowledge that all was well and that she had Harry's blessing, she went her own way, coming home to visit whenever she could snatch time away from the orphanage.

For a long time, Harry stood in the darkened street, oblivious of the rain running down his neck and soaking through to his shirt. 'We shouldn't have done it, Bridget,' he muttered. 'But I'd do it again. If only it was possible, I'd take you away and love you and care for you . . .' From somewhere deep inside a sigh of regret rose to stifle him. 'But we both know you're not mine, and never can be. And I don't blame you for avoiding me at the big house. I know how it is, and I'm sorry. Once we were good friends, but even that's gone now. My fault. Not yours.'

From where he stood he could see his father bent at his work;

weekday, weekend, he toiled away, sixty years of age, grey-haired and weary but with a sparkle in his eyes that only his work could ignite. Silas Little had been a respected tailor in these parts all his working life. His work was his great pride, even above his family, and only the call of a higher master would take him from it. But the price of such devotion was cruel, for now he walked as bent as when he slaved over his table. His spine was crooked and so too were his fingers; the curvature of his neck had become more prominent these past few years, and his knees gave him great pain when he walked. Even his eyesight was suffering, so that often he would sew a seam where none should be. But, for all that, he was still the best tailor in Blackburn.

From upstairs, Alice spied Harry in the rain. 'What the devil's he been up to?' she asked herself. 'If ever there was a man with a guilty conscience, it's him.'

The fevered tapping on the wall sent her running into her mother's room. 'For heaven's sake, Mother, what now?' she demanded impatiently, at the same time snatching away the stick her mother had used to summon her. 'I can't keep running in here all hours of the day and night. I'm not a strong woman, you know that.'

'Stuff and nonsense!' Maud was fifty-eight, quick and shrewd, but only in short spasms. She called these lucid periods her 'real' time. The rest of the time she was in another world, a make-believe place where nothing could hurt her. Right now she was enjoying one of her 'real' moments.

'You're a fit, able woman who likes to imagine she's too delicate to lift a cup, but I know better, Alice Little, and I'll thank you not to lie to your mother. Now then, fetch me a jeremiah and be quick about it, before I wet the sheets.'

'You do, and I'll rub your nose in it!' Alice threatened.

'You'll never live to see the day, my girl!' Nevertheless,

Maud didn't doubt for one minute that her daughter would take pleasure in doing such a thing.

'I mean it, Mother. Wet your bed and you'll be sorry!'

Scurrying downstairs to the washroom, Alice grabbed up the jeremiah and returned, puffing and panting, into her mother's room. Throwing back the sheets, she stuffed the jeremiah under her mother's backside. 'It's Harry's turn to see to you,' she grumbled. 'He should be in here, not messing about outside in the rain. What's he playing at, that's what I'd like to know!'

'Oh, shut up, girl!' In Maud's eyes Harry could do no wrong.

Under her breath, Alice replied peevishly, '*You* shut up, you old hag!' Wrinkling her nose with disgust, she watched her mother's expression change from agony to bliss. The tinkle of water sounded through the room; the smell was vile, for her mother's urine had grown stronger with age. 'Hurry up!' Alice cried. 'I've things to do.'

'I can't hurry up, silly girl,' came the curt reply. 'Anyway, don't stand there watching me. It puts me off.'

Eventually she was finished and Alice slid the jeremiah from beneath her. 'You've *filled* it!' she cried, horrified as a trickle escaped and ran on to the sheet. 'You're disgusting!'

Feeling threatened, Maud began to cry. 'I don't want you. You're cruel. Where's Harry? I want Harry.'

'Yes, and he's welcome to you! I told you, he's outside in the rain. If he had any sense he'd clear off from these parts, and me with him!' Sometimes she pitied Harry, and sometimes she hated him. Right now, she pitied him. Herself too.

She emptied the jeremiah and returned to her own room. Going to the window, she looked out, in time to witness a startling scene in the street below.

Harry was on the point of entering the house when he noticed a figure striding determinedly towards him. It was only when the man was almost on top of him that he saw it was Tom Mulligan. 'Is it me you want?' Harry suspected it must be. Strange how sometimes your thoughts could summon up reality.

Amazed at the other man's coolness, Tom clenched his fists. 'You know bloody well it's you I want!' Legs apart, he stood facing Harry, itching to smash his fist into that quiet face but biding his time until he had some answers. In a voice trembling with emotion, he asked, 'Answer me straight, you bastard. Did you take her against her will?'

A look of surprise crossed Harry's features. 'Did Bridget tell you that?'

'I'm asking you!'

Harry wondered what had made Bridget confess to Tom. 'Bridget and I were caught up in circumstances not of our own making,' he admitted reluctantly. 'It wasn't meant to happen, did she tell you that?'

'*Did you take her against her will?*' Tom's raised voice carried through the sound of thunder to Alice, who had opened her window and was listening to every word, despite the rain lashing down on her.

Harry shook his head. 'I think you know I would never do such a thing, especially not to Bridget.'

'You're a filthy liar!' With a roar, Tom launched himself at Harry, catching him off guard and sending him sprawling to the pavement. 'Liar! Liar!' With every blow Tom cursed and yelled, straddling Harry on the ground and punching at him with such manic strength, it seemed he would finish him off there and then.

For a terrible time Harry was pinned beneath him, until he was on the verge of losing his senses. Then with an almighty burst of strength he thrust his attacker aside. In seconds, the two of them were on their feet. Equally matched, they fought like tigers. There was no mercy, and no victor. Each drew blood, which washed to the pavement and was taken by the rain.

From her vantage point, Alice thought she would be the only witness to murder. The street, which consisted mainly of lock-up shops, was deserted, as it usually was on a Sunday evening. Struggling on the cobbles, Harry seemed to be getting the upper hand as he held Tom down with one fist. But before he could hit him, Tom was back on his feet and dragging Harry across the street by his hair. When he brought his fist up and under Harry's chin, the crunch of bone was sickening.

Greatly excited, yet not wanting Harry to be left dead on the ground in case she was lumbered with looking after their elderly parents, Alice ran down the stairs and out of the front door. 'Leave him alone, Tom Mulligan!' Running towards them as they tumbled and fought on the other side of the street, she threatened to call the police if they didn't stop.

Through swollen eyes Tom saw her coming towards them. Harry turned to see who it was, and in that split second was knocked down yet again by a cowardly blow to the head.

Before he could recover, Tom had him by the throat, squeezing so hard that Harry could not breathe. 'One word to anyone about what's happened between you and Bridget, and I'll throw her out on the street without a second thought. If I remember rightly, you've enough on your plate without taking on a harlot. Believe me, you bastard, I'll ruin her name and yours with it – your father's too! He won't be the respected tailor *then*, will he, eh? So think on what you're doing to others before you open your mouth!'

With that he thrust Harry aside and made off, a bizarre sight with his clothes torn, his face swollen and bloody, one arm hanging limp by his side, and his legs hardly able to keep him upright.

'I've done what I set out to do,' he muttered through swollen lips. 'I've salvaged my pride, and made sure he'll keep his mouth shut. He'll never know he fathered a bastard. And neither will anybody else.'

* * *

Behind him, Alice was firing all manner of questions as she helped Harry into the house. 'What the devil have you been up to, you bloody fool? Why was Tom Mulligan here? Why did he go at you like a mad bull? Crazy, he was! Answer me, Harry. What have you done to antagonise him like that?'

Shaking her off, Harry bent over the sink and washed the blood from his face. Then he tipped a jug of cold water over his head and ran his hands through his hair. 'None of your business,' he said through his dripping hair. He sat down heavily in a kitchen chair, leaned forward and covered his face with his hands. 'It's between me and Tom Mulligan.' Gingerly, he felt his jawbone. From the pain he had thought it must be broken, but thankfully it wasn't.

'I won't go till you tell me what you've been up to.'

Harry scowled at her, his voice rasping, 'Didn't I just say it's none of your bloody business?' Raising the back of his hand, he wiped a trickle of blood from his mouth. 'Go to your room, Alice,' he snapped. The last thing he needed right now was Alice and her sense of righteousness.

The wickedest of smiles crossed her plain features. 'You might as well tell me, Harry, because I heard most of it anyway.'

'You *what*?'

'I heard.'

'Oh? And what did you hear, eh?'

'You and *her* . . . Bridget Mulligan.' Seeing the shocked look on his face, she dared to come nearer. 'He asked if you took her against her will.' Softly laughing, she went on mercilessly, 'Did you, Harry? Did you take Tom Mulligan's wife against her will?'

'Shut your mouth, Alice!' Leaping from his chair, Harry went to grab her, but when she laughingly dodged him, he turned awkwardly and fell back, crashing into the chair.

'Sounds to me like you had your wicked way with her,' she taunted him, 'and now the whole town will know. Did you never stop to think about Mother and Father, and how it would affect their good name?' Suddenly, as another, more unbearable thought struck home, she gasped, 'And what about *me*? I'll never be able to hold my head up in this town again! Then there's Fay. I shouldn't be at all surprised if she doesn't lose her job at the orphanage. I mean, they won't allow her to carry on working there, will they? Not with a placard over the front door saying, "Outcast the sinners". It's *us* they'll outcast, Harry. The entire family, and all because you couldn't keep your hands off another man's wife. Why didn't you think what you were doing to us?'

When Harry did not answer, she changed tack. 'Did she lead you on, Harry? Was that it? I might see you in a different light if that were the case. Was it, Harry? Was it her fault and not yours?'

'Forget that kind of talk, Alice,' he warned gruffly. 'Bridget Mulligan is a good woman.' Realising his sister could ruin Bridget's name if she set her mind to it, he added, 'She wouldn't know *how* to lead a man on.'

Insensitive as ever, Alice made the mistake of going too far. 'I'm right, I know I am. A slut like Bridget Mulligan should be marched through the streets for all decent folk to spit on.' Her face was too near, her eyes too wild. 'And you with her, because as far as I can tell, you're no better than she is. What's more—'

Her words ended in a cry as Harry lunged at her. He grabbed her by the collar, twisting it tight as she tried to resist. 'You seem to have trouble understanding what I'm saying,' he hissed. 'So I'll say it again. Bridget Mulligan did *not* lead me on, nor has she laid claim to me in any way. If she did, things might be very different. As it is, you had better be very careful what you say and to whom, because if you aren't, Alice, the repercussions will indeed be serious.'

Throwing her aside, he went back to the sink to bathe the wound on his temple, which was once again oozing blood.

'Look what you've done!' Alice shrieked. 'You've dripped blood all over my sleeve. Damn you, Harry! You've ruined my best blouse!'

Harry ignored her.

Suddenly she was at his side, tugging at his arm. 'And what did you mean about me having to be careful or the repercussions could be serious? It seems to me that it's you and Bridget Mulligan who should have been careful and the repercussions are all your fault.'

Swinging round, Harry regarded her with pity. 'You still don't understand, do you? If you open your mouth and let it be known what happened here tonight, then the scandal that will follow most certainly *will* be your fault.'

His words infuriated her. 'The two of you should be shown up for what you are,' she snapped, 'and the Mulligan woman should be shunned by every decent person in Blackburn. It's only what you deserve, so why should I care?' With that she turned and swept across the room. 'In fact, I think Father should be told how you've disgraced the family. I shall tell him first, and then I shall talk to Mother. You've always been her favourite. Goodness knows what *she'll* have to say about all this. Her precious Harry, bedding another man's wife, and the poor fellow seeking you out on your own doorstep. And the pair of you fighting in the street like a pair of dogs.'

She had the door half open, unaware that Silas was in the passage outside. What he heard struck him to the heart. He hurried back to his work.

Harry strode across the room and quietly closed the door. 'Remember what you said before, Alice,' he urged. 'The whole family would suffer if the truth ever got out. It would be the end of your ladies' afternoons because none of your so-called friends would set foot over the threshold again.'

'I knew it!' As always, her thoughts were only for herself. 'I'm ruined.'

'That's not all.' Harry was concerned not so much for himself as for his family, and for Bridget. Trying to keep the desperation out of his voice, he outlined the future in harsh terms. 'Our parents would be shunned, and Father would lose the reputation he's built up over many hard years; decent folk would stop bringing work to him, and money would get scarcer and scarcer until you might be forced to find a husband who could support you.'

Alice's eyes widened with horror.

Encouraged, Harry went on, 'Fay would lose her job like you said and she would have to come home again – you and her, arguing the whole time like you used to. I would never be able to support all of you, not if I worked from morning to night, seven days a week. We could lose the house.'

She stared at him, eyes glittering, hating him with every part of her soul. 'You deserve to burn in hell for what you've done to us.'

Taking her by the shoulders, he said, 'Listen to me, Alice. It's all up to you. Tom Mulligan will keep his mouth shut because he obviously loves Bridget. He wouldn't want the world knowing how his wife had slept with another man. He'd be too shamed by it. Bridget won't talk of it, and neither will I. Don't you see, Alice, if you keep quiet, no one will ever know, and life can go on as before.'

'So now you want me to be part of a conspiracy.'

'It's your decision. That's all I'm saying.'

'How do I know it will never happen again – you and *her*?'

'Because I give you my word.'

'I can't trust you.'

'All I can do is give my word.'

For a long moment she continued to stare at him, at his bloodied face and the look of despair in his eyes, and she felt nothing but contempt.

With her eyes fixed on his, she raised her hand and summoning all the force in her body she brought it down across his mouth. The shock of it stunned him. 'You're no brother of mine!' she hissed. She intended to make him suffer for what he had done. It wasn't the shame that drove her. Deep down she was consumed with jealousy. She had never known what it was like to have a man hold her in his arms, while Bridget Mulligan had both husband and lover.

Without another word, she flung open the door and was gone, leaving Harry staring after her. 'God help us,' he murmured. Would Alice keep his secret or would she ruin them all out of spite?

Closing the door, he searched in the dresser for a clean shirt and a towel. Then he set about strip-washing at the sink.

When he was clean and feeling fresher, he put on his coat and went out into the street. Here, in the light from the street lamps, he searched for the bottle of medicine he'd brought for his mother. It was only a matter of minutes before he found it, half hidden at the foot of the steps where it had skidded from his pocket when he fell.

Thankfully it was not broken, though it had landed near a shard of broken glass which pricked his finger when he reached down. 'Not my night at all,' he said sardonically. Dropping the bottle into his pocket he went inside and up to his mother's room.

Alice brushed by him on the landing. 'Have you thought over what I said?' he asked hopefully, needing to know.

With a cold, hostile glare she passed him by without a word.

'Hard bitch!' Agitated, Harry went into his mother's room, and was concerned to find her wide awake. 'You should have been asleep ages ago,' he chided. 'I've brought you your new bottle of medicine.' He gave her a kiss and set the bottle on her bedside table. 'You look pretty,' he said with a smile.

Laughing with delight, Maud took hold of his hand and with surprising strength pulled him down to sit beside her. 'What I want to know is, where have you been? I thought you'd be back ages since.'

'Met a friend,' he lied. 'You know how it is, Ma.'

'Have you been fighting with one of them bloody horses again?' she asked, fingering his wounded temple. 'I've told you before, they're dangerous beasts.'

'Aw, they wouldn't harm a fly,' he replied. 'The master has two carriage horses and an old mare that's past her prime. You'd hardly call them fighting horses.'

'So how did you hurt yourself then?'

'Never you mind.' He had lied enough for one day. 'It doesn't bother me, so it shouldn't bother you.'

'I expect you did it in the stable, and didn't even know you'd done it. Cracked it on a beam or something like that.'

'Happen I did, and happen I didn't. What does it matter?'

Maud shook her head, smiling at him. 'I remember when you were a lad you were allus falling down or tripping up. Oh, but you were such a happy little soul, allus laughing and looking for mischief.' She gazed on him a moment longer, before closing her eyes. 'Oh, lad, I'm that tired. Give us a kiss and be off with you.'

Leaning over, he kissed her softly and squeezed her hand. 'Sleep well, Mam,' he murmured. 'I'll see you in the morning.'

For a time he stood outside the bedroom door, wondering whether he should go after Alice and find out what she had decided. Until he knew what was on her mind, he couldn't rest. He felt like a man with an axe hanging over him. 'She's making me stew in it,' he muttered. 'Oh, bugger it! I'll not give her the satisfaction.'

He hurried down the stairs. When he reached the bottom step, he sat down, his fists under his chin and his elbows resting on his knees. 'What a bloody mess I've caused,' he muttered regretfully.

He wondered how Bridget was faring. Tom Mulligan seemed to love her enough to want to hold on to her, and that being the case, she should come to no harm as far as he could see. 'You've got a man who values you enough to fight for you, Bridget, my love,' he whispered, 'and I'll not come between you ever again.'

He could hear Alice moving about in the kitchen. From where he sat, he had a view of the kitchen door; it was closed but even if it hadn't been, he would still not have been seen. There was a certain comfort in knowing he was hidden from sight.

His gaze travelled down the passageway to the front door. Above the door was a fanlight, and set in the fanlight was a peacock in coloured glass. The light in the passage made it seem almost real; when the light flickered, the peacock seemed to dance, and when he blew softly into the lamp wick, he could swear the bird actually raised its wings and took flight.

As a boy he would delight in mimicking the movement of the bird. It was only when he reached an age when children stop believing that he realised with great sadness that the bird could not move, let alone fly, and that it was all in his imagination. It didn't stop him dreaming though, so after a time the bird recovered its freedom.

Harry had been brought up in this house, and he would rather cut off his right arm than leave it. If anyone might have tempted him to do so, it would have been Bridget, but not now. The price of love was too high. The house was his sanctuary, just as it had been for his parents and his father's parents before. He knew every corner, every nook and cranny. He knew its every mood, and he recognised every smell exuding from its walls. He could smell it now, the warm and musty smell that lived in the passageway, the damp brought in through the ill-fitting front door, the particular odour of worn rugs over a wooden floor, and that comfortable smell of old coats hanging on the pegs by the door.

He got to his feet and made his way down the passage towards his father's workroom. One tap on the door brought the familiar response, 'Come in, son.'

As he entered, Harry was assailed by the smell of cloth, new and old, fabric from bygone days and cloths brought in only yesterday. Roll after roll of material in every colour was stacked on the shelves all around the room. The only light was from the street lamp outside the window and a narrow shaft which glowed from the lamp on his father's bench.

His father was bent over his bench, needle in hand, tiny glasses perched on the end of his nose; even his father carried a particular smell, old and heady, like a pressed flower preserved in time. 'I'm not disturbing you, am I, Father?' The thought that by his actions he may have destroyed this gentle man who had never done anything wrong in his life filled Harry with remorse.

Silas smiled at him. 'Come in, son,' he urged. 'Close the door.' Laying down his needle and spectacles, he gestured for Harry to be seated. 'You'll take a drop of brandy with me, won't you, son?'

'I'd like that, Father, thank you.'

Rising from his chair, Silas went to the tallboy and took out a bottle and two glasses. 'Is there something you want to tell me?' he asked pointedly. He poured a small measure of brandy into each glass, handed one to Harry and sat down opposite him with the other.

'No, there's nothing I want to tell you,' Harry said, his heart beating faster. Did he know about him and Bridget Mulligan? Had Alice been in to see him already?

His fears were allayed when his father smiled disarmingly. 'That's all right then,' he said, 'only you normally tell me what's been going on at the big house. Is the master well?'

'Very well. He's talking about buying a new horse to replace the old mare. She might be taken out of active service and put to foaling.'

Silas nodded. 'I see.' He sipped at his brandy, wondering if Harry would tell him about the row he had overheard. In his heart he wanted his son to confide in him, but he could not make him. Harry was his own man, and had been for a very long time.

For the first time that he could ever recall, Harry felt uncomfortable in his father's presence. 'Are you well, Father?'

'I'm very well, son, and you?' There was always this degree of respect between them, but beneath the surface lay a great deal of love.

'Father?'

'Yes?'

Harry bit his lip. 'It doesn't matter.' For a moment he had been on the verge of telling his father about himself and Bridget. God almighty! What was he thinking of?

Silas sensed his dilemma. 'I'm very proud of you, son, you do know that, don't you?' When Harry was about to reply, he put up his hand to silence him. 'I know we don't see much of each other, and we don't get the chance to talk man to man as we should. We both work hard, and there is nothing wrong with that. But it saps a man's strength, steals his time until after a while he can't see beyond the work he's doing.'

'I know that, Father.'

'And you do know how much I love you, don't you, even if I haven't been much of a father?'

Choked with emotion, and growing surer by the minute that his father knew something, Harry could not open his mouth to reply.

'Sometimes, son, we make terrible mistakes. It can't be helped, you know. We're all human. We're all weak.'

'Not you, Father.'

'Oh yes, son, especially me.'

'Are you trying to tell me something, Father?'

'No.' Silas shook his head. He had said all he needed to. 'Except maybe to remind you that I regret the time we've wasted, you and I. I was never there for you. I had to make a living, you see.'

'I know that.'

'Of course you do, son. Responsibilities bind us all, like a millstone round a man's neck.' His smile was serene. 'The only way we can survive is by learning to love the millstone as if it was part of our very soul.' Suddenly he was bright and alert, like a weasel popping up to see who was about. 'There, you see, I'm just a silly old man feeling sorry for myself. Do you know the biggest regret of my life?'

'Please, I would like to know.'

'That you never took up tailoring. You remind me of your grandfather. Like him, you have a natural eye for good cloth and the way a suit should hang on a man. You've proven that many a time when you've watched me fitting. As a boy you'd say, "It's too long," or, "Look, Father, it's all loose." I recall a time when you even tucked a sleeve with your own tiny hands. And you've sat with me often enough as a boy to see how I make a suit out of a roll of cloth. Why did you never take it up? You could have been a better tailor even than your grandfather. For all my striving, I have never really matched him. Why, son? Why did you never turn your heart that way?'

Before Harry could answer, Silas waved his hand and took

Harry's glass from him. 'I have to finish Squire Arnold's waistcoat before tomorrow evening. Leave me now, son.' Laying a hand on Harry's shoulder, he said softly, 'You've been a good son. I hope, in my own way, I have been a good father.'

'Would you like me to stay?' Harry asked. 'I could watch you, like I used to.'

Silas shook his head. 'Not tonight, thank you all the same.' With that he bade Harry goodnight and watched him leave the room. He closed the door behind Harry and returned to his bench, but he did not resume his work. Instead he sat thinking over their conversation, and how he might have been a better father to that fine young man. It was too late now, he thought with a heavy heart.

For the first time in his life, the old man let his emotions spill over. Softly, all alone in that room, he allowed himself to weep. And the tears that rolled down his face were a blessed relief.

That night, Harry couldn't sleep. He lay awake, his mind on Bridget, then on his father. He thought of Alice and what she might do. Driven by tortured thoughts, he saw the worst in everything.

When the morning skies were filled with ribbons of dawn, he finally closed his eyes and snatched a few precious hours of sleep.

When, some time later, he awoke, he thought he must be late and leaped out of bed. Quickly he washed and dressed, thinking of the day ahead, and how he was to take the mare to a yard some distance away. She would remain there for a month, and while there would be mated with the best stallion in Lancashire. Thinking of work gave him a certain peace of mind.

His first port of call every morning was to look in on his mother. She was sleeping peacefully. 'See you later, Ma,' he whispered. When his new-found love for Bridget was weighed against his old love for this dear soul, and the kindly man downstairs, Harry realised that he could never leave them to fend for themselves.

Every day for as long as he could remember, his father had been the first to rise and the last to bed so he knew that Silas would already be at his bench. Harry wanted to have a word with him. Silas's words last night still preyed on his mind. His father must not think he had not been a good father, for he had been the best he could. Harry wanted to reassure him of that.

In his stockinged feet, he went softly downstairs, afraid to wake the others; it was all on his mind – work, his father, Alice, and Bridget. Thoughts of retribution. 'Concentrate on your work,' he muttered, pulling on his walking boots. 'It will help clear your mind.'

It didn't though. What if he saw Bridget going about her duties up at the house? How would he react? What should he say? But maybe she wouldn't be there. Because of what had happened, Tom might well have forbidden her to work at the Grange. And who could blame him for that?

Going along the passage he tapped gently on the workroom door, waiting a moment for his father's 'Come in, son.'

The answer didn't come, so he tapped again. 'It's me, Father. I'll be off to work in a while, but if you can spare me a few minutes, I need to talk.'

He waited patiently. Often his father would be in the middle of a difficult task, or he might be on the ladder reaching up to sort a roll of cloth; either way his mind would be preoccupied and he would not hear the tap on the door.

When, after a further moment or two, there was still no answer, Harry took the liberty of peeping in.

A smile lit his face. It was just as he'd thought. As usual, Silas was bent over his work, concentrating so hard he hadn't heard his knock.

'I won't keep you too long, Father.' Harry started across the room. 'It's something you said last night – I just want to put your mind at rest.'

Silas made no answer. Instead, he kept his head down, seeming not to have heard.

'Father?' Gingerly, Harry came nearer.

When he was close enough to see his father's face, his heart froze. Silas was looking down, his forehead touching the work still clutched in his hands. His eyes were wide open, almost as though he was inspecting the sewing he had just completed. But there was no life in those old eyes, and for a terrible moment Harry found he couldn't move.

He stood there, looking down on that kindly old man. His heart felt like a stone inside his chest as he struggled to believe what his eyes told him to be the truth. His father, the man who had been his mentor for all his life, was gone from this world. And the world was suddenly a lonely place.

With a great searing gasp, Harry took the old man in his strong arms and rocked him back and forth, shocked to find that the frail figure was still warm to the touch. 'No!' Over and over, he cried out, 'Oh, dear God, no!' The grief took hold of him and tore him to shreds. He learned pain of a kind he had never known before. In that moment, when he held his lifeless father in his arms, willing him back but knowing it was futile, he realised that nothing in the world mattered but what he had lost.

He did not hear the door open. He did not see Alice come into the room, brought there by his awful cries. When she saw what had happened, she fell to her knees beside Harry.

For a long time, neither of them spoke, each suffering in their own way. Then, after a while, Alice stood up. 'He's gone,' she said softly. 'Leave him, Harry. You can't bring him back.'

When he merely stared at her, she said, 'I'll have to get the doctor, but you can see there is nothing he can do.' Reading his mind, she told him, 'I haven't got the courage to tell Mother. You will have to do that.' She looked once more at the face of her father, a man she had never been close to. Then she left them there, father and son, together for the last time.

Harry spoke to his father as if he could hear. 'I needed you to know how much I love you,' he murmured, stroking that dear face. 'I wanted to say how wrong you were in thinking you had not been a good father.' Pausing, he choked back his grief. 'I would not have wanted any other but you.'

There was something else too. 'You said your greatest regret was that I had not taken up your trade. I mean to put that right. I promise you now, Father, I'll carry on your name. I won't let all your good work come to nothing.' It was the least he could do. 'Besides, it will be a fitting penance for my sins.'

When he couldn't speak any more, and the tears blurred his vision so he couldn't see that familiar face, he lifted the small figure and carried him up to his bedroom. He laid him on his bed and covered him over. 'Sleep now, old man,' he said. 'You've earned your rest.'

As he went towards his mother's room, Alice emerged from there. 'Mother is still fast asleep. I'll go for the doctor now.'

There was a softness about Alice that he had not seen for a long time. 'Was it my fault?' he asked. 'Did he hear the row between us? Was it that that killed him, do you think?' He couldn't bear to think of it.

Alice shook her head. 'It was *work* that killed him, Harry,' she said kindly. 'Not you, and not me.'

'I hope so.' He shivered.

'There is no way he could have known about you and that woman,' Alice assured him. 'And no one ever will know because I won't tell. What happened between you and her will never see the light of day from me.'

'Thank you for that.' His mind was easier now, but not his

heart. In the room behind him his father lay, and with him the greater part of his own life. 'I owe you a debt of gratitude.'

The merest suggestion of a smile lit her eyes. 'I'll keep your secret, Harry,' she said slyly, 'but you must realise that it falls on you alone to take care of us now.'

As she walked away, Harry knew he would always be at her mercy.

Chapter Four

Halfway up the hill, Bridget paused to get her breath. 'By! I'm like an old cow ready for the knacker's yard.' Almost eight months pregnant and with the August sun blazing down on her, she thought she would never make it to Fanny's house. 'Keep going,' she urged herself. 'It's only a step or two further.'

In fact it was another half mile, but she caught her breath and was soon on her way again.

Fanny herself was only a fortnight from birthing, but she couldn't believe her eyes when she opened the door to see Bridget there. 'My God!' Propelling her inside, she chided, 'Will yer look at the state o' you. Face as red as a ripe tomato and sweating like you've done two rounds in a boxing ring. Whatever do you think yer playing at? D'yer want to drop the bairn in the street, is that what yer after?'

'I thought the walk up Montague Street would do me good,' Bridget explained.

'Did yer now? Well, yer a silly mare, that's all I have to say.' Shoving Bridget into a chair she told her, 'Sit yer arse there, me darlin', and don't move.' Waddling away, she grinned over her shoulder. 'I reckon you and me 'ave got summat to celebrate.'

Glad to remain in the chair, Bridget stretched out her legs while Fanny rummaged in the sideboard. 'I'll be glad when this baby's born,' Bridget said. 'I'm getting so I can hardly breathe.'

'All the more reason why yer shouldn't be draggin' yerself all over Blackburn!' Fanny leaned further into the sideboard. 'I'm bleedin' sure there was a bottle o' good stuff tucked away in 'ere.'

'I'm *not* draggin' meself all over Blackburn,' Bridget protested. 'I've come to see you because if I didn't get out of that house, I think I might go mad. The nearer I get to birthing, the more bad-tempered Tom gets. Honest to God, Fan, I'm at my wits' end.'

'Aye, well, you can understand him being bad-tempered,' Fanny mumbled. She'd found a mangy humbug and, after removing the layer of dust and grit, popped it into her mouth. 'I mean, what man would take kindly to his wife carrying another man's child?' The humbug clattered against her teeth, making her speak through half-closed lips. 'I'd be the very same,' she went on. 'What! I'd have sent you packing through the door a long time ago.' Fanny prided herself on her outspoken nature. 'The man loves yer, it's plain to see.'

Bridget agreed, but it didn't make life any easier. 'Sometimes I wish he *had* thrown me out on the streets. At least I'd know where I stood. Now, the way things are between us, it's like living with a stranger, only worse, because he has a right to both me and the child. I had to give up work two months ago and he knows I have no means of support. It's as if he takes pleasure in having power over me.'

'When the bairn's born, come here and stay with me.' Accidentally swallowing the humbug, Fanny gave a strange little gulp. 'I mean it,' she emphasised, her eyes watering. 'The two of us could look after each other.'

Bridget had thought long and hard about that, but it wasn't the answer. 'I know you mean well,' she said gratefully, 'and I won't forget it. But in a funny way I'm hoping that when the little one's born Tom will come to love it like his own. And maybe, after a time, he might come to love me again. Either way, the bairn will have a father – and his name. Deep down Tom's a good man. He always was. It's just that right now, with the way things are, he's going through a bad time.'

'Hmm. Good man or not, he's got something out of all this too, and don't you forget it.' Pausing in her search, Fanny popped her head up and peered over the table. 'He's a canny bugger an' all.'

'What do you mean?'

'I mean there's only you, me and Tom who knows the bairn isn't his. Even Harry doesn't know. Ain't that right?'

'Yes, thank God.'

'Well then. As far as everybody else is concerned, Tom Mulligan is about to become a father. And, that being so, he's a better man than his brother, and a better man than folk took him for.'

'He's still been shamed.'

'Does he know you've told me?'

Alarmed, Bridget sat up. 'No! And I hope he never does.'

Groaning, Fanny shifted her position and resumed her search. 'Don't worry,' she called, her head deep inside the cupboard. 'He'll not find out from me. But it only goes to prove what I'm saying. As far as he knows, it's just you and him keeping the secret.'

'Come to think of it, Nelly Potts said she heard how the men from the quarry celebrated soon as ever they heard the news.'

'There you are then. It's just like I said. Tom Mulligan's reputation is all the better for what you and Harry did.'

'I can't deny that. In fact, before it happened, he was intending to leave the quarry and the area where he's lived all his life. We'd have been uprooted to God knows where. He might not have found work, and we might have been miserable. All because he couldn't hold his head up among the other men. They'd all fathered bairns and he hadn't, you see.'

'Men! Scourge of the bleedin' earth, they are.'

'It's awful though, Fanny.' Tom's life may have been improved in some ways, she thought, but in others they were both victims of what happened the night of the snowstorm. 'He won't talk. He gets up of a morning and has his breakfast. I pack his snap can and off he goes. The same of an evening when he gets back. He comes in and I put his tea in front of him. He eats it in silence, then takes himself off to the front parlour where he stays till bedtime. We're like a pair of strangers.'

'Oh, Bridget, that's bloody terrible!' There was a scraping and scuffling from the sideboard. 'I can't find the bleedin' bottle an' I know it were in 'ere.'

'He knows I've no one else to talk to,' Bridget said quietly, 'but it doesn't seem to bother him. The only person I see from morning to night is Nelly Potts. She runs in and out all bloody day, getting on my nerves and making a right nuisance of herself. She comes to the door under any pretext, borrowing this, returning that. The other day she frightened the life out of me.'

'Oh?' Fanny looked up, knocking her head as she did so. 'Frightened the life out of you how?'

'It doesn't matter.' Bridget wished she'd kept her mouth shut. She didn't want Fanny frightened too.

'No, go on!' When Fanny's curiosity was aroused, there was no getting away from it. 'How did the old bugger frighten you?'

'You don't want to hear.'

'Oh, yes, I bleedin' well do. What's the silly cow been saying?'

'Something and nothing.'

'Bridget!'

'All right. She told me how, when her sister had her first bairn, it took a week for it to arrive. The next day she gave up the ghost, leaving the bairn to be looked after by her mam.'

Fanny laughed aloud. 'You don't believe that, do you? You know how the old'uns make up stories to frighten the young. The old biddy were just having you on. Take no notice.'

Bridget clung to the idea, and it gave her a crumb of comfort.

After a few more minutes scraping about in the cupboard, groaning and grunting, Fanny dragged herself upright. 'It's not there! *He* must have had it away when me back were turned. I'll skin the bugger alive when I get me hands on him.' Rubbing the rising bump on her forehead she grimaced. 'There ain't nothing safe. Not even my little treats.'

'Who are you talking about? Who's had what away?'

'Bill Norman, that's who.' Pointing to her swollen belly, she cried angrily, 'The randy devil who did this. What! The next time I clap eyes on him, he'll wish he'd never been born.'

'Don't get yourself in a state, Fanny. Whatever it was, we can do without it. Look. I'll make us a cup of tea and we'll have some of that nice fruit cake you keep.'

'You'll do no such thing. Stay where you are.'

'Please, Fanny. You've got yourself all flustered about something that doesn't really matter.' In fact, Fanny worried her; she was breathing heavily and her face had gone a shade of grey.

Fanny would have none of it. '*I'll* get the tea,' she said stubbornly. 'I ain't got no fruit cake, but I reckon there's a barm-cake left. We'll share it.' Before Bridget could answer, she was off to the kitchen, her steps a bit slower, and no wonder, considering she was two weeks off giving birth.

Feeling rested, Bridget followed her to the kitchen, and while Fanny buttered the barmcake, Bridget made the tea.

Settling themselves in opposite chairs by the empty fireplace, they looked at one another and began to giggle. 'What do we look like?' Fanny spluttered. 'Too fat to be comfortable in the chair, and too bleedin' awkward to walk across a room without us arses draggin' the floor.'

'You speak for yourself,' Bridget laughed. 'Yours is bigger than mine any day.'

Reluctantly, Fanny had to agree. 'Here's to us,' she said, raising her cup in the air, 'and bugger the men. Who needs 'em?' She smiled wickedly. 'Matter o' fact, I've a bit o' news to tell yer. Bill's wife found out about us, and now she's threatening to pack her bags and clear off. When he managed to sneak away and see me, he had a prime black eye she'd given him. He's in a right state, I can tell yer. She's leading him a right merry dance, and that's a fact. Poor old sod. I feel really sorry for him.'

'I thought you said you two were discreet.'

'We were.'

'So how did she find out?'

'According to Bill, somebody shoved a note under the front door. Told her everything, it did. Well, she just went mad, as you can imagine.'

'And you've no idea who it was?'

'I might have.' The smile spread slowly over her face until she was grinning from ear to ear.

Bridget's mouth fell open. 'It was *you*!'

'It were Bill who forced me to it. If he'd been man enough to tell her before I looked like a ship in battle, I'd never have had to stoop so low.' She began giggling. 'Matter o' fact, when I bent to slide the note under the door, I could hardly get up again. I thought she'd open the door and catch me at it there and then.'

'So now she knows. He'll have to make a choice. Is that why you were looking for a drop o' the good stuff to celebrate with?'

'No matter.' Chinking her cup with Bridget's, Fanny laughed. 'Yer should hear the old sod whining on about how he'd like to strangle the bastard who told his missus. I tell yer, Bridget, it's all I can do to keep a straight face.'

But she couldn't keep a straight face now, and neither could Bridget. They laughed until their sides ached, and Fanny warned,

'I'll have to calm down, gal. I've a funny pain coming.' Clutching her side, she gave a weird little groan, but it took a minute or two before the two of them were sober enough to talk without collapsing into fits of laughter. It did them both good.

'You were telling me about things at home,' Fanny reminded Bridget. 'Is there no chance yer might move back into Tom's bedroom?'

Bridget shook her head. 'It's over,' she said sadly. 'Tom vowed he would never again take me as his wife, and he meant it.'

'So he's claimed the big front room, while you're still in that poky room at the back?'

'That doesn't bother me. It's a cosy enough room. I've changed the curtains and put more rugs on the floor, and I can see the fields from my window.' A note of nostalgia crept into her voice. 'I don't sleep much these nights,' she said. 'I'm always up round about five to get Tom's breakfast. 'Patting her belly she explained with a smile, 'Anyway, the little one won't let me sleep for too long at a time. I expect you know all about that.'

'Not me!' Fanny laughed. 'I sleep like a log, and woe betide any bugger who wakes me afore I'm good and ready.'

'Do you think Bill's wife will really leave him?'

'I bloody hope so, otherwise I might as well not have bothered, eh? Mind you, as long as he turns up every Friday with my wages, happen I shouldn't give a sod whether he comes to me or stays with her.'

'But you do? Give a sod, I mean?'

Fanny nodded, her sorry expression betraying the depth of her feelings. 'Oh, aye. I do. I want him here with me, to be a proper husband to me, and a proper father to this bairn.'

'It's not much to ask when all's said and done.'

Fanny shrugged her shoulders. 'We don't always get what we want though. You of all people should know that.'

Bridget wasn't listening. Already her thoughts had moved on. 'I miss him, you know.'

'Who? Harry?'

'No. *Tom.*' Smiling shyly, Bridget explained, 'I miss him cuddling me when we used to lie in bed of a Sunday morning. I miss him at breakfast, then again when he comes home from work. I want things to be like they were. We used to talk and laugh, and though things were never perfect, we were content enough. I miss all that.'

'I expect you do, gal, but—'

'I know what you're trying to say and you're right. I've made my bed and now I'll have to lie on it.' She leaned back in the chair and regarded her friend through quiet eyes. 'I'm not complaining. I've lost Tom's respect and all that went with it and, God knows, it's only what I deserve.'

'We all have to pay a price, gal.'

'And I'll pay mine, for however long it takes.'

'You mustn't let it ruin your life though.'

'I have no life outside of Tom and the bairn.' The warmest smile lifted her features. 'Oh, Fanny, I can't wait for it to be born.' Even though her child was being delivered into an uncertain world and she was destined to be both mother and father to it, Bridget wanted it with all her heart.

Fanny laughed. 'You can 'ave mine an' all if yer want it.'

'You don't mean that.'

'I bloody do!' Fanny retorted. 'What do I want with a brat? I never asked for it in the first place. It was an accident. But now I'm lumbered, and here it is.' Patting her stomach, she smiled and shook her head. 'Big as a barge and ready to show its face any time now.'

Bridget was concerned. 'You wouldn't really give it away, would you?' she asked worriedly.

Fanny took a moment to answer, then, in a soft, regretful

voice she admitted, 'Naw, when all's said an' done, I couldn't give it away, gal.' With a raucous laugh she added, 'Unless it's an ugly bugger. In which case I'll sell it to the Gypsies for half a crown.'

'You're a devil.' Bridget couldn't help but smile.

There followed a quiet moment when the two of them reflected on their situations. Neither of them knew what the future held, and neither was completely secure. But these two were made of stern stuff, and whatever trials they had to face, life would never get the better of them.

Fanny's quiet voice shook Bridget out of her thoughts. 'What about Harry?' she asked gently. 'Do you miss him too?'

Bridget gave it some thought. Yes, there had been times when she did miss Harry, but it wasn't so bad these days. 'Me and Harry went our separate ways a long time ago,' she answered. 'After his father died, he took over the tailoring, and from what I can gather he hardly ever goes out.'

'Aye, I've heard that said.'

'Before I left the big house, I often heard the servants talking about him, saying how sorry they were to see him go. Harry was well liked by everybody, so it was only natural they'd want to know how he was getting on. Cook even visited him once, to pay her respects when she heard about his father. Then, when the butler started having his suits altered by Harry, we got to hear more snippets of gossip. I swear men are worse gossips than women.'

'What kind of gossip?'

'Oh, the usual kind. How he was, the way he worked from morning to night, just like his father used to do. According to the butler, he took to tailoring like a duck to water, and folk respect him almost as much as they did his father.'

'It takes years to build up that kind of respect.'

'Cook says Harry will never get over losing his father. He

works in lamplight, with the curtains drawn, and hardly speaks a word to anyone except his mother. He idolises her.'

'Some say she's got worse since her husband passed on. Is that the truth, Bridget?'

Bridget shook her head. 'Since I left the big house two months ago, I've heard nothing of her.' Pity touched her heart, but her real concern was for Harry. 'I can imagine how Harry must miss his work, driving the horse and wagon, and always outside in God's fresh air. He loved every minute of it, and now he's shut himself away.' If she let herself think too long about that, it would break her heart. 'So you see, we're *both* paying the price.'

'You know his father left a small fortune.'

'So they say.'

'I've heard the eldest sister got the lion's share.'

'I don't know about that, but it wouldn't surprise me. She and Harry both cared for their parents, but Harry had a job and could always earn a living. The younger sister, too, has work, and she's well thought of at the orphanage. Harry told me about her. He said she was a lovely-natured girl, with ambitions far and away above her age. He described her as a strong-minded young woman who would go places on her own merit.' Bridget had never met Fay, but she would have liked to. Harry was very fond of his younger sister, she could tell. 'It isn't easy for a woman,' she said to Fanny, 'particularly a woman like Alice who's never had to work. I suppose her father thought it his duty to set her up so she would never have to go without.'

'From what they say, she'll never wed, too plain and miserable from all accounts.'

'Don't believe everything you hear. You know as well as I do that some people can be very cruel.'

'Do you know Alice?'

'I've never spoken to her.' Bridget didn't like talking about Harry's sister in this way. 'I only know her by sight. Harry pointed her out once, when we were washing the master's dog in the tin bath outside the kitchen door. The old devil had rolled over in fox's muck and smelled to high heaven. Harry was ploughing in the field when he saw the dog run off. Dripping wet, he was, where I'd soaked him with carbolic. I were yelling and screaming for him to come back and Harry heard me. He chased the dog and fetched him back, then stayed with me till the job was done.'

'What was his sister doing there?'

'Visiting the mistress. Something to do with one of them charitable affairs that ladies get involved in.'

'Hmh.' Fanny put on mock airs and graces. 'Fancies herself as a lady then, does she?'

'Harry said it was all she had to keep her occupied.'

'It's all right for some, ain't it, eh?'

'For all I've got my own problems, I wouldn't want to swap places with her.' Bridget thought it must be a very lonely existence. 'At least I've got a man about the place, and a new bairn to look forward to.'

'You're too easily pleased, that's your problem, my gal.'

Glancing at the mantelpiece clock, Bridget gave a cry of horror. 'By! Look at the time! It's nearly four o'clock. I'll have to be quick about it or he'll be home before me. If his tea's not on the table when he walks in, he can be a real misery.'

'Let the bugger wait for his tea.'

'No. I'd best get going, Fanny, or he'll have the sulks worse than ever. I've been through it all before. Sly little glances that make me feel guilty, and pacing the floor while I'm rushing about getting the food.' Tom could make life unbearable when he took a mind to it. 'No, Fanny,' Bridget clambered out of the chair, 'I can't be doing with it.'

'Hang on a minute, me darlin'. It's a lovely afternoon, and I don't want you rushing about like some lunatic. We'll walk to the bottom of the hill together and I'll see you safely on your way.'

Ignoring Bridget's protests, Fanny followed her along the passageway, chattering on about the father of her own child. 'Bill Norman ain't much, but he's all I've got.' Chuckling, she looked in the mirror and tidied her hair. 'Gawd almighty! I look like summat the cat's dragged in!'

'You're nearly nine months gone, Fanny Higgins, so you can be excused for looking a bit jaded. Like me. And you don't hear me complaining, do you, eh?'

'It's *his* fault. That bloody Bill Norman. It's that randy bugger who's put me in this predicament and, by God, he'll face up to his responsibilities or my name's not Fanny Higgins.'

When she opened the door, there was Bill Norman himself standing on the doorstep. 'Would yer believe it!' cried Fanny, throwing her arms above her head. 'Talk o' the devil an' he's sure to appear.' Addressing him, she declared with a huge smile, 'Look what the cat's dragged in. Don't tell me you've left the old battleaxe at long last.'

'I need to talk.' He glanced at Bridget. 'Just the two of us, Fanny,' he stuttered. 'We have to talk.'

Bridget took the hint. 'I'll be on my way.' She stepped across the threshold. 'Take care of yourself, Fanny. I'll try and see you before the end of the week.'

Taking hold of her arm, Fanny said, 'Stay where you are, gal. Let the feller have his say, then I'll walk yer to the bottom of the hill.' Fanny sensed trouble brewing.

'Please, Fanny,' Bill appealed to her, 'we don't want the whole street listening to what I have to say.' With every word he went redder and redder in the face.

Fanny knew him all too well. 'You bastard!' Shoving him aside, she kept firm hold of Bridget. 'You don't need to tell me what's on yer mind, 'cause it's written all over yer bloody face. You're staying with her, that's it, isn't it?' When he dropped his gaze to the ground, she lashed out at him, hitting the top of his head. 'Get away from here!' she screamed. 'I should have known you wouldn't have the guts to stand up to her. You never have before, so why should you *now*?'

'Fanny, please listen to me! She wants to try again. I've too much to lose . . . too set in my ways. You have to understand.'

'Understand?' Raising her voice to such a pitch that doors opened along the street and women popped their heads out to gawp, Fanny gave them enough to gossip about for the next twelve months. 'Does *she* understand, that's what I want to know. I'm carrying your bairn. Does she understand *that*? And does she know you've been leading me on for years, and I've been fool enough to believe yer bloody lies?' When Fanny was in full flow, there was no stopping her. 'Oh, an' have yer told her how you hate the very sight of her, how yer can't bear her to be near yer, and how yer wish she'd bugger off and leave the two of us to make a life together? That's what you told me time and again. Lies, was it, Bill? All lies? Well, o' course it was.' By now the tears were streaming down her face. 'Piss off then! Yer nothing but a lily-livered coward, Bill Norman. An' by God she's bloody welcome to yer!'

With the last statement Fanny lashed out again and caught him hard and true behind the ear. The blow landed with such impact that it sent him sprawling to the ground. 'That's it, Fanny!' he yelled at her from the pavement. 'It's your damned temper that frightens me. That's the top and bottom of it. All right, she's not perfect, but when I come to think of it, I'd rather live with her and know she's not about to take a knife to me heart than live with you and not be able to sleep of a night!'

Fanny's bawling matched his own. 'You'd best bugger off while you've got a chance, Bill Norman,' she cried, 'before I jump off this step and squash yer.'

Scrambling to his feet, he shouted, 'And there's summat else an' all. How do I know for sure it's *mine* yer carrying? It could be *anybody's*. Gawd knows you've been with enough fellers in yer time.'

'*You no-good bastard!*' Incensed beyond endurance, Fanny rushed forward and threw herself at him.

'No, Fan! Leave him.' Seeing the danger, Bridget reached out to draw her back, but it was too late. With a heart-rending cry, Fanny launched herself at him, lost her footing and fell heavily to the pavement. 'Oh, Jesus! Now look what you've done.'

As Fanny lay, face up and dazed, Bill Norman took to his heels and ran off down the street like the coward he was. Behind him a chorus of women's voices called out what a shameful thing he was. 'Yer bloody old man should be chopped off and thrown to the dogs!'

On her knees beside Fanny's prostrate form, Bridget was immensely relieved to see she was not badly hurt. 'It's a good job I'm fat enough to roll, gal,' she quipped. But the tears still lurked, and Bridget could not leave her.

Fanny put one arm round Bridget's neck and another round the neck of a kindly Irish neighbour and struggled to get up. 'I feel drunk as a lord,' she told them with a grin, 'and I ain't even had so much as a sip o' the good stuff.'

With Fanny's considerable weight on their shoulders, Bridget and the neighbour made their way to the back parlour. 'On the couch with her. Gently now, me darlin'. I've a feeling she's started, so I have,' said the neighbour firmly.

A quick examination revealed that Fanny's waters had broken and, ready or not, she was in the early stages of labour. 'We can't let her have the bairn here,' the neighbour decided. 'We'll have to get her upstairs, so we will.' Glancing at Bridget's swollen belly and red face, she remarked wryly, 'Ah, God love us, hold on to it, me darlin'. Sure, I can't be doing with two of youse at the same time.'

With great difficulty, and with Fanny cursing 'the ol' bugger who had his way then buggered off', they finally got her to the bedroom.

'I hope you know what yer doing,' Fanny told the neighbour, between fits of groaning and complaining. 'Yer not one o' these wicked devils who butcher helpless women and charge 'em for the privilege?'

'No, I'm not,' came the haughty reply. 'I've six kids of me own, and I've brought more childer into this world than you've had men grunting atop of you, so stop your chatter and let me and this fine young lady get on with the job.' With that, she tore away Fanny's skirt and took another look. 'Sure, it won't be long now,' she declared. 'Then we'll have the *two* of youse complaining.'

When a small boy appeared at the door, the woman screeched at him, 'Be Jaysus! Where've you come from, our Danny? This is woman's stuff. Be off wit' yer now.'

Before he disappeared, Bridget gave him a sixpence and her home address. 'Please, Danny, give this note to my husband,' she said, and hastily scribbled a few lines to say why she was late. 'Make sure you go straight there,' she instructed the boy. 'He'll be home by now and wondering where I am.'

'And don't be stopping on the way to spend the sixpence,' his mother called out, 'or I'll have your arse for a doormat.'

As he scuttled away, Bridget couldn't help but wonder what sort of a reception she'd have when she finally got home. But right now Fanny needed her and, Tom or no Tom, she would not let her down.

Bridget had never seen a child born, and what she saw happening to Fanny put the fear of God into her.

It was a hard, painful birth. Fanny did a lot of screaming, and the neighbour did a lot of shouting, and Bridget ran back and forth with bowls of hot water and clean towels, and finally, when all three were exhausted, there it was, the biggest, bounciest boy ever seen. 'Oh, Fanny, he's just beautiful!' Bridget was laughing and crying, and as she gazed into those soft dark eyes, her heart turned over with love. All of a sudden, she couldn't wait to hold her own child in her arms.

'Sure, he'll drive the girls wild,' the neighbour said. 'There now, will you look at that! The little feller's winking at me already, so he is.'

Fanny was straining to see. 'Give him here,' she ordered, 'and clear off, so me and the lad can get to know each other.'

Bridget and Fanny embraced. 'I'll come back and see you both tomorrow,' Bridget promised. And Fanny told her how much she valued and loved her as a friend.

'Sure, I'll be downstairs clearing away the rubbish,' the neighbour announced, 'so don't think I'm going yet, because I'm not.'

'You've done more for me than anyone I've ever met, with the exception of Bridget,' Fanny said. 'You're the only one round here who hasn't turned away from me on sight. And, I'm shamed to say, I don't even know your name.'

Wiping the sweat from her brow, the woman smiled. 'The name's Lilian,' she said, 'and don't worry about these buggers round here, because since the day I arrived from Ireland with six kids and no man in tow, they've not had a good word to say about me neither.'

'My door's always open to you,' Fanny promised.

'Well now, that's very kind,' came the grateful reply. 'Sure, I might take you up on that, particularly if there's a drop o' the good stuff on offer.'

'There's none on offer just now,' Fanny confessed. 'That cowardly bugger Bill Norman helped himself to it. But give me a week or two and I'll have a jug tucked away big enough to last the three of us for a month. Isn't that right, Bridget?'

Bridget nodded. 'Whatever you say.' She felt as though she'd been stretched on the rack and, knowing how late she was, she was eager to get home as quickly as possible. 'I'll freshen up and then I'll have to make tracks home,' she told Fanny. 'Look after yourself and, like I said, I'll be back tomorrow.'

Concerned about Bridget walking down the hill in the dark, Fanny asked Lilian if she would walk with her. Lilian said she would. 'And I'll fetch our Danny to keep an eye on you till I get back.' Fanny argued that she was perfectly capable of looking after herself, but Lilian would hear none of it.

While Bridget washed and cleaned up downstairs, the boy was quickly summoned by way of a shout through the back upstairs window. 'What's all them people standing out there for?' he wanted to know as he came rushing into the parlour.

'What folk?' Lilian and Bridget hurried to the front window and peeped through the curtain. 'It looks like an army of neighbours,' Bridget said and, like Lilian, was prepared to do battle.

As it turned out, there was no need.

'We've come to see how she is,' said one proud and well-endowed woman.

'We all know we've not been the good neighbours we should,' said another.

'It's a poor do if us women can't stand together in times of need,' declared yet another.

So, all being friendly, in they came, and no one was more surprised than Fanny. 'Well, bugger me!' she exclaimed as they crowded round her bed to see the newborn. 'Yesterday I were summat to be avoided, and now I'm a bloody peepshow.' But she enjoyed all the attention, and it was another half-hour before Bridget got away, with Lilian in tow.

Before she left her at the bottom of the hill, Bridget thanked her. 'Look after her,' she said, 'and don't take none of her cheek.'

'She'll get as good as she gives if she starts on me,' Lilian promised. With that, and a fond embrace, the two of them parted.

Bridget watched Lilian walk away. She was a fine figure of a woman, well built, with wild red hair and sure green eyes, and there was something about her that gave Bridget confidence. 'Fanny won't get all her own way with that one,' she chuckled. Then she turned her steps towards King Street. 'I wonder what Tom will have to say about all this.' A shadow crossed her face. 'He'll have *nothing* to say, same as always.'

When Bridget came in through the front door, she knew the house was empty; it had that cold, bleak feeling about it. She went through the house calling his name nevertheless, but there was no answer because no one was there.

'That little sod!' Her first thought was that Danny had not delivered the note as he'd been paid to do. 'He probably went off and spent his sixpence and forgot all about the note. I expect Tom came home, found I wasn't here and no tea for him, and off he went in a sulk.'

Dropping into a fireside chair she sighed. 'One of these days I might just pack a bag and leave.' But she knew she wouldn't. Not when she still harboured a hope in her heart that, in spite of everything, all would come right between them.

Her gaze wandered round the room as she thought about how she and Tom had loved this place, how they chose the furniture and arranged it together. Her eyes spotted a note on the table.

Scrambling out of the chair, she plucked the note up. 'So, he *did* deliver it, after all,' she murmured. 'And Tom went out anyway.' She shrugged her shoulders. 'I don't suppose he'll go hungry. He'll be at the pub, tucking into a pork pie and not caring tuppence where I am, or if he never sees me again.'

Feeling the need for sleep, she took off her coat and hung it on the nail behind the door. She splashed her face with cold water at the kitchen sink and then made her way upstairs.

Here she stripped down to her knickers and vest and, because the room grew cold once night set in, she put her nightgown on over her underwear. She sat at the dresser and brushed her brown hair until it shone. Before getting into bed, she dropped her skirt and blouse into the wash basket, as they were splattered with blood.

It made her think of Fanny's new son. 'I hope you don't give me as much trouble as that little lad gave his mammy,' she murmured, spreading her hand over the bulge beneath her nightgown. Seeing Fanny go through the throes of labour and a difficult delivery had frightened her, but even though she thought it horrific, she believed it was a small price to pay for the joy of holding a tiny new life.

'I hope you're a girl,' she whispered, 'then you may not look too much like Harry.' That was one of the fears she had, and it grew with each day that passed. For whatever reason, Tom had vowed to raise the child as his own, but how would he cope if it was made in the living image of its father?

Bridget had another fear. If the child did favour Harry in feature and colouring, how long would it be before people grew suspicious? All it needed was one remark by some nasty-minded individual, and the seed would be sown. 'God forbid that it should ever happen.'

Bridget drifted into a restless sleep, but twice the dreams woke her; dreams of her and Tom, he on one side and her on the other and between them raging rivers of crimson blood. She could see him drifting further and further away and she couldn't reach him. 'I'm sorry, Tom,' she called out time and again, but he seemed not to hear. Then he fell, screaming, into the blackness below. And, to her horror, she saw every awful detail.

That was when she woke, sweating and afraid. 'What does it mean?' She was trembling but she wasn't cold. Not now. Now, she was burning as if with a fever.

When she had paced the floor until her feet felt like two slabs of ice and she was so tired she could hardly put one leg before the other, she lay down again and closed her eyes. This time she slept, a deep, satisfying sleep.

Through her slumbers she heard a noise. At once awake, she ran to the window. Outside it was pitch black. Not a soul in sight. 'What's wrong with me?' she muttered. 'I'm beginning to imagine things.' She wondered whether Tom was back yet. She glanced at the clock. 'Two o'clock. He should have been home ages since.'

She returned to bed but again she was disturbed by a noise, the same as before, like a child sniggering.

On tiptoe she went out to the landing and along to Tom's room. The door was ajar. Gingerly, she pushed it open.

Tom was lying on the bed, stark naked. There was a woman beside him, long and beautiful. She was fondling his private parts. 'It feels strange,' she whispered, 'me being here with you, and your wife asleep in the next room.'

Tom spoke with a louder voice, slurred with drink. 'Forget about her,' he said. 'She goes her way and I go mine.' Purring like a cat, he slid his hand between her naked thighs, growing increasingly agitated when she wiggled towards him.

'Don't you love her?' The young woman tickled his lips with the tip of her tongue.

'I used to, but not any more.'

'Why not?'

'Because she's a slut.'

'*I'm* a slut.'

He laughed. 'Ah yes, but you're *paid* to be a slut.'

'What would you do if she saw us?'

'I don't want to talk about her.'

'What would you do though?' Taking his hardened member in her small hand, she stroked and caressed it, until he could hardly bear it. 'What if she threw me out?'

'She's not woman enough to throw you out, even if she had the right, and she forfeited that right long ago.' Nibbling at her breast, he opened her legs and mounted her. 'Besides, this is *my* house. I'll bring who I like into it, and I don't give a bugger *what* she thinks.' Roughly, he pushed into her. 'Now shut your mouth and earn your money!'

Sickened to her stomach, Bridget turned to flee.

The woman saw her. 'You bastard!' she cried, throwing Tom off. 'You didn't tell me she was with child.'

Running to her room, Bridget locked the door and stood with her back to it, panting as though she'd run a mile. 'How could he? How could he bring a woman of the streets into this house?' The woman herself seemed to have a conscience, judging by what she had said, while Tom was merely out to gratify himself.

'Come back here, you silly baggage!' came Tom's voice as he chased the woman down the stairs. 'She means nowt to me. It were finished long since.'

Bridget heard a scuffle and then laughter, and then a door slamming shut. 'They've gone into the parlour,' she whispered. 'Shame on the pair of them.' But then she recalled her own shame. 'Think how he must have felt when you told him about you and Harry, and the bairn.' It was a terrible thing to see Tom as he had seen her, albeit only in his mind. She and Harry had behaved the same as Tom and that woman, and no matter how she might try to excuse it, she could see no difference between them. 'You're no more than the woman downstairs,' she told herself. 'A slut. Only you're worse because, like Tom said, she gets paid for it while you shamed yourself for pleasure.'

With her world falling apart about her, she buried her head in the sheets and pretended not to hear the cries of passion emanating from downstairs.

Eventually the sounds ceased, the front door was quietly opened and closed, and the silence told her the woman was gone.

Emotionally drained and physically exhausted, Bridget fell into a fitful sleep.

Daylight was creeping into the bedroom when she awoke. It wasn't dreams or noises that woke her this time, it was the pain of contractions.

When they eased, she carefully made her way downstairs. 'Tom! Tom, the baby's started.' Throwing open the parlour door, she leaned against the wall, waves of pain gripping her and growing stronger.

Tom was in a drunken stupor and, try as she might, she could not rouse him. 'Dear God, what am I to do?' Nelly came to mind. 'I'll have to wake her . . . got to help me.'

Nelly answered the frantic knocking on her door with her hair in tin curlers and a look of sheer panic on her face. 'What the devil's up?' she demanded. 'Banging on my door at four o'clock of a morning. I thought it were the police. By heck! You frightened the life outta me.'

Bridget bent double as another tide of contractions engulfed her.

'Jesus, Mary and Joseph,' Nelly cried. 'The poor little bugger's started afore her time.'

Chapter Five

Bridget had been with Nelly for two days.

Lying in bed, racked with pain yet with no signs of the baby arriving, she was losing energy, and losing hope. 'I'm dying, aren't I, Nelly?' And the truth was, she didn't care.

'No, lass, course you're not dying.' Nelly did her best to reassure her, but in her heart she was worried out of her mind. 'Us women are all made different, you see.' She managed a smile. 'There are them as can drop a dozen bairns one after the other, just like they were shelling peas, and there are them, like yerself, who make a hard job of it. You're such a tiny little thing, that's the problem. The babby don't have much room to turn and push.' Picking up a damp rag, Nelly wiped the sweat from Bridget's face. 'But I am worried about you, and that's a fact,' she admitted.

A spasm of pain gripped Bridget. She didn't cry out. Instead she lay, white as a sheet, her eyes tightly closed and her fists clutching Nelly with such force that her fingernails left their mark on Nelly's skin. Bridget knew she could not stand much more of the pain. It came and went, and nothing happened. The child stayed fast, and she grew weaker. She felt that the child, too, was beginning to give up. 'Please, Nelly,' she gasped, 'I need help.'

'All right, lass.' Nelly held her until the pain eased. 'There is somebody I could ask to come and have a look at you. She lives on Armitage Street and goes by the name of Molly Dewhirst. I've never liked the old bugger, and I never shall, but I'll tell you this, Bridget, lass, she knows her stuff. She's brought many a young'un into the world, and there's many a grateful mammy still walking the earth because of her.' And some who weren't, Nelly knew, but beggars couldn't be choosers. 'I'll scour the streets for a runner, then I'll be right back. If the pain comes on you again, take long, deep breaths, and for pity's sake, try not to tighten up.'

'Don't leave me, Nelly. Please, don't leave me.' Bridget had never been so frightened in her life – except perhaps when she had told Tom about what she and Harry had done.

'Aw, lass, I've got to leave you. The truth is, I've done all I can and, God help me, it's not enough.'

'Be quick, Nelly,' Bridget pleaded. 'I'm frightened to be on my own.'

'I'll go like the wind,' Nelly promised. 'With a bit o' luck there'll be childer in the street. Some of them little monsters would run from here to Blackpool if you give 'em a farthing.' Licking her chapped lips, she grinned her toothless grin and, despite feeling like death warmed over, it made Bridget smile.

Nelly took her shawl from the back of the chair, threw it about her shoulders and hurried downstairs. She almost fainted when the front door popped open just as she put her hand on the door knob. 'By! You silly sod, Bob Morris! You frightened the life outta me.'

'I wouldn't do that to you, Nelly, my old love, would I?' said the grinning young man on the doorstep mischievously. 'Not when you're one of my best customers, eh?'

Bob Morris bought milk and eggs from the surrounding farms and then sold them on round the streets. Twenty-eight years old and a familiar sight with his mop of fair hair and his laughing dark eyes, he was well liked by everybody. 'What's the rush anyway?' he wanted to know.

Nelly's answer was to grab him by the arm and march him down the passageway. 'This is your chance to do a bit of good for somebody,' she told him. 'I've a young woman here who'll be carried out this door in a box if I don't get help, and quick.' She propelled him up the stairs. 'Mop her brow,' she instructed, 'and hold her hand when she cries out. If she's not rid of that bairn soon, it's curtains for the both of them.' She opened the bedroom door and thrust Bob inside. 'Bridget,' she said, 'here's a friend to stay with you till I get back.'

Bridget looked up, her eyes huge in her white face.

'I'm sorry,' stuttered Bob, 'I'll go if you like.' In fact he wanted nothing more than to run out of there. The poor creature in the bed was obviously in a desperate way. 'Nelly seemed to think I could help you, but I can't,' he finished lamely. 'I'm sorry.'

Bridget's smile put him to shame. 'I'm glad you're here,' she said. 'I need to tell someone . . . before . . . before . . .' The words caught in her throat. 'I've done a terrible thing, and now I'm frightened to face my maker.'

Softly he came forward, shocked to see who it was. 'Bridget!' His eyes widened with surprise. 'Bridget Mulligan!'

Bridget patted the bed. 'I need to tell someone. Please.'

Deeply moved, and a little afraid, he came and sat beside her.

Out in the street, Nelly spied a lad playing with a hoop. 'Want to earn a penny, do you?' Collaring him by the ear, she gave him as big a fright as Bob Morris had given her.

'What yer after, missus?' He was a crafty young thing and eyed her slyly from beneath his flat cap. He was almost as tall as Nelly, snotty-nosed and smelling as unwashed as he looked.

'Don't ask me to do nuthin' crinimal, missus,' he whined. 'Me dad would flay me alive.'

'Never mind your sodding dad!' Nelly snapped. 'I've a woman badly in there. She's suffering like you'll *never* suffer, 'cause the good Lord saw fit to make you a bloody feller. I've tuppence here, an' it's yours if you'll run to Armitage Street and fetch a lady by the name of Molly Dewhirst. Tell her Nelly Potts has need of her. Tell her it's a matter of life and death.'

The boy thought quickly. If he went about this in the right way, he might earn more than tuppence. 'I ain't going to no Armitage Street!' Cuffing a string of snot over his sleeve, he told her sulkily, 'It must be a good two mile away.'

Nelly clipped his ear. 'Stuff and rubbish,' she retorted. 'It might be two mile for *me*, but for a young'un like you it's nobbut a skip and a jump. And I'll thank you not to try your sly little tricks on, because I know them all. I can afford tuppence for the errand and not a farthing more. So go on, and be quick about it.'

'You're a bit old and ugly to be a bully, ain't you, missus?'

'Old maybe, but I'll thank you not to call me ugly. When I were your age there weren't a feller in the whole of Lancashire who wouldn't have walked me down the aisle if I'd let him.' It was a blatant lie and they both knew it. 'Quick now. You'll find her at number six. Molly Dewhirst. Tell her what I said, and for God's sake run like you've never run before.'

He held out his hand. 'Give us the tuppence then.'

Nelly laughed. 'What! You must think I were born yesterday. You'll get the tuppence when you've done the errand and not before.'

'That ain't fair, missus. If I do fetch this Molly Dewhirst, how do I know you'll give me the money?'

'Because I'm as good as my word, that's how.' Turning, she pointed to her house. 'That's where I live, and that's where you're to fetch her. Now be off, or I'll change my mind. If you don't want to do it, I'm sure there's somebody else as wants to earn an easy tuppence.'

Cursing and muttering, he took up his hoop and ran off.

Satisfied the boy would do as he was bid, Nelly walked the few steps to Bridget's house. She knew Tom Mulligan was home because she'd seen him through the upstairs window. She bent her back to the letter box and called out, 'Mr Mulligan, Bridget needs you. She's right badly.'

The door was flung open and there he stood, the worse for drink, and the same floozy leaning on his arm that Nelly had seen more than once these past two days. 'I want nothing to do with her,' he snarled, 'so I'll thank you to stop banging on this door at all hours of the day and night.'

Nelly wasn't easily put off. 'She needs you, Mr Mulligan,' she insisted. 'She's been calling for you.' And that was no lie.

It was the woman who answered. 'You've been told to bugger off,' she said. 'Are you deaf or what, you old bag?'

Staring at the woman through hard eyes, Nelly told her, 'There was a time, God help me, when circumstances forced me to scour a living on the streets of Liverpool. I'm not proud of that, and never will be, but I can hold my head up as well as any woman and better than most because, however low I sank, I never once lost my sense of decency.'

The woman squirmed beneath her glare, and Nelly turned the knife. 'As far as I know, I never once bedded a feller while his own wife lay dying in the next house, giving birth to his bairn and barred from her own house by this sorry creature standing aside of you.' She spat on the ground. 'Dirt beneath that lass's feet, that's what you are, the pair of you. As far as I'm concerned, you deserve each other.'

As she scurried back to her own front door, Nelly heard the woman's shrill voice shout at Tom, 'Damned liar! You told me she'd packed her bags and buggered off.' Nelly paused to look back. The woman had stalked off down the road and Tom was staring after her. Then he turned into his house and slammed the door. 'May God forgive you,' Nelly murmured. But in her heart she thought He never would.

When she came into the bedroom, Nelly was surprised to see Bob Morris still there. Many a young man would have stayed only as long as it took for her to turn her back, she thought, then he'd have run off like a scalded cur. Instead, Bob was sitting on the side of the bed, holding Bridget's hand and softly murmuring to her.

'She keeps drifting in and out of her senses,' he told Nelly softly. 'I've just been talking to her. I didn't know what else to do.'

Nelly patted him on the shoulder. 'You've done all right,' she said gratefully. She looked more closely at him, at the chiselled features and serious dark eyes. 'How old are you, son?'

'Twenty-eight.'

'Well then, there's nobbut half a dozen years or so between the two of you. But she's a woman and you're not, so you can't fathom out what she's going through, more's the pity. Yet you've given her a deal of comfort when her own husband's turned his back on her. You're a good soul, Bob Morris,' she said, 'and I thank you.'

'I wouldn't leave her,' he said simply.

Bridget was lying so still, for one terrible minute Nelly thought they'd lost her. 'Hold on, Bridget, lass,' she whispered against her face. 'Help's on its way. Molly Dewhirst will have you right in no time at all.'

Bob was appalled. 'Not Molly Dewhirst!' he said in a low, shocked whisper. 'I've heard about her and not much of it's good.'

'She's the best I know. Besides, there's no other way. Doctors hold their hand out for what they do, and we've neither of us got that kind of money.'

'Where's her husband?'

Nelly didn't want to reveal too much. 'None of our business.'

'Has she no mam or dad? No family at all?'

Nelly shook her head. 'Only her husband that I know of.'

Bob was quiet, his troubled gaze resting on Bridget's frail features. 'She felt the need to talk,' he murmured.

Nelly was all ears. 'Talk? What about?'

He smiled quietly. Bridget had sworn him to secrecy. 'Nothing much,' he lied. 'It's just that she seemed to think she were dying and needed to clear her conscience.'

Discreetly, Nelly drew him away from the bedside. 'She *is* dying, son, and it'll take a miracle to save her, poor little bugger. So if you've anything I should know about, I'm her only close friend.' Though her heart was in the right place, Nelly was incurably inquisitive, and nothing in the world would change that. 'I know she'd want you to tell me.'

Bob stood quite still, his eyes going to Bridget, and his heart too. He had no doubt that Nelly had shown great compassion to Bridget, but that quiet soul had imparted her secret to his safe-keeping, and he would not betray her. 'It was nothing,' he lied. 'Just the ramblings of a sick woman.'

Realising he had no intention of revealing anything of what Bridget had said, Nelly let it drop. 'You can go if you've a mind,' she said, 'or you can stay. It's up to you. Once Molly gets here, I dare say she'd be thankful for an extra pair of hands.' Her gaze was drawn to Bridget. 'If it's not already too late.'

Without a word Bob walked back to the bed. He bent and kissed Bridget on the forehead. 'Your secret is safe with me,' he whispered so that Nelly could not hear. 'But it wasn't so shocking that you should pay for it with your life.' He turned to Nelly. 'I'm sorry,' he said, his eyes bright with tears, 'I can't stand by and watch this happen.'

'I understand.' Nelly wasn't at all surprised. She had never yet met a man strong enough to deal with the essentials of life, like birth or death.

When he'd gone, Nelly sat where he had sat, with her hand over Bridget's. 'He's not a bad lad, I suppose. At least he gave you comfort where others wouldn't.' She was thinking of Tom Mulligan, a man she had always respected. Until now.

After a moment, Bridget opened her eyes. She looked at Nelly but didn't see her. Her mind was already closing to all things real.

'Thirsty, are you, lass?' Nelly did not expect, and did not receive, an answer. 'You're not to worry, Molly will be here soon, I promise you.' Under her breath, she muttered angrily, 'Where the hell is she?'

She got up and went downstairs to put the kettle on to boil. That done, she prepared a bowl and clean strips of sheeting. Next she half-filled the bowl with fresh water and carried it upstairs to the bedroom. She bathed Bridget's face and hands, all the while talking to her, trying to stop her from sinking deeper into herself. 'You have to fight, lass,' she urged. 'However hard it is, you have to fight.'

From inside the soft, warm cocoon that encircled her, Bridget heard. She didn't answer. There was no strength left. Just now, she had confessed to the young man, and he had understood. It was enough. And so she smiled, and drifted further away.

Nelly paced the floor, checking the street through the window at every turn. 'If that little bugger's led me a merry dance, God help him!'

She saw a carriage draw up outside the house, and out of it stepped Bob Morris. Behind him came a smartly dressed man carrying a large, dark bag. 'Open the door, Nelly,' Bob called through the letter box. 'I've brought the doctor.'

Nelly ran down the stairs and threw open the door. 'Oh, thank

God! Thank God!' she exclaimed, and ushered the doctor up the stairs and into the bedroom. 'Please help her,' she whispered. 'I've done all I can.'

For the next hour, Nelly worked hard, doing as she was bid, running back and forth, up the stairs and down, until she felt her legs would fall off. 'I'm not so young as I was,' she said breathlessly as she came, puffing and panting, into the bedroom.

When Bob offered to help, she pushed him away. 'This is woman's stuff,' she said proudly.

Once, when she took away a bucketful of soiled sheeting, she caught sight of Bridget looking at her through the pain, and her heart lifted. 'You can do it, lass,' she urged, and her reward was the smallest nod.

'She's in good hands,' Bob told Nelly downstairs as she put the soiled bedding in the dolly tub. 'I'll be off now. Will you let me know how she gets on?'

'Who's going to pay the doctor?' Nelly responded.

'He's paid.'

Choked, Nelly could only nod gratefully.

Some short time later, bending over the range, her head bathed in steam from the boiling water, Nelly didn't hear the door open.

'I've come to take her home,' said a familiar voice.

Startled, Nelly swung round. 'Jesus, Mary and Joseph!' she cried. 'You gave me a fright, Tom Mulligan.'

'Where is she?'

'The doctor's with her. She's in a bad way, and he's the only one who can help.' Standing there, the neck of his shirt open and his hair tousled, he looked exhausted, as though he'd been to hell and back. Yet she knew where he'd been and with whom, and for a moment she was tempted to throw him out.

'Please,' he said quietly, 'I need to make amends.'

Despite herself, Nelly couldn't help but feel sorry for him. 'If you're real quiet, you can go and see how she's doing. But you mustn't interfere. It's up to the doctor now. Like I said, she's in a bad way.'

When he nodded, she wrapped her hand in a rag and took up the kettle. 'Follow me,' she said.

When he walked into that quiet room, Tom saw how serious Bridget's condition was and thought he would never forgive himself for deserting her. He wanted to tell her this, but he knew there was a real fight going on at the bedside, so he kept his distance.

Occasionally, when Nelly helped at the bedside, she cast him an encouraging glance. It helped him bear the sight of blood and Bridget's pitiful moans. At least she's alive, he told himself, but it was no thanks to him. 'God help her,' he murmured. 'God help us both.'

His prayers were answered, for no sooner had he uttered them than there was a flurry of activity at the bedside. Bridget gave a heart-rending scream, and a moment later came the cry of a newborn.

'Oh, Bridget!' Nelly was crying unashamedly. 'It's all right, lass. You've done it, bless your heart.'

While the doctor saw to Bridget, Nelly cleaned the child and wrapped it in a shawl. 'Look here.' Bringing it to Tom, she told him softly, 'You've got a daughter, Tom Mulligan. A lovely little lass, the image of her daddy.'

For a moment he thought she must know the truth. But then he gazed down on the child and his heart stood still. 'My God!' With the brightest blue eyes and a soft down of fair hair, that tiny creature could well have been his own. But he knew differently, and with Nelly's next words, said quite innocently, his illusions were shattered. 'O' course newborns always have blue eyes,' she said. 'Babies change all the time, until they're a few months old, when their colouring sets proper.'

Disillusioned but immensely grateful that all was well, Tom

went to wait downstairs. 'Call me if she asks,' he told Nelly, and Nelly promised she would.

When the doctor took his leave, Nelly brought Tom upstairs. 'A few minutes, that's all,' she cautioned. 'The lass needs her rest. She's lost a lot of blood and she'll be weak as a kitten for some long time yet. Keep her warm and quiet and feed her on broth, that's what the doctor said.' There was something else too. 'She can't be moved, not for at least a week, and maybe longer. I don't have much money, so if you can pay for her keep, I'd be obliged.'

'Don't worry,' Tom reassured her. 'I'll see she has all she needs, and I'll make sure you don't lose out because of all this.' A thought occurred to him. 'The doctor's bill must have cost a pretty penny, I'll be bound.'

Nelly skirted the issue. 'You'd best say hello. She's been asking for you.'

When, a short time later, Tom sat at Bridget's bedside, his heart turned over to see her smiling up at him when he'd been such a bastard to her. 'I'm sorry,' he murmured. 'I wasn't there when you needed me.' Trembling, he held back the tears, but when she reached out, he buried his head in the nape of her neck and sobbed like a child. 'Can you forgive me? Oh, Bridget, can you ever forgive me?'

For a few precious moments, Bridget kept him there, stroking his hair and whispering that she understood, and it was all right.

'I love you,' he whispered. 'I always will.'

'I know,' she murmured.

She slept then, and Tom returned to his empty house.

Evidence of the other woman's presence lay strewn about the Mulligan household: upturned bottles on the floor; stains of crimson wine; a long, silky robe hanging over the foot of the bed. Even the air carried her perfume.

Deeply ashamed, Tom went from room to room and flung open all the windows. He cleaned up the debris, mopped the stains, and tore the robe to shreds. Only when he was satisfied that all traces of the woman had gone did he stop.

He made himself a brew of tea and sat outside on the back yard step. The sun was warm on his face. He felt better than he had done in a long time. 'You've been given a second chance,' he told himself. 'You and Bridget both. So take it and be grateful.'

Leaning back against the door, he closed his eyes and remembered what he had seen just now – Bridget in pain and all alone save for a nosy old neighbour and a doctor she had never set eyes on before. He thought of how he had stood in that room and felt like a stranger looking down on her. And her face, oh, dear God, that lovely, childlike face, drained of energy, the once-bright eyes dull with suffering. And now, for a while, he suffered with her.

He retreated from the suffering into sleep, and in his dreams he saw the child, and its father, and his heart was broken.

When the sun had died down and the air turned colder, he woke with a start, amazed that he had slept at all. Clambering up, he returned his cup to the kitchen. 'Got to get cleaned up and see how she's doing.'

He strip-washed at the sink, brushed his hair and put on a clean shirt. 'Funny how a clean shirt can make a man feel human again.' Regarding himself in the mirror over the fireplace, he took a deep, invigorating breath. 'The house is empty without her.'

Deep in thought, he put on his jacket and went back to the parlour. He stood and looked around at the comfortable chairs and the pictures Bridget had made him put on the walls, pictures of flowers and animals, and bright sunny days. Until now he hadn't realised how precious it all was.

'This is your house, Bridget,' he murmured. 'Never again, for as long as I live, will I taint it with a woman of that kind.'

The image of Harry Little came into his mind. Was Nelly right? Would the child's colouring change and favour her true father? It didn't bear thinking about.

The smallest flame of fury licked his heart at what Bridget had done to him. With a weary sigh, he stifled it. 'We must try and forget all that's gone before,' he whispered, 'or we'll never know any peace.'

Chapter Six

Bridget had been with Nelly for almost a week when Fanny came to visit. 'Why the bleedin' hell didn't yer send word before?' she demanded. 'I had no idea you were badly. I only got out of bed meself day afore yesterday. You could have knocked me down with a feather when the lad fetched the note to the door.' She had a great deal to say, and then there was a great deal of hugging and smiling. 'From what Nelly tells me, you were at death's door,' she chided. 'Oh, gal, if only I'd known sooner.'

'And what could you have done?' Bridget asked. 'You've been through enough yerself, and besides, Nelly forbade me to have visitors until this morning.'

'Oh, Bridget, you look so worn and washed out.' The daylight was streaming in through the bedroom window, lighting Bridget's face and marking the dark rings beneath her eyes. 'Was it awful, gal?' she asked kindly, reaching out to hold Bridget's hand.

Bridget tried to remember, and found she couldn't, not properly. It was as though when the pain went, the memory of it went too. 'It's over now,' she answered softly, 'and I've got the most beautiful daughter to show for it all.' Pointing to the crib, she said, 'You haven't seen her yet. Go on, Fan. Take a peep at her.'

Going on tiptoe in case the baby was sleeping, Fan laughed

out loud when she found herself staring into a pair of curious, dark blue eyes. 'Oh, Bridget,' she purred. 'She's just like you, so small and pretty.'

Bridget fell silent, her eyes downcast and her fingers playing with the fringe on the bedspread.

'I know what you're thinking,' Fanny remarked softly. 'I'm your friend, Bridget. You can talk to me about anything, and it won't go any further.'

Through troubled eyes, Bridget looked at her. 'Do you think she looks like Tom?'

'Maybe,' she answered. 'But then newborns all look the same at first.'

'That's what Nelly said.'

Fanny lowered her voice. 'You're wondering if it might be Tom's after all, is that it?'

Bridget shook her head. 'I know it isn't Tom's,' she said truthfully. 'He knows it too.'

'Well then.'

'I was just thinking . . .' She bit her lip. 'He's better with me now, Fan, more friendly, more tolerant, if you know what I mean.'

Fanny gave a rueful smile. 'But?'

'It seems too good to be true.' Even though he was attentive and forgiving, there was a kind of despair about Tom, and it frightened her. 'I wonder if he'll cope with it all,' she murmured anxiously.

'What do you mean?'

'Once we're home, me and . . . everything.' She glanced towards the crib and smiled. 'I've named her Ruth.'

'Ruth . . . Ruth Mulligan.' Fanny's face lit up. 'Yes, I like it. You've chosen well, gal.'

'What did you name your son?' Bridget hadn't found a chance to ask until now.

'I gave it a great deal of thought, gal. In the end I decided I'd make bloody certain that bugger who fathered him wouldn't forget, and neither would his cow of a wife.'

'You called him Bill, didn't you?' Bridget might have guessed.

Looking immensely proud, Fanny answered cagily, 'Not quite. I've called him Billy. It kinda suits him somehow. But on his birth certificate he's named William, just like his father, the old bastard!' Her expression softened. 'D'you know summat, in a way I owe a debt to Bill Norman, though I would never let him know it. But, as God's my judge, that little lad is the best thing that's ever happened to me.'

Bridget was momentarily taken aback by the love that shone from Fanny's eyes and for one very intimate moment she knew she was witnessing a side to Fanny she had never seen before. 'Bring him up,' she said. 'I want to see what a difference a week makes.'

Fanny shook her head. 'In a while,' she said. 'Billy's happy enough downstairs with Nelly for now and besides, I've a feeling you need to talk.'

'It can wait.'

'There's no time like the present, gal. You say it's better between you and Tom, so why do you think he won't be able to cope?'

Bridget had spent many hours in this room thinking things through, and the more she thought, the more unsure she felt. 'I just wonder if it's too much to ask of him,' she answered. 'You already know how badly he took it all, and how like strangers we were becoming.'

'I know that, gal, but you said he'd been better since you had the bairn.'

'That's true, but deep down I know he's never forgiven me, and never will.' With a sense of shame she revealed. 'On the night I started with the bairn, he was with a woman. He brought her to the house and I saw the two of them . . .' Bridget blushed to the roots of her hair. 'It's no more than I deserve.'

'Did he throw you out? Is that what you're trying to say?'

'No, he didn't go as far as that, but he might as well have. When I started with the bairn, I found him drunk out of his mind. I don't know how I got to Nelly's front door.'

'He was a pig to do what he did, gal,' Fanny said, 'but happen he needed to get back at yer for what you did to him. Have yer thought of that?'

'It crossed my mind.'

'And has it crossed your mind that he's got it out of his system now and he really means to do the best he can with what he's got? He's seen the child and happen he's fallen in love with her. Happen he means to put it all behind him now. He has the family he's always wanted, and nobody knows the truth . . .' Glancing anxiously at the door, she whispered, 'At least nobody who would ever tell.'

'I hope you're right, Fan.'

'Is he rid of the bitch he brought home?'

'So Nelly says.'

'And has he talked it through with you?'

Bridget nodded. 'He says it will never happen again, that he wants us to be a family, and though he knows it won't happen overnight, he swears he'll do his best for all of us.'

'But you don't believe him, is that it?'

Bridget's answer was a long time coming, and when she finally did answer, it was with a long, weary sigh. 'In all the time we've been together, I swear Tom has never lied to me. Yes, I do believe he means what he says. If he tells me he'll do his best to make us a family, then he will.'

'I don't understand, Bridget. It sounds to me as if you've got everything you hoped for. Yet you're still worried. Why?'

'Because I've known Tom for a long time. I know how he

thinks. I know how hard it will be for him to let folk believe that Ruth is his. He's a man of honour, you see.'

'Then he'll keep his promise to you. He'll make you a proper family, just like he said.'

Bridget was not convinced. 'He means well, but can he stand it? Living a lie twenty-four hours a day, seven days a week. Every time he hears the baby cry, every time I have to get out of bed to see to her, he'll watch us. He'll see me feeding her, holding her in my arms. Oh, Fan, I'm so afraid it will tear him apart. He'll see me and Ruth, and in his mind he'll see me and Harry the same.'

'You can't know that.' Privately, Fanny thought Bridget might be right. 'You have to give him a chance to prove he's man enough to deal with it. You owe him that much.'

'Do you think I don't know that?' It was turning her inside out. There had been many times when she would have given anything to turn the clock back to before she became pregnant. Not now though; now the thought of being without that beautiful little bairn was too terrible to contemplate. 'The truth is, I've only now realised just how much I love Tom. Harry was a mistake. Oh, I'm fond of him, and in a way I'll always have a soft spot for him, but it's not right, is it?'

'Do you *want* to go home, gal?'

Bridget looked up, the tears glittering on her lashes. She brushed them away. 'Oh, yes!' Right now she wanted nothing more. 'I want to make it up to him.'

'Then stop torturing yerself.' Taking Bridget by the shoulders, Fanny gently shook her. 'You're not even twenty-one, Bridget, and you've been through more than some women will go through in their entire lifetime. But you've survived, ain't yer? There has to be a reason for that, don't you think? I mean it, gal, don't lie here punishing yourself about summat you can't change.'

'I'm frightened for him . . . for all of us.'

'Look, Bridget.' Fetching the child from the crib, she laid her in Bridget's arms. 'This is your daughter, gal, your own flesh and blood. Her name is Ruth Mulligan, and she's a person all in her own right. She's got nobody else in this world but you, and Tom. Think on that, gal, and everything else will come right.'

'I've thought of nothing else.'

'Then *keep* thinking it.'

Bridget promised she would. But the niggling fear ate away at her. Would Tom's good will last? Or would there be a price to pay?

Nelly came rushing into the room with Fanny's son held out at arm's length. 'The little bugger's pissed all down my apron!' she cried. 'And after I'd near broke me arm rocking him to sleep.'

When the other two burst out laughing, she saw the funny side of it. 'Here, you can have the little sod!' Handing the child to Fanny, she suggested with a cheeky grin, 'I reckon you should teach him which way the wind blows.'

Soon after that, Fanny took her leave. 'I'd better not come and visit you at home,' she told Bridget. 'Tom wouldn't take kindly to that, you know he can't stand the sight of me. Common as muck, that's what he thinks of me, and I'm buggered if he's not right.'

Bridget regarded her friend with affection. The business with Bill Norman had taken its toll on Fanny. There were dark circles under her eyes and the laughter that used to light her smile just wasn't there any more. Yet her spirit was intact, as always, even if it was slightly ragged. 'Has Bill been round to see you?' Bridget asked.

'No, and he'd better not! If he shows his bleedin' face at my door, he'll rue the day, I can promise yer that!'

Before Fanny left, she and Bridget agreed to keep in touch by letter. 'Until I'm strong enough to come to your place,' Bridget said. 'By then we'll have tales to swap, and the babies can start getting to know each other.'

'You've got a good friend in her,' Nelly remarked as she helped Bridget prepare to go home when Tom arrived. He was due soon.

'I've got a good friend in you too, Nelly.' Bridget would never have dreamed that this old gossip had such a heart of gold under her wagging tongue. 'I won't forget what you did for me.'

'It was no more than anybody else would have done.'

'Maybe, but I owe you a lot. I know we've never been that close, Nelly, but from now on, you're welcome in my house any time.'

Nelly laughed. 'In that case you'll have to mind you don't let slip any juicy gossip for me to carry away. I can't help it, you see. I'm a tittle-tat. Always have been.'

'All the same, Nelly. I meant what I said. I honestly don't know what I would have done without you.'

'Give over, lass.' Nelly flushed with embarrassment. 'I'm only too pleased it all worked out in the end.' She helped Bridget on with her coat, picked up the baby and escorted Bridget downstairs.

'I can hold her,' Bridget protested.

Nelly would have none of it. 'You can hardly put one foot before the other,' she chided. 'Anyway, don't deny an old woman the feel of a bairn in her arms. You'll have plenty of time to molly-coddle her when you're settled back under your own roof.'

When Tom arrived to collect his family, he looked as shy as a man on his first date. He had finished work early, been home, washed and changed, and lit a small fire, for the houses in the area were chilly in the evening, even in the month of August.

Standing at the door of Nelly's parlour, cap in hand and his best jacket on, he nearly broke Bridget's heart. 'It's good to see you, Tom,' she said, going towards him with Ruth in her arms.

Dear God above, she thought, it was wonderful just to talk with him: for too long they had been like strangers.

'You look stronger,' he muttered. 'You've got more colour in your cheeks than yesterday.' He felt awkward, as though he didn't know her at all.

Nelly came to stand beside Bridget. 'The roses in her cheeks are there because you're taking her home,' she explained. 'A woman needs to be in her own place. She needs to look round her own kitchen, and sit beside her own fireplace. Give the lass a few days at home and you'll see the sun shine out of her eyes.'

While she spoke, Tom looked at Bridget and felt like a man lost. It would be hard to pick up the pieces, he knew that. But seeing her so weak and vulnerable, and knowing what she had been through, he felt nothing but pity for her. And beneath the pity lay his love for her. He loved her too much, that was the trouble. He was tormented by thoughts of how she had lain in another man's arms. Did she give herself easily? When in the throes of coupling . . . when he entered her . . . did she have no thought in her mind for her husband? How did he make love, this other man? Was he gentle? Rough? Exciting? Or, in the end, was he no better than he was himself at satisfying her? But he must have been, because here was the child to prove it! Here, in Bridget's arms, was the result of it all.

As so often before, anger began to rise in him. Anger, and a terrible sense of despair.

With a surge of inner strength, he pushed it away. Don't let it destroy you, Tom! he told himself. You're not blameless. We've both made mistakes. I mustn't let the past stand in the way of starting afresh with Bridget.

Nelly's voice interrupted his thoughts. 'Don't let her do too much at first,' she told him. 'Doctor says she's to build her strength up afore she tackles a full day's housework. She'll have enough with the bairn for a time, that's what he said.'

'Will he be calling on her again?' Tom asked. 'Only they don't come cheap, these bloody doctors.'

'No. He'll not be seeing her again.'

'You never said how much I owed you for his visit.' Digging into his pocket, Tom brought out a folded wage packet. 'I'll settle with you now. How much?' Carefully, he opened the packet.

Nelly calculated on her fingers. 'Well, if yer give me a shilling for the food and keep, that's enough for me,' she said. 'And a florin for the doctor.'

'A florin? By! That's bloody steep, isn't it?'

'You wouldn't have thought so if you'd seen him at work,' Nelly argued. 'Why, the man performed a bloody miracle. This lass were knocking on death's door and he pulled her back, and the bairn with her. Thanks to him, you've still got a wife, and a bonny bairn into the bargain. I reckon they're worth a florin. So pay up and look big.'

As Tom dropped the coin into her hand, Nelly caught sight of Bridget giving her a strange look. She smiled in response. 'Look after yourself now, lass,' she said disarmingly.

When they had left, Nelly leaned on the door and wiped the sweat from her brow. 'I reckon the little sod rumbled me,' she chuckled. 'But she'll not give me away, even if she does remember Bob Morris. A grand feller, the way he fetched the doctor and dipped into his own pocket to pay him too.' Still chuckling, she spat on the coin for good luck.

In the kitchen, she cleared the table, whipped the cloth off, and inched the table top along. Within the framework underneath was a carved hole the size of a man's fist. Reaching into it she withdrew a small, round bag and tipped its contents on to the table. The coins spilled out and she rubbed her hands with glee. 'While I've got this, I'll never be lonely,' she giggled.

For a brief moment she reviewed her life. 'When it comes right down to it, Nelly Potts,' she muttered thoughtfully, 'there's nobody else in this whole wide world who really gives a sod about you.' It was a sobering thought. Yet, as she set about counting the coins for the umpteenth time, she didn't care a bugger. 'Sod 'em all, that's what I say. As long as I've got me little bag o' cash, I'll be happy as a pig in muck.'

Well into the evening, Nelly sat at the table, counting her hoard, missing a coin and starting again. She was never happier.

'Is it warm enough?' Tom took Bridget's shawl and laid it across the back of a chair.

'It's lovely, Tom. Thank you.' When she raised her face and their eyes met, she saw the goodness there. There was something else too, a kind of fear. 'Would you like to hold Ruth?' Bridget looked down, smiling into that tiny face, so incredibly like Tom's.

She heard a sound behind her and when she looked up again Tom was gone. 'I'll make you a hot drink,' he called from the kitchen.

Bridget's heart sank. True, Tom had not refused to hold the child, nor had he been unkind in any way, but clearly he wanted to keep his distance. And towards herself he had shown only concern, not affection. He had got the house ready and displayed more kindness than he had done in a long time, but he had not kissed her, or even touched her. He had followed her into the house and he had lifted the shawl from her shoulders without any kind of contact. More disturbing than that, when she looked into his eyes, she saw that same desperation as before.

When Tom returned to set the drink beside her, she reached out and held his hand. 'I do love you,' she murmured sincerely. 'Please believe that.'

Taken aback, he stared at her for a moment before drawing away. 'I know,' he said simply. 'Just give me time.'

Bridget wondered how much time it would take. Days? Months? Years?

There was nothing she could do other than be cautious, and let him know how much she truly loved him. Everything else rested with Tom himself.

The next two weeks were the worst of Bridget's life.

But day by day she grew stronger and she soon learned the ways of a mother, and kept the home as cosy and welcoming as ever.

Baby Ruth was a delight; at night she slept well, and during the day she lay in her crib, often wide awake and looking at everything about her, gurgling with contentment, her small, chubby fingers curling round each other, as though comforting herself.

Today was Friday. 'Come on, my beauty.' Having got herself washed and changed and ready to go out, Bridget returned to the bedroom to collect Ruth. 'We're off to see Fanny today. This will be the first time since we came home that we've set foot outside the door.' Oh, but she was so looking forward to it. 'You'll see Billy, and Fanny said in her letter that she's got a surprise in store for us.'

Ruth was already fed, so now Bridget bathed her and brushed the fine cap of soft, fair hair. 'There!' Raising the child into her arms, she was caught by the perfection of that small, trusting face. 'I wish he could love you like I do,' she sighed. It was her greatest regret. 'However you were made, Tom *is* your daddy when all is said and done, because, God help me, you will never know another.'

In the shaft of sunlight streaming in through the window, she looked at Ruth more closely. 'Nelly was right, your eyes *are* changing colour . . . darker . . . more like Harry's.' In spite of herself, Bridget's thoughts went back to that stormy night in the barn with Harry.

Holding the child close, she began to tremble. 'There's no

denying it,' she whispered. 'You're Harry's child. And I will never love you the less for that.'

With Ruth swaddled in the same long grey shawl Tom had brought to fetch her home, Bridget wheeled out the pram, a deep-bodied thing with great wheels and a towering handle. 'Aren't you the little smartie?' she teased as they went away down the street. 'Your mammy's proud as punch, that she is.'

Bridget, too, looked smart in her best blue blouse, a broad belt at her waist, and her grey, wide-hemmed skirt dancing about the top of her boots. She cut a handsome, youthful figure. Gone were the hollowed eyes and slow, painful walk. Forgotten, too, were the harrowing nightmares that had plagued her for a week after coming home. Now as she went down the street at a jaunty pace, her cheeks glowed and her step was bouncy, and everyone who saw her thought the same.

'My! You do look a picture, lass. Pretty as I've ever seen.' Nelly was on her way back from the baker's. 'It's heartening to see you out and about,' she said approvingly.

Bridget stopped to chat. 'Thank you, Nelly. I'm taking Ruth for her very first outing.'

'Quite right.' Curiosity got the better of her. 'And where might you be off to?'

'Well, as it's such a lovely day, I thought we might walk along the canal.' Knowing how Nelly liked to talk, Bridget made no mention of Fanny in case word got back to Tom.

'Aye, well, like you say, it is a fine day, and I'm sure the bairn would get a deal of pleasure from watching the ducks on the water.' Clucking at the sleeping child, Nelly discreetly scrutinised Bridget, noting the bright hazel eyes and the way her long brown hair shone in the sunlight. 'You go on and enjoy yourself, lass,' she said. 'Lord knows you've earned the right.'

When Bridget said cheerio and carried on, the old biddy stared after her. 'Nobody has a right to be as pretty as that,' she grumbled, 'especially after what she's been through. Anybody would think she had a man friend waiting in the park.'

She started walking on; then she stopped and looked at Bridget once more, her inquisitive mind busy. She recalled the raised voices from next door, and the way Bridget had fled to her in her hour of need although her own husband was at home. She remembered how, right up to the day Bridget gave birth, Tom Mulligan never once inquired about her, even though she herself had warned him that his wife might not live. Then there was the floozy he'd taken to his bed. What kind of man would do such a thing with his wife lying desperately ill and his child's life threatened too? Her mind ticked over like a clock. No man would behave like that, surely – unless he had good reason.

As she stood considering all these things, Bridget turned and gave her a wave, making Nelly feel ashamed. 'You're a born troublemaker, Nelly Potts,' she chided. 'Why! That lass never gave him no good cause to do what he did. The plain truth is, Tom Mulligan is the same as most other men. A wife on one arm and a floozy on the other. I've never met a man yet who needs a reason to cheat. Randy buggers, each and every one!'

Thinking of it, she chuckled out loud, wishing she had a randy bugger to keep her warm of a night. 'I might be toothless and dried up, but it's never too late, isn't that what they say?'

It was a farfetched idea and she doubted if any man would even look at her, let alone take her to his bed. All the same, just thinking about it put a spring in her step.

A glance at the clock on the church spire told Bridget it was already quarter past midday.

'I'm sure Fan said she'd be waiting here at quarter to.' Plucking her bag from the pram, she took out the note Fanny had sent. 'I'll meet you at quarter to twelve where the canal crosses the bridge at Penny Street,' said the note.

Growing anxious, she scoured up and down for a sight of that familiar figure; she even walked to the top of Penny Street and back again. There was no sign of her. 'If she's not here in ten minutes,' she decided, 'I'll make my way up to Montague Street.' It was a fair way but she had time enough, she thought.

The minutes came and went, and as the church clock chimed the half hour, Bridget turned towards William Henry Street. 'It's not like her to be late,' she murmured. 'I hope there's no trouble.' She was thinking of Bill Norman and that wife of his.

She had got as far as the top of the canal walk when she heard the faint clip-clop of hooves behind her. At first she took no notice; the canal walk was a short cut to the market and, like the bargees, many a farmer ran his goods along this way.

When the sound got closer, she thought she had better step aside. At that point Ruth started crying. Pressing the pram close beneath the trees, Bridget bent to calm her. 'It's only the farmer,' she cooed. 'It's all right, sweetheart. He won't run us over.'

'That's the first time I've been called a bleedin' farmer!' came a familiar voice. 'And yer right, gal, I ain't gonna run yer over. I've handled horses afore.'

'Fanny!' Bridget couldn't believe her eyes. Fanny was perched on the scruffiest Gypsy wagon Bridget had ever seen, driving an old piebald horse complete with feathers round its fetlocks and a hay bag tied beneath its chin. Fanny jumped down from the seat, her face split by a grin and on her head a bright, spotted Gypsy scarf. 'What in God's name are you up to?' Bridget demanded, the smile on her face as wide as Fanny's.

Fanny hugged her fiercely and said how well she looked. Then she turned to the wagon. 'What d'yer think, gal?' she asked excitedly. 'Is it pretty or what?'

Momentarily lost for words, Bridget could only stare at it; the horse looked as if it was on its last legs, and the wagon the same. No doubt in its day this colourful ensemble cut a dash along the highways and byways, but now, with the swirls of colour faded on the side of the caravan and the wheel rims worn away, it was a sad sight. The door was sagging, and the scalloped skirting had come away in places. 'Is it safe?' Bridget wanted to know.

'Course it's bloody safe!' Fanny was indignant. 'Yer don't think I'd have bought it if it weren't safe.' She went to the front of the wagon and lifted Billy from his cradle.

'Are you telling me you spent good money on this . . . this . . .' Bridget thought it better to say no more.

'Yer don't think much to it, d'yer, gal?' Fanny's disappointment was evident.

'I don't understand. Is it really yours?'

'Lock, stock and barrel, gal. Come inside and I'll tell yer all about it.'

Bridget flinched. 'I'm not going in there. It might collapse.'

'Stuff and nonsense,' said Fanny. She climbed back into the seat and, with surprising skill, edged the ensemble away from the footpath. That done, she took the bairns one at a time from Bridget. When they were settled comfortably, one at the top of the crib and one at the bottom, she helped Bridget up. 'Inside,' she ordered, lifting the crib containing both babies out of the way as though it weighed nothing at all.

The next hour was an experience Bridget would never forget.

Seated on a bench, drinking cool sarsaparilla, she looked about her, and was amazed. The inside of the wagon was like a little house, with pretty curtains and a table, and there was even a bunk high up in the front. In the centre of the room was a cast-iron stove, and at the back a run of cupboards. Above them, a wooden rack displayed plates and such. But it was also dirty and shockingly neglected, and a kind of musty smell pervaded it.

'Whatever made you buy it?' Bridget asked. 'And where did you get the money? I thought you said Bill had cut your allowance?'

'Bill did cut my allowance,' Fanny admitted, 'but his wife had other ideas.'

'Oh?'

'She came to see me. She said as how Bill and her were closer now than they'd been in a long time, and I was a threat to all that. She offered me a deal to stay away from him.'

'What kind of a deal?'

'In return for a sum of money, I was never to get in touch with Bill again, and if he was to come to my house, I was to send him on his way without mercy.' Creased with laughter, Fanny shook her head in disbelief. 'Poor cow! You'll never believe what story the old bugger told her. He said we'd had a little fling, and now he couldn't get rid of me. He wanted nothing at all to do with me, and he were worried sick about it all. One night, he told her, one stupid mistake, that's all, he said, and now I were driving him insane going on my knees for him to come and live with me.'

'What? And she believed all that?'

'Not only believed it, but came and asked me to leave him be. And if I agreed, she'd make it worth my while,' Fanny's eyes lit up, 'to the tune of four guineas.'

'By! That's a bloody fortune!'

'I had to sign papers and such to say I would stick to her conditions. I reckon she knew he were telling a pack o' lies but chose to turn a blind eye. Anyway, I signed the papers and got me money. I went straight out and paid for the house, and then I bought this. I've allus fancied a wagon. And there's still enough money left for me and little Billy to live on for a good while yet.'

Bridget admired her. 'You're mad as a March hare,' she said, laughing. 'I never know what you'll do next.'

'We'll go for a little ride, shall we? You can tell me what's been happening between you and Tom. The bairns can get to know each other, and when they start bawling for their titty, I'll take you home – well, as far as the bottom end of King Street.

We don't want your old man knowing you've been out with me, do we, eh?'

Fanny edged the horse and wagon out towards the main road. Soon they were heading towards Pleasington and open country. While the bairns gurgled and played, she and Bridget talked about anything and everything. They talked of Bill, and how Fanny would miss him, and Fanny confessed, 'To tell the truth, gal, I'd rather have had the old bugger aside o' me than sell him for a bag full o' money. I've a son now, and so has he, though he denied all knowledge of it to his wife. But my little lad needs a father, and when all's said and done, I reckon Bill would do as well as the next feller.'

'Are you sure it's not too late?' Bridget asked. 'Can't you go and see him? Explain the way things are?'

'I might have considered it some time back,' Fanny answered thoughtfully, 'but not now, gal. Not since the old battleaxe told me what he'd been saying. He made me out to be a mad woman, wanting him at any cost. I can't forgive that. Bill Norman has proved himself to be a liar and a coward, and there ain't no room in my life for that kind of a creature. I've got security now, though I know it won't last for ever, and I've got my pride. Whereas Bill Norman is saddled with a monster of a wife and a life I wouldn't want if they gave me the Crown Jewels as consolation.'

When they'd exhausted Fanny's news, Bridget told her that she and Tom were getting along well enough. 'He's finding it hard though,' she said. 'He can't bring himself to hold Ruth. He can't even bear to be near her. In fact, he's deliberately working all hours, spending more time at the quarry than he does at home.'

'What about you?' Fanny asked. 'Can he bear to be near you?'

'We talk,' Bridget said resignedly. 'It's a start.' But it was never enough for her. She needed him to be a husband, like he used to be. And a father to Ruth, God willing.

When all the serious issues were covered, Bridget asked, 'What made you buy a wagon?'

'Ah, well now, I don't know if I ever told you, but I come of Irish stock, so I'm used to the horse and wagon. My old daddy was a tinker, you see, gal. With my mammy and infant brother we travelled all over the place – spent a magical summer in Scotland once. Daddy said he had relatives there, but I reckon he were lying. He liked the ale there, that's what me mam said.' Suddenly she was silent, her eyes fixed on the road ahead, and her gaze sad. 'Two years later my brother died of the fever. Mammy went the same way soon after.'

Bridget was filled with compassion. 'Oh, Fan, I never knew. I'm so sorry. What about your father?'

Fanny laughed, a dry, harsh sound. '*He* didn't die, but he might as well have. When it was just the two of us, he hardly spoke two words from one day to the next. At night, when I was in the back, I could hear him sobbing his heart out. If I tried to comfort him, he'd shrug me off. I've never forgotten how bad that felt. One day he lent me out to a market trader for sixpence. "Polish the apples and smile at the customers," he told me, "and I'll be back for you later."'

'He never came back, did he?'

'No.' Fanny gave her an old-fashioned look. 'The old market trader took me in but he didn't want me and neither did his missus.'

'What happened, Fan?' Bridget thought it a terrible thing. 'Why did he never come back?'

'Because he'd taken up with a woman from Burnley and thought I might cramp his style.'

'How did you find out?'

'One night I heard the market trader and his missus talking about me. The sixpence he gave my dad wasn't for a lend. He actually *sold* me for that.' She grunted, shaking her head.

'*Sixpence!* That's all I was worth to my dad, one bright, shiny sixpence.' Taking a deep breath she went on, 'The trader told his missus he wasn't happy with me. "No good at selling fruit and veg," he said, "but there's many a desperate man who'd pay well for an hour or two with her."'

Bridget had heard about these things, but never at first hand. 'Dear God, what monsters!'

'Fortunately for me his missus refused to be a part of it. Instead she pushed me out the back door with a bag of food and a shilling and told me to watch out for the bad men.'

'Oh, Fan, no wonder you don't trust anybody.'

'It taught me a lesson, gal,' came the answer. 'From that day on, I knew I had no one but meself. One way or another, I managed to scrape a living. It was hard, but I survived. I learned how to hate and cheat and, yes, steal if I had to. I also learned how to play men off one against the other. But it cost me, gal. I could never make friends easily . . . never knew if they were out to hurt me or do me down.'

'Fan, please, look at me.' Reaching out, Bridget put her hands round Fanny's face and turned her. When Fanny was looking into her eyes, she said softly, 'I'm sorry for what happened to you but I'm really glad you chose me for a friend. If I never had another friend in the whole world, it wouldn't matter. Not as long as I had you.'

Bridget's words were so moving, Fanny had no answer, but tears of gratitude shone in her eyes. 'It's time I got you home, gal,' she said. And for the rest of the journey they were content just to sit beside each other, thinking their own thoughts.

Fanny brought the horse to a halt just a step or two from the mouth of King Street. 'Go on, gal,' she urged, 'afore your old man claps eyes on us.'

She watched Bridget climb down and when she handed Ruth to her, she murmured, 'This wagon might seem a strange thing to you, gal. But it's a piece of my past, you see, and it gives me a deal of comfort.' Suddenly, in that unpredictable way she had, she was smiling again. 'Besides,' she joked, 'I can take off for weeks on end if I want, travel the highways and byways, and who knows,' a strange, faraway look came into her eyes, 'one of these fine days I might decide to go and root out the bugger who sold me. That would give him a shock, don't yer think, eh?' The smile erupted into laughter. 'There'd be him with his ageing floozy, and I'd turn up with a grandson for him. By! That'd take the grin off his face, I reckon.'

Scampering from the wagon, she untied the pram from behind. 'I'll be in touch,' she said with a kiss. Then she was up on the seat again and off down the street, the sound of the wagon wheels echoing from the cobbles.

'You're a mystery, Fanny Higgins,' Bridget laughed. 'Mad as a hatter and stubborn as a mule. But, so help me, I love you like you were my own flesh and blood.'

As Bridget put the key in her front door, Tom watched from the other end of the street. He had seen her come into King Street, and he had seen Fanny Higgins draw away in her curious contraption. 'So, you defied me, eh?' he muttered angrily. 'Damn and bugger it, doesn't what I say mean anything any more?'

In the blink of an eye, his mood changed. 'Well, it doesn't really matter, does it? There are more serious issues at stake here. Issues that concern you and me, and the child.' With slow, heavy steps he made his way to the house. At the door he paused, reluctant to go in. 'I can't face her just yet. I don't know what to say any more.' Covered in sweat and quarry dust, he turned away. 'I'll go where I feel more comfortable,' he decided. 'After a jar or two of good ale, I'll feel like a man again.'

Quickly, before she might look out of the window and see him, he hurried along King Street, up to the top, and across to the

Swan Inn. Here he knew he would find a friend or two to help him drown his sorrows.

He strode in and ordered a jar of best ale.

Within moments of his appearing, he was surrounded by men from the quarry, laughing and joking, warmed by the ale inside them. 'Don't you lot have homes to go to?' Tom joked. And they asked him the same.

It was a merry evening, but though he drank a few more than he intended, Tom didn't laugh along with the others, nor did he join in when they gathered round the accordion and sent out the loudest, most awful medley of songs. 'Keep on like that,' the landlord protested, 'and you'll have the sodding authorities knocking on the door!'

The only response he got was a roar of laughter. 'Garn, you miserable old bugger!' yelled one. 'If we can't let off steam on a Friday night, what's the world coming to, eh?'

'Daft buggers!' grumbled Tom, looking enviously at the men and wondering what they had to be so merry about anyway.

Choosing a quiet corner, he sat himself down and concentrated on his ale; one wasn't enough to dull the pain inside, nor two, nor three, and pretty soon the landlord was telling him he'd had enough. 'It's a long walk home, Tom,' he reminded him. 'You don't want to be falling down in the street.'

Tom nodded. The old feller meant well, he knew. 'I'll be away soon,' he promised.

As he gazed at the familiar faces of the men, one caught his eye.

Tom cringed as he recognised Ted Louis, his old enemy, the man who had taunted him when it was thought he could never father a child. 'And he was right,' Tom thought bitterly, 'though God willing he'll never have the satisfaction of knowing it.'

When Ted continued to stare, Tom looked away, but the sound of the man's voice carried across the room.

Silencing the others with a yell, Ted raised his jar of ale. 'To Tom Mulligan!' he cried. 'A man I've set meself against time and again, with never a good word on his behalf. But I stand here tonight to raise my glass to him.' Taking a step forward, he called out drunkenly, 'Here's to you, Tom, father of a young'un at long last, and no doubt with another one on the way before too long, eh?' Digging a mate in the ribs, he laughed lewdly. 'Happen now he's got the hang of it we'll have a *dozen* Mulligans before we know it. And if he gets tired from all that loving, I can always make meself available for someone as young and pretty as Bridget Mulligan.'

It was too much for Tom. He was across the room in two strides and punched Ted's chin. The blow sent Ted to the floor, and before he could get back to his feet, Tom hit him again, and again.

'Whoa! That's enough, Tom. Yer don't have to kill him, for Christ's sake!' said one of the men. Two more grabbed his arms and marched him across the floor and out of the building.

'Cool off, man,' one said. 'You've had too much to drink. You know what Ted Louis is like. He didn't mean it badly. He's just a loud-mouth, and when he's had a jar or two of ale down him, he doesn't know when to shut it.'

Deep in thought and the worse for drink, Tom made his way back to King Street.

Bridget, too, had been doing some thinking. Holding the sleepy child, she talked softly, unburdening her heart. 'I was hoping he might be home before I put you to bed,' she murmured, 'but he's working late again, same as always.'

Turning back her blouse, she put Ruth to her breast, and while she greedily sucked, Bridget looked wonderingly into her tiny face. When the child was filled and content, Bridget covered her breast and stood up, disappointed that Tom was still not home.

'Come on, sweetheart. It's late. Time you were in your bed.'

Washed and fed, the small bundle was carried upstairs and laid in its crib. 'Asleep already, eh?' Ruth was a good bairn, and Bridget was grateful for that.

Returning to the parlour, she went to the stairs cupboard and brought out the tin bath which she set before the fire. She hurried to the kitchen and filled two large pans with cold water. In the parlour she wedged them on the coals, and while the water was heating, she laid out a bar of carbolic, a towel, and her best blue nightgown.

Testing the water several times, she was eventually satisfied that it was hot enough and poured it into the tub. Stripping off, she lowered herself into the water, sighing with pleasure as the warm, soothing liquid flowed over her bare skin.

Lying there, eyes closed, Bridget didn't hear the front door open and close. She had no idea that Tom had walked down the passage and was standing there, his eyes feasting on her nakedness.

It was only when she climbed out of the bath and reached for the towel that she saw him. The cry froze in her throat as she realised with relief that it was only Tom. 'You frightened me,' she gently chided. 'Give me a minute and I'll have your meal ready.'

Barefooted and with only the towel draped about her, she went into the kitchen.

Unsteady on his feet, Tom followed.

Leaning on the door jamb, he told her angrily, 'I thought I told you not to mix with that bloody slag.'

His slurred voice surprised her. Swinging round, she accused him, 'I thought you were at work, and all the time you've been drinking!' She thought of how she and Ruth had waited for him. She saw now how blind she had been. If he preferred the alehouse to his wife, what kind of future could they have together?

'Where I go and what I do is *my* business, damn you!' He strode across the room and grabbed her by the hair. 'I said you weren't to see her, and the minute my back's turned you're meeting up with her, riding in that God-awful contraption, brassy as you please. What will folk think, eh? That you're as bad as she is, that's what they'll bloody well think!'

'Let them think what they like!' Bridget retaliated. 'Fanny Higgins is the best friend I've ever had, and I'm not about to stop seeing her just because you say so! And what about *you*, eh? There I was, fool that I am, waiting for you to come home from work so we could have a quiet evening together. I thought we could talk about . . . everything, sort it out and get it over with.'

He just stared at her.

She took a deep breath, unleashing all the agony inside. 'Don't you see, Tom, we need to talk it through. It's all wrong, you know that. What happened is still eating away at you, and until we can talk about it, there's no hope for us.'

'Shut your mouth, damn you!'

Angered by his reaction, she yelled back, 'Look at tonight! I thought you were at work, and all the time you were at the bloody alehouse, not caring a bugger about me or the bairn. So don't talk to me about who I can and can't see. You have your mates, don't you? You enjoy being with them, and it doesn't matter to you whether I approve or not. Well, it doesn't matter to me what you think of Fanny Higgins because I intend seeing her whenever I please.'

Staring him in the eye, she said quietly, 'Do you understand what I'm saying, Tom? I've had enough. Either we live together as a family, the three of us, or we call it a day and go our separate ways. Which is it to—'

Tom slapped her face hard. 'Don't *ever* question my authority again,' he said, incensed. 'Now get out of my sight.'

Silenced but determined, she stared at him for what seemed

an age; when the blood trickled from her nose, she wiped it with the back of her hand, and all the while her sad, brown eyes looked unflinchingly into his. After a while, she lowered her gaze. 'The pity of it all is,' she murmured softly, 'you'll never know the love I have for you.'

She would have turned away then, but when he asked quietly, 'Why did you do it, Bridget?' all her resolve melted.

'It was a mad, bad thing,' she whispered, her brown eyes pleading. 'I promise you, Tom. It meant nothing.'

It was a time for confessions. 'I had a woman here when you were at Nelly's house, did you know that?'

'Yes, I knew.'

'So Nelly told you after all.'

Bridget shook her head. 'She didn't have to. A woman has a way of knowing.' She raised her hand to wipe away the blood again. To her surprise, Tom reached up and put his hand over hers. With the other hand he tenderly wiped away the crimson trail. Softly, he slid the towel from her body. Gasping with delight, he stroked her shoulders, the silky, warm breasts, licking at the drop of milk that rose like a tear on her nipple.

Ripples of joy coursed through her. This was the way it used to be, she thought, she and Tom together as man and wife.

Yielding beneath his touch, she let him take her into his arms and carry her upstairs, laughing when he almost lost his balance. In the bedroom, he laid her gently on the bed and gazed on her nakedness. Then he threw off his clothes and lay beside her.

They touched and fondled, and raised each other to the heights of pleasure. When the pleasure turned to passion, and the passion could not be contained, he spread her body beneath him and, with a soft, pained cry, he positioned his erect member and tenderly entered her, pushing into her like a man starved.

Deeply roused, Bridget surrendered body and soul.

When it was over and he fell asleep beside her, she prayed it was the start of everything good for them. Because now she knew he loved her. If they had a love this strong to bind them, surely it was enough.

She covered him with a blanket and nestled down beside him. The bairn was asleep in her crib, her husband was lying next to her, and her heart was more content than it had been in a long, long time.

With these pleasant thoughts on her mind, Bridget drifted into a deep, comfortable sleep.

Tom was not so content. Soon after midnight he woke and lay there, perfectly still, eyes wide open and his mind quick with memories.

Oblivious to his anguish, Bridget slept on.

She slept when he stood over her, gazing down and thinking how beautiful she was, and she slept when he bent to kiss her, saying softly, 'I want to forget, but I can't. I need to love you but *he's* always there, spoiling everything we ever had.'

Since Bridget had brought Harry's child into the world, he had thought long and hard about what he must do. Now, his mind was made up. 'If only you knew how hard I've tried.' There was so much regret in his voice, so much pain, and love. 'It's no good,' he whispered. 'He'll always come between us. The child too. I know now I could never take her as my own.'

Softly, he gathered his clothes. Before leaving the room, he peered into the crib and to his astonishment the child was wide awake, looking up at him with those big, knowing eyes. When she reached out with a tiny hand, it brought a smile to his face. 'It's not your fault,' he whispered. 'But you're not mine, and I was a fool to think you ever could be.'

In a move that surprised even himself, he took hold of that tiny hand, his heart torn in two when the fingers wound round his thumb. 'I love your mammy too much,' he murmured. 'That's the trouble.'

Quick and soft as a shadow he left the house and made his way to the quarry.

The night watchman was surprised to see him. 'Why, Mr Mulligan! Whatever are you doing here at this time of a morning? These days you're the first here and the last to leave.' Cocking a quizzical eye at him, he asked, 'I didn't realise you were booked in for this morning though. As I remember rightly, you worked last Saturday.'

'Your memory serves you well, Jack,' said Tom. 'I did work last Saturday and as a rule I don't do two Saturdays on the trot, but the foreman got a message to me last night. It seems they're a man short, so I'm it.'

'That's hard luck, and you just being a daddy an' all.'

Tom smiled resignedly. 'Oh, I don't mind,' he said. 'What with the bairn bawling all night, I couldn't get off to sleep anyway.'

The old man laughed. 'Aye, well, that's bairns for yer. Thank God I'm past all that.' Just then the little cast-iron pan of water began to boil and spit on the brazier coals. 'I'm making a brew,' he said. 'Yer welcome to share it. I've an extra cup, and it's clean, I promise yer.'

Tom played along. 'Why not? Thanks, Jack, I dare say it'll warm me up.' Though the days were still warm, the early hours and late evenings had a real bite to them.

Jack rolled the sleeve of his coat over his hand and plucked the pan from the fire. 'Two sugars or three?' he asked, pouring the hot water over the tea leaves.

'One sugar,' Tom answered. 'Plenty of milk though.'

The two of them sat by the fire, chatting. 'So, you've got yerself a bairn at long last, eh?' The old man smiled at Tom. 'They're no trouble when they're small,' he declared wisely. 'It's when they get old enough to answer back, that's when you feel like wringing their bloody necks, the buggers.' He fell into serious mood. 'Aye. Me and the missus had six childer, and I'll tell yer this, they've none of 'em ever done us any good.'

'How long have you been married?'

'Forty year come Sunday, and I love her like it were yesterday when me and 'er used to stroll in the park together. Mind you, the ol' darlin' ain't as pretty as she were.' He roared with laughter. 'But then neither am I.'

'Has she ever done anything that made you think you'd be better off apart?'

Jack stared at him. 'What, you mean other men? Is that what you're saying?'

Regretting his impulse, Tom shrugged his shoulders. 'Just wondered, that's all.'

The old man was emphatic. 'Good Lord, no. Loyal and true as the day's long, that's my missus. I've been the same, never cheated on her. And I've never raised me hand to her neither in all the years we've been together.'

Tom's mind went back to Harry Little . . . and the floozy he himself had taken to Bridget's bed. He recalled how, only a few hours ago, he had hit her, and her only weeks from coming close to losing her life. 'Sometimes life leads us along a route we'd rather not take,' he murmured softly.

'What's that you say?' Cupping his hand to his ear, Jack strained to listen. 'Didn't hear what you said. That bloody factory hooter deafens me at times.'

'Nothing.' Tom was glad he hadn't heard. 'I'd better be making a start.'

Jack leaned forward. 'There's a drop o' brandy tucked away under me barrel. What say we have a tickle in our tea?'

'Go on then.'

Rising from his seat, the old man dipped into the barrel he was sitting on and pulled out a small flask. 'This'll take the edge off,' he grinned, pouring a measure into each of the cups. That done, he returned the flask to its hiding place, replaced the barrel lid and sat down again. 'Don't let on you've seen it,' he urged, 'or the buggers will have it away when I'm not looking.'

A short time later, Tom stood up to leave. 'I'd best be off now. Thanks, old feller.'

'What's bothering you, son?'

Made uneasy by the observation, Tom replied firmly, 'Nothing's bothering me. What makes you ask?'

Jack slurped the remains of his tea and wiped finger and thumb down his moustache to catch the drips. 'I never tell what's told me. Never have, and never will.'

'There's nothing to tell.'

'I've been a bad enemy to some in my time. But I can be a good friend when I'm called on. Do you need a friend, Tom? Are you in some kinda trouble?'

'No trouble.' Tom flexed his muscles. 'Sitting here so close to the fire makes a man lazy.'

'No need to rush away. There's time enough yet.' He glanced at the clock on the nearby factory. 'You've a good half-hour afore the others start arriving.'

'All the same, I'd best be off. Before you know it they'll be at the gates and a man won't have time to call his own.'

'Well, *I've* time enough yet. I shall sit here and contemplate, warm me arse and have another drop of brandy. Then I shall go home and climb in bed aside o' my missus.' Winking cheekily, he laughed, 'Happen she'll warm me arse a bit more, if you know what I mean.'

As he walked away, Tom muttered enviously, 'You lucky old bugger. It seems all your troubles are behind you.' A quiet smile crossed his face. 'And so are yours, Tom Mulligan,' he whispered. 'God willing, so are yours.'

The old man watched him go. 'There's summat troubling that young feller.' He saw Tom take the key from the wall of the storehouse, and he saw him go in. But he didn't notice him come out.

A short time later Ted Louis arrived. 'Mulligan's been here ages,' Jack told him. 'Couldn't sleep, that's what he said.'

'Is that right?' Ted was still sporting the black eye given him by Tom the night before. 'Gone in the storehouse, has he?'

'That's right.'

Ted squared his shoulders. 'The sly bastard's trying to get on the right side of the foreman, I shouldn't wonder. He might wish he hadn't come in at all today. But now that he has, I'd best root him out. Me and him have a score or two to settle.'

More quarrymen were making their way down the lane. 'I'll be off soon,' the old man said. Truth was, he didn't want to witness any violence. He glanced at the clock on the factory. 'Five minutes, then I'm away.' And the way things were shaping up, the five minutes couldn't pass quickly enough.

Ted's raised voice could be heard all over the site. 'Mulligan! Are you in there? Come out, ye bugger, we've business to finish.'

The old man hurriedly scooped up a handful of dust and threw it on the fire. When it sizzled out, he gathered up his belongings and prepared to leave. 'A man-sized fried breakfast then a warm bed,' he muttered, 'and let the buggers fight it out among theirselves. Old Jack's off out of it, quick as a wink.'

The foreman came through the gates and Jack made a beeline for him. 'You'd best sort these men out,' he warned. 'Ted Louis is on the warpath, and he's got Mulligan in his sights.' Considering he'd done his duty, he hurried away.

He'd gone only a few yards when there was a frantic shout. The foreman ran towards the quarry. Ted was standing on the edge, his mouth open with shock and his eyes stricken with horror. 'Jesus!'

Jack retraced his steps at a run. 'What's the mad bugger done now?'

As he drew nearer, he could hear other men chasing up behind him. 'What the hell's going on?' they asked. From the look on the foreman's face, it was obvious something was very wrong.

When they reached the quarry mouth, they could hear Ted muttering over and over, 'It weren't me! I swear to God, I never touched him.'

The foreman ran towards the winch. 'For Christ's sake, somebody get over here!' he yelled, and two men dropped their tool bags and dashed towards him.

Jack stood beside Ted, his curious gaze following Ted's stricken stare down into the quarry. Below was the great bucket, filled with sand and ready for raising. Above that was the boom, and hanging from it was Tom Mulligan. 'Oh no!' Jack cried, his face ashen. 'Dear God, why would he do a thing like that?'

By the time they cut Tom down, it was too late.

For a long, terrible moment nobody spoke. The foreman was on his knees, desperately trying to force a spark of life into that young, still body. 'It's no good,' he said. 'There's nothing I can do.'

The old man was trembling from head to toe. 'We were just supping a drop o' brandy together . . . the lad never said . . . he never said . . .' And yet he knew there had been a weight on Tom Mulligan's shoulders. He knew, and had not been able to help.

Ted stared down at his old enemy; he would have given anything to change what had happened. 'I thought he were in the storehouse,' he murmured. 'I never dreamed he'd do such a thing. Somebody's got to tell that lass.' The words choked in his throat. 'She'll be out of her mind at this . . . My God, whatever possessed him?'

The foreman sent a man to summon the authorities. His own duty lay elsewhere; he knew it was up to him to tell Bridget. 'Cover the poor bastard up,' he ordered. And, head bowed, he hurried away.

* * *

It was just striking seven when they knocked on Bridget's door.

Half asleep, she stumbled out of bed to peep through the window. She couldn't see who it was because they were too close to the front door. She went to the crib where Ruth was beginning to whimper. Bridget picked her up and held her close to her breast. Instinctively, her gaze went to the bed. 'Tom?' She ran into the other bedroom. He wasn't there either. Leaning over the banister, she called downstairs. 'Tom! There's someone at the door!'

No answer.

She didn't understand. 'I thought he wasn't working today. He promised we'd spend the day together. We'd talk things over, that's what he said.'

Bridget returned to the bedroom and put on a robe. She hushed Ruth, who seemed to sense her anxiety. 'He must have changed his mind and gone off to work,' she decided. 'But why didn't he wake me?' It was very strange.

A dreadful thought occurred to her as she hurried downstairs, the child fretful in her arms. 'What if he's sorry about last night? What if he's changed his mind and everything is just as it was?' It didn't bear thinking about.

Cautiously, she opened the door. 'I'm sorry, Mrs Mulligan,' the officer said. 'Can we come in?'

Confused and afraid, Bridget led them through to the parlour. Ruth was quiet now, nuzzling close. 'What is it?' Her heart was beating like a mad thing. 'What do you want with me?'

'I think it best if you sit down. Let me hold the child.' It was a kindly voice, but not one she knew. 'I'm Tom's foreman . . . at the quarry.' Swallowing deeply, he stepped back a pace. He hadn't realised it would be so hard.

The officer intervened. 'I'm afraid it's bad news.'

Bridget's eyes opened wide. 'Bad news? What do you mean?'

The foreman took the child. Bridget made no protest. 'Please,' he said. 'Bridget . . . won't you sit down?'

Woodenly she obeyed him and he handed Ruth back to her. All manner of ideas were rushing through Bridget's mind, turning her heart inside out and making her blood run cold. Had Fanny come to a sorry end in that bloody old caravan? Or Nelly next door? She liked her tipple – had she got drunk and caused an accident? Was she badly hurt? Another, greater fear lurked deep in her consciousness but she refused to acknowledge it. Tom . . . it was Tom . . . Defiantly she shook her head, pushing the thought away.

'I'm sorry, Mrs Mulligan,' the foreman was saying, 'an accident at the quarry . . . I have to tell you . . .' His voice went on, like a hammer in her brain. '. . . nothing we could do. I'm so sorry.'

She sat rigid, her eyes staring but not seeing, her face pale and quivering.

Softly at first, she cried out. The cry became a piercing wail and, shaking from head to toe, she clung to Ruth. 'He's not coming home,' she sobbed. 'Your daddy's not coming home.'

It was a long time before they left her, and when they had gone she didn't even realise they had brought Nelly to comfort her.

She sat so still and quiet. In her mind she could see Tom as he had been only a few hours before. She remembered how they had made love, and how wonderful it was. She recalled how he'd smiled at her, and how she'd believed everything was all right now. All was forgiven. Now he was gone, and she would never see contentment on his face.

The truth was unbearable. Because of her, Tom had done this terrible thing. *Because of her!* She knew that beyond any doubt.

And try as she might, Nelly could do nothing to ease her pain.

In blazing sunshine, beneath a flowering cherry tree, Tom Mulligan was laid to rest.

Though he might have cursed her, Fanny Higgins was there

to pay her respects. 'God rest his soul,' she murmured, bowing her head and making the sign of the cross. 'And may God forgive him.'

Nelly, too, was there, standing some way apart from Fanny and Bridget. Huddled close to another neighbour from King Street, Nelly dabbed at her eyes with a spotless white handkerchief. 'He did a terrible thing,' she muttered angrily. 'A young man like that, with a bairn only weeks old. Whatever came into his mind to make him take his own life?'

All the quarrymen were there. None of them spoke. They stood like proud sentries round Tom's open grave, looking down into that deep, wide hole, and thinking how one day they would all return to the earth. It was a sobering thought.

Of them all, Ted Louis was most affected. The shock of what Tom had done had changed him beyond recognition, some said.

When the prayer was finished, Bridget stepped forward, a small, tragic figure clothed in black. In one arm she carried Ruth; in the other she clutched a slim bunch of yellow roses. Gazing down for a long moment, she let the tears fall, her eyes red from crying. Throwing the roses into the grave, she told Tom in a whisper that she would never forget him, and that she understood.

But understanding did not make the bearing any easier.

'Come away now, me darlin',' Fanny's voice murmured in her ear. 'He's in God's hands now.'

Bridget nodded and turned, and made her way back to the carriage. The other mourners followed.

Out of the corner of her eye, Bridget saw a solitary figure standing to one side. It was Harry, the father of her child. His gaze enveloped her, his eyes scarred by what he had done to Tom. He must have been there all the time, she thought. He had come to pay his respects, but he, like her, was responsible for putting Tom in the cold ground.

A feeling of repugnance came over her.

She saw his mouth move. She knew he was saying sorry, but she walked on without acknowledging him.

Harry's gaze followed her. Dear God, if only he could turn the clock back, he would have moved heaven and earth.

'Don't blame yourself.' Alice took hold of his arm. 'And don't think you can do anything about it, because she doesn't want you. Anyone can see that.'

The look he gave her was murderous.

She didn't seem to realise, or care, that she was stirring him to hatred. 'If you're thinking of approaching her, you'd better think again. All you'll do is make matters worse. Besides, Mother needs you at home far more than Bridget Mulligan *ever* will. I have a trip planned to Europe, remember, and I'll be away for weeks.'

With that she flounced away. 'I wonder,' she muttered, 'is that child Harry's?' She hoped not, for if he thought the child was his, nothing on earth would keep him from Bridget Mulligan's side.

Harry took small notice of his sister. He didn't need her to remind him of his duties. He watched Bridget climb into the carriage. She has no love for me, he thought, I saw that in her eyes. But one day she might come to need him. If that day ever came, he would be there for her. The child too, for he had robbed it of its father. Seeing it just now, nestling close to Bridget's heart, had sent a shiver of regret through him.

Sighing, he turned and left that place.

Bridget saw him go, and her heart was cold. Tom was gone and she was alone, with a child. There was no one to lean on now but herself.

Part Two

1854–59

UPS AND DOWNS

Chapter Seven

Brrr! It's enough to freeze the balls off a pawnshop sign!'

Old Joe Tidy had kept a stall in Blackburn market for nigh on twenty years, and his loathing of winter never wavered. 'Bloody wind!' Drawing his coat tighter about him, he blew into his cold, cupped hands. 'It never stops, does it, eh? Never bloody stops, day and night, blowing a gale, like it were straight from Siberia!'

Bridget finished serving the customer. 'Thank you, have a lovely Christmas.' Turning to old Joe, she chided, 'If you got yourself a little brazier like the other market stallholders, you wouldn't feel the cold so much.'

He glared at her. 'Oh aye! I haven't got money to burn, lass. What profit I make buys the goods, and while you're thinking of ways to spend my hard-earned cash, don't forget it pays your wages an' all.'

Suppressing a grin, Bridget looked suitably penitent. 'It were just a thought. Sorry.'

'The cold doesn't bother you, does it, lass? Here's me, my lips are chapped and raw, and I can't feel my fingers, and there's you, all bright-eyed and rosy-cheeked, charming the customers.'

'I've still got some broth left in my billycan,' Bridget told him. 'It's probably stone cold by now, but you're welcome to it. It might help keep the cold out.'

'Go on then, give us the broth. It can't do no harm.'

Removing the billycan from the pram, Bridget checked to see if Ruth was still asleep. 'Just look at her,' she said, calling Joe over. 'Sleeping like an angel.'

Joe peered into the carriage. 'Pretty little thing,' he said. 'And she's such a good little bairn. You'd think she'd get fed up with you hanging round here the best part of a day, but not her. She'll sit and play, and keep herself occupied. The customers think the world of her.' He clicked his tongue sadly. 'It is a pity though. The lass deserves a daddy.' He was immediately contrite. 'Me an' my big mouth, I should never have said that. I'm sorry, lass.'

'It's all right, Joe.' Never a day passed when Bridget didn't think the same. In spite of all the problems she and Tom had had, she missed him sorely.

Pouring the broth into a large enamel cup, she handed it to Joe. 'Drink it slowly. There are some fair-sized pieces of meat and turnip in there, and it wouldn't do for you to choke on them, would it?' She grinned. 'I'd be short of my wages then, wouldn't I?'

'Heartless hussy,' Joe chuckled. 'But you'd find other work, I've no doubt. Hard-grafting lasses like you are few and far between.' He slurped at the broth. 'By! This is good. Warm too.'

'Tom always said that billycan kept his tea warm.'

'Ah! So this 'ere was the one Tom used, eh?' Holding it out in front of him, Joe took a look at it. 'It's just an ordinary billycan, lass,' he remarked quietly. 'Sometimes it's best to put such things away, especially if they remind you of things you'd rather forget.'

'I don't need a billycan to remind me of Tom,' she answered. 'I only have to look at Ruth, and Tom is in my mind.' For all the wrong reasons, she thought.

'You're right, lass, and I should mind my own business.'

Bridget watched the old man, hands round the cup, smacking his lips. His name was a giggle, because in truth Joe Tidy was anything but tidy. Short and sturdy, with vivid blue eyes, a drooping moustache, and a halo of silver hair round a bald pate, he dressed like a tramp, and until Bridget had had a word with him he smelled like a dog in a ditch. His stall was a nightmare. Rolls of unkempt cloth competed with piles of offcuts and overflowing boxes of buttons and ribbon and tape. At least that was how it had been before Bridget came to work for him – four times a week, travelling about: Mondays it was Accrington; Tuesdays, Bolton; Wednesdays, Darwen; and Saturdays her home town of Blackburn. Now, everything on the stall could be seen at a glance. Large rolls were set out to the sides of the stall; finer material was hung by hooks from the framework and attractively draped over the canvas. Everything else was in its proper place, and customers would comment on how much better it was when you could see what you wanted.

Joe came to rely more and more on Bridget, and she on him. He was her only source of income, the means by which she could pay the rent and feed herself and Ruth. The work gave her pride and independence. It had helped her to cope with what had happened to Tom, and she met all kinds of new and interesting folk. All in all, she had come to enjoy the travelling and the work. Joe was a dear old man, and Bridget treated him with the regard and respect he deserved.

But Joe was no angel. He could be a bugger when the mood took him. And it took him now. 'Well I never!' Pointing to a woman who was eyeing him curiously, he whispered, 'Cor, take a gander at that one, eh? By! If I were a year or two younger, I'd lead her a merry dance an' no mistake.'

Bridget discreetly regarded her, quickly coming to the conclusion that she was a woman of the streets. Her face was thick with rouge and lipstick, a crimson shawl was flung haphazardly about her shoulders, and her dress was cut so low at the breast it was a wonder she didn't catch her death of cold. The woman was obviously touting for business.

'Behave yourself, Joe!' Bridget chastised with a smile. 'She's too much for a man of your age.'

'Don't you believe it, my girl. I might be longer in the tooth and dafter in the head, but I've not lost my touch where women are concerned. What! When I were a young man, women flocked from everywhere just to get a glimpse of me.' Brushing the palms of his hands over his balding head, he sighed. 'Mind you, I had a full head of hair then, and a smile of flashing teeth.' Reality seemed to sober him. 'Aw, who am I kidding? I'm just a silly old man whose cock stopped crowing years ago. You're right, lass, I should know better.'

Bridget heard the genuine regret in his voice. 'That one wouldn't be suitable for you, Joe,' she consoled him. 'Look at her now.' The woman was chatting up a younger stallholder with broad shoulders and pockets bulging with money. 'You want somebody less brazen and more . . . homely.' That was the kindest way she could put it, without offending.

'I know what you mean,' he conceded. 'You think I should settle for a woman of my own age, who'd be content to wash my socks and have a good meal waiting for me of an evening.'

'Something like that.'

'Happen you're right, lass.' He eyed the woman with a glint of naughtiness in his eye. 'All the same, I wouldn't mind keeping that one warm of a night.' Like a schoolboy imparting a secret, he muttered, 'Mind you, there'd be no need of that, would there? Judging by the flimsy frock she's wearing, the bugger's too hot-arsed to feel the cold.'

'There you go then.' Bridget thought he must have been a real terror in his day.

Just then Ruth sat up in her carriage, big eyes looking about.

Joe saw her first. 'Hello, young'un. Bless 'er heart, she never wakes crying, does she, eh?'

Bridget gave her a hug. 'Hungry, are you, sweetheart?'

'Tired, Mammy.' Ruth yawned widely. Then she threw her arms round Bridget's neck and seemed to go back to sleep.

'Hey!' Gently raising her daughter, Bridget warned, 'I don't want you going back to sleep just now, you won't sleep tonight else. And anyway, we'll be away home in a few minutes.'

Ruth wouldn't be budged.

'Better put her back in the carriage,' Joe laughed. 'She's gone right off to sleep again.'

Bridget nodded. 'Must be the fresh air,' she commented, smiling at Joe. 'Usually I can't keep her still for a minute at a time.'

'She's a pretty thing, an' no mistake.' Much to his regret, Joe did not have a daughter. 'I'd have given anything for a lass, but all I got were three boys, and none o' the buggers turned out well. They were off on their own as soon as they knew they weren't gonna live off me. Then their mam ran off with the coalman ten years back, and I've been on my own ever since.' A look of anger darkened his face. 'I hope to God I never clap eyes on any of 'em again!' And though the anger remained, there was a note of sadness in his trembling voice as he told Bridget, 'If she turned up tomorrow, I'd never have her back. I'm far better on my own.'

Not wanting to get caught up in Joe's family troubles, Bridget gazed down at her daughter. 'You're right, Joe,' she said. 'Ruth is a pretty thing, and she has a lovely temperament to go with it.'

Putting his own troubles aside for the moment, Joe came to stand beside her. 'With her dark blue eyes and mass of brown hair, she'll set some lad's heart atrembling one o' these days,' he said. 'I admire you, though. It can't be easy fetching up a bairn all on your own.'

'When you've got no choice, you just get on with it. But, like you said, she deserves a father and that's the one thing I can't give her.'

'Away with you, lass! There'll be a time when you find the right man to be a daddy to the young'un. I know it's difficult, what with Tom and everything, but it's been, what, three years now. You have to remember, it's not only the bairn that needs to be taken care of, it's you an' all.'

Bridget shook her head. 'I'll never remarry,' she said decisively.

'You can't be sure of that.'

'Oh, but I can.'

'You're a woman in a man's world. It won't be easy for either of you.'

'As long as I've got two strong arms, me and Ruth will be all right.'

'What about that nice young man who walks you home now and then?'

'Bob Morris, you mean?'

'Aye, that's the one. Buys the milk from the farmers and touts it round the streets.'

'He's a friend, that's all.'

'I see.'

Bridget smiled at him. 'No. He really is just a friend.'

'Ah, but does *he* know that?'

'What do you mean, Joe?'

'I mean he has a certain twinkle in his eye whenever he catches sight of you. I reckon if you were to give him a chance, that fine young man would take on you and Ruth without a moment's hesitation.'

Bridget was quiet for a moment, her gaze going to Ruth; when she looked at her daughter, she saw Harry, the same wild brown hair. But sometimes the child bore an uncanny resemblance to Tom.

Yet, Ruth was Harry's, there was no doubt of that. She had Harry's nature, sometimes shy and quiet, sometimes painfully outspoken. There was nothing of Tom's complex nature about her. Bridget had mixed feelings about that. 'I do miss him.' She seemed to be speaking to herself, but Joe heard and was understanding.

'I expect you do, lass,' he said. 'It's only natural.'

'Tom would have made such a wonderful father.' If only he had allowed himself to love that innocent child, she thought bitterly.

'It were a tragedy. You've borne it well, lass.'

He would never know how hard it had been. 'Like I said, Joe. When you have no choice you get on and do the best you can.'

'Listen to me, Bridget. You're a very pretty young woman. God willing, you've a long life ahead of you, both you and the bairn. Don't turn your back on Bob Morris. He seems a fine young man. Take your time. See him with the child. See how she takes to him. Then, if you both feel right with him, happen you an' he could make a go of it, eh?'

'I don't know.' She did like Bob, there was no denying, and she would always be grateful to him for what he did for her when Ruthie was struggling to come into the world.

'I know it's none of my business,' Joe persisted, 'but if I'd ever had a daughter I like to think I'd have given her the same advice. It's not right for you and the bairn to be on your own.'

To his astonishment, Bridget gave him a fleeting kiss. 'I know you mean well, Joe,' she acknowledged, 'and nobody wants Ruth to have a daddy more than I do. But it's not easy. Bob Morris is a good man, and I'm very fond of him, but I'd rather Ruth had no daddy at all than the wrong one.' She smiled wistfully. 'Besides, though he walks me home occasionally, Bob has never given me reason to believe he feels anything other than friendship.'

Joe tapped the side of his nose. 'A man knows different. There's more in that young man's mind than friendship. You see if I'm not right.'

'You're an old witch.'

'And too nosy by half, I know.' Softly laughing, he turned to serve a customer. As he did so, he caught sight of a familiar figure making its way towards them.

Smiling as always, Bob Morris came straight to Bridget. 'I was just passing,' he lied. 'As it's getting dark, I wondered if you might like me to walk you home.'

'Well, thank you, Bob.' To tell the truth, Bridget didn't savour the walk home to King Street. It was a long trek, and there were a number of suspicious dark alleys leading off it. 'If you're sure.'

'My pleasure,' he answered.

When Joe had finished serving the customer, Bob nodded to him. 'All right, are you?'

'I'm fine, lad, and yourself?'

'Glad to be finished for the day. Christmas Eve is always my busiest time.'

While Bob manoeuvred the baby carriage from behind the stall, Joe handed Bridget her wage packet. 'There's a little Christmas bonus inside. I'm not very good at knowing what to buy, so I thought it best to give you the money instead,' he told her. 'Mind you have a good Christmas, and I'll see you the second day of the New Year.'

'I don't like to think of you spending Christmas on your own, Joe. You know you're welcome to spend it with me and Ruth. Won't you come?' She didn't see the downcast look on Bob's face when she made no mention of him.

Much as Joe would have loved to accept, he refused yet again, thinking that if he wasn't there, she might turn to Bob. 'I'll not be on my own,' he lied. 'I've an old friend coming to see me, somebody I knew when I was a lad. Anyway,' he joked, 'don't you think I see enough of you all year round?'

Bridget gave him a hug. 'Take care of yourself.' She took a small parcel out of the pram and gave it to him. 'Happy Christmas, and don't open it until tomorrow morning.' It was only a pouch of his favourite tobacco, but she knew he would appreciate it.

'God bless you,' he murmured as she and Bob went on their way. 'You and the bairn have brought me more joy than you'll ever know.'

Neither Joe nor Bridget noticed the solitary figure lingering beneath the market clock. Harry Little saw her leave with the young man, and he knew he had missed his chance yet again.

'Stop fooling yourself, Harry,' he muttered as he walked slowly away. 'Even if she'd been on her own, you would never have approached her. If you had, she might have torn your heart out. Tom Mulligan was driven to take his own life, Bridget was widowed, and the child was made fatherless, and all because of what you did. For too many reasons there was never any chance for you and Bridget. And the sooner you forget her, the better.'

By the time Bob and Bridget got to the top of King Street, it was pitch black. 'Are you coming inside for a while?' Bridget thought it was the least she could offer.

'Thank you, yes, I'd like that.' His dark eyes shone with pleasure. 'I can't believe Ruth slept all the way.' Peering into the carriage, he saw she was only now beginning to stir. 'Is she always this good?'

Finding the keyhole, Bridget inserted the key, turned it and flung open the door. 'She's a real sweetheart,' she replied. 'In all her three years, I've never had one bad day with her.'

When she went to take charge of the carriage, he politely told her he could manage. Skilfully manoeuvring the cumbersome thing all the way down the passage and into the parlour, he was delighted when Ruth put up her arms to him. 'Oh, look, she's wide awake!' Lifting the child into his arms, he sat himself down, cooing and chatting and making her laugh. 'She's so pretty,' he exclaimed. 'She gets it from her mammy.'

Making no comment, Bridget hung up her coat and went straight into the kitchen where she prepared porridge for Ruth and hot cocoa for herself and Bob.

When she came back into the parlour, he was lighting the fire and keeping Ruth at bay all at the same time. 'Have you no guard for this fire?' he asked with concern, and when Bridget answered that she used the cot side to keep Ruth away from the fire, he promised to make her a special guard. 'One that will hook to the wall either side.'

The next hour was one of the most pleasant Bridget had spent in a long time. Ruth sat at the table, and she and Bob talked about his work, and how she saw her future, but while the subject of marriage hung heavy in the air, neither of them mentioned it.

Ruth ate every last spoonful of her porridge. 'That's a good girl,' Bridget said, lifting her down from the chair. It was half past seven. 'Tired, are you, sweetheart?'

The child shook her head. 'Want to play.'

'All right.' Bridget normally liked to put Ruth to bed before eight o'clock, but tonight was Christmas Eve after all. 'You can stay up an extra half-hour,' she said. 'Then it's off to your bed and no argument.'

While Bridget prepared the turkey, Bob watched, in love but not daring to say so. 'I'd better go,' he said eventually; if he stayed much longer he might say something to frighten her, like 'Marry me, Bridget'.

Bridget saw him to the door.

'Bridget . . . er, there's something I've been meaning to ask,' he said hesitantly. 'I wonder if . . .' Overcome with shyness, the words stuck in his throat.

Bridget wondered what was coming.

Summoning the dregs of his courage, he blurted out, 'Will you let me take you and Ruth out? There are some baby rabbits on Tomson's farm. I'm sure Ruth would love to see them, and afterwards we could have a bite to eat at the Tickled Trout along Preston New Road.'

Bridget thought quickly. What would be the harm? And, like he said, Ruth would love to see the baby rabbits. 'Yes,' she answered. 'Thank you, we'd like that.'

He was so excited he hopped on the spot. 'Oh, Bridget! That's wonderful!'

Bridget had an invitation of her own. He seemed such a lonely man, and she owed him so much. 'I've been thinking. You've been so good to me and Ruth, seeing us home these dark nights and everything. If you want, you're welcome to join us for Christmas dinner.'

He was on the point of accepting when Bridget added encouragingly, 'Fanny will be here, and her son Billy. Nelly Potts is coming from next door – you remember her?' Of course he did! How could he forget the day Ruth was born? When Bridget recalled the things he had seen – and heard – she blushed to the roots of her hair. 'I'll pay you for the fire guard,' she finished lamely.

'I'm not likely to forget Nelly Potts,' he declared with a grin, 'and I don't want your money, Bridget. I've told you many a time, I'm just glad to be of help.'

'So will you come for Christmas dinner?'

It was the thought of all the others being there that put him off. If it had been just himself and Bridget, with only Ruth to worry about, he might well have reorganised his workload. As it was, he didn't see that it was worth it. 'I can't, thank you all the same,' he told her. 'I've work to do. But you will make it soon, won't you? I mean the farm and everything.'

'When would you suggest?' she answered.

'Next week, after the holidays.' He could hardly contain his excitement. 'Oh, Bridget, it will be lovely, just the three of us.' Laughing, he grabbed her round the waist, lifted her clean off her feet and kissed her long and hard. Then he put her down and walked away down the street, merrily whistling.

Bridget was stunned by the suddenness of it all. Quietly she closed the door behind him and fingered her mouth. 'Well, Bridget Mulligan,' she chuckled, 'you walked right into that one.'

Going down the passageway, there was a smile on her face. As she walked into the parlour, she saw Ruth playing at the foot of Tom's chair. In her mind's eye she saw Tom sitting there as he used to when they were first married, his legs stretched out and his eyes turned towards her; eyes that were filled with love.

The smile slid from her mouth. She was tied when he was alive. And, one way or another, she was still tied.

Christmas Day was wonderful.

Fanny turned up, large and colourful, wearing a flowing skirt and carrying two presents, one for Bridget and one for Ruth. 'Open them now,' she ordered, looking on proudly while they tore away the wrapping.

'Oh, Fanny, I love it!' Bridget's present was a vase which Fanny had painted herself. The base had a halo of daisies, and the neck a ring of bluebells.

'Took me a whole week, that bugger did!' Fanny told her, and Bridget was pleased as could be.

To Ruth Fanny gave a small rocking horse. 'I got it for a tanner off a rag-and-bone man,' she confessed. 'Then I rubbed it down and varnished it all over.'

Ruth was mesmerised by its hairy tail.

'That there's a *real* tail,' Fanny informed her proudly. 'My old horse had such a mass of hair I stripped a bit away, and he didn't even miss it.' Giggling, she added, 'Mind you, he squealed a bit when I accidentally stuck the scissors in his bare arse.'

At this, Nelly fell about laughing. Bridget, though, thought it was wicked and said so.

Bridget had found time to knit a beautiful blue shawl for Nelly, and for Fanny she'd found the prettiest hat, large enough to keep the sun off in summer, and small enough to be cosy in winter. Both Fanny and Nelly were thrilled to bits.

Nelly had brought pots of her own homemade jam from last summer for both Fanny and Bridget. 'There's nowt wrong with it,' she declared. 'My jam keeps longer than most.' She gave the children each a pair of mittens that she had crocheted herself.

Having colluded with the old woman, Bridget was able to give them each a scarf to match the mittens.

Bridget's main present to her daughter was a doll she had bought on weekly instalments since early August; and when Ruth cried out with delight, hugging the toy to her breast, she knew the scrimping and scraping had been well worth it.

They had a meal of turkey, with potatoes and cabbage, and afterwards an apple pie with thick, sugary custard.

'By! That were grand!' Nelly said, patting her belly.

Later, she snored contentedly by the fireside. The children played at her feet, and Fanny helped Bridget with the washing up.

'Right, gal,' Fanny said. 'Tell me all your news.'

When Bridget told her that Bob had asked her out, Fanny winked naughtily. 'I knew it!' she cried. 'He fancies yer rotten, gal. Afore you know it, he'll have yer walking down the aisle, I'm buggered if he won't.'

Thinking about it afterwards, Bridget hoped she hadn't got herself into something she would live to regret.

* * *

Christmas Day was no different for Harry than any other day.

Seated at his workbench, he sewed and measured, just as his father had done before him.

The customer watched admiringly. 'You're as good a tailor as your father ever was,' he said, 'and you'll never know how grateful I am that you gave up your Christmas to help me out.'

'Nonsense!' Harry put the finishing touches to the jacket. 'We can't have you turning up for a function with a jacket that's too tight.' He snipped off the thread and handed the jacket over. 'Try it now,' he urged. 'It should fit a treat.'

Sure enough, the jacket fitted like a second skin. 'You've saved my life.' Reaching into his purse, the man pulled out four silver shillings. 'My boot boy said you were a treasure, and he was right.'

Picking up two of the coins, Harry instructed the man to return the others to his pocket. 'I have a set fee for altering jackets,' he said. 'Two shillings, that's the charge.' He smiled and the gentleman was struck by how handsome Harry Little was. He had a reputation as a sombre man who never smiled or indulged in conversation. 'A miserable bugger', that was how the boot boy had described him.

'You've done me a great favour,' the man argued. 'I really would like you to have the extra two shillings.'

'If you should need other alterations on your expensive clothes, will you seek me out again?'

'Without a doubt!'

'Then it's your boot boy who's done *me* the favour. I suggest you give the two shillings to him.'

'If that's what you want.'

'It is.'

Surprised and humbled by such a generous act, the gentleman picked up the coins and returned them to his pocket. 'Then that's what I shall do. Good day to you, sir, and thank you once again.'

Harry saw the man to the door, then went straight upstairs to his mother's room. 'All right?' he asked fondly.

Propped up in her bed, the old woman was pleased to see him. 'I heard the front door close. Did you have a visitor?'

'You don't miss much, do you?' he laughed.

'Who was it?'

'A gentleman – a customer.'

'Well, he had no right to disturb you on Christmas Day.'

'He needed a jacket for an official function. Apparently he hadn't worn it for some time, and when he tried it on, it was too tight. I altered it while he waited. Twenty minutes, that's all it took. And anyway, Ma, I don't mind. Christmas Day is just another work day as far as I'm concerned.'

'Where's Alice?'

'Somewhere about.'

'Why isn't she here? Fetch her. Tell her I want a word.'

Before he went he made sure Maud had everything she needed; he checked her water jug and her tablets, and asked her if she was ready for something to eat.

'Stop fussing,' was what he got for his trouble. 'I need to talk to my daughter, damn and bugger her.'

'Has she upset you?'

'No.' Maud gave him a fond smile. 'But you will if you don't do as I ask.'

'Then I'd better get a move on, eh?' He kissed her and departed, wondering what had unsettled her.

Maud sighed wearily, a tear shaping in the corner of her eye. 'Oh, lad! You should be wed, with childer and a house of your own, a table set for Christmas cheer, and a fire to put your feet up against.' It broke her heart to see her son so lonely. 'Instead of that, you'll spend the best years of your life looking after an old woman who doesn't deserve it.' A scowl darkened her face. 'I only wish your sister were as loyal as you, my boy. It's always been the same. You were always the giver and Alice the taker – she still is. Where you're good and reliable, that madam is selfish and spiteful, and I rue the day she were ever born!'

A moment later Alice appeared, dressed to the nines and made up like a painted doll.

'You look like some floozy off the streets!' her mother accused. 'I hope you're not off on your travels again, leaving your brother to do all the work round this place. It's not right for a man to clean and cook and see to the needs of a lady like myself. Then there's the tailoring. He never stops. He'll work himself into the ground, that's what he'll do. If he goes under, God help us all!'

Sweeping into the room, Alice snapped back, 'For heaven's sake, Mother, don't be so dramatic. I have things to do, so what is it you want? Harry said you were most insistent.'

'I want to talk to you about Harry.'

'What about him?'

'He needs to get out more. At his age he needs other company. He can't survive with an old woman and an embittered creature like you.'

'If you mean to insult me, I'll take my leave right now!'

'You'll stay and hear what I've got to say, that's what you'll do.'

'What makes you think I have any influence over Harry?'

Maud eyed her with suspicion. 'I don't know what goes on between you two,' she said, 'but I know there is something. He seems almost afraid to stand up to you.' It was as though Alice knew something Harry didn't want made public. 'I can sense it whenever you're near, and it's gone on too long. I don't understand it and I don't like it. I want it to stop so that Harry can start to live a proper life.'

'Don't be silly, Mother.' In her arrogance, Alice had not realised how astute the old woman was, and it came as a shock. 'Why would he be afraid of me?'

'I didn't say he was afraid of *you.* I said he seemed to be afraid to stand up to you.'

'Well, you're wrong. He's always on at me, don't do this, do that. If he got the chance, he'd run my life.'

'It needs somebody to run it, my girl. You don't seem to know what you want from one day to the next. First you have these "ladies' days" when you have all and sundry parading about my house, no doubt poking their noses into this and that. Then you get fed up with their company and go gadding off to God knows where whenever the fancy takes you. And now you've picked up with this fellow who looks like he's into all sorts of shady dealings.'

Alice was furious. 'How dare you spy on me?' Rushing closer to the bed, she thumped her fist on the pillow, only inches away from her mother's face. 'Who I see and what I choose to do with my life is my own business, and I don't want you or Harry telling me what I should and shouldn't do.' Eyes blazing, she pressed her face close, her voice falling to a harsh whisper. 'If you had your way, you'd have me in chains, but you won't. I'll see to that.'

Equally incensed, Maud shouted back, 'If you think I want you chained to me, then you're more of a fool than I took you for! You're getting on for thirty and here you are, still without a man. There is nothing I'd like more than to see you get wed. I'm your mother, God help me, and what mother wouldn't want her daughter settled and bringing her grandchildren?'

'If that's true, why do you always put obstacles in my way?'

'Because you're going about it all the wrong way! I've looked through this window time and again this past week and I've seen the fellow you're walking out with. He has no intention of marrying you. Quite likely he's got a wife and six childer at home, and he sees an opportunity here to set himself up very nicely, thank you.'

'You're jealous! You lie here day and night, with nothing to do but dream up these foul notions.' Shaking with anger, Alice was close to hitting her mother. 'You want to hurt me, that's it. You've always hated me.'

'I've never hated you or anyone else in my life.' Taking hold of her daughter's arm, Maud insisted, 'Take a good look at him, Alice! Listen to what I'm saying, before it's too late. He's up to no good, I can tell.'

Tearing herself away, Alice glared at her mother with raw hatred. 'What are you saying, you silly woman?'

'That man has the look of a villain, that's what I'm saying, and I want you to stop seeing him. Do you hear? I want you to stop seeing him!'

'No, Mother, that's not what you want at all. What you want is for me to run up and down the stairs after you, day and night. Well, I've had enough. Do you understand what *I'm* saying, Mother? I'm sick of waiting on you hand and foot. Villain or not, if he wants to marry me, I'll go to him with open arms.'

Exhausted, Maud fell back against the pillow. 'You've always had a wicked streak,' she said. 'If you're making up to this fellow just to get away from me, then I've failed you, and may God forgive me. But, like you say, you'll do as you want, and neither I nor Harry nor anyone else can stop you.' She turned her face away. 'Go away now. Please.'

Unconcerned and triumphant, Alice hurried to the door, startled when Harry burst into the room.

'What the hell's going on?' he demanded.

'Don't know what you mean.'

'I was crossing the hallway when I heard shouting.'

'It was Mother. You know how excited she gets.'

He rushed across the room to his mother's side. As always, she greeted him with a smile. 'I thought you were working.'

Ignoring her obvious attempt to distract him, he asked softly, 'Has she been getting at you?'

Maud shook her head. 'No.'

'I heard shouting.'

'You're mistaken, Harry. It must have been someone out in the street.'

Harry could have argued. He could have insisted that he had heard her and Alice rowing, but what good would it do? His mother was obviously not prepared to admit it. Maybe he was questioning the wrong person. 'You could be right,' he said, hoping that would settle her. 'I'll get back to my work. Is there anything you want before I go?'

'A drink maybe.'

Going to the dresser, he took up the jug and poured a small measure of water into her glass. He lifted her head gently and waited until she had drunk. 'Sleep now,' he said, and she closed her eyes.

Softly, he went out of the room. Alice had things to answer for, he thought angrily.

But when he went into the parlour, she was gone. Going to the window, he stared out, to see her and her man arm in arm beneath the gaslight. 'I envy you,' he murmured. 'At least you have a choice. As for me, I've lost all chance of ever making Bridget mine. But there is no one else to blame. I did what I did, and now I'm paying for it.'

He returned to his bench. For what seemed an age, he sat there reviewing these past turbulent years. A smile crept over his features. 'All in all,' he whispered, 'I did a wrong thing, but I'd do it again, for I love her with all my heart.' He thought of Bridget, with her long hair and brown, honest eyes, and his heart swelled. 'You'll never know how I long to hold you again,' he murmured. But his moment of loving was gone, and deep down he suspected there would never be another. He recalled how

Bridget had looked at him after Tom's funeral. The coldness in her eyes had shocked him to his roots.

It was painfully obvious that Bridget deeply regretted the night they had lain in each other's arms. But for him it was a night he would carry in his heart to his dying day.

Laying a measure of thick, woollen cloth over the bench, he bent his head to his work, deliberately pushing away the memory of that wonderful, terrible night.

Chapter Eight

'Well, gal, what have you got to say for yerself? Is it getting serious between you and Bob Morris, or what?' Lounging on the grass by the canal, Fanny squinted into the sun as she tried to focus on Bridget. 'No lies, mind,' she warned. 'I'll know if you're not being honest with me.'

Quietly contemplating her answer, Bridget watched the two children playing on the grass. 'I can't believe how much Billy has grown,' she commented evasively. 'He's a proper little gentleman.'

'Makes me proud, he does,' Fanny declared, a mother's light shining in her eyes.

'He's like you.'

'So they say.'

The boy was taller than Ruth, with long, lean limbs and a thick, wild shock of dark hair. He had a hearty laugh like his mother, and a way of teasing Ruth that made her giggle.

Allowing Bridget the time she needed to gather her thoughts, Fanny went along with the conversation. 'The boy does seem to have shot up all of a sudden. But then, so has Ruthie. She's making a real beauty, an' no mistake,' Fanny declared. 'I tell you, gal, when she grows up, that long, chestnut-coloured hair and them big saucer-blue eyes will drive the fellers up the wall.' She pointed to Billy who was seated beside Ruthie, his arm round her small shoulders and a smile on his face that made both women chuckle. 'See that, the little bugger's in love with her already.'

'It's hard to believe that the day before yesterday Billy was six years old, and today Ruthie the same.' Bridget could recall the day Billy was born as if it was yesterday. Ruthie's birth, however, was less vivid, but that was hardly surprising.

'Time flies, gal,' Fanny sighed. 'That's why we should live every minute as though it were our last.'

'I know what you're trying to say, Fanny, and I know what you want me to tell you.'

'Oh, aye, and what's that?'

'You think I should marry Bob Morris, don't you?'

'That's for you to say, gal. There's nobody on this earth who can help you make up your mind where that's concerned. But while you're deciding, think on this. The poor sod's been asking you to be his missus long enough. I reckon it's time you gave him an answer one way or the other, and put him out of his misery.'

'I *have* given him an answer. Time and again I've told him I'm not ready to marry again, and still he won't go away.'

'Is that what you really want, gal? For him to go away?'

'I'm not sure what I want any more.'

Fanny changed her tactics. 'Tell me what's bothering you, gal. Is it that you don't like Bob enough to settle down with him?'

'No. I do like him enough. It's just that I . . .' She shrugged, reluctant to go on.

'Is it Ruthie? Has she taken against him?'

'Ruthie seems happy enough when he's around. Remember, Fan, he's known her since she was a baby. He used to push her round in her carriage. He takes a real interest in everything she does.'

'So, it's not that you don't like him enough to settle down with him, and it's not because Ruthie doesn't like him. In that case, why can't you tell him yes? Marry him, gal. Let him take care of you and Ruthie. From what you tell me, he's built his business up to a thriving concern. He's contracted to buy milk and eggs from eight farms hereabouts, and he's got enough eager customers waiting to pour money into his pockets. By! He must be earning a small fortune.'

Bridget gave a wry smile. 'That's true, and if he had his way, he'd spend it all on me and Ruthie.'

'There you are then. You could give up your job at the market, become a lady of leisure, or raise a horde of young'uns, if that's what you want.'

Bridget's answer came swift and decisive. 'It's *not* what I want.' Memories of the way it was with Ruthie were still too painful. 'I have Ruthie. It's enough.'

'All right, but either way, I'm sure he'll see you never do a day's work again.'

Bridget lapsed into silence. If only Tom wasn't so clear in her mind. If only she could forgive herself. And Harry. Only then could she start looking forward instead of always looking back. Her voice was barely audible as she murmured, 'I still miss him.'

In contrast, Fanny's voice startled the ducks on the water as she yelled, 'Billy, yer bugger! What have I told you? Keep away from the water's edge. Get back here now! Or I'll put you in the wagon and bar the door on yer!'

Billy ran back to Ruthie who was lying face down on the grass, peeking at him out of one eye. When he got within a few feet of her, she jumped up and ran between the trees. 'Can't catch me,' she called, squealing with terror when he chased after her.

Chuckling, Fanny turned to Bridget. 'Little sods! They don't give a bugger for anything.'

'It's good to see them enjoying themselves.'

'What was that you said just now?'

'What? About them enjoying themselves?'

'No, silly arse!' Fanny had a way with words. 'Just now, when I yelled at Billy, you were saying something about missing somebody.' When Bridget didn't answer, Fanny went on, 'It's Tom, ain't it, gal? After all this time, you still miss him, don't yer?'

Pressing back against the tree, Bridget nodded. 'I can't help it,' she said. 'I go to sleep at night and he's in my dreams, and when I wake up in the morning he's sitting at the table, looking up at me. Then . . . he's . . . he's . . .' she gulped hard before going on, 'he's hanging in the quarry where they found him. Day and night he's never far away.'

Taking hold of Bridget's hand, Fanny wasn't surprised to find it trembling, for she could see the horror in her friend's eyes. 'You've got to try and rid yerself of all that,' she urged. 'Tom's been gone these past six years, and you've got a life to live. There's Ruthie an' all. You have to put it behind you, for her sake.'

Snatching away her hand, Bridget gave vent to her feelings. 'You don't understand,' she cried. 'How can I forget? Don't you think I've tried to put it all behind me? Don't you think I know I have Ruthie to consider? It's no good, Fan. I was the one who caused Tom to take his own life.' Her voice rose to a sob. 'What I did must have haunted him so much that he couldn't stand it any longer. We'd agreed that he would be Ruthie's father in all but blood, but soon after Ruthie was born and I asked him to hold her, I saw the pain in his eyes. I knew then that he couldn't do it. But I hoped. Oh, dear God, how I hoped it would all come right.'

Sobbing helplessly, she confessed, 'I did love him, you see. What Harry and I did had nothing to do with the kind of love I felt for Tom. It was more to do with excitement, and wanting something you couldn't have. I never stopped loving Tom. But he didn't believe that. He thought I didn't want him any more. Oh, Fan, if only I could have told him how much I did want him, how much I still loved him. If only I could have made him believe.' Her eyes brimmed with tears. 'But there was Ruthie, you see. For the rest of his life, Ruthie would be there to remind him. And he just couldn't bear that.'

'What happened to Tom was a terrible and tragic waste of a young life,' Fanny said, 'but it was not your fault. These things happen, wrong as they are. Women the world over make mistakes, the same as men do. Remember how he took a woman off the streets and let her into your house – into your bed. You forgave him that, didn't you? And don't say it were nothing compared to what you did, because in my book it were.'

'He did come to me though, in Nelly's house.'

'Oh, aye! When you were inches away from drawing your last breath, and probably only then because his conscience pricked him.'

Bridget thought about that. It was easy to see that Fanny was only trying to make her feel less guilty. 'I won't marry Bob Morris,' she said flatly. 'Somehow, I'll have to make him accept that.'

'Then you're a bloody fool.'

'It wouldn't work,' Bridget argued. 'Whatever Tom did, I can't let another man come into his house, sleep in his bed, make love to me there.' She shook her head. 'I'd rather not marry at all than marry and regret it for the rest of my life.'

Fanny nodded, only now beginning to realise how deeply the tragedy of Tom had rooted itself in Bridget's mind. 'Listen to me, gal, and listen carefully,' she said. 'You must learn to accept that what you and Harry did was *not* the root cause of Tom's problem. What you did with Harry may have triggered it off, but it went deeper than that, didn't it? You know I'm right.'

'What are you getting at?'

'Think about it, gal. Here was a man who couldn't father a bairn. Some men just can't stand that kind of humiliation. They see it as a failing, a constant reminder that they aren't real men.

I think Tom was one of them. The signs were all there. You said so yourself – being tormented at work and wanting to leave the area because of it, always desperate for you to say you were with child five minutes after you'd made love together. Watching you like a hawk, hoping against hope you'd bear him a child.' Bending her head to look straight into Bridget's eyes, she said gently, 'Am I right?'

Bridget nodded, but said nothing. It was all true, everything Fanny had said.

'Maybe it was Ruthie who got to him. When you asked him to hold her, he should have had the strength to love her for what she was, an innocent bairn who had no part or say in her making. But don't you understand, Bridget? He looked at her and could only see Harry, not you, but Harry. A man who had fathered a child when he could not.'

When she saw that Bridget was listening intently, Fanny went on urgently, 'Don't you see, gal? It didn't matter that you were Ruthie's mother. It only mattered that Harry was her father. That was what rankled with him. Harry had fathered a child when he could not!'

'All this time,' said Bridget, 'and you've never spoken like this before. Why now?'

Fanny looked at her tear-smudged face, and her heart was sore. 'Over the years, for one reason or another, we've both bottled up our feelings, but there comes a time when you have to let it all out.'

'I'm glad we talked like this.'

'Will you think about what I've said, gal? Will you give yourself a chance to enjoy life? You're still young and lovely, and here's a man who could make you forget all the bad things. So will you think about it? For Ruthie, and for me.' She smiled. 'And most of all, gal, for yourself.'

Just then the children ran up. 'We're hungry,' Billy yelled, running rings round them, and with an excited shout Ruthie threw herself on top of Bridget.

'Billy says we've got jelly,' she cried. And the women knew their time for privacy was over.

'Right, you two!' Fanny's voice rose like a sergeant major's above the din. 'It's party time!'

She got out the tablecloth and laid it on the grass, while Bridget began setting out the food. First came the sandwiches she and Fanny had prepared, then the tiny pieces of chicken cooked and cut up by Bridget the night before, together with some very dainty pork pies from a local farm and supplied by Bob Morris. The plates were laid out, then the cutlery and some very pretty napkins bought by Fanny in the market the week before; and two beautiful, hand-made birthday cards for the children which Bridget had been keeping hidden for the past three weeks.

Fanny had baked scones and made up little bags of sweets – six for each child to celebrate their sixth birthdays. There was cordial and sarsaparilla, and a drop o' the good stuff for the women.

Billy was considered to be the hero of the day because he had had to wait two whole days for his birthday party. 'And yer mam's right proud of yer,' Fanny told him.

Billy reminded them how last year Ruthie had had her party early so they could have it together, as always. Ruthie, never far away from him, slid her hand into his. When he smiled down at her, it gave Bridget a lump in her throat. 'I hope they'll always be such good friends,' she told Fanny.

Fanny said nothing but secretly she hoped that when they were grown up they might be more than that.

While the children looked on with big, excited eyes, Bridget went back inside the wagon and reappeared with a magnificent birthday cake, complete with twelve candles, a circle of six blue ones, and another circle of six pink. 'We'll light one set at a time, like always,' she said as she came down the steps. 'Last year Ruthie got to blow hers out first. This time it's Billy's turn.' She almost tripped on the steps.

'Watch what yer doing, lass!' Fanny cried. 'We don't want the cake splattered all over the place.'

'Oh, I see,' said Bridget. 'So it doesn't matter if *I'm* splattered all over the place.'

'We'd 'ave scraped yer up,' Fanny grinned. 'Wouldn't we, eh?'

'I don't want Mammy splattered all over,' protested Ruthie.

Billy laughed. 'It were only a joke.'

'No touching until we say so.' Setting the cake down on the tablecloth, Bridget returned to the wagon for the jellies.

'We've got four jellies,' Fanny said, sitting cross-legged on the tablecloth. 'Red, green, orange and pink.' Billy opted for the red one and Ruthie for the orange. 'Oh, look! They're not set proper,' Fanny groaned when the jellies dripped off the spoons. But it didn't matter to the children.

First Billy's candles were lit, and he blew them all out with one great breath. Ruthie then blew hers out, but missed one and had to do it again.

They ate almost everything, and even the horse had a slice of birthday cake, but there were enough crumbs left over for the ducks.

When the children were so full they could hardly move, Bridget and Fanny cleared away and a short time later, they were all aboard the wagon and heading for King Street. The children were inside, telling each other stories, and Fanny and Bridget were side by side on the driving seat.

'Has Bill ever seen his son?' Bridget wanted to know.

'No, he ain't,' came the curt answer. 'Billy's better off without him. We both are.'

Bridget felt sad about that. 'Do you really mean it? If he came to you on bended knees, would you find it in your heart to turn him away?'

Fanny gave her a sideways grin. 'Depends.'

'On what?'

'On how much I'm worth.'

'You're a wicked devil,' Bridget laughed. 'I don't know who's worse, you or him.'

'You needn't worry,' Fanny told her, 'he's too much of a coward ever to leave the old battleaxe.'

'If you did get back together, what would happen about the money she gave you? She'd want it back, wouldn't she?'

'Well, she wouldn't get a penny. It's out of her reach now. I've paid for the house and bought meself this wagon. The rest I've put aside to draw on. And Bill does still send me a few shilling regular like. I'm not too proud to take them neither! When all's said and done, me and the lad need food and clothing, don't we?'

'Course you do.'

'Anyway, it don't matter any more, because he'll not be back. He had his chance. He knew she paid me to keep away, and he stood back and let her do it. Like I said, Billy's dad is all kinds of a coward, and to be honest I don't know as I'd have him back even if he did go down on bended knees. We've managed well enough without him all this time, gal. And, God willing, we'll go on managing.' She was silent for a moment. 'D'yer reckon he will be back, gal?' It might not be so bad after all, she thought wistfully, not now she'd got this beautiful wagon. They could take off and he could kiss goodbye to the farm, and the old battleaxe with it.

'I wouldn't be at all surprised,' said Bridget. 'There have been rumours that Bill and his battleaxe have been rowing and falling out, and that he's at the end of his tether. Maggie Batley said in the paper shop the other day how the pair of them were going hammer and tongs at each other at their vegetable stall. The very next day, so I've heard, Bill were seen sporting a black eye.'

At that, Fanny laughed, and so did Bridget. 'Poor thing,' said Bridget.

'Poor thing nothing! If he came near me he'd have *two* black eyes.'

'Don't you feel anything for him at all?'

Sighing, Fanny answered cautiously, 'To tell you the truth, gal, I do. I allus have. I'm angry, though. Angry that he could let himself be dictated to by her and angry that he's never once acknowledged his son. But it's been six years since Billy's birth, and he hasn't shown his face. I swear I ain't had a man since him.' Turning to grin at Bridget, she added, 'What yer ain't had yer don't miss, ain't that right, gal?'

'I know what you mean.' Bridget had almost forgotten what it was like to have a man make love to her. Occasionally Bob Morris held her in his arms and kissed her, but it was nothing to get excited about.

'I'm worried about the lad though,' Fanny went on. 'There's bound to come a day when he asks after his daddy, and I'll have to tell him some kind of a tale.'

'Will you tell him the truth?'

'If I don't, somebody else might.'

'When will you tell him?'

'That's my dilemma, gal. Do I wait until he asks me or he hears some nasty piece of gossip? Or do I sit him down and tell him now, before he gets much older? I'd tell him tomorrow but for three things.'

Bridget was ahead of her. 'You're frightened of telling him in case he thinks you've deliberately kept him away from his father. And, if you do tell him, you think he might seek Bill out. Then there's the worry that Bill might reject him yet again. Am I right?'

'Yer bugger! Yer know me better than I know meself.'

'All I can say, Fan, is follow your instinct. Billy adores you, anyone can see that. I'm sure the love between you and your son can stand up to the truth.'

Slapping her knee with delight, Fanny cried, 'Yer right, gal.'

'So you'll tell him?'

'Aye, I will. When the time's right, I'll tell him the truth.'

From inside the wagon came the sound of young voices singing.

'Listen to them little buggers,' Fanny exclaimed. 'They ain't got a worry in the world.'

'Let's hope it stays that way.'

As they turned into King Street, there, eager and moon-eyed, was Bob, waving at Bridget from the front door of her house.

'Will yer look at that,' Fanny laughed. 'There's yer very man, waiting for yer to come home. Think yerself lucky, my gal,' she sighed. 'I ain't got no man waiting for me, and not likely to have neither.'

Bridget returned Bob's eager wave. Yes, she was lucky, she thought. But as she got down from the wagon and he came running towards them, she couldn't help but feel that he was too good to be true.

Chapter Nine

In October of the following year, things came to a head.

It was eight o'clock on a Saturday morning when a knock came on Bridget's door. 'God love us! Whoever's that at this time of a morning?' The memory rushed into her mind of the day Tom had killed himself and someone had knocked on her door just like that. She hardly dared get out of her bed.

From the next room, Ruthie called, 'Mam! There's somebody at the door!'

Taking a deep breath, Bridget clambered out of bed and hurried across the room. The knocking continued, and Ruthie's voice grew anxious. 'Mam! Who is it?'

'It's all right, sweetheart, I'm on my way.' She looked out of the window, straight into Fanny's upturned face.

'Come on, gal!' Fanny cried. 'I've been here ten minutes. Cor! It's like trying to wake the bleedin' dead.'

Throwing on her clothes, Bridget ran down the stairs and along the passageway. 'You'll have the street out with your clamour,' she teased Fanny.

With her son in tow, Fanny marched into the parlour. 'Me mind's made up,' she said. 'I'm off. I'm getting out of here, and it'll be a bloody long time afore I come back.'

Bridget couldn't believe her ears. 'What do you mean, you're off?'

'Just what I said. I'm going. Leaving. Buggering off from these parts once and for all.'

'Who's upset you now? Is it that woman from the corner shop? I said she'd cause trouble if you kept parking the wagon right in front of her window.'

'No, it ain't the woman from the corner shop, and she's not likely to cause trouble, not when we've come to an arrangement where our Billy delivers her stale old muffins to all and sundry without a penny for his trouble.' Suddenly she put her hand over her face as if she was quietly crying. 'I knew all along it would come to this, gal.'

Shocked, for she had never in her life seen Fanny cry, Bridget looked from her to Billy. 'Who's upset your mam, Billy?' she asked softly.

The boy hung his head. 'Me mam's had a fight.' His voice shook. 'It were awful.'

At that moment, Ruthie appeared. Billy's eyes were drawn to her straightaway. For a moment they looked at each other, not certain what to say.

'Here's a sixpence, Ruthie,' said Bridget briskly. 'We need a loaf of bread.' She smiled at the boy. 'Happen Billy will walk with you to the shop.'

Quick-minded, Ruthie understood the situation. 'We don't need to hurry back, do we, Mam?'

'Not if you've a mind to stroll.'

Sliding her hand into Billy's, Ruthie asked, 'Have you made any more of those tiny wooden trains, Billy?'

His face lit up. 'Oh, yes! Me mam took me to the railway bridge last week and I drew all the trains that went past. I've made one from the drawing, but it was hard, all those funnels and things.' Pride shone in his face. 'It's in the wagon. Do you want to see?'

Ruthie looked at her mam, and when Bridget nodded, she grabbed up the sixpence and the two of them scuttled away.

With the children out of the way, Bridget turned her attention to Fanny. 'What's happened?' she asked. 'I've never seen you like this before.'

Fanny managed a shaky grin. 'Go on, gal, make us a brew. Getting meself in a state like that, me throat's parched as a bloody pea.'

'You gave me a turn, I can tell you.' Bridget carried on talking as she went to the kitchen. 'Who's upset you? What did Billy mean? You haven't really had a fight, have you?'

By the time she'd finished asking questions and getting no answers, she had brewed the tea, poured it out, and was on her way back with it. 'I hope you didn't mean it when you said you were leaving.'

'Billy was right,' Fanny said. 'I did have a fight.' And to prove it, she rolled up her sleeve to display a large, purple-coloured bruise.

'Oh, Fan!' Bridget knew her friend had a wicked temper, but she had never known her to resort to fisticuffs. 'Why?'

'Because it needed to be done,' came the answer. 'It were the ol' battleaxe. She came round last night, high and bloody mighty, threatening me with all and sundry if I ever claimed that Billy belonged to her husband. She found out he were paying me a few shilling towards the lad's keep, and it made her furious. I told her straight, the lad were Bill's and there was nothing she could do about it. I said as how I meant to tell the lad when he were old enough, and like it or not her precious husband would have to face up to his responsibility.'

'My God! What a bitch to come round and threaten you like that. What about Billy? Did he hear all this?'

Fanny nodded. 'The lad heard everything.'

'Oh, no.'

'That's why I were so bloody angry! The lad stood at the top of the stairs and she saw him there, yet she still ranted on. "You'll get no more money out of me," she said. "And if you start spreading your filthy lies, you'll be the one to come off worse, believe me. I'll make sure folk round here know that lad is not my husband's. He could belong to anybody." That's what she said.' Fanny was growing angry just talking about it.

'Don't let her get to you. She was bluffing, that's all.'

'Oh no, she weren't! But I tell yer, gal, I saw red. When I bundled her out the door, she started lashing out, so I gave her a taste o' my fist. She couldn't handle that. What! She were off up that street like a scalded cat.'

'And young Billy?' Bridget recalled how distressed he had seemed just now, before Ruthie came down. 'How did you explain?'

'I told him everything. I said as how me and his daddy had known each other a long time, that we'd loved each other, and that I'd fallen with child. I told him his father had had to make a choice, and he'd chosen to stay with his wife.'

'So you didn't paint him in too bad a light then. I mean, you didn't tell Billy how his father deserted you when you needed him most. You didn't say how she bought you off, and he let it happen. And you didn't tell Billy how his father had never once asked after him, nor come round to see him. You left all that unsaid?'

'Aye. I came to the conclusion that some things are best left unsaid.' A troubled look shadowed Fanny's face. 'Did I do right, gal?'

Bridget nodded. 'Yes,' she said. 'You did right.'

'Would you have done the same?'

'You know I would. If you'd told young Billy all those things, he might have thought you were being too hard on his father.'

'My very thoughts exactly.' Already, Fanny was beginning to feel better.

'This way, he'll have an open mind,' Bridget went on. 'He'll either find out what a coward his father really is, or he'll touch a sense of goodness in him, and maybe one day they can be friends. Either way, you'll have done the right thing. To my mind, there's nothing worthwhile to be gained from setting the lad against his father.'

Fanny's soft smile enveloped Bridget. 'No wonder I think the world of yer,' she said fondly. 'Whenever I need to talk, yer allus there, allus willing to lend a helping hand.'

'You've done the same for me over the years,' Bridget murmured. 'It's what best friends are for. That's why I don't want to hear any more talk of you leaving.'

'Oh, but me mind's made up.' Sitting up in the chair, Fanny looked unusually serious. 'I'm setting off for pastures new.'

Bridget was shocked. 'You can't mean that, Fan,' she protested. 'Where would you go, and why? She'll not be back to bother you now. She's had her say and you sent her packing. You've seen the last of her, you can bet on it.'

Placing her cup in the hearth, Fanny shook her head. 'No. She'll not give me any peace now. But that doesn't bother me. I've come up against harder cases than her afore. It's the lad I'm worried about. She'll not let him alone. I know her sort. If she were to see him in the street, she'd be going on at him, calling him a bastard and saying how his mam was a scruff who'd let anybody into her bed. She's a wicked bugger, gal. I have to get away. Not for meself, but for my Billy. He's the one who'll suffer.'

'I see what you mean.'

'If his father was a proper man, I could turn to him. But he's so frightened of the old battleaxe and desperate to keep her because he can't run the business without her, I reckon he'd stand by and see her tear that lad apart – his own flesh and blood too.'

'Don't leave,' Bridget pleaded. 'Come and stay here, with me and Ruthie. There's room enough. You'll come to no harm here. The first time she turns up on my doorstep, it'll be the last, I promise you.'

'Bless yer for that, gal. I know you'd take us in, and I'll be eternally grateful for the offer. But I can't.' Fanny smiled warmly. 'There are three people who mean the world to me, my lad Billy, your lovely lass and, long before they came on the scene, you. It were allus you and me.' Fanny gave a long, deep sigh. 'We go back a long way, gal, and wherever I go, I'll allus make me way back to make sure you're doing all right.'

'Don't go, Fanny. Please, stay with me and Ruthie.' Bridget was close to tears.

'No, gal, I'll not stay. But you've made me an offer,' she said, 'and now I've got one for you. Come with us, you and Ruthie.'

Bridget's eyes opened wide. 'What?'

'Come with us, gal. There's nothing to hold you here, is there?'

'Memories,' Bridget told her. 'This is where my life is, Fan. It's where I belong. I have a good job at the market, I'm paid well, and Joe really needs me. He's getting old. Besides, Ruthie is due to take lessons at the charity school next month. I can't deny her the chance to learn.'

Fanny understood. 'Course yer can't, gal. It's just me being selfish, same as usual. I can't bear the idea that I won't see you so often, or that you might need me and I won't be here.'

'Where will you go?'

'Anywhere and everywhere. We'll give the old horse his head, and he can take us wherever he fancies. Who knows where we'll end up.'

'What will you do with the house?'

'Happen I'll sell it. I don't want to, but we might need the money.' She crinkled her face, as she always did when she was thinking. 'But not yet. I've got enough put by to keep us going for a while, and we'll pick up odd jobs on the way, I'm sure.'

'What about Billy's schooling?'

'Billy will be all right. He'll learn about the trees and the brooks, and the way a bird glides through the skies. He'll see foals being born in the fields, chickens hatching, and sheep licking their newborn. Of a night he'll see a bat or an owl so close he'll be able to reach out and touch it.'

While she spoke her eyes shone with such wonder that Bridget was mesmerised. She never knew Fanny had such an imagination.

'Oh, an' the little bugger will watch the trains churning out their steam. He'll sit astride a bridge and draw them to his heart's content, bless 'im. That's what he loves, gal, like me, though I never knew what lay out there until I got meself that old wagon. It's opened my eyes, gal, I can tell yer.' Her smile was bright with pleasure. 'God's world, gal. That will be my boy's schooling, and when he's old enough he can take up whatever work he sees fit.'

Bridget couldn't argue with that. 'You really have thought it through, haven't you?'

'I lay awake all night thinking about it. It's a big step, I know that, gal. But I'm convinced it's the right decision. For me, and for my lad.'

Bridget did not try to change her mind. Instead, she talked of other things, of Ruthie, and how she would miss Billy. 'They get on so well,' she said. 'He's like a brother to her.'

'Ah, well now, if you get wed to Bob Morris, you might well have another bairn. Have yer thought o' that?'

'I've told you before, I don't want another bairn.'

'There's summat about Bob that worries yer, ain't there?'

'I never said that.'

Fanny smiled a knowing smile. 'Aye, well, yer don't have to, my gal,' she said. 'I know you only too well.' Settling back in her chair, she regarded Bridget through beady eyes. 'Come on then, gal. Out with it.'

Bridget wanted to tell, and she didn't want to tell. All these years she had kept it to herself, not telling a soul, yet always it had been at the back of her mind, gnawing away, making her feel beholden. She couldn't see the point of telling anyone about it after all this time, but then again, there was surely no harm in telling Fanny. She knew she would feel better for it, especially as Fanny wouldn't be here for her to talk to in the near future.

'There are two things bothering me,' she began. 'Like I said before, I don't mind Bob. In fact, to tell the truth, I really like him. But I've a feeling his father doesn't approve of me.'

'What makes yer say that?'

'I don't know really. Just a feeling. Bob often talks of his mother – she passed on some years ago apparently, before he and his father moved to Blackburn. But he never talks of his father. Bob's an only child, and his father is a very wealthy and important man, part of the committee that runs Blackburn Corporation. Old Joe Tidy told me that, not Bob. According to the gossip, whatever decision is made at the corporation, Bob's father has the last word on it. But he's not an easy man, and he's not well liked. In fact, according to Joe he's made a lot of enemies.'

'He sounds like a nasty piece of work to me, but it doesn't mean to say he's taken a dislike to you. You've never met the man, have yer?'

'Never been asked. And, if what Joe says is true, I'm not sure I want to meet him.'

'Course yer do. Happen Bob's just waiting for yer to say yes afore he brings the two of you together.'

'Maybe. But why does Bob never talk about him? When you come right down to it, I don't know all that much about Bob himself, except that he works from morning till night, and has a reputation for being fair and honest. The farmers hereabouts like him a lot, and he's built up a round that fetches a handsome profit. I also know he still lives at home with his father.'

'That's enough to be going on with.'

'But why is he so secretive about his father? And if he's serious about us getting wed, why hasn't he invited me to his home? He's been here often enough. I've got nothing to hide.'

'There could be all manner o' reasons, gal. If yer ask me, I think you're worrying over nothing at all. He'll ask you round to his father's house when you agree to be his wife. There's no point in taking yer home afore then, is there?'

Bridget laughed. 'Everything is always black or white with you.'

'Don't cross yer bridges afore yer get to 'em, that's my motto. Now then, gal, yer said there were two things bothering yer.'

Hesitantly, Bridget told her. 'It's to do with Harry.' A slow, pink flush spread over her face. 'When I was having Ruthie, I really thought I might die. If it hadn't been for Bob, I daren't think what might have happened. He was the one who saved me and Ruthie. Nelly told me what he did – brought a doctor and paid for him out of his own pocket. And I can't even talk to him about it, can you understand that?' She wanted to, but somehow there was never a right time. 'I'm in his debt and it worries me.'

Fanny was staring at her intently. 'I can understand how yer might be bothered about that, gal.'

'And I told him about me and Harry, and how Harry was Ruth's father, not Tom. I've never mentioned it since, and neither has Bob. It's just that I don't know what he thinks of me, knowing I had another man's bairn.' Shame engulfed her. 'I would never have told him if I hadn't thought I were dying. Later, when Tom killed himself, how much did Bob think it was because of me?'

'Yer say he's never mentioned it?'

'Not once.'

Fanny could see only one solution. 'You'll have to talk to him about it, gal. Ask him outright what he thinks of you and if he's ever told anybody else. Yer must get his promise that he'll *never* betray yer trust, especially not to Harry, or Ruthie. Tell him that Harry doesn't know the child is his, and that the lass has been brought up thinking her father died in a quarry accident.'

'God willing, she'll never know anything different.'

'Happen Bob's forgotten what you told him. You're sure yer told him, are yer? I mean, from what Nelly said, you must have been out of yer mind at the time.'

'I'm sure,' said Bridget. 'But you're right, the very next time I see Bob, I'll ask him if he remembers what I said that day.'

Fanny started giggling. 'I'll tell yer what, gal, it's a good job it weren't *me* making me last confession.'

'Why's that?'

'Well, I've so much to confess, the poor bugger would have been there till Doomsday!'

Outside in the wagon, the children were also confiding in each other.

'I know who my daddy is,' Billy was saying. 'He's called Bill, and he lives with this horrible woman. She came to our house and started fighting with Mammy.'

'Did you see your daddy?' Ruthie was sitting cross-legged on the bench, her attention riveted by what Billy was telling her. 'Did he send the woman away?'

Billy shook his head. 'No. The woman said my daddy didn't want me, and if I ever showed my face at her door, she'd kick me all the way down the street.'

'Do you want to see your daddy?'

Bill shook his head determinedly. 'No! If he doesn't want me, I don't want him, and anyway, me mammy says we're better off without him.'

'I'm sorry, Billy.' Ruthie didn't fully understand, but she wanted whatever Billy wanted. 'Is that why you're going away?'

'Me mam says it's for the best.' He bowed his head. 'I want to go, but I don't want to leave you behind.'

Close to tears, Ruthie said, 'I don't want you to go away. I'll miss you too much.'

Older than his years, Billy put his arm round her. 'I'll never forget you,' he promised. 'And Mammy said we'll see you every birthday.'

Ruthie looked up at him, her big blue eyes wet with tears. 'You're my bestest friend, Billy,' she said. 'Please don't be gone for ever.'

'I won't.' Holding her close, he tightened his arm about her and said with childish innocence, 'I do love you, Ruthie.'

From the doorway, Bridget and Fanny watched. 'Will yer look at that. Bless their hearts,' said Fanny, deeply touched by the children's obvious affection for each other.

'We'll both miss you,' Bridget murmured. 'Keep safe, and keep in touch.'

Like the children, they embraced tearfully. All these years they had been like family, and now they were going their different ways.

'Remember what I said,' Fanny told Bridget. 'Me and our Billy will be at the canal every fourth of August to celebrate the childer's birthdays.'

'Meanwhile, you know where I am if you need me.'

'Come with us, gal. It's still not too late to change yer mind.'

'No.' Bridget shook her head, and Fanny understood.

They hugged again, and the children too. 'Which way are you headed?' Bridget wanted to know.

'South,' Fanny replied, looking up at the sky. 'I reckon we'll just follow the sun.'

A last embrace then Fanny slipped a small bottle of gin into

Bridget's hand. 'Just a wee drop o' the good stuff,' she said with a wink. 'Sometimes it helps to clear yer mind.'

Bridget laughed. 'In that case you might need it more than me.'

'Cheeky bugger!' Fanny grinned. She slapped leather against the horse's rump, and off they went. Bridget and Ruthie stood, hand in hand, watching the wagon roll away down the street.

'Will we ever see them again?' Ruthie asked tearfully.

'Course we will, sweetheart,' Bridget replied. But in her heart she was asking the same question. 'Take care of yourselves,' she murmured, 'and may God keep you safe from harm.'

That night, Ruthie cried herself to sleep. Downstairs, Bridget sat at the table, her heart heavy. 'Happen I were a fool not to go with her,' she muttered. 'After all, what is there to keep me here?' She looked at the bottle which Fanny had given her. 'You bugger, Fan!' she laughed, and straightaway her heart was lighter.

Picking up the bottle, she turned it over and over in her hands. She opened the top and took the tiniest sip. She might have put the top back on, but the sip had made her feel warm all over. She took another sip, then another, and soon she was feeling so sleepy she could hardly keep her head up.

Replacing the top on the bottle, she folded her arms on the table and rested her head on them. It had been a long day, and at the end of it she had lost her dearest friend. She had no way of knowing if she would ever see her again, and now, even with her beloved Ruthie upstairs, she felt lonelier than at any other time in her life.

For no particular reason, her mind went back over the years, to Harry . . . Tom . . . the way it was. And she wondered how she had lived through it all.

But then there was Ruthie, and everything was worthwhile.

A knock on the door startled her. 'My God! It's Fanny come

back!' Feeling dizzy, she got up from the chair and went at an unsteady run down the passageway. 'I knew you'd come back!' she cried, flinging open the door, and her arms as well.

Bob was taken by surprise. 'Well now, that's a warm welcome if ever I saw one,' he joked, realising from the astonished look on her face that she had expected someone else.

'Come in,' she said, feeling rather foolish.

Stepping inside, he took her into his arms and kissed her on the mouth. When she drew away, he asked with concern, 'Is something the matter?'

'Fanny's gone away,' she explained, returning to the parlour. God, but her head was spinning. So much for Fanny's good stuff, she thought.

'What? You mean she's gone away for good?' He wasn't sorry. Fanny was a good sort, but she took up a great deal of Bridget's time when it could have been his.

'Yes, she decided to take Billy away for a while.'

'And just now, when you threw open the door, you thought it was Fanny come back?'

Bridget smiled. 'It doesn't mean I'm not glad to see you,' she assured him, and strangely enough, she was delighted that he'd chosen to come round tonight of all nights, even if it was going on for ten o'clock.

He held out his arm and opened his hand to reveal a small, velvet box. 'Open it,' he urged softly. 'I've been carrying it around for weeks. Tonight, I plucked up the courage, and here I am.'

Nervously, Bridget took the box; it was smooth and soft in her fingers. Unsure, she glanced up at him.

'Open it, my love,' he whispered. And she did.

There, nestling in the box, was the most striking ring she had ever seen. Set astride slim gold shoulders was a dazzling blue opal, its iridescent colours flashing and burning in the lamplight. 'Oh, Bob, it's beautiful!'

Tenderly, he took the ring from her hand and slid it on her finger. 'I've known you for so many long years,' he murmured, 'and I've loved you all that time. I know I've asked you, time and again, to be my wife, and each time you've backed away. But I won't give in. I mean it, Bridget.' He looked into her eyes and saw there the smallest encouragement. 'All I ask is to look after you and Ruthie. I can provide you with the best that money can buy. All I want is to love you, to see you happy and content, without worries or burdens of any kind.'

Placing his fingers under her chin, he made her look up at him, saying in the tenderest voice, 'I know you love me, Bridget. It may not be a burning love, or a love that will move mountains, but I know you feel something for me.'

'Yes,' she admitted, 'I do, but—'

He pressed his finger to her lips. 'No. Don't give me an answer right now. I don't want to rush you into saying the wrong thing. Just promise me you'll sleep on it.'

Just then, Ruthie came downstairs. Half asleep and rubbing her eyes, she saw who it was and ran to him. 'Uncle Bob!' she cried, the tears starting to flow. 'Billy's gone away. I want him to come back. Please make him come back.'

Astonished that she had gone to Bob and not to her, Bridget wondered if Ruthie blamed her for not keeping Fanny and the boy here. Or maybe she had heard her refuse when Fanny invited them to go along.

She watched the two of them together, and it was only then that she realised how fond Ruthie was of Bob. Maybe, by not accepting Bob's offer, she was doing Ruthie a disservice. They seemed so good together, so natural with each other.

Ruthie poured out her heart to him, and Bob listened sympathetically. Then, very gently, he led her back upstairs and saw her off to sleep. 'She's very upset,' he said when he returned to the parlour. 'I'm sorry. It must have been me knocking on the door that woke her. It was thoughtless of me to come round so late.' He took Bridget's hand in his and smiled at her. 'I'd better go.'

Bridget held him there. 'You're right,' she said. 'I am very fond of you, and yes, I would be happy to be your wife.'

His eyes widened. For a moment he was speechless, staring at her in disbelief. 'Oh, Bridget! Do you mean it? Do you really mean it?' When she nodded, he pulled her into his arms, holding her so tightly she could hardly breathe. 'You can't know what this means to me,' he murmured, his mouth against her neck. 'Oh, Bridget, my love, you've made me the happiest man alive.'

Quietly, he went to the door and closed it. Still with his gaze on her, he turned the lamp low.

When he swooped her into his arms, she did not resist. When he laid her down on the floor and began to remove her clothes, she made no protest. Instead she responded, helping him, taking off his clothes and casting them aside. If she knew anything at all, it was that he loved her; not like Harry, not even like Tom. It was a different kind of love, steadfast and undemanding. And to be loved was a wonderful thing.

When she lay before him, naked and yielding, he gasped with astonishment at her beauty. 'You have the figure of a girl,' he told her. For endless minutes he fondled and caressed, licking the edge of her nipples with the tip of his tongue, running his hands through her hair, luxuriating in the feel of it against his skin.

He moved against her, teasing, toying, making her want him, making her stretch up and draw him down to her. She could feel his hardness against her, the brush of his chest hairs tickled her breasts. Longingly, she opened herself to him, and he took her, in one deep push. Gasping, she held him there, remembering what it was like to have a man so close.

When finally the loving was over, she lay beneath him, drained. There was no shame. No guilt. Just an overwhelming and wonderful sense of belonging.

* * *

The shame and the guilt crept up on her in the early hours.

Bob had gone home, and after she had bathed and brushed her hair, she checked on her daughter and then went to her own bed. It was only a matter of minutes before she fell into a sound, deep sleep.

When she awoke, the downstairs clock was striking the chimes. She counted them. One . . . two . . . three. Only three o'clock, she thought, disappointed.

She went softly downstairs to make herself a hot drink. She sat at the table, slowly sipping the burning liquid, her active mind going over the night's events.

She spied the bottle of gin, surprised to see how much of it she had drunk. 'When I said I'd marry him, was it me talking, or was it the gin?'

Absent-mindedly, she rolled the cool bottle against her face, thinking of Fanny, and how she had always wanted her to marry Bob. 'Put him out of his misery, gal,' that's what she'd said. 'Well, now I've put him out of his misery,' Bridget muttered. 'Have I done the right thing?' Taking a deep sigh, she nodded her head. 'I reckon so.'

Again, she looked at the bottle, then to the floor where she and Bob had writhed together in their nakedness. It swam through her mind as if she was seeing it through another person's eyes.

'Dear God! What if Ruthie had come down and seen us?' But then she recalled how Bob had dimmed the light and closed the door, probably with that very thought in mind. All the same, what if Ruthie *had* come down? It didn't bear thinking about.

Now, with the sleep gone from her, she returned to her room and dressed. 'There's work to be done,' she muttered, 'and a great deal to think about.' She put clean sheets on the bed, gathered together a pile of washing, and dumped it in the dolly tub downstairs.

By the time the clock struck eight, the clothes were washed, mangled and hung out on the line, she had made a small fire, dusted, polished, and cooked her and Ruthie's breakfast.

'Come on, sweetheart.' Climbing the stairs, Bridget gently shook the sleeping child. 'Time to get up. Breakfast is ready, and I've got something special to tell you.'

While Ruthie stretched, peering curiously out of sleepy eyes, Bridget felt this was the start of a whole new life. It feels right, she decided.

'What have you got to tell me, Mammy?'

'You like Uncle Bob, don't you?'

'I think so.' One arm went round Bridget and the other scratched her head.

'Would you like to have him for your daddy?'

'My daddy was killed in the quarry.' Thoughts of what Billy had told her came to mind. His daddy didn't want him. Her daddy was dead. Mammy had told her so.

'I know that, sweetheart, but sometimes we get a second chance. Uncle Bob wants to marry me, and that would make him your new daddy. Would you like that?' Bridget held her breath. If Ruthie was set against the idea, she wouldn't know how to handle it.

Ruthie blinked and yawned. Then she fixed her gaze on Bridget's troubled brown eyes and declared matter-of-factly, 'Mammy, I'm hungry.'

Taking that as a yes, Bridget hugged her hard. 'Things will be different from now on,' she promised. 'You see if I'm not right.'

'What the devil do you mean?' Edward Morris was a big man, with long, drooping whiskers and a hard, hostile face that forbade anyone to get too close. 'Explain yourself, my boy!'

When he was a child, Bob had been in awe of his father. He had endured hours of standing in corners and even now he bore the scars of spiteful, severe beatings; not physical scars, but mental and emotional scars. Now he was a man and he was not afraid any more but there was still a part of him that squirmed at the look in his father's eyes. It might be suppressed, but that scared little boy was still there, deep inside.

'Answer me, boy. I asked you to explain. What do you mean, you're getting married? This is the first I've heard of it. I want to know who she is, what family she's from. How long has this been going on?' Seated behind his desk, his formidable presence filled the room.

Bob stood proud, his eyes unflinchingly on his father's face, his hands calm and still by his sides. 'I've known her for many years,' he said proudly, 'though it's only these past three years that we've grown closer. Her name is Bridget, and she is not from any notable family. In fact, there is only her and her little girl. Her husband was . . .' He paused. There was no need to go into too much detail. 'He was killed in an accident some years ago.'

The older man was appalled. He leaned forward across the desk. 'A *widow*!' He spat out the word as though it had a bad taste. 'You've been seeing a *widow*? And she's got a child?' His face straightened, suspicious. 'It's not yours, is it?'

'No, it is not.'

'Was she left well-off by her husband?'

'No.'

'So what does she do? How does she live?'

Bob took a deep breath. This would be difficult, and he must stand firm. 'Bridget works with a man called Joe Tidy. He has a draper's stall in the market.'

For what seemed an age Edward Morris stared at his son, his eyes as hard as marbles. Presently, he opened a drawer. He took out a book, opened it and picked up his pen. 'How much does she want?' he asked quietly.

Bob was across the room in two strides. He slammed his fist on the desk. 'How dare you!'

Coolly, Edward looked up. 'This woman, who has no husband but owns a child and works at a market stall, obviously knows who I am. It's very clear to me that she's looking to be paid off.'

Bob shook his head in disbelief. 'You disgust me, Father. You think money buys everything, don't you?'

'In my experience it does.'

'Not this time. Bridget wants nothing from you, and neither do I. I've built up a thriving business, and I've done it without your help. We have more than enough to live on.'

Edward laughed at him. 'Business? Buying and selling milk and eggs? You have no idea how you embarrass me! *Me!* A man of importance, a man people look up to, and I have a son who *buys and sells dairy produce*! I hoped my son would follow in my footsteps, but you haven't got it in you. I've always known that. You're too soft. You always have been. Soft and deceitful.'

'If I'm deceitful, I've you to thank for it.'

'Get out!' Shaking with rage, Edward Morris clenched his fists on the desk. 'Go to your widow – and God help her,' he added, his voice heavy with meaning.

Suddenly the tension in the room became almost palpable.

'Don't, Father,' said Bob, his face white. 'That was a long time ago.'

'Does she know about it?'

There was fear in Bob's eyes. 'Don't rake it all up, not now, after all this time. Please, Father. It won't happen again, not now I've found someone worthwhile.'

'You haven't told her, have you? No, of course you haven't, or she would never have agreed to marry you.' He smiled wickedly. 'You can't have forgotten how we were hounded out of our home, and all because of you. The shame of it killed your poor mother.'

'Please, Father. I promise you. It's different this time.' He was a small boy again, and his father was the master. 'It wouldn't do you much good if the truth ever got out. Of the two of us, you have the most to lose.'

'Of course, you're right. I would be foolish if I let it be known, even to rid ourselves of this poor widow who can't see what's before her eyes.'

'I love her, Father. I really do.'

'Maybe. Maybe not. I hope and pray for both our sakes that you really have put it all behind you.' Weary now, he looked away and bowed his head. 'Get out. I want nothing more to do with you.'

Chapter Ten

On the first day of November, Bridget delivered Ruthie to the charity school.

The matron seemed a stern woman, but in truth her crust of hardness hid a kind heart.

'Name?' She sat before them in her office, pen in hand, and a form a mile long in front of her.

When Ruthie hesitated, Bridget gave her a nudge.

'Ruthie Mulligan, ma'am.' Ruthie did not want to be here at all.

'Age?'

'Seven, ma'am.'

'Date of birth?'

'August . . . er . . . August . . .'

Bridget came to her rescue. 'August the fourth, eighteen fifty-one, ma'am.'

She received a hard stare, a wag of the finger, and the strict instruction, 'Let the girl speak for herself.'

Resuming the interrogation, the matron went on, 'Do you know what the Bible is?'

'Yes, ma'am. It's the book of the Lord. But it's hard,' Ruthie added innocently. 'I don't understand it very well.'

'Hmm.' Another long entry on the form. 'Now then, Ruth

Mulligan, aged seven. Do we have a queen or a king on the throne?'

'A queen, ma'am.'

'Good girl.' Matron actually smiled. 'I don't suppose you know her name, do you?'

'Yes, I do, ma'am.' Ruthie's chest puffed out with pride. 'She's called Queen Victoria.'

Matron's face positively beamed. 'Wonderful!'

'Mammy told me.' Ruthie gave Bridget a big smile, and was quickly reprimanded.

'Look at me, girl!' With the tip of her fingers, Matron drummed the desk top. 'Count to ten.'

Ruthie did so.

'Spell "education".'

Ruthie was in trouble now. Bridget was not a good speller and had taught Ruthie only short words like 'milk' and 'school' which she had taught herself.

'Come along, child. I haven't got all day.'

Ruthie gave it a brave try. 'Ed . . . yookay . . . shun.'

Matron scribbled something on the form. 'Do you have lice?'

'No, she does not!' Bridget cried angrily. 'My lass's hair is washed and combed regular.'

Matron ignored the outburst and stood up. 'Bend your head, child.'

Ruthie gave her mother a nervous glance, but when Bridget nodded reassuringly, she bent her head and let the woman rummage through her hair. Leaving Ruthie's hair all of a tumble, Matron returned to her desk and wrote on the form, saying aloud, 'Clean head. No lice.'

'That's what I said,' Bridget told her. 'Washed and combed regular.' A well-directed scowl shut her up.

'Right then.' Laying down her pen, Matron stepped forward.

'Do you know what kind of things we do here at the charity school?'

'Mammy said I have to learn how to read and write. And I have to be a good girl.'

'What do you think about being a good girl?'

'I'm not always a good girl.'

'None of us are,' Matron murmured caustically.

Bridget looked at her curiously.

Matron noticed and cleared her throat. 'I see no reason why you shouldn't start school straightaway. Collect her at three thirty, Mrs Mulligan.' And before Bridget could reply, she was away down the corridor with Ruthie following like a sorry shadow.

''Bye, sweetheart.' Bridget waved and smiled, but Ruthie was whisked away round a corner, and even the sound of their echoing footsteps was soon gone. 'I feel like she's been taken to be hanged,' Bridget murmured, sorely tempted to go after her. Then she reminded herself firmly that Ruthie was only going to school, and that three thirty would soon roll round.

Joe Tidy was rushed off his feet. 'I'm glad you're here,' he told Bridget as she came hurrying towards the stall. 'I've not had a minute's peace this morning.'

'The train was late,' Bridget apologised. 'I've just taken Ruthie to school and I miss her already.' She didn't have time to say much else because the customers were queuing.

Accrington was always busy on a Monday. It was as if people huddled indoors all Saturday and Sunday then came rushing out on Monday morning to spend their Friday wages.

The rush went on until gone midday. After that, it slowed to a trickle, and Bridget had a favour to ask. 'Being as it's quiet, do you think you could spare me for half an hour?'

'What for?' Old Joe felt the cold more and more these days.

Blowing into his hands and stamping his feet as always, he moaned, 'First yer late in, and now you're wanting to be away afore we've even closed up shop.'

'When I got off the train just now, I saw a blue dress in Taylor's shop window. If it fits me, I reckon it'll be perfect to get wed in.'

'Oh, go on then.' He was a kindly soul, was Joe. 'But don't be gone long. I can't manage on me own any more. And anyways, there's summat important I want to ask yer.'

Bridget went at a run to the shop. The dress was her size, and fitted beautifully. 'You look right lovely,' cooed the assistant. 'I wish I were as slim as you.' Unfortunately she was 'twice round the gasworks and three times on Sunday' as Fanny would have said.

The dress was two shillings. 'I'll have it.' Bridget felt good in it. The blue was the same colour as Ruthie's eyes, and she loved the way the hem swung as she walked. The neck was high and pretty, with a folded-back lapel, and the waist fitted snugly beneath a narrow belt.

The assistant wrapped the dress carefully, and brimming with happiness Bridget made her way back to the stall.

'I see you bought it then.' Old Joe beamed from ear to ear. 'I hope I'm getting an invite to this 'ere wedding o' yours.'

Bridget was surprised he should even doubt it. 'Of course. It wouldn't be the same without you.' Nor without Fanny, she thought sadly. There must be ways of finding out where she was. Bob had promised to look into it, and she trusted him to come up with a plan. Getting married without Fanny standing beside her was unthinkable.

Bridget brought her mind back to Joe. 'What did you want to ask me?'

'I want you to take over the stall.' When her mouth fell open in astonishment, he said, 'Don't look so surprised, lass. It's you who's kept it going through thick and thin. I'm feeling the cold so bad, I ache in every bone of my body. I've been thinking I might take it easier.'

Bridget couldn't believe what she was hearing. 'Joe, are you serious? You really want me to take over the stall?'

'Never more serious, lass. I could concentrate on the buying, and you could do the selling. That way, I'll not be standing about in freezing weather, and I'll have time to choose more quality stuff. Folks keep asking for better goods – you've said so yerself, many a time.'

'I know that, Joe, but you've allus loved the selling side of it, the noise and bustle of the marketplace.'

'Well, now I don't 'cause I'm too bloody old and weathered. So! Do yer want it or not?' He knew she couldn't resist. 'Instead of me paying you a wage, we'll split the profits. How's that?'

'I don't know what to say.' It was everything she'd ever wanted. 'It's a wonderful offer, Joe.'

'Then say yes afore I change me mind and offer it to somebody else.' There was a twinkle in his eye all the same.

'You wouldn't!' She smiled at him. She knew he had thought long and hard about it, and she was immensely grateful.

'Well, what's yer answer, lass?'

'Oh, yes, Joe!' She flung her arms round his neck and gave him a loud smacker on the mouth. 'Thank you, Joe. I won't let you down.'

'Right then. We'd better start making plans. There's a deal to work out atween us – money, which goods we should concentrate on, that sort o' thing.'

'Hey! You there! I want two rolls of that tweed, and I ain't got all day!' The voice of an irate customer set their minds to the task in hand. Later, they could talk about their new partnership, and maybe they'd have a small celebration, just the two of them – a drop o' the good stuff perhaps, Bridget thought, and a cake from the baker's across the square.

For the rest of the afternoon she was so excited she could hardly think straight, and once she almost gave a customer change for a shilling instead of a sixpence. 'We'll soon go broke if you keep that up,' Joe chided, but he was just as thrilled. At his time of life it was good to take things a bit easier and to know he had an honest, hard-working lass in charge. And, when all was said and done, it was no more than Bridget deserved.

At three thirty Bridget was waiting at the school gates for Ruthie, hoping against hope that she had enjoyed her first day.

Eventually, a long, orderly line of children marched out into the yard. Straightaway, Bridget spied her daughter. 'Ruthie!' she called, and, after seeking permission from Matron, Ruthie ran to her.

'How did you get on, sweetheart?'

'It's not so bad. We had to stand in the hall and say prayers, then we sang hymns. One girl was taken out because she was sick on the floor. Freddy Jackson fell asleep and they carried him out, and afterwards we had to sit in long rows to learn our numbers.'

Bridget smiled. 'Sounds like we've both had quite a day.'

And it wasn't over yet. Halfway home, Bridget caught the heel of her boot in a grating and it was only Ruthie's strong arm that stopped her from falling face down on the ground. 'It's been one of them unforgettable days,' Bridget laughed, and as they went into the house on King Street, the sound of their laughter echoed round the walls. They were home at last. It was a good feeling.

After dinner, Bridget showed Ruthie the dress, and Ruthie made her put it on and walk up and down the room. 'Oh, Mam!' she breathed. 'You look like a princess.'

'I feel like one,' Bridget admitted. 'And there's something

else I have to tell you.' Joe's offer was high in her thoughts, and she couldn't wait to tell her daughter.

An odd little smile came to Ruthie's face. 'I know what it is,' she cried excitedly. 'You're not getting married after all.'

Bridget was concerned. 'Don't you want me to get married?'

Ruthie frowned. 'Course I do.'

Sitting beside her, Bridget gently questioned her. 'Just now, when you thought I might not be getting married, I thought you seemed pleased.'

Ruthie shook her head.

'You do like Bob, don't you?'

Ruthie nodded, but she couldn't look her mother in the eyes. Not long ago she had discovered something about Bob that her mother didn't know about.

'I want you to tell me the truth now. If me and Bob get wed, will you be unhappy?'

'I want *you* to be happy, Mammy.'

'I know that, sweetheart, but I want you to be happy as well. You would tell me if you weren't, wouldn't you?'

Throwing her arms round Bridget's neck, Ruthie whispered, 'I love you, Mammy, and I think you'll look beautiful in your frock.' Drawing away she asked impishly, 'Can I wear a pretty frock too, with bows and frills and things?'

'You bet!' Bridget felt relieved, but not altogether reassured. 'And when me and Bob get wed, you'll be standing right next to me, looking like the princess you are.'

'Will Billy be there?' Ruth had so many things to tell Billy, especially about Bob Morris. Billy would know what to do.

Bridget nodded. 'And Fanny too, if we can find them.'

'What if we don't?'

'Look, sweetheart, the wedding isn't until Easter, so that gives us at least four months to track them down. I want them there as much as you do.'

* * *

When Ruthie had gone to bed, and the house was quiet, Bridget sat at the kitchen table. 'We didn't even talk about my taking over the stall,' she mused sadly. 'But that can wait.'

In her mind she went back over her and Ruthie's conversation. When she got right down to it, there was no real reason to believe that Ruthie was unhappy about the wedding. But she hadn't really denied it either. 'What then? What am I to believe? It wasn't what Ruthie said so much as what she *didn't* say. No, there's something wrong somewhere.'

She pottered about, washed the dishes and put them away, folded the tablecloth and returned it to the dresser, then she sat by the fire, warming her toes. Half an hour later, Bob arrived.

'Why is it you nearly always show up when I'm getting ready for bed?' she asked him, though she was pleased to see him.

'Happen I'm hoping you might invite me along,' he said cheekily. 'Will you?'

'No, I won't,' she laughed. 'I've had a day and a half, and I'm worn to a frazzle.'

'Well, that's a fine how-do-you-do,' he teased. 'Here's me, come to see my future wife, and she's turned me down before I've hardly asked.' All the same, he didn't seem to mind too much.

Nudging up to him on the settee, she said, 'I've got something to tell you.'

'Oh?' His gaze shifted to the door. 'Ruthie in bed, is she?'

'Yes, why?'

'Just wondered, that's all.' His smile was as bright as ever. 'Did she say anything?'

'What about?' Bridget was genuinely puzzled. 'School, is that what you mean?'

'Of course I mean school. What else did you think?' Curiously, he seemed relieved. 'How did she get on?'

'All right, I think, but . . .'

'But what?'

Bridget shrugged. 'Nothing really. From what I can make out, she likes it but she's missing Billy. That's all. She wonders if we'll find him in time for the wedding.'

Drawing her close, he said, 'We'll do our best to please her.' Thank God, he thought, Ruthie had said nothing. She knew better!

'Do you really think you can find them?'

'Don't know until I try.' He gave her a sound kiss. 'You wanted to tell me something – and from the look on your face I imagined it was something important.'

'It is important! Joe wants me to take over the stall. We're going to be partners and split the profits. Oh, Bob, I'm so excited. I've got so many plans.'

He seemed disturbed by her news. 'Have you forgotten we're about to get married?'

'Course I haven't, and I'm excited by that too. It's all happening at once, Bob, and oh, you can't know what it means to me. Being in charge of my own stall – it's like having a shop. It's what I've always wanted. Joe must have great faith in me. It's a real honour, do you realise that?'

'Of course I do,' he murmured, stroking her hair. 'And of course you should accept. It will be fun, I'm sure – at least until after we're married.'

She twisted round in his arms. 'Oh, no,' she said firmly. 'If Joe's pleased with me, I'll keep on with the stall even after we're married. In fact I have plans to expand. There are all manner of opportunities coming up. There's talk of an indoor market being built soon, with proper little shops and cafés and things. I'll have time off for the wedding and everything. But when we're settled, I mean to carry on with Joe.'

'I see.'

'I know you earn good money, Bob, and I know you worked hard to build up your business. So you must understand how I feel. I want to do my share. I want the same opportunities. Trust me. I'll make you proud.'

Smiling, he cupped her face in his hands. 'Well now, you're an independent little bugger, I must say.' His smile stiffened. 'I can see I'll have to take you in hand.'

They talked of the wedding, the date, the arrangements; they argued about where the reception might take place – Bob wanted it in a posh hotel but Bridget preferred the church hall. 'Some folks might feel embarrassed in a posh hotel,' she said. And for the moment Bob left the matter open.

A short time later, he got up to leave. At the door he said, 'Perhaps we'll visit the farm this weekend. I promised Ruthie she could see the new filly foal.'

Bridget smiled. 'That would be wonderful.'

'Goodnight then, my lovely.' He seemed happy and content, and reluctant to leave, but as he went down the street, his face hardened, and his voice was harsh as he muttered, 'The reception will take place where I say, and as for working behind a market stall after we're married, you can forget that, my lovely!' At the bottom of the street he paused. Looking back, he gazed at the house, at the upstairs window. 'You're a sensible girl, Ruthie,' he smiled. 'I knew you wouldn't upset your mammy by telling silly stories.'

Bill Norman was born a coward, and a coward he would be to his dying day.

But even for a man like him, there were limits to what he would endure. 'You had no bloody right to go round there!' he yelled. 'I told you it was over between us . . . that I wasn't interested in her or the boy. I told you to let it be, that there was nothing to be gained from raking over dead coals. But, oh no!

You had to go and poke your snout in, as usual.'

'And I've every right to poke me bloody snout in!' Standing at either side of the table, glaring at each other, they were like two mad dogs setting up for a barney. 'I had to make sure she didn't imagine the boy was an easy way back into your life. You married *me*, Bill Norman, and by God, I'll not let some other woman get her claws into you, not after all these years, and all the hard work I've put into our marriage. And God only knows it's not been easy.'

'The trouble is, you don't trust me. You never have!'

'Huh! And I never will neither!'

'You should have kept away. You've made me look a damned fool.'

'That's because you *are* a damned fool. You're a lazy, useless bugger, and you'll never be anything else. Fanny Higgins saw a soft, easy life in you. She imagined her and the boy would live it up at my expense. Well, she knows different now. I told her a thing or two, and I'm not sorry. That woman won't get her hands on you, not if I can help it. Nor will the boy, however much she lies about him belonging to you.'

'She's not lying. The lad is mine.'

'Rubbish! She's been with all sorts. He could belong to anybody. For all you know, he could be the coalman's, or the street-sweeper's. But I'll tell yer one thing, Bill Norman, he ain't yourn, and that's for sure.'

'You're a wicked woman.'

'Oh? Wicked am I? Because I want to keep you away from slags like that? Are you too bloody dozy to understand I went round there for your own good? Not mine . . . but yourn.'

'The lad is mine.' He wasn't shouting now, but trying to convince her. He knew the lad was his. There was no doubt.

Laughing hysterically, she tormented him. 'D'yer still want her, eh, is that it? Want yer wicked way, eh, 'cause you can't get it with me?' Rushing at him, she raised both her fists and brought them crashing against his chest. 'Well, go on then, you useless devil! Get after her. And let's see how long it lasts, shall we? She'll soon have you out the house and down the street. The woman is no fool, and neither am I. You've no money to call yer own, and you'll get not a penny from me.' Flinging open the door, she goaded him to the last. 'Go on! Go to her. Tell her you're penniless. Whether the lad's yours, or whether he ain't, I'll warrant she'll not give you the time of day.'

For a long moment he stood there, his hands on the table edge and his eyes fixed on her face; hard and accusing they bored right through her, but she didn't flinch. Instead, she coolly returned his stare, her lips curled in a smile.

'Well! Are you going or what?' Her laughter was piercing, like the peals of high-toned bells.

He didn't answer. He calmly collected his coat from the nail at the back of the door, and put it on.

Having gone at a smart pace, Bill arrived at Fanny's house in record time.

Pausing outside the door, he straightened his tie and rubbed the front of his shoes over his trousers to make them shine. When he was satisfied, he tapped on the door. 'I hope she's up and about,' he muttered worriedly. 'Fanny gets in a powerful bad mood when she's woken out of her beauty sleep.'

When after a few minutes there was no reply, he knocked again. After a third knock he began to get worried; peering in through the window and calling through the letter box, 'Fanny! It's Bill . . . Where the devil are you?'

A woman's amused voice sounded directly behind him. 'She's not in there, dearie.'

Startled, he swung round. 'I beg your pardon?'

'I'm Lilian . . . from next door. I heard you shouting and, like

I said, you'll not find Fanny Higgins at home . . . not now and not for some long time, I shouldn't wonder.'

'Why not?'

'Well, because she's gone away.'

'Fanny . . . where did she go?'

'No idea. She just took off, and said not to expect her till I set eyes on her, that's all I know.'

It was half an hour later when Bill returned home.

'I knew you'd be back,' his wife smirked.

His knuckles tightened at his sides. If only he had the courage, he thought.

But courage was difficult for a man like Bill Norman. So he bore her abuse in painful silence.

Chapter Eleven

It was Saturday morning on a cold February day. The young woman was a bit on the round side but very pretty, with fair hair and pale eyes. She had a lovely smile. But as she fingered the fabrics on the stall, she seemed disappointed. 'I don't think you've got what I'm looking for.'

Ever keen to please a customer, Bridget said, 'If you tell me what it is you're after, I might be able to get it for you.'

'I'll need it by four o'clock at the latest.'

'I'll do my best. What is it you're wanting?'

'I've been invited to Blackpool with a friend of mine, and she's bringing along a couple of young men. I don't go out all that often, so I don't have much in the way of fancy clothes.' Smiling shyly, she confided, 'I really would like a pretty dress, and a coat, with big lapels and frilled cuffs. I can make it myself. I'd like something in a deep blue. I seem to suit blue.'

'That's because you have pretty blue eyes.' Bridget thought she was a shy, nervous little thing, and she had taken an instant liking to her. 'I'll get you your material,' she promised. 'Come back here at half past three and I'll have it waiting for you.'

The young woman was thrilled. 'Are you sure? Oh! That would be wonderful. I've looked all over the market and I can't find the colour I want.'

'I'm due a delivery of material any minute now,' Bridget informed her. 'I've an idea there'll be a roll of midnight blue in there somewhere.'

Delighted, the young woman went on her way.

Ruthie appeared from her place at the back of the stall. 'Have you really got a delivery?' she asked.

'Sort of. When Joe brought us in this morning, he was short of all manner of things on the cart.' According to him, he'd simply forgotten to put them on, but Bridget knew he hadn't been too well lately, so made no fuss. 'Bob promised he'd fetch them on his wagon later. I know there were a few half rolls of material, including one of blue. Let's hope I'm right.'

Ruthie returned to her makeshift parlour at the back of the stall where Bridget had draped towels and such to make it more cosy.

The young woman in question was only minutes from Bridget's stall when she was spotted by an older man, a short, weasel-faced creature who seemed surprised to see her. He stood a moment, his poky features twitching with excitement. 'Well, I never. Here I am, minding my own business and thinking about a certain pretty young thing, and she turns up right out of the blue.'

Quickening his steps, he went after her. 'Fay!' he called. She didn't hear. He hurried after her across the cobbles and down towards an alley. 'Fay!' he called again. 'Fay Little!'

She turned, and he ran up to her, gasping and smiling. 'I thought it was you,' he said. 'Where are you off to?'

He was her boss at the orphanage, and knowing what a quick temper he had, Fay was worried that he might become angry with her. 'It's my break,' she explained nervously. 'I swapped with John so I could come to the market, and anyway I'm owed a whole day off because I worked six days in a row.'

'Ah! Then you deserve a break,' he said sweetly. 'And the

minute you get back, you must remind me that I owe you a day off.'

Relieved, she gave a small curtsy. 'Thank you, sir.'

'Call me Mr Noosan,' he purred. 'I don't mind us being less formal, out of working hours.' She looked so deliciously innocent, he had an urge to take her in his arms. 'Are you on your way back to the orphanage?'

'Yes, sir . . . er, Mr Noosan.' She felt embarrassed. 'I've only been gone about half an hour, and if it's all right with you I'll take the other half-hour to return here at three thirty. I have to collect some material.'

'Of course! As a senior member of staff you are allowed one full hour off in every ten, and if the young man has swapped his time with you, then you are quite free to do with it as you please.'

A boy with a hoop came rushing by and almost knocked her over. If it hadn't been for Mr Noosan catching her, she might have ended up on the ground. 'Young lout!' He shook his fist at the boy, who simply jeered at him.

'Are you all right, Miss Little?' he asked. 'Did he frighten you?'

'I'm fine,' she answered. 'Thank you.' In truth, the boy had given her a fright but she didn't want to make a fuss.

'Look. I've finished my business here and I'm on my way back to the orphanage this very minute. Please, let me offer you a lift in my carriage.'

'Goodness me, sir,' she looked away, smiling shyly, 'I can't do that. Whatever would the others say?'

'Let them say what the devil they like!'

She would not be persuaded. 'No, sir. There's no use causing jealousy. It's better if I walk back.'

'Very well. But after the fright you've just had, I insist on coming with you for some of the way.'

It wasn't much to ask, so Fay agreed. 'You're very kind, sir.'

The two of them set off down the alley, which was the shortest route to the orphanage. At night it was frequented by prostitutes and rogues, but Fay did not know this. She worked such long hours, she very rarely stepped foot outside her beloved orphanage. Narrow and cobbled, full of little niches and dark places, the alley was usually deserted in the daytime.

Shivering, Fay drew her cloak tighter about herself. 'I don't suppose this alleyway ever sees the sun,' she said. 'I don't think I'll use this short cut again.'

Reaching out, Mr Noosan lifted her cloak higher over her shoulders.

Instinctively she turned, and as she did so, he grabbed her shoulders and shoved her to the wall. 'You're so pretty,' he leered. 'A man can't be blamed for wanting you.'

Shocked, she pushed him away, but he was far too strong.

'Please, don't fight me,' he groaned, undoing his trouser buttons. 'You'll only make me want you more.' When she opened her mouth to scream, he pressed the palm of his hand over her face. 'I won't hurt you,' he promised. 'It will only take a minute, then we'll be on our way.'

Smiling into her terror-stricken eyes, he bent to lift her skirt, one hand tearing at her underwear while with the other he stroked his erect member. 'You mustn't say anything about this to any of the others,' he said casually. 'People don't understand these things, especially women. Oh dear me no. If Matron found out, she would never forgive me. So you see, my sweet Fay, it just wouldn't do to report any of this, would it? Especially when I'm a man of responsibility. I can make or break anyone I please with the stroke of a pen or a click of the fingers. If you were to cross me, no one would believe you. Besides, you've done so well at the orphanage. There's even talk that you should be put in charge of your own department, and at such a young age too. We wouldn't want to spoil all that, would we, eh?'

Giggling like a schoolboy, he spread her legs. 'Only a minute,' he murmured, his face close to hers and the palm of his hand pressing her head against the wall. 'There's a good girl.'

In a surge of desperation, she opened her mouth far enough to bite his hand. With all the force she could summon up she sank her teeth deep into his flesh. With a yell he reeled away. 'You bloody bitch!'

When she broke away, he lunged at her, but she was too quick for him and in a moment he was alone in the alley, his trousers round his ankles and his naked member – a pitiful thing now – hanging limp and wrinkled between his legs.

'Oh my Gawd, what we got 'ere then, eh?' Two street women were out early looking for a likely treat, and here, right before their eyes, was one for the taking. 'Bugger me if he ain't that eager he's got his trousers down all ready to be at it!' laughed the red-headed one.

Her friend regarded him with avaricious eyes. 'I don't think he'll do much damage with a shrunk-up tool like that,' she sniggered. 'But from the cut o' that jacket 'e looks like he's worth a bob or two.' Moving towards him, she cried excitedly, 'Let me 'ave first go.'

'No! I saw him first!'

'Fair dos, gal. I know how energetic you are an' I don't want him worn out afore I even get a look in.'

The sight of these two painted slags coming for him struck terror in Mr Noosan. 'Help!' he shouted. 'Help!' and was off up the alley with the pair in hot pursuit. Desperately trying to pull up his trousers he fell to the cobbles twice, but such was his terror that he managed to reach his carriage unmolested.

From his lofty seat the driver couldn't believe his eyes. 'Cor, luv us!' he exclaimed. 'What's all this then?'

Holding up his trousers with one hand, Mr Noosan leaped into the carriage like a man possessed. 'Away with you, man!' he yelled. 'And don't stop till you get to the orphanage!'

Will you watch the stall for half an hour, sweetheart?' Bridget asked Ruthie. 'I have to see the manager of the market before he takes his leave.'

Ruthie was delighted. 'I'm a big girl now, aren't I, Mammy?'

Bridget couldn't argue with that. After all, Ruthie was eight this year and she knew the trade almost as well as she herself did. 'Oh, look at your snotty nose, child!' she tutted. Taking a handkerchief out of her pinny pocket, she wiped her nose and then tucked the hankie in Ruthie's pocket. 'Don't let the customers see you with a runny nose,' she warned, 'or you'll put them off.'

Before she went, Bridget made doubly sure Ruthie would be all right by discreetly asking Aggie, the woman on the next stall, to keep an eye on her.

Going at a fast pace, Bridget hurried along the stalls and down towards the quieter part of the market, on the alley side. 'Got to be quick,' she muttered. 'Don't want to leave Ruthie on her own for too long.' There were some shady characters strolling these areas and a mother couldn't be too careful.

As she moved away from the stalls, she heard a whimper. Swinging round, Bridget was astonished to see a girl pressed against the wall, her head bent, softly crying. Cautiously she walked towards her. She saw it was the same girl who had come to the stall earlier and rushed forward. 'Whatever's wrong? Are you in trouble?' The girl was obviously in deep distress.

Recognising her, Fay flung her arms round Bridget's neck. 'It was Mr Noosan,' she cried tearfully. 'He attacked me.' Her clothes were torn, and she kept glancing about as if afraid the offender might still be there.

'Hold on to me,' Bridget urged, leading her away. 'We're

going to a friend of mine. Marge is a kindly soul who keeps herself to herself and never repeats other folk's business.'

'I don't want people to see me.'

'They won't. We'll go the back way.'

Bridget gently propelled Fay round the corner and along an alley behind Penny Street. Halfway down it they went through a green-painted door which led to a small, cobbled yard. Through the yard was another door which led straight into Marge's kitchen.

Fay had never seen its like before. The room was small and warm, with a smell of lavender and herbs. From every wall hung lace of different lengths and patterns, some cream, some white, and even a spill of black. Across the ceiling was a rack, and slung over the rack were more festoons of lace. The room was a sheer delight.

Working at the table was a wizened old woman with bright, inquisitive eyes and a perfectly round bald patch on the top of her head. She looked up and smiled from ear to ear. 'Bridget, lass! I were wondering when you'd come and see me.' Her sharp gaze drifted to Fay. 'I see you've brought a friend.'

'She's in need of our help, Marge.'

'What's happened to her?'

'She was attacked.'

The lined features took on a look of disgust. 'A feller, was it?' When Bridget nodded, she sighed. 'Poor little bugger.'

'Sorry to burst in on you like this,' Bridget apologised, 'but you were the only one I could think of.'

'Well, don't hang about then. Get the lass sat down afore she falls down.'

Bridget led Fay to a chair. 'Her clothes are torn too,' she said. With a sheepish grin she added, 'I know how good you are with a needle and thread.'

'You're welcome here any time you like,' Marge told her. 'Your friend too.' She hobbled towards them and looked closely at Fay. 'You're a bit bruised and battered, lass.' Taking the torn hemline between finger and thumb, she examined it carefully, then the undergarment. 'Bloody men!' she snapped. 'They want their doings chopped off.'

Her comment brought a smile to Fay's face.

'That's better, lass,' the old one chuckled. 'You sit there and rest while I go and put the kettle on. Me and Bridget will soon have you looking good as new.'

Fay couldn't believe that strangers could be so kind. 'Thank you,' she said. 'I'm really grateful.'

'Pah! I dare say you'd do the same for us.' And with that Marge made her slow way into the kitchen.

Before too long, Fay's bruises were treated and her clothes stitched to perfection. After a toddy of brandy, there was a pink glow to her cheeks, and all was well.

'Where is it you live, lass?' Marge asked.

'I live and work at the orphanage.'

The old woman was horrified. 'What! You mean with childer?'

'They're not all ruffians.'

'Mebbe not, but they're still childer, and the further away from me they are, the better I like it.'

Bridget had an idea she knew Fay, or at least knew of her, but she wasn't sure. 'What exactly do you do at the orphanage?'

'I mind the children, and sometimes I take them outside to walk the yard. On Sundays I lead them to the chapel and get them to stand in line.' A smile of joy swept her young features. 'But what I like best of all is when we have a new child and I'm the one who looks after it.'

'Good Lord!' cried Marge. 'You're nobbut a child yourself, lass.'

'I'm in my twenties,' Fay said indignantly.

The old woman regarded her with amusement. 'You don't look above fourteen or fifteen to me,' she said.

Soon, Fay and Bridget took their leave.

'Don't forget to come and see me now and then,' said the old woman.

Her answer was a smile from Fay and a kiss on the cheek from Bridget.

'By!' Marge went pink all over. 'Nobody's ever kissed me afore.'

'Then it's high time,' Bridget said, and for the first time wondered about the old woman's past.

Once outside, Fay thanked Bridget profusely. 'I don't know what I would have done without you. Now, though, I'm wondering how I should deal with Mr Noosan.' It was a real worry. 'I know if I tell he'll make Matron think it was my fault, and I'll lose my place at the orphanage.' Tears came to her eyes. 'I wouldn't know what to do if I was made to leave.'

Bridget regarded her. 'You really love it there, don't you?'

'More than I can say. I would never want to work anywhere else.' In a softer voice she confessed, 'The children are so frightened when they come in, and Matron is so hard. Nobody seems to realise how lonely they are. When I make them laugh, it makes me feel happy too.'

'Don't you worry about it.' Bridget had an idea. 'Soon as ever the material is delivered, I'll come to the orphanage with it and I'll have a word with this Mr Noosan.'

'I don't want any trouble.'

'You won't get any neither,' Bridget promised. 'If he's not very careful, it will be our friend Mr Noosan who finds himself in trouble.' She shook her head. 'Here I am, promising to speak to this feller and I won't even know who I'm talking about. What's your name?'

'It's Fay, Fay Little.' She laughed. 'When I was small, my brother Harry used to call me little Fay.'

'My God!' Bridget was shocked. '*Harry's* sister! He told me all about you. I should have known, what with the orphanage an' all.'

Fay was surprised. 'You know my brother then?'

Momentarily lost for words, Bridget could only nod.

'Are you friends?'

'We used to work together, at the big house.' God! If this innocent young thing knew the truth about me and her brother, Bridget thought, what would she think of us?

'Harry is a very special brother,' Fay said. 'When Father died, he took on the burden of the family. My sister Alice is worse than useless and causes Harry no end of trouble. I offered to leave the orphanage and help out so Harry might have a life of his own, but he wouldn't hear of it.' A tear glistened. 'He's so kind and thoughtful, and he has such a lonely life. It's so unfair. He would make somebody a wonderful husband.'

Bridget remained silent, not trusting herself to speak. In her mind's eye she saw Harry's handsome face and agreed it was a waste of a splendid man. But because of what they had done, another good man had died. Such a thing was not easily forgotten.

'You won't tell him what happened today, will you?' Fay pleaded. 'Please don't. Harry is so protective of me. He has a real temper when he's roused, and I'm afraid he might take this whole thing on himself.'

'I won't tell,' Bridget promised. Harry obviously had enough trouble on his plate as it was. 'Now you do as I say. Ignore this Mr Noosan. Carry on as if nothing happened, and I'll be down there as soon as I can.'

They parted, and Bridget went back towards the market and on to the manager's office.

The manager was called Mr Crouch, and true to his name he walked in a peculiar bent-over manner. Even when he sat down he seemed to be crouching. Nobody knew whether Crouch was his real name or a nickname bestowed on him by cruel tormentors, but either way he answered to it without animosity.

'It's always a pleasure to see you, Bridget.' He greeted her with a smile as bent as his back. 'Come in, my dear. Sit down.'

Bridget did as she was bid. 'I've heard you've got the handling of the new indoor stalls,' she began. 'Is that right?'

'Yes, but they won't be stalls. They'll be proper shops, with their own entrances and storerooms. There'll be a big window for display purposes, and a large serving area.' He tucked his thumbs in his waistcoat and beamed at her from across his desk. 'There are others who could have done the job but it's me they've asked to take on the responsibility for it. I'm to write down the names of all interested parties and recommend certain of them to the authorities. You see how they trust me?'

'And so they should.' Bridget had always thought Mr Crouch worked harder than any of them. 'You know this market like the back of your hand, and you know the folks who work here. Who else has that kind of knowledge? Certainly not the men who sit inside plush council offices, nor the inspector who walks round once a month to see the cobbles are kept clean and swept.'

'You're absolutely right.' His small beady eyes peered into hers. 'So, my dear, what business have you come on this morning?'

'I want you to put my name down for one of those shops,' Bridget told him straight out. And before he could get his breath, she went on, 'I think I have a bigger turnover than anyone here, and I always keep my part of the market cleaned and swept – the inspector will tell you so. I sell quality goods, and I've built up a sizeable core of loyal customers.'

'The rents will be far higher than with a stall, you do realise that?'

'I would be surprised if they weren't.'

'The outdoor market will remain functional, so it's likely that if you get a shop, you'll lose your stall to someone else.'

'I understand that.'

'I can only put your name down. At this stage I'm not prepared to recommend anybody. We'll have to wait and see.'

'I understand that too.'

He looked at her with a hint of a smile on his face. 'I must admit you've done wonders since Joe put you in charge. And you've got an eye to the future, I can see that, my dear. To tell the truth, I already had you in mind for one of the shops, only I didn't know if you'd be interested.'

Thrilled, Bridget leaped up. 'Oh, Mr Crouch, that's wonderful! I've come a long way since Joe gave me my first chance, and I know he's never regretted it. He makes more money and I do most of the worrying. A proper shop, though, that's what I've always dreamed of.'

'So, you've proved yourself to Joe, and now you want me to give you your second chance, is that it?'

'I know Joe will back me all the way.'

'He'd be a bloody fool *not* to back you.'

'What are my chances then?'

'Nothing is decided,' he warned. 'You must remember that.'

'All the same . . .'

'What's been said here is between you and me, and nobody else.'

'You can trust me.'

'I'll do my best, that's all I can promise.'

'I know you will, and thank you, Mr Crouch. You're an honest man, and since taking over the running of the stall, I've come to realise there are very few honest men in business.'

'Ah, well now, the trick is to learn which men are honest and which are not. Off you go then, my dear. Get back to your work, and earn Joe a small fortune.'

As she neared her stall, Bridget caught sight of a man talking to Ruthie; tall and rugged, with broad shoulders and a certain authority, she quickly recognised him as Harry Little. 'Good God! What's he doing here?' The nearer she got, the more her stomach turned somersaults.

She was almost alongside him when he turned and she found herself looking into his quiet brown eyes. They widened in surprise when he saw her. 'Hello, Bridget!'

With her heart beating nineteen to the dozen, she heard herself say, 'Hello, Harry,' but the voice was thin and shy, not like hers at all.

He smiled that easy, quiet smile that had touched her heart so many times before. 'I've been talking to your daughter. She's a credit to you, Bridget, a lovely child.' In a quieter voice he added, 'I'm so sorry about her daddy. You must both miss him.'

'Thank you.' Tom isn't her daddy, she was thinking. *You* are. And every day I see more of you in her. She has your ways, Harry, and your shy, handsome smile. She's thoughtful, like you, and she laughs like you; and sometimes, when I'm not looking, I can feel her eyes on me, quietly studying me, just like you used to.

She went behind her stall, putting a barrier between them. 'Was there something you wanted?' she asked, her voice cooler.

He noticed, and was sorry for it. 'Your daughter will tell you,' he answered. 'I have to get back to my work. You look . . . very well, Bridget,' he finished lamely. Then he turned and walked away.

'He's a nice man,' Ruthie declared. 'I like him.'

Bridget thought it interesting that she should have taken to Harry so quickly. As a rule, Ruthie was not easily won over. Even Bob had not yet completely won his way into her affections – which was odd, Bridget thought, because at first he and Ruthie had got on really well. Lately, though, Ruthie made all sorts of excuses to be out of the way whenever Bob called.

She silently chided herself. She took to Harry because he's her father, that's why. The bond is there, whether I like it or not. In fact, she wasn't certain how she did feel about it. Just now, when she caught the two of them chatting and laughing, a warm feeling had come over her. But a moment later she'd felt wary, almost hostile. It was a defensive reaction, that's what it was. She had to defend herself against her own feelings, for, if the truth be told, she still had a lingering affection for Harry.

'What did he want, sweetheart?'

'Who?' Ruthie had been counting brown buttons and had lost one. She was on her hands and knees searching the cobbles for it.

'Harry. What did he want?'

'He wanted Joe at first, but when I told him Joe had passed the stall to you, he asked who you were. I told him you were Bridget Mulligan, and he laughed.'

'The cheeky sod! Why did he laugh?'

Ruthie shook her head. 'Oh no, I didn't mean it like *that*. It's just that when I told him you were in charge of the stall now, he was so pleased, he laughed and clapped his hands, and said he was delighted to hear it.'

'Oh, he was, was he?' Though she sounded annoyed, Bridget was secretly pleased. Harry had always said she'd do well, and now that she had, he was obviously proud of her. 'Fay is right,' she muttered. 'Harry *is* a special man, and maybe I shouldn't be so hard on him.'

'He said he needed to talk to Joe about work.'

'What kind of work?'

'Dunno.'

'All right, sweetheart. Thank you.' She wondered if Harry had material he wanted to sell, or maybe he needed something Joe could get, and he couldn't.

'I've kept an eye out for her all the while you were gone.' Aggie's face peered in from the adjoining stall. 'She's been a good lass. No trouble at all.'

Bridget thanked her. 'I'm sorry I was gone longer than I hoped, but I helped a young woman who'd been attacked.'

There followed a host of questions which Bridget answered with few details so as not to reveal Fay's identity.

'Things is getting from bad to worse,' Aggie complained. 'It's coming to summat when a woman can't walk the streets in peace.'

When Bridget was left alone with her thoughts again, she was unable to get Harry out of her mind. 'Oh, Harry!' she murmured. 'Every time I think of what we did, I'm drowned in shame. The truth is, what happened between us, and then afterwards with Tom, was more my fault than yours.'

'Talking to yourself is a sign of insanity, so they say.'

Startled, Bridget turned to see Bob standing there. She felt the blood rise to her face. 'Just working out how much I've taken this morning,' she lied.

'Well, here's more for you to sell.' He had two rolls of material over his shoulders. With a heave he dropped them on to the stall, but not before he noticed how Ruthie shrank away on seeing him.

'It's good of you to help out, Bob.'

'Only 'cause I love you.' He winked. 'Now then, I'll be late coming over tonight,' he said. 'When I've finished here, I need to make tracks to Meaker's Farm – he owes me money and if it's left for too long it's one hell of a job getting it out of him, the old bugger!' He emptied his pockets of small brown sacks of buttons and sewing cotton, and parcels of lace. 'Well, I must say, you don't seem very pleased to see me.' Grinning, he took Bridget in his arms and kissed her.

'I'm sorry,' she apologised. 'I didn't expect you so early, that's all. And about tonight. It won't matter because I've decided to have an early night. I'm tired out.' Harry was still on her mind, and somehow Bob didn't measure up.

'I can leave the farm for another time if you'd rather.'

'No, Bob. It's all right, honestly. You go and collect your money tonight, and I'll cook you dinner tomorrow. How about that?'

He was obviously not pleased. 'If you say so.'

'Have you half an hour to spare?' Bridget thought she might take advantage of him being there; she had taken one favour from Aggie and it wouldn't be fair to ask another.

Smiling with anticipation, he murmured, 'Why? Have you got something in mind?'

Returning his smile, she dashed his hopes. 'I've promised to make a delivery to the orphanage.' While she spoke, she rolled out a measure of blue cloth and snipped it off.

He was aware of Ruthie cowering at the back of the stall. 'Half an hour, you say?'

'Three-quarters at the outside.'

'I think I can manage that.'

'Mammy! I want to come with you.' Ruthie rushed forward and tugged at Bridget's skirt. 'Please, Mammy, let me come with you. I don't want to stay here.'

Taking her by the shoulders, Bridget leaned down to explain. 'I have to see someone there, and I won't be able to discuss business if you tag along. Bob's here, sweetheart. He'll take care of you, and I won't be long, I promise.'

Bob stepped forward. 'We'll be all right, won't we, Ruthie? I mean, we wouldn't want to upset your mammy, would we now?' Stooping lower, he looked her in the eye. 'Anyway, I thought we were friends?'

Bridget kissed Ruthie and hurried away, but at the pit of her stomach there was an uneasy feeling. She looked back and saw Bob laughingly tickle Ruthie under the chin.

Reassured, Bridget pressed on. 'Anyone can see he thinks the world of her.'

Once Bridget was out of sight and he thought he was safe, Bob's attitude changed. Taking Ruthie to the far end of the stall where they could not easily be overheard, he shook her hard. 'Are you trying to turn your mammy against me?'

Ruthie shook her head.

'Then why did you let her think you were frightened to stay with me?'

Her bottom lip trembled. 'I didn't.'

He shook her again. 'Oh, but you did!'

'I'm sorry.'

'That's not enough, is it?'

'I won't do it again.' Tears swam in her eyes.

'Did you tell . . . anyone?'

'No.'

'And you *won't* tell, will you, Ruthie?'

'But I saw you!'

'Yes, and I explained. She was a friend. Just a friend.'

'You were kissing her.'

'There is nothing wrong with kissing a friend, but your mammy might not be pleased if she knew.' He laughed softly. 'She might be jealous, and then we might fight and your mammy could get hurt. We wouldn't want that, would we, eh? You *won't* tell, will you, Ruthie?'

When Ruthie appeared sullen, he asked again, and when she still refused to answer, he gripped her arms so hard she cried out in pain.

'Ruthie! Is that you? Are you all right, lass?' Aggie's voice sailed through the air and in a moment her face appeared at the opening between the two stalls. 'Ruthie! Ruthie, where are you, lass?'

Bob hurried over. 'It's all right,' he answered. 'Bridget had to make an urgent delivery and I'm left to watch Ruthie. She's been playing under the stall, but she's all right now. Kids! They get stuck in the most unlikely places, don't they, eh?'

Aggie looked at Ruthie. She was rubbing her arms. 'Do you want to come and help me till your mammy comes back?' she asked.

'Yes, please, Aggie.'

'Come on then, lass.'

As she made to follow Aggie, Bob grabbed her and hissed, 'Keep your mouth shut or I'll make sure your mammy knows what a terrible liar you really are!'

Mr Noosan, still shaken by events in the alley, was not in the best of tempers when Bridget was admitted to his office. He glared at her. 'Well? What is it that's so important? What do you mean by demanding to see me?'

Undeterred by his manner, Bridget put her case, and as she did so his face changed colour. 'So you see, Mr Noosan,' she finished, 'I know all about your attack on Fay Little, and I know that should this ever be made known to the authorities, your place here wouldn't be worth a farthing. I did consider going straight to the top, but I didn't think it fair that the young lady should be put through the ordeal which would surely follow.'

'She's a liar! It was her who tempted me.'

'Very well, Mr Noosan. Then I think I had better speak to her brother. I had hoped to avoid that. I believe he has a foul temper and is very protective of his little sister. But if you mean to lie through your teeth and hound Fay out of her place here, then I'm afraid you leave me no alternative but to give him your name and let him take it up with you.' She turned to leave.

'Wait!' Mr Noosan leaped out of his seat. 'There is really no need to take this business any further than this room.'

'Isn't there?'

'No, no . . . I mean . . . she wasn't altogether lying.' He wiped the sweat from his brow. 'Maybe I was a little exuberant, but I meant no harm, I assure you.'

Bridget stared at him coldly.

'I'll make amends,' Mr Noosan hurried on. 'There has been talk of promoting the young lady in question. I shall make sure it goes through.'

'And you swear never to lay a hand on her again?'

'I swear. Never again!'

'And you will personally see to it that her position here will go from strength to strength?'

'I will.'

Bridget looked him up and down, making him squirm. 'Could you see to it that she gets this material – urgently?' she asked coolly, laying the fabric on his desk.

He snatched up a small hand bell and rang it loudly. A maid in a frilly cap and apron appeared at the door. 'Yes, sir, Mr Noosan?'

He thrust the material into her hands. 'Deliver this to Miss Little at once.'

When thc maid had gone, Mr Noosan scurried behind his desk again but did not sit down. He looked at Bridget nervously.

He was a pitiful thing, she thought. She had no doubt that he would keep his word with regard to Fay. Like all bullies, he was a coward.

'Good day to you then, sir,' she said, and swept from the room.

The market clock told her she'd been gone only half an hour. 'Not bad going,' she told herself. As she approached, her eyes were searching for Ruthie.

'I'd best be off, my lovely,' Bob greeted her. 'Are you sure you wouldn't rather I came round tonight? Like I said, I can always make the farm visit another day.'

'No. Not tonight.' She was firm about it. 'Where's Ruthie?'

'She bumped herself. Aggie took care of her.' Bridget swung away but he took hold of her. 'No need to get alarmed. She's all right.'

Aggie assured her of the same. 'The lass is fine,' she said. 'I heard her cry out and thought she might be better helping me out here till you got back.'

Ruthie ran into Bridget's arms. 'You're not going on any more errands, are you, Mammy?'

Bridget assured her she was not.

'Well, you ain't missed nothing, lass,' Aggie said. 'It's been quiet as the churchyard round 'ere. Folks must have gone off for a bite to eat but give it another hour and they'll be out in force.'

And she was right.

For the rest of the afternoon, Bridget was run off her feet. She took a healthy pile of money and, just before she shut shop, Joe turned up on his horse and cart. 'I'm feeling better,' he said, 'but I'll have to ask you to load up, lass, 'cause I'm not ready yet to take any weight.'

Bridget was soon ready for off. 'By the way,' she said, 'Harry Little dropped by when I was out on an errand. He told Ruthie he needed to talk to you about work.'

'Fine. I dare say he'll catch up with me.'

While Joe and Ruthie climbed aboard, Bridget thanked Aggie again. 'You've been a pal,' she said. 'But I won't be leaving Ruthie on her own again. She seems to have got herself all upset. Thanks again, Aggie. Take care now.'

'Er, d'yer mind if I say summat, lass?'

'Course not. What's on your mind?'

'Are you really intending to marry that feller?'

Bridget was shocked. 'Well, yes, I am.'

'Only, if you don't mind me saying, the lass seems to have taken agin him.'

'What makes you say that, Aggie?'

Aggie tapped her nose. 'Just an old woman's instinct. But I dare say there's nothing to it. Kids are funny creatures. They take agin all kinds o' folk, for all kinds o' reasons.'

On the way home, Ruthie slept in the back of the cart. Bridget was preoccupied by what Aggie had said. She decided to sound out Joe. 'Aggie says Ruthie's taken against Bob. Do you think there could be any truth in that, Joe?'

'Aggie might be a good soul, but sometimes she talks out of her arse. You've only got to see him with Ruthie to know he thinks the world o' the lass.'

Bridget said no more about it, but when they reached home and she undressed Ruthie for her wash, she was startled to see the small, dark bruises forming on her daughter's arms. 'Good God, Ruthie. How did you do this?'

There was a moment's hesitation before she answered. 'It was when I got stuck under the stall and I had to squeeze through.' She didn't dare say how Bob had got hold of her arms and squeezed them until they hurt. She could never tell her mammy. Not after what Bob had said to her.

The furthest contract on Bob Morris's round was Meaker's Farm on the outskirts of Lancaster. Jack Meaker was a well-respected, hard-working man who had the misfortune to have married a woman with an insatiable appetite for the opposite sex. It was known far and wide by many but Jack himself lived in ignorance and, because of that, was fairly content.

Over a number of months, Bob Morris had found favour with the farmer's wife and never lost an opportunity to show his gratitude. They had an arrangement whereby he would collect his money at the back door and minutes later he would hide his wagon round by the barn and there she would come and meet him.

A dark-haired beauty, she loved to be gently persuaded, but on this particular evening Bob was in no mood for niceties. He was at her almost the minute she walked in the door. 'I've been ready for you all day,' he groaned, pawing at her like a dog at a bone.

'Had a row with your pretty market girl, have you?' she teased.

He closed her mouth with a rough kiss, biting her lips until they bled.

Save for an owl and the crunch of hay as they rolled in it, it was quiet there.

Quiet. And wicked.

Chapter Twelve

Fanny was homesick.

There was something about velvet skies and moonlit nights that broke her heart and made her sad. 'Shall we make us way home, lad?'

Billy sat on the wagon step beside her, his legs stretched out and his chin resting on his hands. He was so deep in his own thoughts that he didn't hear.

Softly smiling, Fanny studied her son. This past few weeks he had seemed suddenly to blossom before her eyes. He looked so handsome and grown up that it made her proud. Billy was a mingling of herself and his father. He laughed like her but he had his father's irritating way of slouching against a tree or a door with his hands in his pockets. And yet he was his own man, with those wonderful eyes that seemed always to be gazing far away, and a lazy, easy smile that filled her with wonder.

Billy was her pride and joy, and even though they had not seen Bridget or Ruthie for some long time, Fanny still hoped that one fine day Ruthie and Billy would find their future with each other.

Seeing how preoccupied he was, she let him alone for a time, thinking that he, too, must be missing their friends back in Blackburn. And so they sat, hunched together on the wagon steps, with the moon shining down and the lake shimmering before them. The old horse stood close by, eyes closed and head bowed, enjoying his rest.

It was a marvellous, magical evening, and for a time it seemed as though they might be the only two people in the whole world. But there was another, so close he could have reached out and touched them. Instead, he remained hidden from sight, watching and listening.

Fanny stretched and yawned. It was time to prepare the evening meal. The watcher's stomach rumbled with hunger as the sizzle and aroma of bacon cooking over an open fire reached him, and the smell of coffee wafted through the air, with just a whiff of brandy mixed in.

When Fanny and Billy had eaten, Fanny repeated her question. 'D'yer reckon we should mek us way back home, son?' she asked.

Billy's eyes lit up. 'What, to Blackburn, you mean?'

'If yer like.'

He flung his arms round her neck. 'Oh Mam, yes! Yes!'

Releasing herself, Fanny told him through her laughter, 'If yer choke me to death, yer bugger, you'll 'ave to find yer own way back.'

'*When*, Mam?' She had not seen him so happy for a long time. 'When can we go home?'

Teasing him, she looked solemn. 'Well now, let's see. It'll be a shame to miss the harvest. We could mek a bit o' money there. Aye, happen we should bide our time for a while yet.'

'But it's *months* away yet!'

'Well, that's right. Then o' course there'll be the autumn and the apple picking. We could mek a few bob there.'

'Oh, Mam!'

Laughing, she caught him to her. 'We'll start us way home first thing in the morning,' she promised. 'And when I clap eyes on that Bridget, I'll give her the biggest bloody cuddle she's ever had.' She had missed her so.

'Do you think Ruthie will be glad to see me?' he asked shyly.

'She'd better bloody be, my lad, or she'll hear from me.'

Thrilled and excited, they talked well into the night, long after the watcher had stolen away. Even after they went to their beds, they lay awake, unable to sleep, Fanny thinking of Bridget, and Billy thinking of Ruthie. Fanny even gave a thought to Bill Norman. 'For all yer faults, yer still the lad's daddy and, God help me, the only feller I've ever wanted in the whole o' me miserable life.'

Bill Norman's wife was a devious woman, and when it came to keeping track of her husband's goings-on there was no depth to which she would not sink. Showing the seedy-looking character into the back room, she stood before him, hard-faced and impatient. 'What have you found out?'

Though they were two of a kind, he had taken an instant dislike to her. 'You won't like what I have to tell you,' he smirked.

'Neither will you if you don't get on and do what you're paid for. I asked you a question and I expect you to answer it without any fuss. What did you find out? Be quick, now!'

Sullen, he told her, 'She and the boy are on their way back.'

'What? How do you know that?'

'I found them camped in a wood some twelve miles the other side of Lancaster. I tell you, missus, it's been one of the hardest cases I've ever handled. I've travelled miles, and it's worked out far more expensive than I thought.'

'Then you should price your work right. Hard case or not, you'll get no more money from me. I'm paying you more than enough as it is. So, go on. What exactly did you find out?'

'She and the boy were set up for the night. They talked about coming back. The woman seemed sad, I thought, as if she was missing someone.'

'Did she now?'

'They seemed well enough, content in a way, but eager to be making tracks back home, that's how it came across to me.'

'Were they alone?'

'Well, yes, I think so.'

'So you didn't see anybody else then, a man maybe?'

'There was no man there, not as far as I could see. Mind you, I don't know who might have been inside the wagon. It was dark. I only caught sight of these two in the light from the camp fire.'

'Pity.' That would have been a pleasant turn-up for the book. If some other man had come along and taken charge of that witch and her bastard, her own husband might not be so restless. When she'd heard that Fanny Higgins had taken herself and her boy off and out of Blackburn, she'd been delighted. But ever since he'd found out, Bill had been withdrawn and moody. She felt her power over him slipping away, and it frightened her. All she could do now was keep one step ahead of her rival by having her watched.

'What would you like me to do now?'

'Get on her tail. I want to know her every move. I want to know where she is at every turn, and who she's with, especially if you catch sight of a man friend.'

Long after he was gone, she paced the floor, then some half hour later she made her way back to the vegetable stall. Bill had been waiting to leave. 'Took you long enough to get here, didn't it?' he grumbled. 'You know I've work to do back at the farm. The cartwheel still needs mending, and there's all manner of odd jobs going untended.'

She looked at him, wondering not for the first time what Fanny Higgins ever saw in him; come to that, what did *she* ever see in him? But this man was hers, and they had a business to run. Neither of them could run it without the other. The fact was, they needed each other.

'We've been all right, you and me, haven't we, Bill?'

He looked away.

'I'm talking to you! I said, we've been all right, haven't we, considering everything.'

'If you say so,' he grunted, and swiftly left the stall.

We'll see Fanny and Billy on my birthday, won't we, Mam?'

'I should hope so,' said Bridget, 'or I'll want to know the reason why.' She turned to serve a customer. As soon as she had finished, Ruthie resumed her questions.

'Why has she never sent word, Mam? She promised.'

'Who knows.'

'Do you know why?'

'I might do.' Stooping low, Bridget murmured, 'I think it's because she can't write an' doesn't like folks to know that.'

'But you know.'

Bridget held her close. 'Not because she told me, sweetheart.'

'How then?'

'Because I love her, and when you love somebody, you just know these things.'

'D'you miss her?'

'Yes, I do,' she answered softly. Not a day passed when she didn't think about Fanny and Billy. But it was up to Fanny to get word to her, because there were no means by which she could find out where they were, or even whether they were all right.

'I miss Billy too.'

'And I'm sure he misses you, sweetheart.'

When Joe arrived at two thirty, he beamed with pleasure at the handsome takings. 'You're a magnet, lass,' he chuckled. 'The customers love to chat with you and, more importantly, they love to part with their money.' He counted the coins and slipped them into a drawbag. 'By! You make more in a day than I used to make in a week.'

The afternoon was drawing to a close when Harry turned up with an offer that had Joe beaming even more widely. 'I've a society wedding coming up,' he told Joe, 'and I urgently need another three reams of silk for the waistcoats and such. Can you help me out?'

Joe slapped him on the back. 'I know just the cargo. It's sitting in Liverpool docks at this very minute and, would you believe, the master is a friend of mine.' The two of them sat down, talking colour and quality, and arranging delivery.

While they talked, Bridget got on with serving, though several times she turned to find Harry quietly studying her. He would smile and she would blush, and from her place at the back of the stall, Ruthie would giggle.

When the men's business was concluded and it was time for Harry to leave, Bridget dared not bring herself to look at him although she knew he was looking at her, and her heart beat faster because of it.

When Harry had gone a short way, Ruthie ran after him. 'I like you, mister,' she declared solemnly.

Deeply moved, Harry smiled. 'I like you too,' he replied.

'And you like my mammy, don't you?'

Harry laughed out loud. 'You don't miss much, do you?'

Her face fell. 'I miss Billy.'

'Oh? And who might Billy be?'

'He's Fanny's boy.'

'Ah!' Now he understood. 'You mean Fanny Higgins, your mammy's best friend.'

'They've gone away and we don't know where they are.'

'Don't you worry. In my experience, folks always make their way back home sooner or later.'

Encouraged, Ruthie launched into a long and detailed account of how Fanny and Billy had gone away, and how they promised always to meet down by the canal when it was her birthday.

'You can come too, if you like,' she invited excitedly. 'I'm sure Mammy wouldn't mind.'

As they chatted, Harry's sister Alice swept towards them. Unobserved by the two, she was stopped in her tracks by the sight of Ruthie.

'My God! If I had ever wondered whether the brat was his, I need wonder no more.' They had the same long limbs and easy smiles, and the same handsome profile. 'That girl is his, and nobody could ever tell me otherwise.' But she wouldn't make it known, for if she did, he might feel more responsibility for his child and her mother than he did for his own mother. If she was to continue to live the free and flirtatious life she had manipulated for herself, Alice knew she would do well to keep her mouth shut.

Having seen enough, she went to him, impatient as usual. 'Mother is being difficult,' she complained. 'And, as always, she will not be consoled by anyone but you.'

'Is she ill?'

'No, just cantankerous.'

'You mean she won't let you have your own way.'

'I hate it when you leave me alone with her.'

'You have a responsibility, Alice, whether you like it or not. I told you when I came out that I had several business matters to attend to.'

'I won't go back without you.'

'Oh, yes you will,' he declared angrily. 'I shan't be home for at least another hour or so yet. No man can run his business from inside closed doors. Now, take yourself home and don't aggravate her or you'll answer to me.'

'I'm not going back without you, Harry. She hates me.'

Visibly controlling his anger, he closed his fingers over her wrist and drew her sharply to him, his voice low and trembling. 'Is it any wonder she hates you? What kindness have you ever shown her? You'll do as I say and make your way back *now*! For once in your life have a thought for those who put the clothes on your worthless back!'

Realising she had goaded him too far, she snatched herself away and hurried towards Penny Street.

Ruthie had heard it all. 'Is she your missus?'

Harry was still boiling inside, but Ruthie's innocent question brought a smile to his face. 'Good Lord, no,' he chuckled. 'She's my sister, and not a very good one at that.'

'She's very rude.'

'Through the eyes of a child,' he murmured. He noticed Bridget coming towards them. 'Look, here's your mammy come to get you,' he told Ruthie. To Bridget he said, 'She's like you. Warm and honest.'

'No,' Bridget replied softly. 'She's not like me. Ruthie is her own special self. I'm just . . . Bridget Mulligan.' A smile lifted her face and soon he, too, was smiling.

They looked at each other, and something sparked between them, a bond that only memory and love could bring.

Reaching down to stroke Ruthie's hair, Harry said, 'I have to go now. Take care of your mammy, because whether she believes it or not, she *is* very special too.' And as far as he was concerned, she always would be.

Less than an hour later, having hurried through his business and concerned about leaving Alice alone with their mother, Harry made his way home at a fast pace.

As he strode towards the house, even before he set foot inside he knew something was not quite right.

The old lady hated the dark and he always left the stairway lamp burning, but he realised the lamp must be out because there was no flickering light shining through the glass door panels. In fact, the whole house was in darkness, and when he let himself in, he could hear the sound of someone softly crying upstairs.

Deeply concerned, he quickly lit a lamp and mounted the stairs two steps at a time. When he opened the door to his mother's room, she held out her arms to him. 'Oh, Harry! Harry!' she cried. 'I'm so glad you're home. Come in quickly. Shut the door.'

He put the lamp down on the dresser and went to her. 'What is it, Mother? Where's Alice? I told her not to leave you on your own. And why is the house in darkness?'

'She turned out all the lamps, Harry,' Maud quavered. 'Alice left me in the dark. I don't like the dark.'

'Why did she do that?'

'She's going off her mind,' the old lady whispered. 'Stay here with me, Harry. Don't leave me.'

'Hush now. There's nothing to be frightened of. I'm not going out again but I must go and find Alice.' He kissed her on the forehead. 'You do understand, don't you?'

She nodded, and watched him leave the room.

The way was dark. Only the flickering of the lamp he had left in his mother's room helped to light the way.

As he came nearer to Alice's room, he heard silly, childish laughter.

He inched open the door and in the light from the street lamp outside the window he made out his sister lying sprawled on the floor. Beside her was another, masculine figure, laughing as he tried to mount her.

Harry stepped forward into the room.

'Who's that?' The man fell back, startled.

Alice knelt to light the lamp, her eyes filled with fury as she stared at her brother. 'Get out of here, Harry!'

She was stark naked. So was the man.

'Clear off, matey,' he told Harry. 'You'll have to wait your turn.'

Incensed beyond reason, Harry lunged forward and jerked the man roughly to his feet. Without a word, he threw both him and his clothes down the stairs. 'If I see you anywhere near this house again,' he hissed, 'I'll break your neck, so help me God.'

The man scrambled out of the house like a scalded cat.

'You bastard!' screeched Alice. 'You've no right to throw him out. I invited him here. It has nothing to do with you!'

Swinging round, Harry took hold of her. 'You're wrong, Alice. It has *everything* to do with me.' His face was like stone. 'You have no shame. You bring a man like that into our father's home, you terrorise an old woman, your own mother . . . I'd be failing in my duty if I allowed you to stay under this roof.'

Fear rippled through her. 'What are you saying?'

'I'm saying I want you out of here.'

'You can't! Don't forget, I'm not the only one who brought shame on this house. What about you and the Mulligan woman?'

With a cry, he raised his hand to slap her, but with immense control he stopped himself. 'You're not fit to even speak Bridget Mulligan's name. Yes, I did wrong, but it wasn't out of lust or greed. It was something altogether different, something you could never understand. The only mistake I made was that Bridget was not mine to love. I have paid a terrible price for what I did, and so has she. But you've sunk so low you're incapable of recognising goodness when you see it! So don't talk to me about Bridget Mulligan. You're not fit to wipe her boots!'

'You can't throw me out.'

'That's where you're wrong, Alice. With Father gone, I am head of this household.'

'What I've done is not so wrong.'

'You think not? You contribute nothing to this household except trouble. You steal money from my workshop and imagine I don't know about it. You are unwilling to make even the smallest effort to make Mother more comfortable. I've put up with your behaviour for the sake of peace, but when you deliberately frighten a helpless old woman by leaving her in the dark while you cavort with God knows who, do you really think I could risk it happening again?'

'It *won't* happen again, I swear it.'

'Your promises are meaningless. No, Alice, I can't allow you to stay here. I won't see you destitute. There will be an adequate allowance to keep you clothed and fed and provide a modest roof over your head, but from now on you are to keep away from this house and if you ever need to see Mother, you will have to go through me. Is that understood?'

'If you do this to me, I'll make you regret it.'

His easy smile infuriated her. 'In my life I've regretted many things, Alice,' he replied. 'But I will never regret asking you to leave this house.'

'I'm warning you, there are things I could say – *bad* things. Things you don't even know about. Things that might cause you no end of anguish.' She was thinking of the girl – Harry's daughter.

'You could do nothing to cause me anguish that you have not already done.'

She laughed in his face. 'If you think that, you're wrong. I saw you with that brat today, your precious woman's daughter.'

'Ruthie? What about her?'

'The girl is yours, Harry. Anyone can see that.'

Disgust showed on his face. 'Good God, woman! Is there nothing you wouldn't stoop to?'

Alice twisted the knife. 'She didn't tell you, did she? All this time – what, eight years! And she's deceived you all along. Hah! So much for Bridget Mulligan being any better than I am! She's a liar. You have a daughter, Harry, and you never knew. For all my faults, I would never be that cruel.'

The colour had drained from Harry's face. It couldn't be true. Ruthie was not his. Alice was goading him, and no one was better at that than she was. 'Bridget never told me because it's not true,' he said. 'That lovely child belongs to Tom Mulligan. I ought to kill you for soiling that good man's memory. I warn you, Alice, if I ever hear that you've spread one word of this terrible lie, I'll come after you. And I won't be responsible for my actions.'

'Ask her! Make her tell you the truth!'

'That's enough! Go and get dressed. I'm going to make sure Mother's all right, and I want you out of the house by the time I return.'

When Harry began to explain to his mother what had happened, she stopped him. 'I heard it all,' she said, 'and you have done what had to be done.'

They talked for some minutes, he comforting and reassuring, and she feeling that she had spent enough time on God's earth, and all she wanted now was to be at peace. Harry was the best son a woman could wish for, but he was young and, from what she had heard just now, somewhere there was a woman who had loved him and, God willing, a child that was his. Right or wrong, there was something very wonderful about that. Harry deserved love and contentment, and the strength of his own family about him. He had never once complained, but she knew that at times the weight on his shoulders must be intolerable. Harry was right to throw Alice out, but how she wished it had not happened. For how could a mother not love her child, even if that child was selfish and destructive?

A short time later they heard Alice going down the stairs, and then the front door closing. As she looked up at her son, Maud knew a deep sense of loneliness, but not for herself. It was for Harry she felt lonely.

Harry was too disturbed to work. He paced the floor, his mind going over and over what Alice had said. 'It can't be true,' he muttered. 'Bridget would have told me. But maybe she kept it from me because of Tom. And how could I blame her for that?'

Beside himself with anguish, he walked back and forth, scraping his hands through his hair. The clock ticked away the minutes; minutes became hours, and still he paced, thinking and worrying.

Lying in her bed, Maud could hear him pacing the floor downstairs, and she could only guess at the agonies he was going through.

'Bridget Mulligan,' she whispered. And with that name on her lips, she closed her eyes and went to sleep.

Chapter Thirteen

Fanny and Billy had reached the outskirts of Lancaster.

'Look, Mam, over there!' Pointing over the hedge towards the clutch of buildings, Billy cried excitedly, 'It's a farm. And look, there are hundreds of chicks running about. The farmer won't miss a few eggs, and I'm hungry enough to eat the chicken as well.'

Fanny laughed. 'No chickens,' she said firmly. 'But you're right, they'll not miss four eggs.'

'Oh, Mam, only four?' he moaned. 'I could eat them all to meself.'

'Well then, you're a pig, Billy Higgins.'

'If we take six, we can have three each,' he suggested hopefully.

'All right. But only six, and no more. And I've a mind to leave a few pennies in the tin.'

'If you do that we won't be able to buy a new bucket. Remember, we threw the other away because there was a hole in it.'

'Oh aye. I'd forgotten about the bucket.' He was growing more dependable by the minute. 'But we ain't broke, yer know,' she reminded him. 'Yer mammy's just being careful with her money, that's all.' She winked at him. 'Happen we might see if there's a jug o' milk going spare in the churn as well.'

'And mebbe some freshly cured bacon, eh, Mam?' He licked his lips. Already he could smell the bacon sizzling.

As the old horse pulled the wagon into the field, another, younger animal came up behind. Cautiously its rider dismounted and tethered the horse to a tree. 'I'll be glad when this damned job is over,' the man moaned. 'I'm not used to this – cold nights and horses that need feeding. It's too much like hard work.'

He dug into his leather side pack and drew out a small bag of hay which he tied to the horse's nose. Then he dug out a smaller bundle and quickly devoured the bread and cheese it contained. 'This is no way for a man to earn a living,' he told the horse who took no notice as it contentedly munched its hay. 'If it wasn't for the handsome sum of money promised, I'd give it up here and now. I'm cold and miserable, and I never know where I'll end up next. When I dare take my eyes off these two, I have to grab what food I can. I've even gone days without washing in case I lose track of 'em. Not as I'm bothered about *that* in particular.'

He crept towards the hedge and peered through. 'There they go, warm and cosy in their wagon, and here's me, so cold I can't keep a limb still.' In the last hour, with night setting in, a chilly wind had got up. 'The minute this job's done and I've got my wages safe in my pocket, I'll be off to enjoy a night of brown ale and fleshy women.' The thought of holding an eager woman in his arms sent a glow all over, and suddenly the job didn't seem so bad after all.

At a discreet distance from the farm, Fanny drew the wagon to a halt beside a tall hedge. 'You stay here and keep a lookout,' she told Billy. 'I'll be back afore yer know it.'

He was used to the routine by now. 'Here you are, Mam.' He handed her a small earthenware jug from inside the wagon. 'For the milk.'

'I didn't forget,' she declared. 'I were just about to look for it when yer beat me to it.'

They both knew she was fibbing. These days her mind was all over the place, mostly on Bridget and Ruthie, but also on Bill Norman. The truth was, she didn't like being this far away from any of them.

'Right, son.' She pulled out a basket from beneath the seat, placed the jug inside it and scrambled down to the ground – straight into a newlaid cow pat. 'Jesus, Mary and Joseph!' she groaned. 'Now I'll have to wash me feet when I get back.'

She caught sight of Billy trying to suppress a smile, and burst into laughter. 'Ssh!' she warned. 'If the farmer hears us, he'll be after shooting us up the arse with his gun.'

'Be careful, Mam,' Billy whispered as she went on her way.

Inside the barn, Bob Morris waited impatiently. 'Where the devil is she?'

He'd collected the money at the back door as usual, and afterwards parked his cart where the husband couldn't see it. She had given him the wink and he'd been here waiting for her for at least half an hour already but there was no sign of her.

He looked towards the house. 'What's the silly cow playing at? If she doesn't get a move on, I might be seen, and that would never do. A few more minutes, that's all. After that, I'm away.' But he did so want her. He'd wanted her all day. She wasn't like Bridget. Bridget was a lady, with a lady's tenderness, while this one was rough, needing it more than he did, and that always excited him.

Thinking of her, he began to tremble with anticipation. When at last she came rushing in, he threw her to the ground and began to tear at her clothes.

'No!' she protested, struggling against him. 'I think he's on to us! He's been watching me like a hawk. I only managed to get out now because he's tending a fevered lamb.'

When he wouldn't listen but instead began undoing his trousers, she grew frantic. 'No, Bob! I've got to get back before he does. Tomorrow though . . . we'll meet tomorrow.'

'Shut your mouth, woman.' Laying her beneath him, he lifted her skirt and prepared to enter her. 'You kept me waiting, you bitch. *Nobody* keeps me waiting.' He was a man used to getting what he wanted – or meting out punishment if denied. He had killed before and it was all too easy.

The more she struggled, the more determined he was to have her.

Just then Fanny arrived at the barn door. She saw them writhing on the ground but didn't realise the woman was resisting. She thought it was just two lovers having a good time.

Envious, she turned away. 'The eggs can wait.' She smiled wistfully. 'I wouldn't dream of interrupting when they're enjoying theirselves so much.' Through the window, she took another look. 'Lucky buggers. It's a long time since I had a man atween me thighs.'

She sat down on an upturned log, one eye on the barn door, the other on lookout. 'Hurry up, yer buggers,' she whispered, 'or I must be off and our Billy will have to go without his eggs.' Loitering on private property was always dangerous. 'Some o' these farmers only want half an excuse to point a double barrel at yer.' Restless, she got up and walked towards the bushes. 'Best keep well out o' sight. I'm too young and beautiful to have me bleedin' head shot off.'

A few minutes later she heard the woman call out. 'Help! Somebody help me!'

'Gawd almighty!' In a panic, Fanny took flight, but after a few yards, her conscience stopped her. 'The bastard's turned nasty on her.' She knew only too well how men could turn nasty at the drop of a hat. 'He might be killing her for all I know.

I'll have to go back or I'll never forgive meself.'

She ran back towards the barn, her basket lying where she had dropped it and her heart beating nineteen to the dozen. The sight that greeted her through the barn door horrified her.

The woman was fighting for her life. She had been beaten about the head and face, her clothes were torn, and she was pressed against the wall, her arms pinned to her sides as the man brutally forced himself on her. As Fanny watched, he grabbed the woman by the scruff of the neck and with a choked cry brought his fist hard down on her temple, knocking her out.

'Yer bugger!' yelled Fanny. 'Leave her be!' She rushed into the barn. 'You wicked bastard, you've killed her!' He turned and Fanny's heart almost stopped from the shock. 'You! Bob Morris . . . Bridget's feller!'

She saw him quickly button his trousers and walk calmly towards her. 'If you know what's good for you, you'll keep your mouth shut,' he warned.

Fanny came to her senses and took to her heels. But he was too quick for her. In one great stride he had her by the throat. 'One word to Bridget and you'll get the same as that one.' He gestured to the woman lying on the ground, unmoving. 'I can be a bad enemy,' he breathed, 'but I know how to reward a friend.' Nuzzling up to her ear, he made his intention very clear; the longing for a woman, any woman, was still on him.

Wriggling loose, Fanny gave him a hefty kick on the shin. He gave a yell of pain. 'Yer a dangerous bastard,' she cried, 'and you'll not get away with what you've done to that poor woman.' She started running, but again he caught up with her and this time he was not so gentle. 'I warned you,' he growled, crossing his arm over her neck and pinning her to him. 'I can see I'll have to deal with you after all.'

To Fanny's horror, she heard Billy calling. 'Mam! Mam, where are you?'

'Go back, son!' she shouted, and Bob tightened his hold on her throat, almost choking her.

Suddenly the place was alive with people. From one side the farmer Jack Meaker came running towards them; another, smaller fellow was racing from another direction and a big, burly fellow had grabbed Billy by his coat collar.

'What the devil's going on here?' asked the farmer, his gun at the ready. 'Bob Morris, isn't it? I thought you'd left the property ages since. Explain yourself, man.'

Bob did not relax his hold on Fanny and she was horrified when she heard him say, 'My horse picked up a stone in his hoof. I was just finished getting it out when I heard an almighty scuffle going on in the barn. As I ran towards it, I heard a woman scream out for help, and just as I got to the doors, I caught this Gypsy woman running away. I've an idea she was poaching when your wife caught her at it.'

Jack Meaker was shocked. 'Are you saying my *wife* was out here?'

'I'm afraid so, sir.' Lowering his voice to a sombre tone, Bob explained, 'I'm sorry, but it seems this ragbag has done your wife harm.' Tightening his hold on Fanny, he tried to reassure the startled farmer. 'But don't you worry, sir, I've got hold of the culprit, and I don't intend to let go until the authorities arrive.'

At that moment, the smaller man Fanny had seen earlier came running out of the barn. 'You'd better come quick, sir!'

As the farmer went at a run towards the barn, Billy was dragged kicking and shouting across the ground to where Fanny and Bob stood. 'What's happened?' he asked, addressing Bob, obviously assuming he was as innocent as he himself was.

'Gypsies,' Bob answered, looking down at Fanny with a glint of satisfaction. 'This one went for the missus. Wouldn't be at all surprised if she hasn't done for her.'

'Liars! You're all liars. Let me mam go, she ain't done

nuthin'!' Billy got a swift blow to the head for his trouble.

Looking up at Fanny, he seemed to understand when she widened her eyes, giving the smallest shake of her head in a warning. She couldn't speak. She didn't have to. He understood, and remained silent and, like her, very much afraid.

'You say she's done for the missus, eh?' Eyeing Fanny with interest, he spat on the ground. 'In that case she'll be for the rope an' no mistake.'

Grabbing Billy, he swung him in the air. 'As for this one, he'll be lucky if he don't find himself dangling alongside her.'

No excuses and no lies, or you'll not get a farthing from me! I told you I needed to be kept informed of her every move, and you've kept me waiting nearly three weeks. Is she back? Has she changed her mind and isn't coming back at all? Or have you been stupid enough to lose track of her?' Bill Norman's wife was no easy person to deal with at the best of times, but when she paid out good money to be kept informed and nothing came of it, she wanted blood. 'Well, what have you to say for yourself?'

'I stayed away because I thought it for the best. You'll understand when I tell you. You might even consider giving me an extra shilling or two.'

'And I might consider slicing the head from your worthless shoulders too. You've got two minutes.'

'Well now, what if I told you Fanny Higgins were about to be hanged from the gallows?' With that dangerous glint in her eyes, he thought it wise to step back a pace. 'What would you say to that, eh? Would you say it might be worth an extra shilling for all my trouble?'

She gawped at him. 'It might well be worth a few shilling more.' She eyed him with suspicion. 'Why would she be hanged? What did she do?'

He held out his hand. 'I'll have my wages first, if you please.'

'Oh no! Report first, money after, that's the arrangement.'

He tightened his lips. 'Murder. That's what they say she's done.'

'Murder?' She had to sit down. 'I'd never have thought her capable of *murder*. Who was it she murdered then?'

'Happen you heard about the woman who was killed on that farm the other side of Lancaster.'

She shook her head. 'Can't say as I have.'

'Aye, well, give it time. News like that has a way of travelling through the alehouses and on to the streets, even to our corner of the world. I followed the two of them to this farm. She got out of the wagon and took off towards the barn with her basket, no doubt looking to fill it with eggs, or chickens, or whatever else she could get her hands on.' He took a breath before continuing, 'There was a frightful row going on in the barn, some woman calling out for help. I managed to get close enough to see what was happening and I witnessed the farmer's woman being murdered there and then.'

'Good Lord above!' She stared at him through marbled eyes. 'You mean to say you actually saw Fanny Higgins murder this woman? And you did nothing to help the poor soul?'

'Ah well, it weren't as simple as that, being as how it weren't Fanny Higgins as did the murder. It were a feller who was trying to have his way with the farmer's wife. Only Fanny Higgins saw it all, and instead of minding her own business like any sensible body might, she went at him like a mad thing.'

'Mad, yes, that's her all right.'

'The upshot of it all was that he caught hold of her and when the alarm was raised, he said as how Fanny Higgins were stealing eggs when the farmer's wife interrupted her, and the two of them got fighting. Fanny Higgins were the one who murdered that poor woman, that's what he claimed.'

'What? And they believed him?'

He nodded. 'And since then I've heard that both Fanny Higgins and the boy have been thrown in jail, waiting to be sentenced. There's no doubt on it, missus, she'll be hanged right enough, and nobody to plead her case for her.'

By now, she was on her feet and looking triumphant. 'Aye, and it's just as well. I'll be rid of her once and for all.'

'And is it worth an extra shilling, would you say?'

She went to the dresser and took out a box. Out of the box she drew a bag and out of the bag she tipped a cascade of coins. She counted out his wages, and an extra shilling into the bargain. 'If I can rely on you not to open your mouth to anybody about what you saw, I might think a favour like that could be worth a few more shillings. What do you say?'

'I say you can rely on me.' Grinning expectantly, he held out his hand.

'Oh no,' she said, wagging a finger, 'if I pay you now you'll more than likely loosen your tongue over a glass of ale and our little secret will be out. I'll keep the money aside for you. That way I'll feel more secure, if you know what I mean. But I'm a woman of my word. Once Fanny Higgins is under the ground, the money will be waiting for you.'

'How can I be sure you'll pay me? I mean, once she's hanged, you won't care who I tell, will you?'

'Firstly, I don't think you want to tell or you would have done so already; secondly, if some folks knew how you'd let an innocent woman hang, they might well do the very same to you. And thirdly, why should I not pay you when you've given me the best news I've heard in years?' A thought occurred to her. 'This man, the one who did the murder. Who was it?'

'I've no idea.' Why should he tell her? he thought. That might be worth another shilling, another day.

Part Three

1859

A FRIEND IN NEED

Chapter Fourteen

Bob Morris swallowed the last bite of apple pie. 'That was a wonderful meal,' he told Bridget. 'When we're married, I'll be the best fed man in the whole of Lancashire.'

Flattered but not duped, Bridget began to clear the table. 'You're lying,' she laughed. 'I've never been all that good a cook. Throwing together a hotpot is no great achievement, and all you have to do for a pie is drop the apples in the bottom of a dish and cover them with a layer of pastry. That's about it. Nothing fancy there.'

'You do yourself down, my lovely.' Getting out of the chair, he came to wind his arms round her waist. 'I meant what I said, and I can't wait for the day when you lie next to me as my wife. You've already put it off once. Now that we've decided to wait for another month, I'm beginning to get frustrated.'

Bridget had deliberately put the wedding off because of the doubts she harboured. She felt restless and uncertain but as yet, she had managed to make good her excuses to him. When he watched her, as he was doing now, she was almost afraid of him. 'Can you finish clearing the table, Bob?' she asked. 'I need to go up and see how Ruthie is.'

She was deeply troubled. The minute Ruthie knew Bob was staying to dinner, she had taken herself off to her room, claiming she didn't feel well. Bridget knew otherwise, though she didn't argue. She let Ruthie do what made her feel comfortable, and if it meant hiding herself in her room, that was all right. But it was not a good situation, and Bridget meant to get to the bottom of it once and for all.

'That's right. You go and see Ruthie.' Kissing her from behind, he said meaningfully, 'I'll wait for you in the front bedroom, shall I?'

'Not tonight, Bob.'

'What's the matter with you?'

'I'm just concerned about Ruthie, that's all. She's been acting very strange lately.'

'It's been almost a week.'

Bridget shrugged him off. 'I know.'

'If you don't show me some affection soon, I'll begin to think you don't want me any more.' He walked round to face her. 'You *do* want me, don't you, my lovely?'

Not for the first time, Bridget began to wonder. 'Stop feeling sorry for yourself,' she said, which infuriated him. 'You finish clearing the table and I'll go up to Ruthie. Afterwards, we'll sit and talk.'

Before he could argue, she was out of the room and on her way up the stairs.

'Bitch!' He slammed his fist on the table, shaking with anger.

Upstairs, Bridget sat on the bed next to Ruthie. 'What's wrong, sweetheart?'

'Will you and . . . *him* . . . get married, Mam?'

'Would you be very unhappy if we did?'

There was a long pause before Ruthie shook her head. 'Not if you really wanted to.'

'You don't like Bob, do you?'

Ruthie shrugged her shoulders. '*You* do.'

'I suppose I must.' It was a strange thing to say, but these days, ever since she'd seen Harry again, her feelings were all at odds.

'Mam?'

'I'm listening, sweetheart.'

'If I asked you not to, would you still marry him?'

It took a moment for Bridget to give her answer. 'Not just because you asked me. You would need to give me a very good reason. We've already made plans, and I happen to think Bob would make you a very good father. We need a man about the place, and I won't always have you here. One day you'll get married and I might end up a lonely old woman.'

Ruthie hadn't thought of that. 'I wouldn't want that to happen, Mam.'

'Neither would I. So, if you have a good reason why I shouldn't marry Bob, then I need to know.'

When Ruthie started softly crying, Bridget held her close. 'Is there something you want to tell me?'

A moment passed, and then Ruthie shook her head.

'Ruthie?'

'Yes, Mam?'

'You always used to like Bob.'

'Yes, Mam.'

'What's changed to turn you against him?'

'Nothing.'

'Are you jealous, is that it?'

'Sometimes.'

'Do you think I won't love you as much? Because if that's so, then you're wrong, sweetheart. You're very precious to me, and you could never do anything to stop me loving you.'

'I love you too, Mam.'

'And do you think you could learn to like Bob again?'

No answer.

'All right. We'll see.'

'I'm sorry I didn't want any dinner, Mam.'

'There's still some hotpot left,' Bridget replied hopefully. 'And happen a slice of apple pie. Would you like to come back downstairs for a while?'

'Don't want to.'

'Then you don't have to.'

'Mam?'

'Yes?'

'When will Billy come back?'

'I only wish I knew. I can't understand why Fanny hasn't tried to get in touch. I've asked everybody I know, and even strangers, whether they've seen a woman and a boy travelling in a wagon, but nobody seems to know.'

'Why don't we put papers up round the market?'

'You mean like a notice or something?'

'Yes. Like that one about the circus. Everybody sees it.'

'By! You might just have something there.' It was a brilliant idea and Bridget wondered why she hadn't thought of it herself. 'We'll do it tomorrow morning.' Already she was designing the notice in her mind.

'Thanks, Mam.'

'And there's nothing else you want to tell me?'

'No.'

'Goodnight then. Go to sleep now.'

The small face lit up. 'Can I have some hot potatoes from Mack's barrow tomorrow?'

'Only if I can have some too.'

Outside the bedroom door, Bob Morris smiled to himself, satisfied that Ruthie had kept his secret. He crept back downstairs and by the time Bridget returned, he had quickly cleared away all the dishes and was seated by the fire, with a mug of tea waiting on either side of the hearth.

'See what a good husband I'll make?' he said as she came through the door.

'Only because I'm training you well,' she joked. But though she smiled, Bridget was sorely troubled. Ruthie worried her, and she was aware that she still had not got to the bottom of whatever was bothering her daughter. But if pushed, Ruthie would only clam up. So all she could do now was to stay alert and watch for clues to the problem.

'I'll not only be a good husband,' Bob was saying, 'I'll be the best father to Ruthie. Once you and me are wed, I mean to make sure I never work on a Sunday. That'll be our day, you, me and Ruthie. We'll go off to the park in the morning, feed the ducks, and later we'll go down the river to that pretty café where they serve piping hot chips and big squashy cakes. I mean to spoil you both rotten.'

Bridget sank into the chair and sipped her tea. 'You don't have to spoil us rotten,' she told him, 'and you mustn't change your work days to suit us.'

'I might even buy us a small farm. I've saved more money than you know, and I'm thinking it's high time I did something useful with it instead of travelling the highways working from morning till night, seven days a week.'

'But if you had a farm, you'd still be working on the land from morning till night, wouldn't you? You've said yourself that farming is a hard life.'

'Ah well, you and Ruthie would need to muck in.'

'I don't think so, Bob. I want Ruthie to be educated, and I've already mapped out a future for myself. It doesn't mean to say I'll be working any longer hours than I do now, or that I won't always be here for you and Ruthie, because I will. But you have to understand, I've been on my own for a long time now, and circumstances have made me independent.'

'But it's not natural for a woman to be in business.' He could have said more but decided it was best for now to let her have her say.

'Why not?' Bridget demanded. 'Joe didn't care that I was a woman. He had enough faith in my ability to make me a partner and I mean to prove myself. I want Joe to reap the benefits of his judgement. I mean to move up in the world, Bob, and if I succeed, it can only help us all.'

'What do you mean, move up in the world?'

Bridget was cagey. 'I don't want to say too much, Bob, in case I tempt fate and lose it all, but right now I've got a few irons in the fire. With luck, they'll come good.'

'I see.' He was obviously disturbed. 'All the same, I'll not want you working once we're wed. The man is the breadwinner, and that's the way it should be. There'll be no need for you to work. I make more than enough money for the three of us.'

'It isn't just to do with money, Bob,' she explained. 'It's to do with me making something of myself.' She looked at him steadily. 'Would it mean you wouldn't want us to be wed if I was earning?'

'Good God, no!' He was a good liar and he knew how to hide his anger when necessary. 'Like I said, I don't think much to it, but if it's what you want, my lovely, then who am I to stand in your way? As long as we're man and wife, that's all that matters to me. You must do what you feel is right. If you want to build up a business, I'll even help you do it if I can find the time – though I suspect you would want to do it all on your own, wouldn't you?' His smile was wooden as his anger nearly got the better of him.

She nodded. 'Thanks, Bob. I'm glad you understand.'

'All I want is for you to be happy.'

'Bob? Will you do me a favour?'

'I might.' He winked at her, his mind still on the front bedroom.

'No. I'm serious.'

'Go on.'

'Just now Ruthie asked after Billy, and she came up with an idea.'

'Did she now?'

'She said we should put notices up everywhere, like the circus ones. And she's right. Everybody would see them and there might be a chance that someone would know about Fanny and Billy.'

The colour drained from his face. 'Slim chance, I'd say.' Taken aback by her plan, he grew frightened. After all, he was the one who had put Fanny Higgins behind bars; the boy too. So far news of Fanny and her son had not filtered through to Blackburn town, but it would, and once it did, he wanted to have a ring on Bridget's finger. He wanted to have proved what a good husband he could be. He hadn't yet thought up a good enough story as to why he hadn't told her before about what happened that night.

'Well, I think Ruthie's idea is a good one, and tomorrow we'll make some notices and put them up everywhere.' Bridget wondered at his lukewarm response. In fact, he seemed almost hostile to the idea, and yet he had promised to try and track Fanny down himself so that she and Billy could come to their wedding. Nothing had come of his promise; maybe he didn't like being shown up by a child. The thought made her uneasy and she pushed it aside. 'Will you take some of the notices with you when you're out and about? You can pin them on to trees and gates, and maybe ask about to see if anybody knows where she might be.'

'What makes you think she wants to be found?'

'You could be right. Maybe she doesn't, but it's not like her to stay away so long without somehow getting in touch. I'm worried, Bob. I'm wondering if she's in some kind of trouble.'

'Why would she be in trouble?'

Bridget laughed. 'Because trouble seems to root her out, that's why. Please, Bob, will you help find her?'

Putting on a smile, he got out of his chair and went to her. 'You know I'd do anything for you,' he said, kissing her on the mouth. 'Make as many notices as you like and I'll put them everywhere I go. Will that suit you?'

Reaching up, she kissed him back. 'I knew you wouldn't let me down. You never have before.'

'There you go then.'

'And I'm glad you understand about me and what I want to do.'

'It's your life,' he said jovially. 'Who am I to say what you should and shouldn't do?' Until we're wed, he thought, then you'll see another side of me. 'I'd better be off now – seeing as there's nothing doing.'

'Shame on you,' she said. 'You'll have me thinking that's the only reason you come to see me.'

'You know better than that, my lovely. Walk me to the door then.'

At the door, he kissed her long and passionately and Bridget responded warmly; she found a kind of comfort in his arms.

From the top of the stairs, Ruthie watched them, and when she could stand it no longer, she ran back to her room. 'I *hate* him!' she cried, banging her fists on the windowsill. '*Hate* him! *Hate* him! I wish Billy was here. I'd tell him how I saw Bob kissing that woman in the street. And he wasn't her friend, because he kissed her like he kissed Mammy just now. If Billy were here, I'd tell him what a bad man Bob Morris is. I'd tell him I'm frightened because he said if I told Mammy about it, he would hurt her. Oh, Billy, I wish you were here.'

But Billy wasn't here, and she didn't even know where he was.

'Happen I'll run away,' she muttered. 'Happen I'll go and find him.' The longer she thought about it, the more convinced she was that it was the right thing to do.

* * *

As usual, the Saturday market was busy.

All morning, the customers kept coming, and both Bridget and Joe were run off their feet. Only when it got towards late afternoon and the twilight began to creep in did they get a chance to breathe.

'How are the notices coming along, sweetheart?'

Ruthie had not raised her head all day. Tucked at the back of the stall, she had been busy cutting out the sheets for the notices. 'All finished, Mam.'

'You've done well, sweetheart,' Bridget told her. 'Now then, what shall we say?'

'That we want anyone to tell us if they know where Fanny and Billy are.'

Bridget began to write in big bold letters: 'IF ENYONE KNOWS THE WUREABOUTS OF FANNY HIGGINS AND HER SON, BILLY, TRAVLLIN BY ORSE AND CART, PLEESE SEE BRIDGET MULLIGAN OF 24, KING STREET, BLACKBURN. TO SHILIN REWORD IF FOUND.'

'You've spelled that word wrong,' Joe said, when she showed him the notice.

'Which word?'

'That one.' He pointed at the 'To'.

'What's wrong with it?' Spelling wasn't Bridget's strong point, but she thought it looked right, and said so.

'It wants another "o" at the end of it.'

Feeling foolish, and believing Joe to be a better scholar than she was, she corrected it. 'There you are, "Too shilin".'

'That's more like it,' said Joe.

'Oh, Mam, somebody will find them, won't they?' said Ruthie.

'I should hope so, after all the trouble we've gone to.'

Aggie appeared to ask Bridget's advice on a new dress she was thinking of buying. 'I've got it for an hour, then, if it don't suit I have to take it back.'

'Go behind the curtain and try it on,' Bridget suggested. 'It's the right colour anyway – red puts the roses in your cheeks.' Aggie was past her prime but she had a certain jaded vivaciousness that told Bridget she must have been a beauty in her time.

Ruthie was chatting to Joe. 'Joe, do you like Bob Morris?'

'He's all right, I suppose. Why?'

'Just wondered.'

'Well, he *must* be all right, lass, 'cause yer mam wouldn't be about to wed him if he weren't.'

'Who's that other man?'

'What other man?'

'The one who came to see you the other day.'

He patted her head. 'Eh, lass, there's many a feller comes to see old Joe. What does he look like, this man?'

'He's bigger than you, and he's got real nice brown eyes. I think he's a bit shy.'

'Bigger than me, eh? Brown eyes . . . Oh, you must mean Harry. Harry Little, lives on Ainsworth Street. He's a tailor and, yes, you're right, he does seem shy at times.' Chuckling to himself, he added, 'But not when it comes to business. Oh no. Our Harry's sharp as a tack when it comes to business.'

'I like him.'

'Aye, lass, an' so do I. Come to think of it, there ain't many folk who *don't* like him. He's a good sort, is Harry.'

Their conversation was brought to a halt by a flurry of customers. 'We need a hand this side, lass,' Joe called, and Bridget came running, having persuaded Aggie that the dress was made for her.

Soon afterwards, Bob Morris arrived. 'I've finished for the day,' he explained. 'Barnaby's cows have got milk fever and I've had to call off two of my rounds.'

'That's a pity for the cows but I'm glad you're here.' Bridget handed him a number of the finished notices. 'You can take them out with you in the morning. Ruthie and I will put some up around here before we finish for the day.'

Bob promised to take the notices with him in the morning. 'I won't be round tonight,' he said. 'I went over some rough ground and busted two wheels on the cart. It'll take me all night to repair 'em.' Truth was, he fancied a night out with a bit of rough.

In a way Bridget was glad he didn't plan to come round. If she and Ruthie were on their own, Ruthie might confide in her. Bob took his leave, and much to Ruthie's disgust, kissed Bridget as though he wouldn't be seeing her for a month.

He had gone only a short distance when Ruthie saw him discreetly drop the notices into a waste bin. She was horrified but she didn't say anything; she did not dare. But it made up her mind for her.

When Bridget went to get them each a bag of hot potatoes from Mack's barrow, she said to Joe, 'Tell Mammy I've gone to find Billy.'

Joe wasn't as quick-witted as he used to be. 'Billy who?'

'Mam will know.' She put on her coat and hat and was quickly gone, keeping low and winding her way through the stalls so Bridget wouldn't see her.

Only yards away, Bob Morris was preoccupied with a woman of loose reputation. 'I reckon we should find somewhere a bit more private,' he suggested. 'Nothing personal, but I don't want to be seen here with you.'

'Huh! You wouldn't have said that a few months ago,' she snapped. 'I was mixing with the top folk – smart clothes, having tea with the ladies.'

He laughed at her. 'You don't say? And did you visit the palace? Were you invited to have tea with royalty as well?'

'You think I'm lying, but it's true,' she protested. 'I was respectable enough, until my brother threw me out. He's warm and comfortable, damn his eyes, while here I am having to put up with dogs like you because he won't give me more money.'

'My heart goes out to you,' Bob sneered. 'The truth is, you slut, if you want money you must work for it, like we all do. So get a move on and find us a place where we won't be a peepshow.'

Taking him by the arm, she led him away, smiling grandly at the little girl who stood at the mouth of the alley. 'Happen she's here to learn a trade,' she laughed.

Bob swung round to look but there was no one there. 'You're seeing things,' he chuckled. 'You'd better take water with your gin from now on.'

'Whisky's my tipple,' she told him with a nudge. 'I'm a woman with expensive tastes.'

'What's your name then, *lady*?' he mocked.

'Alice,' she replied haughtily. 'Alice Little, and I don't give a sod who knows it!'

Pressed against the wall at the top of the alley, Ruthie prayed he wouldn't come looking. When she realised they'd gone, she ran on, out of the market square, and down towards the open road. 'Got to find Billy,' she kept saying. 'Got to find Billy!'

It was only a matter of minutes before Bridget returned to the stall carrying an armful of cornet-shaped bags filled with piping hot crusty potatoes. 'Quick now,' she said as she rounded the stall. 'Ruthie, take these from me, sweetheart. There's one each for us, and two for Joe.'

'She ain't here,' Joe called out. He was serving a customer.

Bridget dropped the bags on to the wooden crate that served as a table. 'What do you mean, she ain't here?'

'She's on an errand.'

'You mean she's gone next door to Aggie's?' Ruthie often popped round and helped Aggie sort out her bric-a-brac.

''Ere! I'm in a hurry, mister!' Holding out her hand for change, the customer was growing irate. 'Yer can do yer gossiping when I've gawn.'

Joe counted out the change. 'No, she ain't gone to Aggie's. She's gone to fetch Billy.'

'What?' Gripping him by the shoulders, Bridget swung him round. 'What do you mean, she's gone to get Billy?'

Joe was so startled by her reaction that he dropped the change all over the stall. 'Bugger me, lass, what's wrong with you?'

'What did she say, Joe? What *exactly* did Ruthie say?'

'The lass told me she were going to find Billy and you'd know all about it, that's what she said.'

'Oh my God, Joe, she's gone looking for Fanny and her boy!' The colour drained from Bridget's face. She looked frantically up and down the stalls. 'Which way did she go?' When he seemed slow to answer, she shook him. 'Answer me, Joe! Which way did Ruthie go?'

The old fellow was beginning to realise just how serious it was. 'Fanny's boy?' he said frowning. 'But I thought you didn't know where they were.'

'Joe! *Which way did Ruthie go?*'

'Down towards the clock, I reckon.' He had never heard Bridget raise her voice like that before.

'I've got to find her, Joe, I've got to find my lass,' she called as she took off after Ruthie.

Aggie poked her head round the stall. 'What's going on? Where's Bridget gone running off to?'

'The young'un's gone to find Billy and his mam,' Joe told her. 'They're on the road somewhere, God only knows where!' Frantic now, he asked, 'Will you watch the stall, Aggie, while I go after her?'

'Get going! Don't worry about the stall. I can keep two as well as one.'

Joe was quickly joined by others who had heard the commotion and wanted to help. 'Is there anything I can do?' asked the customer who had stood open-mouthed as the drama unfurled. 'I used to keep a stall meself some time back, when I were younger, and you've customers waiting.'

Relieved, Aggie beckoned her round. 'By! Yer a blessing in disguise,' she said gratefully. 'But didn't I hear you telling Joe you were in a hurry?'

'Not now, I'm not,' came the reply. 'There's more important things in life, gal, and if there's a child missing, the old man can get his own bleedin' tea.' With that, she took off her hat and coat and set to.

All evening they searched, and well into the early hours, but there was no sign of Ruthie. 'Tell the authorities,' one of the helpers said. 'Some do-gooder might have marched her off to the police station.'

'Aye, it's worth a try,' another said. 'The lass might have got frightened in the dark and found her own way there.'

At the police station the constable was unsympathetic. 'Lasses go missing all the time,' he said wearily. 'Usually it's a family row or summat o' that sort.' He peered at Bridget. 'You haven't had a fall-out among yourselves, have you? You didn't throw the lass out, and now you've come to regret it?'

'No! Find her, that's all I want. Please, just find her.'

'Not easy, but give me the details anyway.'

It seemed to take an infuriatingly long time; Bridget had to go over everything again and again. 'Ruthie's been lonely,' she told the constable. 'Her friend went away and she were pining. We haven't heard from 'em and now she's gone looking, but they could be anywhere. There are bad people out there, and I'm frightened for her.'

'Aye, and summat as pretty as yourself shouldn't be wandering the streets neither, especially at this time of a morning.' Close to retirement, the constable had a daughter much the same age as

Bridget. 'You look washed out, lass. Go home. Get some sleep and start again tomorrow.'

'Please, you will do everything you can to find her, won't you?'

He nodded. 'You've given me all the details we might need,' he assured her. 'If there's anything else I think of, we'll be in touch. Now go on, lass, get some sleep. You'll be no good to your girl nor anybody else if you can't think straight.'

Bridget knew that what the constable had said made sense but it didn't help her to come to terms with Ruthie running off like that. 'Why would she do that? Summat were eating away at the lass, not just me and Bob getting wed, but summat else. Oh, I wish to God I knew what it was.'

Taking the longest route home, Bridget scoured every alley, hurrying past dead cats and drunks and brazen floozies who offered themselves for a tanner. The only thing on her mind was her child, all alone in such a world. Time and again, she called out Ruthie's name, and a few heartless mischief-makers mimicked her as she passed. Others gave their sympathy. 'She'll come running 'ome soon as ever she's 'ungry,' one painted creature promised, while another made her want to weep when she snarled, 'Serves yer right, lady. You should never have let her out o' yer sight.'

The market clock was striking three when, distraught and blaming herself, Bridget let herself into the house.

She was so tired she could hardly keep her eyes open, but she couldn't sleep. How could she sleep when her only reason for living was lost out there in the night?

She splashed her face with cold water to revive her senses. She made herself a cup of tea but she couldn't sit still long enough to drink it. She walked back and forth, peering out of the window, and sometimes taking a brisk walk down the street in the hope that Ruthie might be making her way back.

An hour later there was a knock on the door. She ran up the passageway and flung open the door. 'Ruthie . . .' It wasn't Ruthie. 'Oh, it's you, Joe. What's the matter? Have you heard anything? Have they found her?'

Inviting himself in, he closed the door behind him, gently escorting her down the passageway and into the parlour. 'I couldn't sleep, lass, that's why I'm here. I were worried about you. I should never have let you go off like that.'

'Thank you, Joe.' He was an old friend, and old friends were precious. 'I'm glad you're here.'

He looked about. 'I wondered if Bob might be here. You shouldn't be on your own at a time like this.'

'I haven't told Bob,' she confessed. 'I don't want him searching for her.'

'Why ever not, lass?'

'If Ruthie caught sight of him, she would only hide.'

'Why would she do that?'

Suddenly it was all too much and she couldn't hold back the tears any longer. 'She doesn't like him, Joe. Don't ask me why, because I don't know. She's been upset about me and Bob getting wed. I tried to ask her what was wrong, but she wouldn't talk to me. I think that's why she's run away, to find Billy and tell him what's worrying her.'

Cradling her face in her hands, Bridget cried bitterly. 'Why couldn't she talk to me, Joe? I'm her mammy, aren't I? We've never kept secrets from each other before.'

'Ah, well, sometimes young'uns get all manner of strange ideas in their heads. They might tell other young'uns what's on their mind when they'll not tell anybody else, especially grown-ups.' He put his arm round her. 'Did you go to the authorities, lass?' She nodded.

'Did they say they would help?'

She nodded again.

'Then there's not much you can do except snatch a few hours' sleep. I'll stay down here if you like, and when you wake, we'll root out some help. You've more friends than you realise, lass.'

'I can't sleep, Joe. Not until Ruthie's home safe.'

'Eh, lass,' Joe tutted, 'you'll drive yourself insane.' Another thought occurred to him. 'You never got to eat the 'taties from Mack's barrow, so have you eaten anything at all since yesterday?'

'I can't eat.'

'I'll take a look in the scullery, see what you've got, eh? Happen I'll make us a brew while I'm at it.'

She grabbed hold of him. 'Sit here with me, Joe. Tell me again what Ruthie said before she ran off. Think hard, remember every word, no matter how silly it might seem to you.'

Joe sat down on the sofa beside her. 'She's a right little chatterbox an' no mistake,' he said with a smile. 'Well now, let me think.' He scratched his head and screwed up his eyes. 'Well now, she told me she were off to find Billy.'

'You already told me that, Joe.'

'Oh, aye, and summat else while I think about it. She asked after the nice man.' He chuckled. 'She were talking about Harry. I tell you, Bridget, she seems to have taken a real liking to him. He were bigger than me, she said, with lovely brown eyes.'

'Did she mention anybody else?'

'Only Billy.'

'She does like Harry,' Bridget mused. 'Did she ask where he lived?'

'No, but I've a feeling I did say as how he were a tailor from Ainsworth Street. D'you reckon she might have gone to Harry's house? Is that what you're thinking, lass?'

'Will you take me there, Joe? I know it's early of a morning, but I have to know.'

'Think what you're saying, lass. If she'd gone to Harry's, he would have brought her straight round.'

'Happen he doesn't even know she's there. She might have sneaked into the cellar or got inside the house without him being aware of it. Happen she's waiting her chance to talk to him. You said yourself she's taken a liking to him. Harry listens to her, you see.' Her voice softened. 'I've seen them together and they get on so well, she might feel she can trust him enough to confide what she won't confide in me.'

'But the lass said as she were going to find Billy. If that were true, why would she want to talk to Harry?'

'Maybe she thinks he could help her find him, or maybe she wasn't going to find Billy at all. I don't know, Joe, but if there's the slightest chance she could be at Harry's house, I have to go.'

'Course you do, lass,' Joe agreed. 'Come on then, and wrap up warm. It strikes cold outside this time of a morning.'

A few minutes later, Bridget and the old man were on their way, and ten minutes after that they were outside Harry's house. 'Well, I never.' Joe pointed to the lighted window downstairs. 'Look at that, lass. There were me, concerned about getting him out of his bed so soon, and I'm damned if the bugger ain't already up and working.' He manoeuvred the horse and cart closer to the road edge. 'You stay here a minute, lass, while I go and knock on the door.'

'No, don't do that.' Bridget jumped down from the cart. 'His old mam's bedridden. We wouldn't want to disturb her if we can help it.' Hurrying across the pavement, she tapped on the window. When he looked up, startled, she pointed to the front door. 'Let me in, Harry,' she mouthed, and he was on his feet immediately.

In a moment he was at the door. 'What's wrong?' He looked from her to Joe, and back again, his eyes intent on her face. 'Are you in trouble?' Because of their past, and the strained relationship that had followed, he dared not feel too easy in her presence.

'It's Ruthie.' Bridget felt all manner of emotions as she stood before him. 'She's gone missing. I thought she might have come here.'

Shocked at the news, and concerned by how tired and unwell Bridget looked, he took her gently by the arm. 'You'd better come in.'

The three of them went down the passageway to the back room where a cheery fire was blazing. It took only a few minutes to tell him the problem.

Harry was seriously concerned. 'We have to find her,' he said. 'The police will no doubt do what they can, but in my experience the more we can do ourselves, the better.' He smiled at Bridget. 'Besides, I can't see you sitting and waiting while others search for her.'

'What can we do, Harry? She said she was going to find Billy, but she's got no idea where to look, and neither have I.'

'What made you think she might be here?'

'Because she's grown fond of you, and before she left she was asking Joe about you.'

'Aye,' confirmed Joe, 'that's right enough. Bridget reckoned the lass might have summat to tell you.'

Harry looked at Bridget. 'Such as what?'

'She was worried, that's all I know. I asked her time and again but she wouldn't confide in me.'

'Bridget seemed to think it was summat to do with Bob Morris,' Joe explained, trying to be helpful.

Sensing there was more here than met the eye, Harry said tactfully, 'None of that matters right now. The main thing is for us to find the girl. After that, maybe we can get to the bottom of what's been worrying her.' He strode to the cellar door and took his coat from the peg. 'If she's gone to find Billy, I expect she'll be making for the Gypsy camps. You look all in, Bridget. Stay here, and keep warm. But I might need your help, Joe.'

'You don't have to ask.' Grabbing his hat from the chair arm, he hurried across the room to take up his place beside Harry. 'There are others out there an' all, just waiting for the word.'

'I'm coming too,' Bridget insisted. 'I *won't* be left behind.'

Harry gripped her by the shoulders and in the kindest voice told her, 'I don't want you along. I might have to go places where I wouldn't want you to be. There are men out there who would slit your throat for a shilling, and I don't want to be watching out for you as well. So please, Bridget, for your own sake, and for Ruthie's, do as I ask.'

With his hands on her shoulders, Bridget felt the warmth of his body flow into hers. It was a frightening, wonderful feeling. 'Please, Harry,' she pleaded, tears of anguish flowing down her face. 'Take me with you.'

He shook his head. 'I can't do that, Bridget. I've already told you why, and besides, I need you to mind my mother while I'm gone. Alice no longer lives here, and though it is Fay's morning for visiting Mother, she doesn't arrive for another half hour or more. We can't wait that long, and even if we could, I wouldn't take you along.' Tenderly stroking the tears from her eyes, he said, 'We'll find Ruthie. I won't come back to you without her. And besides, I love her too, you know.'

Through blurred eyes, Bridget studied his face, the brown eyes that Ruthie had taken to, and the tiny dimple in his chin that deepened when he smiled, and her heart was full. 'I understand,' she said, 'and you mustn't worry about your mother. She'll be safe with me.'

When he and Joe left, she ran to the window and watched them climb on to the cart. Harry didn't look up as he went by, but for the first time in years Bridget felt a great sense of trust and reassurance.

It seemed strange to be here in Harry's house, a place she had never set foot in before and yet which she had often wondered about.

Restless, she wandered about, thinking about Ruthie. She would not let herself think that they wouldn't find her, only where she would be found, and whether she would be all right.

As she walked from room to room, she got a feeling of contentment, and when she opened the door to Harry's workplace, she could feel his presence. The room was somehow like him, with its sturdy brown shelves and rolls of material, all neatly labelled and stacked; it was a room with character, the kind of room a man might feel comfortable in. In one corner was a beautiful old desk with deep drawers and brass handles. On top was a leatherbound ledger and a splendid bronze shire horse.

Intrigued, Bridget studied its long shaggy mane and the beautiful feathers at its fetlocks. It took only a moment for her to recognise it as a model of the horse that had drawn Harry's cart when he worked at Weatherfield Grange. 'You loved that horse, didn't you, Harry?' she whispered. 'You were pals for a long time. You must have hated saying goodbye.'

Bridget thought she understood why he had left a job he loved to follow in his father's footsteps as a tailor. Joe had mentioned how Harry's father had always wanted his son to follow the trade, and she suspected he had done so partly to make amends for disappointing his father, and partly as a penance for the sin he and she had committed.

Gazing about at the room where Harry and his father before him had worked all the hours God sent, Bridget felt humbled. 'So this is where you work, is it, Harry? Here, in this confined place, surrounded by the things your father loved, when in your heart you would rather be out there in God's green land.'

She walked to the workbench where Harry had been sitting when they arrived. Reverently, she sat in his chair; it was high-backed and surprisingly comfortable. A wistful smile flitted across her face. 'Do you sit here and dream of the countryside, Harry?' A feeling of sadness swept over her, sadness for Harry, and the past; sadness because of Ruthie, and because deep inside her she knew now that it was Harry she loved, and no power on this earth could make her wed Bob Morris.

Reaching out, she touched the wooden rule Harry used to measure cloth; sensually she fingered the cloth he was working on and the scissors he must have held in his hand only that very morning. She could imagine him holding the scissors, imagine him carefully cutting a ream of silk or skilfully rounding the hem of a waistcoat.

Closing her eyes, she shivered at the memory of their one night of passion in the barn with the snow and wind howling outside. Filled with wonder, she realised the magic was still there. It always would be.

She made her way out of the room again. As she closed the door, an old voice called from upstairs, 'Harry, is that you?'

Startled, Bridget ran to the foot of the stairs. 'It's all right,' she replied. 'Harry won't be long.' She hoped to God it was the truth, and that when he returned he would have Ruthie with him.

'Who's that?' Fear had crept into the voice. 'I don't know you.'

Quickly, Bridget made her way upstairs and followed the old lady's voice to the right room. 'There's nothing to worry about,' she said, opening the door and peeking in. 'Harry's on an errand. He should be back soon.'

The old lady was propped up against the pillows, pale and frail, yet with the bright, curious eyes of a child. 'What are you doing in my house?'

Feeling like an intruder, Bridget remained at the door. 'I'm a friend of Harry's,' she said. 'I'm to mind you until he gets back.'

'Come in, child, come in.' A gnarled finger beckoned.

Bridget went forward. 'I'm sorry if I frightened you.' As she neared the bed, she detected scents of rosemary and lavender.

Through the half-open window a gentle breeze wafted. The sun was waking the skies and the room was filled with the coming morning.

'You were in Harry's room, weren't you?'

Embarrassed, Bridget flushed pink. 'I'm sorry, I . . . was just . . . looking around . . . seeing where Harry worked.'

'That room is directly beneath mine, that's how I knew you were in there.'

'I'm so sorry. I had no right.'

'Well, at least you're not a liar. You could have denied you were there, but you didn't.' Maud patted the bed. 'Sit beside me, dear.'

When Bridget did so, the old woman regarded her closely, noting her youth and how her lovely blue eyes were sad and troubled. 'You're very pretty.'

Bridget smiled. 'I haven't been called that in a long time,' she confessed.

Maud thought that a sin and a shame. 'How do you know my son?' she asked curiously.

'We worked together at the big house, a long time ago now.'

'How long?' The old woman's memory wasn't what it used to be.

'Some eight years now.' Only eight years, she thought, when it seemed like a lifetime.

'What's your name?'

'Bridget.'

The old woman was suddenly alert. 'Bridget Mulligan!'

'Yes.' Bridget was surprised. 'How did you know? Did Harry tell you?'

Overcome with emotion, Maud fell back against the pillows. 'Bridget Mulligan,' she kept saying. 'Bridget Mulligan.' She caught hold of Bridget's hand. 'They were rowing . . . him and Alice. She said he was bad . . . and you had a child . . . *his* child.'

Looking at Bridget intently, she asked, 'Has my Harry got a daughter?'

Bridget stared at her, not knowing what to reply. 'I have to go,' she said, getting up from the bed. 'I have to watch out for Harry.'

The old lady was already sinking into a world of her own. 'It's all right, dear,' she said, smiling sweetly. 'You go about your business. What day is it now?'

She had been in such turmoil these past hours, Bridget took a moment to think. 'Sunday,' she replied. 'It's Sunday morning.'

'Sunday.' Maud closed her eyes. 'Mustn't go to sleep. *Fay* comes to see me on Sunday.'

Softly, Bridget left.

So Harry had been told Ruthie was his daughter. How could his sister have known? And had Harry believed her? That could explain what he had said to her just now, about him loving Ruthie too.

It was all too much for Bridget. 'How can I face you with the truth now, Harry?' she murmured. 'What would you think of me if I confessed that I've deceived you all these years?' It didn't bear thinking about.

Ten minutes later Fay arrived.

Bridget was looking out of the window and recognised her at once. Before Fay could put the key in the lock, Bridget was there, a torrent of words spilling nervously from her lips. 'Ruthie's run away. Harry and Joe have gone looking for her. I wanted to go but they wouldn't let me. I'm minding your mother. She's all right. She's sleeping now, I think.'

Astonished at seeing Bridget there, and shocked by the reason for it, Fay did what she could to comfort Bridget. 'If Harry's gone after her, you can be sure he'll find her,' she said, when the two of them were settled before the fire. 'Look, you just sit there while I go and see if Mam's awake. When I come back down, we'll have a drink and a bite to eat. I don't suppose you've had anything since Ruthie's been gone.'

By the time she came back down, Bridget had made the tea and was just bringing it to the fireside. 'I can't eat anything. I can't think of anything but Ruthie.'

They got talking, and after only minutes it was as if they had known each other all their lives. 'I shouldn't be burdening you with all this,' Bridget told Fay gratefully, 'but there's nothing worse than having no one to talk to.' She thought of Fanny and Billy, and wondered where they might be. 'I had a good friend,' she said. 'The best. Only she went away and I've no idea where she's gone. That's where Ruthie went, you see, looking for them. She was close to Fanny's lad, right from when they were born. Two peas in a pod, that's them.'

'If she was a friend, she'll be back, I'm sure,' said Fay. 'And if you feel the need to talk, then I'm happy to listen.' She hadn't forgotten what Bridget had done for her. 'You saved my job. Nobody's bothered me since, and I've been given even more responsibility. So you see, I could never do enough to thank you.'

Bridget told Fay all about Fanny and Billy, and how she and Ruthie missed them so. 'Before she got the wanderlust, Fanny was always like a sister to me.'

Fay smiled, a small, sad smile. 'Sometimes friends can be kinder than sisters,' she said. 'Harry and I have a sister but she might as well be a stranger. Alice is a selfish creature. She's also lazy and spiteful. She and Harry had a terrible row, and it ended in him throwing her out.'

Bridget was amazed. 'That's terrible! I never imagined Harry could do a thing like that, however much he was provoked.'

'He had no choice. I would have done exactly the same. She lived very comfortably in this house but made no contribution at all. She wouldn't care for Mother, and she wouldn't help Harry in any way. He bought her clothes and food, he worked hard to keep a roof over her head, treated her with consideration, and still she wasn't satisfied.'

'I'm sorry.'

'My mother's always been terrified of the dark,' Fay went on, 'and one night Harry came home to find all the lamps deliberately turned out. Mother was crying . . . Harry found Alice, naked as you like, rolling about the bedroom floor with a man. That's when Harry told her he no longer wanted her here.'

'Do you see her at all?'

'No.' But she had heard her. Once when she passed through town in the evening she heard Alice laughing down some alley. When she looked, she saw her sister locked in the arms of a man.

Fay went to check on her mother again. Maud was awake and Fay stayed to talk to her for a while. Then she had to leave. 'I have to go to work now,' she apologised to Bridget, 'or I'll be late. We're due a new arrival of children – two orphan girls, a boy found wandering the streets, and another young lad come straight from the cells.'

'What dreadful thing did he do to be locked in the *cells*?' Bridget asked.

Fay shook her head. 'It's a sorry state of affairs. Apparently the lad's mammy is waiting to be tried for a murder. There's talk that she'll be hanged for sure, but they're not certain how to deal with the lad. It's said he took no part in the killing, so he's to remain at the orphanage until they decide what to do with him.' Tutting, she added angrily, 'I expect they'll ship him off. That's what they usually do.'

'Dear God! I hope Harry and Joe find Ruthie before the authorities do. I feel so helpless.'

'If you'll stay here with Mother, I'll try and get back so you can go looking for her, though I'm not sure I'll be helping because you can't do any more than is already being done.'

'Thanks. There's always the chance Ruthie might make her way back home to King Street, so if you really can get away to stay with your mam till Harry gets back, I'll go and wait for her there.'

When Fay had gone, Bridget went to the front parlour and sat by the window. 'Please, God,' she prayed, 'bring Ruthie home safe.'

Dressed in drab grey uniforms, the children stood in a line.

The matron sat at the desk, pen in hand and the great red ledger open before her. 'Send them down one at a time,' she instructed Fay. 'Make sure they have their hands at their sides and their heads up.'

'Do as she says,' Fay told them kindly, 'and I think I might be able to find you an extra ladle of porridge for breakfast.' In fact, she treated all the children the same, and they all had enough porridge to keep them satisfied till dinner time.

Matron's voice sailed through the room. 'Name?'

'Maisie.' The child was trembling in her shoes.

'Ma'am! Remember who you are speaking to, child.'

'Maisie . . . ma'am.'

'Maisie *who*?'

'Just Maisie . . . ma'am.'

'Wait over there. Next!'

Each child took less than a minute and soon it was the turn of the last boy in line. 'Remember to say ma'am,' Fay reminded him.

'What's your name, boy? Speak up.'

In a proud but shaking voice he answered, 'Billy Higgins, ma'am, and me mam shouldn't be in jail 'cause she ain't done nuthin' wrong.'

Matron was speechless at such effrontery. She sucked in her breath to give him a blast but Fay quickly intervened and ushered him and the other children out of the hall and along to the dormitory.

She showed the children to their beds and then took Billy aside. Fay could see he had been crying. 'What's your mammy's name, Billy?'

'She never killed nobody.'

'Is she called Fanny?'

Billy nodded. 'I want to see her.'

'You can't see her yet, Billy. I'm sorry.'

'Well, can I see Bridget?' he asked tearfully. 'She'll know what to do.'

Now there was no doubt in Fay's mind. 'Do you mean Bridget Mulligan?'

Hope lit his eyes. 'Yeah, Bridget Mulligan. She'll tell 'em my mam never done nuthin' wrong.'

'They won't let you see anybody just now, Billy,' she said sorrowfully, 'but I'll let her know what's happened.'

'Promise?'

She nodded. 'Meanwhile, you just do as you're told. Don't break any of Matron's rules and you'll come to no harm.'

Increasingly anxious, Bridget remained by the window. Once or twice she ran down the street to the corner and looked about, and when there was no sign of Harry or Joe, she hurried back to the house, checked that the old lady was all right, and resumed her vigil at the window. 'Come on, Harry,' she fretted, 'or I'll have to come and find you.'

It wasn't Harry who arrived moments later. It was Fay, and she had some news for Bridget. 'I'm positive this lad we've admitted is your friend's son.'

'What? Billy, you mean? Billy Higgins? Are you sure?'

Fay sat her down, describing Billy in detail. 'He told me his mother was Fanny Higgins, and I had it checked out. He was telling the truth, Bridget.' Swallowing hard, she didn't relish having to bring more bad news. 'It's a shocking tale,' she warned. 'Remember what I told you this morning, about a boy coming to the orphanage because his mother was awaiting trial for murder.'

'No!' Shaking her head, Bridget couldn't believe what she was hearing. 'It isn't right. Fanny would never kill anybody.' With trembling hands she took hold of Fay. 'They've made some dreadful mistake. They've got to let her go.' What in God's name was happening? she thought. Her whole world was falling apart. 'Fanny will go crazy in jail. And what about Billy? We have to get him out of there right away.' She buried her face in her hands. 'Ruthie! She went looking for them. What if she found them and got caught up in it? Where is she, Fay? Where's Ruthie?'

'Ruthie couldn't have got caught up in it because the murder was done before Ruthie ran away. As for the police letting Fanny go, as far as I understand it, there's small hope of that, I'm afraid. There was a witness apparently. He was there when the murder took place, and he saw it all. He saw your friend murder the farmer's wife and caught her as she tried to run away.'

Bridget leaped out of her chair. 'If he said that, he's a liar! Fanny never murdered anybody! She's too soft to kill a spider, let alone anything else. Who is he, this witness?'

Fay shook her head. 'I wasn't given his name. All I know is that the woman killed was Lucy Meaker, of Meaker's Farm – some half a mile the other side of Lancaster.'

'Summat's wrong here,' Bridget insisted. 'I'd stake my life that Fanny never killed that poor woman. I don't care what they say, she just couldn't do such a thing.'

'I really am sorry, Bridget, but these are the facts as I was given them.'

Bridget wasn't listening. Her mind was racing ahead. 'Ruthie must have gone there, I'm sure of it! She meant to find Fanny and Billy, and when she makes up her mind about summat there's no shifting her. She would have asked all manner of questions from all and sundry, I know her!'

'Keep calm, Bridget, you're not thinking straight.'

'I know you mean well, and I'm grateful, lass, but the truth is I'm only just beginning to think straight. I might well be wrong, but what if Ruthie's enquiries *did* lead her to that farm?' There was no changing her mind now. 'I've got to go there, Fay, and while I'm there I'll make it my business to find out who this witness is that says Fanny committed murder. For some reason of his own, the bugger's lying. I know he is! And if he's harmed my Ruthie, I swear there *will* be murder done.'

She picked up her coat. 'One way or another, I have to find my girl, and once I've found her, there's Fanny to be got out of that jail.' Now that she knew what to do, she felt a whole lot better; if only the task was not so terrifying.

Wishing she hadn't said anything, Fay tried to dissuade her from leaving. 'Wait until Harry comes back,' she pleaded. 'You can't go out there all by yourself. There'll be trouble, you might get hurt, and if you're right about Fanny being innocent, there's no telling what you might be getting yourself into.'

Bridget was adamant. 'If Harry comes back, tell him where I've gone. Tell him I can't rest. I need to be out there.'

Bridget hurried out of the house and went down the street at a run. She hailed a hansom, gave the driver directions, and then climbed in and was on her way.

The ride out to the farm seemed to take for ever, but the driver knew the place and went straight to it.

'Drop me out here.' Bridget didn't want to go too close to the house. She needed to take stock, weigh up what she had to do. Now that she was actually here, she wondered if she had done the right thing after all. But then she reminded herself of her own arguments, how Ruthie might well have tracked Fanny here.

The driver took her coins and dropped them in his pocket. 'D'yer want me to wait?'

'No thanks. I'll find my own way back.' If she cut across the fields, it would take only half the time.

She watched him go, and then she crept towards the house. 'Must be a rich bugger,' she muttered. 'Happen Fanny chanced along at the right minute. Happen he killed his own wife and paid this witness to throw the blame on Fanny.'

Nothing could have prepared Bridget for what she saw through the drawing-room window. 'My God! What's *he* doing here?'

Bob Morris was standing at a table facing a second man who was meticulously counting out bank-notes. Bob was smiling smugly, hands in his pockets, obviously waiting for the other man to finish counting so he could collect the money and be on his way.

Sick to her stomach, Bridget fell away from the window, hands at her throat as she tried hard not to cry out his name.

After a moment she heard them talking. Creeping to the window once more, she remained hidden, listening to their every word.

'You did a good job,' the farmer was saying. 'Though you didn't have to make such a bloody mess. I wanted it quick and clean.' He grinned. 'Or did you want to have your way with her one last time? God knows it took you long enough to make up your bloody mind.'

Bob Morris stuffed the money in his pocket. 'Can you blame me? She was a looker, your missus. I didn't think you'd mind me taking my time. Besides, I reckon I earned a few weeks of fun, before it were all to come to an end.'

Striding to the dresser, the farmer poured two drinks. 'I knew there would come a day when she'd had enough of me. I couldn't let that happen, could I?' He handed Bob his drink. 'Not when she owned every inch of land I ride across . . .' He looked up.

'Even this house . . . been in her family for generations.'

'You had to have her done away with, guv.' Bob Morris sipped his drink. 'No one could blame you for that.'

'Here's to you, my man, and a good job done.' The farmer raised his glass, then, beckoning Morris to sit, he laughed. 'Lucky the Higgins woman turned up when she did . . . saved you the task of burying my poor wife.'

'Have they set a date for the trial?'

Growing merry with the wine, Morris congratulated himself. 'There'll be no doubt about the outcome,' he promised. 'There are people baying for her blood . . . they're all for breaking into the jail and hanging her on the spot. Take it from me, guv, the authorities daren't do anything but string her up, or they'll be made to take her place.'

'Quite so. But the sooner she's hanged the better for us all.'

'What about the boy? He knows she didn't do it.'

'Ah well, that won't matter, will it? You see, I've got friends who will make sure he never grows up on English soil.'

'Ship him out, is that what you have in mind?'

The farmer grinned wickedly. 'Something of the sort.'

Outside, Bridget was in fear of her life. If she was caught here she would be done away with – she was certain of it. 'So, Ruthie didn't get this far, thank God,' she murmured. If she had, there would have been mention of it. She had to tell the authorities . . . Fanny *didn't* do the murder. They'd have to let her go . . . Billy too.

Backing off, while keeping her eyes on the two men, Bridget told herself, 'Get away, Bridget lass. Quietly now.'

Being too careful, and too intent on watching them, she didn't see the fallen tree behind her. With a cry she fell backwards, knocked senseless when her head hit the upturned root.

When she came round, they were standing over her. Her arms were spread out, tied by the wrists to the stable wall. 'Ah!' The farmer was smiling. 'Awake at last. I'm sorry if you're uncomfortable, but we can't let you go now, can we? And we couldn't possibly kill you before we knew how much you had heard, or whether there was anyone else with you.' Prodding her shoulder with a stick, he demanded to know, 'Was there anyone else here with you?'

Defiant, Bridget refused to answer.

Another prod, this time more spiteful. 'I asked . . . was there anyone with you?'

Again there was no answer. Instead she stared him out.

Stepping forward he grabbed the horse-whip from the stable door. 'Stubborn little bastard, aren't you?' he sneered. 'Well, let's see how brave you are.' Throwing the whip to Bob, who had stood in the shadows all this time, he ordered, 'You deal with her. I haven't the stomach for it.'

While he stepped back, Morris stepped forward. Leaning down to her, he urged, 'Tell him what he wants to know, Bridget. He's in a mood to see me flay the skin off your back.'

For a second or two she really believed he was worried for her. The moment swiftly passed when she remembered what he had done. 'You killed a woman for money,' she accused. 'Then you let Fanny and the boy be taken for it.'

'I mean it, Bridget. If you cross him, he won't show you any mercy.' Glancing back at the farmer, Bob seemed afraid. 'You don't know him.'

'What? Like I don't know *you*?'

'I've always loved you, Bridget, you must believe that.'

'Then let me go. Let me find Ruthie.'

Befuddled with drink, something snapped in his mind. 'Oh!' He began to smile. 'Of course . . . *Harry's* brat . . . the snooper. She saw me with a woman and thought it was the end of the world. But she daren't tell you, not when I asked her not to. Besides, the woman meant nothing to me . . . they never do. Not like you.' His features hardened. 'Run off, has she? Well I never. And what makes you think I care whether you find her or not?'

So, *that's* what Ruthie was worried about. Now it all began to make sense. *That* was why she had run off. She was frightened to tell Bridget, but not Billy.

'What was it like with him, Bridget? Making Ruthie . . . was it more exciting than with me?' Bob's eyes hardened. 'Is that why you've grown cold on me . . . because you think he's a better man?'

Turning her head away, Bridget was shocked when he flicked the whip before her eyes. 'Look at me when I'm talking to you, bitch!'

'That's it!' From the back of the stable where he was swigging booze, the farmer egged him on. 'Show her you mean it, Morris. Loosen her tongue. Find out if there was anyone else with her.'

The first stripe of the whip fell across her shoulders, slicing her blouse, making her scream with pain. 'Well? You prefer him to me . . . do you?'

'Yes, I do! Harry is twice the man you are, and I love him.'

To the delight of the farmer, Morris raised the whip once more. 'You weren't lying when you said the girl was his . . . were you? Were you lying, damn your eyes?'

'Kill me,' she said quietly. 'But it won't change the truth.' The pain seared her back and her senses were fading; she truly believed this was her last hour on God's earth, but it didn't matter what happened to her. What mattered was Ruthie, and Harry, and all the lost years. 'Harry is Ruthie's father, and I'm proud of that.'

Tired of the time it was taking, Meaker stepped forward, shotgun in hand. 'Enough!' he yelled. 'If you haven't got the guts to do it, then get out of the way. She's playing us along. There was no one else with her.'

As he lowered the gun to take aim, the doors were flung open and Harry burst in, followed by Joe. Startling the culprits, Joe tackled Morris, while Harry leapt at Meaker, knocking the gun out of his hands. As it fell there was an almighty bang. Joe was sent sideways to the wall, but all eyes went to Morris, his body sprawled across the floor at Bridget's feet. There was a look of panic on his face as he clutched his chest. 'Oh Jesus!' His shocked face was turned up to Bridget, the eyes bright with tears.

Quickly Harry lashed the farmer to the centre beams while Joe pushed Morris aside and began untying Bridget.

Rushing across the room, Harry fell to his knees, tearing at the ropes that bound her. 'Watch the other one, Joe,' he said. 'I'll see to Bridget.'

When he had her free, he took her in his arms. 'You're safe, sweetheart,' he whispered. 'I've got you.'

When, with a twinge of sadness, Bridget looked down, it was to see Bob smiling at her. 'I'm sorry, my lovely.' His voice shivered with pain. 'I did love you though.' Then he closed his eyes and was no more.

With the culprit tied to the cart-shaft, and Bridget wrapped in a blanket in the back, they began their way home; along by the spinney, and travelling slowly so as not to jar the cart too much.

Up front, Joe drove carefully, while Harry stayed close to Bridget, his arms about her and his face close to hers. 'I heard you tell him,' he whispered. 'Is it true? Do you really love me?'

Through her pain Bridget smiled. 'Did you find Ruthie?'

Smiling secretly, he reached over her to a nearby blanket. Lifting it at the corner, he revealed a small sleeping face. 'I think this belongs to us,' he said, and when she saw Ruthie there, fast asleep without a care in the world, she cried in his arms. 'Where did you find her?' she asked and taking hold of the girl's tiny hand she pressed it lovingly to her face, tears of joy welling over.

As they reached the other side of the spinney, Harry pointed to a wagon half-hidden there. 'Fay told me how you thought

Ruthie might have tracked Fanny and the boy out here, and you were right. Fanny must have parked the wagon here when she went to the farm that night. Ruthie found it, though God only knows how. Anyway, that's where I found her . . . sleeping off the adventure.'

'How can I ever thank you?' Bridget touched his face, her heart filled with gratitude. 'Just now, you asked me a question,' she whispered. 'And yes, I do love you, with all my heart.'

'And is Ruthie mine?'

Bridget nodded. 'How could you not know,' she asked, 'when every gesture, every smile, reminds me of you?'

Ashamed, she asked his forgiveness for deceiving him all these years.

'I know why you did it, and I can't be angry.' He held her to him. 'I'm a lucky man,' he murmured.

Bridget closed her eyes. On one side she had the man she loved, and on the other their precious child. I'm the lucky one, she thought.

And as they travelled back to Blackburn, she held on to them for all she was worth.

Chapter Fifteen

It was two weeks since the night when Ruthie was found, but to Bridget it seemed like only yesterday.

Downstairs, she spoke to Alice, while Harry went up to say goodbye to his mother, and to tell her how he would never be far away, and that he would see her often. It had been the right decision for him to move in with Bridget and Ruthie; at least until they were able to make a new start not too far away.

Alice was a changed woman. Emotionally bruised by her recent experiences she had found her way home. 'I've been stupid,' she told Bridget. 'I had it all, and it was never enough.'

'We all make mistakes,' Bridget consoled her. God knows *she* had made enough in her time.

Alice looked at Fay, who had been with her these past two days. 'How can you ever forgive me for what I did to you all?' she asked. 'I've been bad . . . shamed you all, and still you don't punish me for it. Instead, you're kind and generous and I will never deserve it.'

Fay wound an arm round her shoulders. 'You're family,' she said kindly. 'We love you.'

Alice had been punished enough; by the very people she chose to turn to. Now, humbled and repentant, she had come to realise who her true friends were.

Harry came down just then. 'We'd best make tracks, Bridget.'

'I'm ready.' Bridget had spoken to Harry's mother earlier, and had promised that she and Harry would come to see her as often as they could. The old woman seemed content with that. In a couple of months she and Harry would be man and wife, and even now Bridget dared hardly believe it.

It was strange, coming back to Weatherfield Grange after being away for so long.

Peter Doyle had not changed much, Bridget thought: still pathetic; milder; rounder maybe, with slivers of grey in his sideburns. A fast man burned out quickly, she decided.

'We've come to thank you,' Harry explained. 'Fanny Higgins was too shy to come herself, but we couldn't let your kindness go. If it hadn't been for you intervening, she might still have taken the blame for what happened.' Bridget thought it had been an uncharacteristic move on his part, but was grateful all the same.

'I'm sure she would,' came the reply. 'Meaker had friends in high places . . . people who might have squashed his "confession" as the ramblings of a grieving man.'

Bridget had never understood that. 'But how could that happen,' she demanded to know, 'when all along she was innocent?'

'Miscarriages of justice are not uncommon,' Doyle replied knowingly. 'These things have happened in the past, and no doubt they will happen in the future. But, all that aside, I have a proposition to put to the two of you.'

Gesturing to a sofa, he bade them sit. 'One of my tenants has moved on, and I intend to make a few changes.'

Harry wondered, 'What kind of changes, sir, and how does that affect us?'

'The departing tenant ran one of my smaller farms – a hundred acres, with a small thatched cottage. The land has fallen into poor condition, and the cottage needs work on it.'

Anticipating his proposition, Harry stood up. 'Thank you all the same, and don't think Bridget and I are not grateful, but we've set our hearts on owning our own business, lock, stock and barrel. We can't even consider taking on a tenancy, however attractive.'

'Quite right too.' Doyle bade him sit again. 'Now then, I mean to sell all my tenancies, and this is by far the best. It lies in the south valley, overlooking the Blaketon Hills.' He wagged a finger at Harry. 'You know the farm. You've helped work it often enough.'

Harry did know it well. 'It is a beautiful position,' he admitted. But he was a practical man. 'I could never afford it.'

Brushing aside Harry's protests, Doyle went on: 'As I have already explained, the land is in a dire state . . . the cottage too, and it will cost time and effort to put it right. So, as you can see, I'm not being over-generous. I have no intention of pouring good money after bad. I want shot of all the small farms, and, because you were always hard-working and loyal, I'm offering this one to you. And before you say any more, think on this . . . I would be a rogue if I were to ask more than it's worth at this moment in time; which, I have to admit, is not a great deal. So? What do you say?'

He needed an answer. 'I have a selfish reason for asking. I intend spending much time abroad, and I have need of a reliable person to oversee my interests here. I can think of no man, other than yourself, who has my trust. And of course, I will pay you well.'

Thrilled, Harry turned to Bridget. 'What do you think? Could we do it, the two of us?'

'Take your good woman to see it,' Doyle commanded. 'Then come and give me word.'

* * *

That same afternoon, Harry took Bridget to the farm in the valley.

'Oh, Harry, it's beautiful,' she said. 'We have to make it ours.'

'I knew you would say that,' he told her. 'I've always loved this place. I used to stand here and dream that one day you and I would find happiness together. There is no other place I would rather be.' He loved the countryside. Working enclosed in his father's room had been hard to bear. Now, though, he felt he had paid the price for what he had done, and his heart was at peace.

The sound of laughter made Bridget look down to where the cottage stood. 'Come outa there, yer buggers!' Fanny yelled. 'Else I'll tan yer arses, so I will.'

Bill Norman sat on the grass beside her. When he reached out to tickle her under the arms, she screeched with laughter.

Harry and Bridget laughed too. 'I hope he never regrets the choice he made,' she said. 'He could find his new wife quite a handful.'

Harry kissed her long and lovingly. 'A man knows what he wants,' he murmured. 'Bill has found his happiness with Fanny, and I've found mine with you.'

In the distance the children played, and Bridget's heart was full. 'I once thought owning a shop would be the top of the world,' she confessed. 'But that was before I came here.'

'You'll see, sweetheart,' he promised. 'We'll be happier here than we've ever been.'

And as he held her hand and ran with her down the hill, Bridget knew he was right.

JOSEPHINE COX

Don't Cry Alone

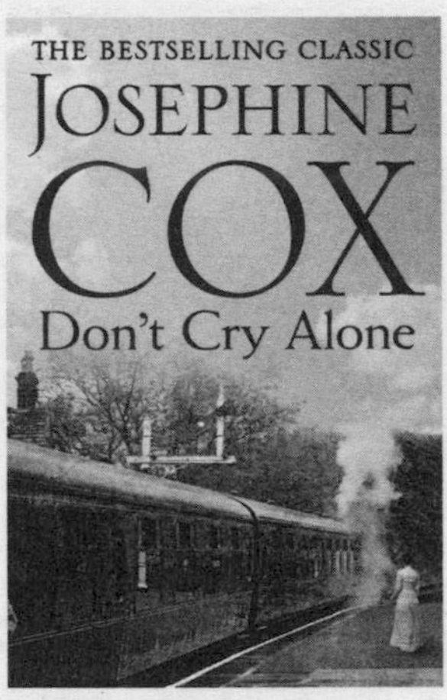

Beth Ward and Tyler Blacklock share a love they know will last forever. But Beth's mother, Esther, is jealous of the girl and seizes an opportunity to be rid of her daughter.

Banished in disgrace from the family home, Beth takes the northbound train and alights at Blackburn, friendless and alone. On this day, fortune smiles, for Beth is taken in by warm-hearted Maisie Armstrong, a widow with two children. Money is scarce, but love abounds in the cosy house on Larkhill, and Beth is content there to await the birth of her child.

But she cannot forget Tyler, and is tormented by the belief that he has betrayed her . . .

JOSEPHINE COX

Let It Shine

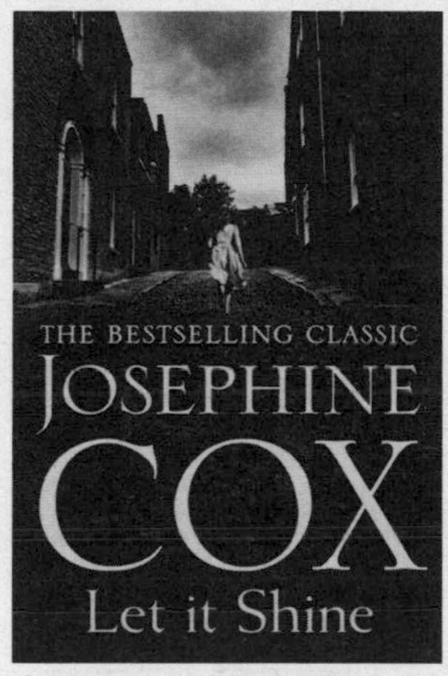

Ada Williams once believed money and power would bring her happiness. But now she is all alone in the world except for her greedy son Peter, who waits only for the day he will inherit her fortune. Ada, however, has a different plan altogether.

A few miles away in Blackburn, the Bolton family may be poor – but the love they share means they can overcome almost any adversity. But no one could foresee the shocking events of Christmas night, 1932, which split the family asunder, leaving Larry crippled and the twins, Ellie and Betsy, in a foster home. Events that Ada Williams, all these years later, will never forget.